# IMPOSSIBLE!

# IMPOSSIBLE!

## MICHELLE MAGORIAN

troika books

Published by TROIKA BOOKS

First published 2014

Troika Books, Well House, Green Lane, Ardleigh CO7 7PD, UK

www.troikabooks.com

A CIP catalogue record for this book

is available from the British Library

ISBN 978-1-909991-04-0

1 2 3 4 5 6 7 8 9 10

*To*
*Dudley Rogers*
*and in memory of Anne Dugon*

# Contents

—

# Act One

——•◦•——

## Through Josie's Eyes

# I

# September 1959

'I'LL BE FRANK WITH YOU,' SAID MISS DAGLEISH, her long, lean figure towering over a polished mahogany desk. 'You resemble a boy in a gymslip.'

Josie stood smartly to attention in her navy uniform, squeezing the muscles in her nostrils in an attempt to prevent the pungent stench of lavender seeping into her nose. But there was no escape. Its aroma continued to hover above the ancient furniture in the dimly lit headmistress's study. The smell always reminded her of the time her mother used to wash the knickers of an elderly neighbour who kept wetting herself. Whenever the neighbour visited their flat, she always ponged of it, and ever since, the slightest whiff of lavender brought back memories of stale wee.

'What on earth possessed you to have it cut again?' demanded Miss Dagleish. 'It was far too short three weeks ago when you started here. Did someone force you?'

'No, madam,' replied Josie. 'I asked the hairdresser to do it.'

'Hairdresser! My dear, you have the appearance of someone who has been dragged into a barbershop and had clippers taken to their head.' She gave an exasperated sigh. 'It's difficult enough to find acting roles for a red-headed girl as it is. And yes, I know you have the advantage of being small for your age and of possessing freckles, and freckles are what producers want nowadays. Unfortunately for us you have an overabundance of them. It would have been more beneficial to have had a handful scattered either side of your nose. Talking of which, is there something the matter with yours?'

'No, madam.'

'Then will you kindly have the courtesy not to twitch it when I am speaking to you.' Miss Dagleish shook her head as though lost for words. 'Good wigs are so expensive these days. You realise this means I am now quite unable to put you up for any work until your hair grows and that's hardly fair on your aunt when she has been generous enough to make a substantial contribution towards your fees.'

'What about boys' roles, madam?'

'That's not why you had it cut short, is it?'

'Yes, madam. Boy's parts aren't so soppy. I always played boys in me last school. Me sister had her hair cut short when she was twelve too, and she got a boy's part.'

'And what kind of educational establishment was she attending at the time?'

'A grammar school, madam.'

'Ah. She played a boy in an amateur production. That explains it.'

Before Josie could tell her that Elsie had played the role in a professional production in the very theatre where she was now working, Miss Dagleish's arm shot up, the palm of her hand directed at Josie. Her sign for silence.

'This is a London stage school, Josephine,' she said icily, 'not a small town dramatic society. Our pupils work in the world of the theatre, film and the BBC – where girls play girls. In spite of the fact that you are a mere beginner, as a pupil of this establishment it is vital that you think and behave like a professional. Is that clear?'

'Yes, madam,' murmured Josie.

'I had assumed that since your brother and sister are in the profession, they would have made this clear.' She wrenched her lips sideways into a taut smile. 'Is your sister in work at the moment?'

'Yes, madam. On Saturdee I'm watchin' the run-through of the play she's rehearsin' at Winford rep.'

'Ah. *Life With Father*. One of our junior pupils has a role in it. Michael Bailey. He's playing one of the four sons.'

'I know the boy playin' the youngest son,' added Josie.

'Really? How?'

'He's the half-brother of my sister's fiancé.'

'I see. And what of *your* brother, Ralph Hollis? Which Shakespeare play is he appearing in at present?'

Josie suppressed a smile. It always sounded funny when people pronounced his name *Rayfe*.

'He ain't in a Shakespeare one. I mean, *isn't*, madam. He's in a play called *The Hostage*.'

'*The Hostage*! But your aunt told me he was working in Stratford.'

'He is. He's in the Theatre Workshop Company.'

The muscles in Miss Dagleish's face went into spasm. It

was then that Josie remembered that Auntie Win had called the director of the Theatre Workshop Company, 'That Joan woman who swears like a trooper.' It was obvious that Miss Dagleish knew what her aunt knew.

'This play you mentioned, have you seen it?' she asked Josie.

'No. Me mum says it's only for adults.'

'And a certain class of adult, I'm afraid. Not what I call theatre. No style.' She cleared her throat hurriedly. 'Now, although it's impossible for you to be put up for any auditions this term, I do have some good news for you. You are to move up to the next form.'

Josie was puzzled. She had already been moved into the row of Form II desks when it was discovered she had covered all the Form I work at her previous school.

'Please, madam,' said Josie hesitantly, 'I'm already in the Form II row.'

'I am quite aware of that, my dear. On Monday, you will move your books into the Form III row. From what the teachers tell me, the work in Form II is far too easy for you. You will remain in the same ballet class and will join Form III's acting, singing, make-up lessons and etiquette classes.'

Josie was speechless for a moment. Miss Dagleish stared at her.

'Oh. Yes, madam,' Josie blurted out hurriedly. 'Thank you, madam.'

'You may go. And remember, Josephine, in future I want more hair from you.'

'Yes, madam.'

Josie curtsied and backed out of the room, only to bump into a tall, gangly girl called Doris and her mousey-haired, dumpy friend, Thelma, both of whom had been lurking in the corridor.

'What audition is she putting you up for?' Doris demanded.

'And why weren't we chosen?' said Thelma. 'We've been here far longer than you.'

'It wasn't about an audition,' said Josie.

'Oh? What was it about then?' asked Doris.

'I'm being put into the Form III row.'

'Ooh, clever clogs!' they chorused.

'We'll have to start calling you *Professor*,' said Thelma.

'You'll end up like Clive,' Doris added. 'This is his second year in Form IV and he says he has to do exactly the same work as he did last year.'

It was at that moment Josie realised that if she was going to be with the thirteen and fourteen year olds in Form III from Monday, she would be put into the last form the following year and stay there for three years doing the same lessons.

As they ran off shrieking with laughter, Josie headed down the large hallway towards a door at the side of the staircase. She pushed it open and hopped down the stairs to the rear room in the basement. At the back and in the middle of the room were long wooden benches with square cubby-holes underneath for shoes. Attached to each bench was a wooden wall with pegs for clothes. Josie hurried over to the one in the centre to get changed for her dance class, took off her long grey socks and sat down to put on her black tights, lifting her knees away from the floor to avoid the splinters in the floorboards. Three other girls were chatting and changing on the other side. They were in her Grade IV ballet class and had been at the stage school since the juniors. They avoided talking to her because she was small – the smallest in the senior part of the school – and they were jealous. The smaller you were, the more chance you had of being given work because you could play roles your age and younger. During her first week she had overheard one of them saying loudly enough for her to hear, 'She has no talent. She was only accepted because of her size.'

Seated cross-legged at the end of her bench in leotard and tights was Hilda, a thirteen year old with long chestnut-brown hair scraped into a bun. Oblivious to everyone, she had her nose in one of her Lorna Hill ballet books.

Even when she was reading, Hilda appeared graceful. She was the best dancer in the school. One of the boys in her class had told Josie that she had broken her leg in an accident, and that although she had recovered, it meant that she wasn't good enough for the high standards of a ballet school, so her parents had decided to send her to a stage school instead. It was her second term. She and Josie were the only pupils who had received proper ballet lessons and had taken Royal Academy of Dance examinations. Back home in Sternsea, Josie's ballet teacher was a down-to-earth retired ballerina, whereas the elderly dance mistress at the stage school, Miss Frobisher, did nothing but sway from side to side in a long skirt, tossing a silk scarf into the air. Her assistant, an ex-pupil called Miss Peabody, couldn't demonstrate any dance positions either and had a back as straight as a ramrod. It was so stiff Josie wondered how she was able to bend over to tie up her shoelaces.

Every class would begin with a few stretching exercises after which Miss Frobisher would produce pictures of women posing in Grecian robes. Miss Peabody, who knew these tableaux by heart, would make the pupils imitate the poses by placing their arms and legs into the correct positions. They then had to walk gracefully into each pose over and over again.

Josie remembered the day she and her aunt had visited the school and how impressed she had been to see Hilda twirling in graceful pirouettes around these tableaux as the other pupils glided effortlessly into them. Sadly, once she was a pupil, Josie discovered that they were rarely allowed to be too energetic because dance classes were always accompanied by gramophone music. If they jumped too high it would cause the needle to scratch a record, and their parents would be sent a bill to pay for the cost of a new one.

The gramophone was also used for singing lessons, where they had to sing songs accompanied by more records. They were usually sickly sweet ones about roses and violets and the humming of the bee-ee-ees. During one of these classes, Miss Tilbury, the singing mistress, had told Hilda that she had a lovely voice and that when she was older she would be ideal for Noel Coward musicals where *elegance* was essential. 'None of this rock and roll nonsense,' she had added firmly. Josie had been tempted to ask Miss Tilbury what she

thought of the musical her Auntie Win had taken her to see
the previous week but a warning instinct made her keep her
mouth shut.

The musical, *My Fair Lady*, was the story of a cockney
dustman's daughter who had been taken from the gutter
where she had been selling flowers, and had been turned into
a young lady for a bet. It was the scenes with the cockneys
leaping up and whirling round each other that Josie loved
best. She longed to be allowed to dance with the same gusto
and energy. That same night, she had overheard people in
the seats behind them talking enthusiastically about another
new musical, *West Side Story*. It was the most revolutionary
musical they had ever seen. Auntie Win must have been
eavesdropping too because as they made their way out
through the crowded auditorium she said, 'I'll take you to
see that one in your half-term.'

Just then there was the sound of a bell ringing.

She gave a start and ran, towards the stairs.

*Please let today's dance class be less boring*, she thought.

At breaktime, stepping out into the small, scrubby garden at
the back of the school, Josie dashed over to where a group of
boys were kicking a ball. The fourth form girls had gathered
in their usual spot by the far wall, drinking in Esmeralda
Havilland's every word. Esmeralda was the head girl, a
curvaceous fifteen year old with short, wavy blond hair
who walked regally about the corridors as though already
touched by fame.

Because she bragged about her meetings with famous

actors and actresses, the girls ate up her stories about them, as though knowing what they had said and done put themselves in their hallowed company.

'So then what happened?' she overheard Brenda Mackie, one of the awestruck admirers, ask.

'He escorted me into a coffee house in Kensington where they played Latin American music. The coffee was served in flat glass cups. It was very sophisticated. And we ate open sandwiches. That's without bread on top. *Swedish style*, they call it. So exotic!'

'Gosh!' said a skinny girl called Merle.

Josie suspected Esmeralda was about to describe every garment she was wearing at the time to her open-mouthed audience and it was the last thing she wanted to hear. Without asking if she could join in the boys' kick-about, she weaved in among them, chasing their ball until, with a balletic touch, she whacked it sideways with the inside of her foot towards a tall dark-haired boy with spots. Her older brother Harry had taught her the rudiments of the game before emigrating to Australia with his wife.

The boys said nothing, but unbeknown to her they peered over her head, their eyebrows raised. As Josie continued to swerve happily around them, she kept glancing over her shoulder, expecting her two friends, Jack and Derek to appear. She had missed their company that morning. Their lopsided grins always made the ordinary lessons like history and geography bearable, and in the acting lessons the three of them would always gravitate towards one another. She stopped short, having realised that from Monday they wouldn't be in the same form any more. But then she remembered she would still see them in the dance classes.

'When are Jack and Derek coming back from the auditions, Gordon?' she asked one of the Form I boys.

'Haven't you heard?' said Len, a stocky boy with frizzy hair. 'They've been offered a tour with the Scottish Shakespeare Travellers' Company. Lucky so and sos.'

Josie froze.

'Both of 'em?'

'Yes. They're sharing the same role. They start rehearsals on Monday. They've got a three-month contract.'

Josie felt as though someone had kicked the football directly into her stomach.

'That's good,' she forced herself to say.

After the deportment class where they had to walk around a room with a book on their head, remembering to pull in their tummy muscles and imagine they were wearing a corset, Josie dived back into the cloakroom and heaped her enormous duffle coat around her shoulders. It was several sizes too large for her so that she could grow into it. On her first day, Esmeralda Havilland had commented loudly to Merle that it looked as though Josie was wearing a blanket, and had laughed at her. But Josie didn't care. Sliding her arms into the sleeves, it was as though her family were wrapping their arms round her. She plonked her wide-brimmed navy hat onto her head, pulled on her white gloves, grabbed her bottle-green attaché case and climbed up the stairs to the hall.

Outside, it was already growing dark. With a heavy heart she walked down the stone steps and headed for the bus stop hauling herself onto the first double decker that pulled up. She dragged her case up the stairs. She was in luck. Her favourite seat, the single one at the front, was empty and it cheered her a little. As the bus juddered between stops, she rested her cheek against the window, drinking in the blazing London streets below and the scurrying commuters on their way home. She wondered what her parents were doing in their ground-floor flat in Sternsea, and wished she were going back there . . .

She thought back to the day of her audition, how she had stood on the pavement, taking in the grand houses surrounding the square. Her aunt, who had visited the school earlier on behalf of Josie's parents on one of their visitors' days, had been impressed to find that a school whose fees were half those of other London stage schools stood in such 'genteel' surroundings. And Josie, who had had always been at her happiest when acting in school productions, had gazed up at the old house that was Miss Dagleish's stage school and had thought, *This is where I want to go!*

It had taken a few days to adjust to its smallness. She had been used to being in a school where each form had its own classroom. At the stage school, the four senior forms shared one room. The row of double desks on the left was Form I, the two rows in the middle were Forms II and III and the row on the right by the display board was Form IV. Each form took it in turns to have lessons while the other forms attended singing, acting and dance classes in the other rooms.

It suddenly occurred to her that from Monday she would no longer be eating dinner at the school but would be expected to join the third- and fourth-formers at a tea house where Miss Dagleish had an arrangement with the manageress. Only she wasn't to call it dinner; she had to call it lunch. Dinner, she had been informed, was the meal you ate in the evening, unless you had something on toast instead, in which case you must call it supper. It was all part of their training in dining-room etiquette, which involved not only knowing how to hold a knife and fork correctly but which piece of cutlery to pick up first.

She remembered her first bewildering etiquette lesson when Miss Bentley-Higham had announced grandly, 'Remember, gels, it's *napkins* not *serviettes.*' Glancing at Josie she had immediately added, 'And for those who don't know what a napkin is, it's a square piece of starched white linen that you place on your lap or tuck into the front of your collar to prevent food spillages soiling your garments when eating a meal.'

The bus gave a jolt. It was her stop. She snatched up her case and leaped down the stairs. It was time to put on a cheerful face for her aunt.

# 2

# Auntie Win

JOSIE RACED UP THE ORNATE 1930s CIRCULAR stairway past the other flats to the second landing and her aunt's familiar door. Her aunt had only been in the flat for a few months. It was the first time she had lived on her own since leaving the Women's Royal Army Corps. For years she had saved every penny of her pay so that she could afford a radiogram and rugs, never dreaming that one day she would win enough money on the premium bonds to buy herself a posh flat in London.

Unfortunately, she was always losing the key. Several times Josie had needed to ask Mrs Jenkins from one of the other flats if she could borrow a chair so that she could stand on it and push open the window above the door. Her aunt would lift her up so that Josie could slide backwards through it on her stomach, jump down into the hallway and open it with the spare key that was kept in the cutlery drawer under the kitchen table. It was either that or climb up the fire escape at the back of the building and enter by the kitchen door, which was usually unlocked.

Josie glanced up at the light above the door and hesitated

for a moment. Should she tell her aunt she had let her and her parents down by making it impossible for a producer to cast her in a play this term? She thought back to the day she had left Sternsea, how her father had stood on the railway platform as she and her mother leaned happily out of the train window, chatting to him. Her mother had travelled with Josie and her luggage to help her settle in with her aunt.

'When you come 'ome at 'alf term and you're talkin' like a toff,' he had said, 'will you still speak to us?'

Miss Dagleish had explained to her parents that any pupil with a working class accent would be taught to speak RP – Received Pronunciation.

'Don't be daft. Of course she will,' said her mother. 'Elsie and Ralph still do.'

'And Auntie Win,' added Josie. 'She talks posh too, Dad.'

'Ah. That's cos she caught *officeritis*,' he had said, grinning. 'As soon as she started goin' up in the ranks, she started talkin' different. You can't 'ave an army major soundin' as though she's sellin' spuds dahn the market. A major in the WRAC 'as to speak wiv a plum in 'er mouth, don't she?'

'That's enough!' her mother had warned, fighting to control her laughter.

They had been interrupted by the sound of a guard's whistle. Her father had stepped back, and as the train pulled out Josie had waved frantically, startled to feel a strange ache in her throat.

What was she going to say when they rang that night?

She opened the door into the wide, carpeted passage. As she hung her coat up on one of the hooks on the wall, she was reminded of Miss Dagleish's disapproving gaze when she had first spotted it, preferring Josie to have worn a neat navy blue girl's coat, not an enormous boy's duffle coat that was brown. But it was so comfortable. All boys' clothes were comfortable. Girls had to put up with dresses with fiddly bows and pastel cardigans with endless buttons. It wasn't fair.

From the sitting room, she could hear Julie Andrews singing *Wouldn't It Be Loverly* from *My Fair Lady* and then there was silence, broken a few moments later by an American chorus singing '*Papa-pa-paya! Papa-pa-paya!*' She couldn't help smiling. Within seconds there came the mellow, relaxed tones of Perry Como singing,

'*Don't let the stars get in your eyes.*

'*Don't let the moon break your heart.*'

A tall, middle-aged woman with a pointed face and a dash of grey in her permed brown hair peered round the door. She was wearing a pair of old slacks and a man's white shirt covered in royal blue paint. She beamed and began dancing, flinging her arms and legs about.

'*Too many nights,*' sang Josie, joining in with Perry Como.

'*Too many stars,*' Auntie Win sang in answer.

'*Too many stars. Too many stars,*' they sang together. '*You're the only one. You're the only one I'll ever love!*'

When the record had stopped playing they leaned back against the coats and laughed.

'Beans on toast?' asked her aunt.

'Yeah. Please.'

*Or would that be too dangerous?* thought Josie.

Her aunt wasn't the greatest cook. Mum said it was because she had been used to years of other people cooking for her in the army. When Auntie Win attempted to boil an egg, she would either approach it like a military campaign or lose herself in a detective novel until the sound of dried shell breaking caught her attention, which was why her mother had arranged for Josie to stay at Mr and Mrs Carpenters' place every weekend. That way she was sure Josie would be eating some decent meals and would also have the opportunity of seeing Elsie who rented a room there. Henry, her fiancé, was Mrs Carpenter's son. For the last three Fridays, as arranged, Josie had taken her washing with her so that Mrs Carpenter could add it to her family wash. Auntie Win didn't have a washing machine. Like most of the other residents in the flats, her basket of laundry was picked up weekly by a laundry service.

Josie poked her nose into the room that was being turned into a bathroom. The garish flowery wallpaper had been stripped off and in its place hung plain white lining paper. The legs of the newly installed bath were now hidden from view by a long piece of freshly painted board. Three of the walls around the old fireplace, the windows and behind the bath were white but the fourth wall was the same royal blue as the side of the bath. She noticed that the airing cupboard in the corner was now encased in white doors. Carefully avoiding the tin of blue paint stuck to an old sheet on the floor, she opened them. This was luxury. Her mother had always dreamed of having an airing cupboard. She climbed over cardboard boxes to the new basin and turned on the taps. Water came out of them! This meant that she and Auntie Win would no longer have to strip wash at the sink in the kitchen.

'On Sundays, I'll switch on the hot water!' she heard her aunt yell. She had obviously heard the water running.

Dashing back to the passage, Josie flung off her clothes in the room she shared with her aunt and opened the wardrobe door. Facing her was Auntie Win's old army uniform: a bottle-green jacket and skirt and, on the shelf above, her bottle-green cap with a badge of a lion below a crown.

She hung her school uniform next to it. Hardly had she slipped into a pair of corduroy trousers and a woolly jersey when there was a loud crash from the kitchen. Josie raced down the passage, through the half-decorated sitting room and empty dining room area towards the kitchen and the smell of burning, where she found her aunt scrabbling round the black and white floor tiles, attempting to pick up the charred remains of two pieces of toast.

'I forgot to put the oven gloves on when I pulled out the tray,' she explained, blowing on her fingers.

'The beans!' cried Josie, leaping towards a small saucepan on a glowing electric ring. A hot spoon was stuck inside. Using a damp, slimy cloth to hold the handle, she prized it out. As she stirred the congealed beans she could see that half the contents were now firmly attached to the bottom of the blackened saucepan. She forced them loose with the edge of the spoon while Auntie Win waved the billowing smoke out through the doorway onto the fire escape.

Later, after crunching her way through the scraped toast and dried baked beans, followed by a handful of fig rolls to take away the taste, Auntie Win brought two cups of tea over to the red Formica-topped table. It was a different world to tea-making at school. Josie heard that once the girls reached Form IV they had to use sugar tongs and learn how to pour tea properly into small china cups through a tea strainer. Already Josie had gathered that her mum poured tea *incorrectly*, always putting the milk in first to draw the tea leaves to the bottom to prevent them sticking to your teeth.

Her aunt planted herself in the chair opposite, clasping her cup.

'So what did you do today?' she asked, peering over the rim.

Josie looked away hurriedly.

'In diction class we had to recite, "If you play *gof* with no coat on you could *cetch* a cold. Always remember to take a *handkerchiff*. Oh my goodness! My *forrid* is *frahtfulli* hot! I must *jest git* my *medcin*. I do hope my temp*eratu*re will have *gorn* down by the morning."'

Auntie Win stared at her.

'It means, if you play golf with no coat on, you could catch a cold. Always remember to take a hankie. Oh my goodness! My forehead is frightfully hot!'

'Yes, yes. I get the picture,' said Auntie Win.

'And in etiquette,' Josie continued, 'we were taught how to tell a visitor where the toilet is, I mean, the *lavatory*, in case they're too shy to ask, I s'pose. When they arrive –'

'You say let me show you where the lavatory is?' interrupted Auntie Win.

'No. You say, "Let me show you the geography of the house."'

'Sounds like you need a map and compass.' Auntie Win looked puzzled. 'I don't remember seeing any plays with people wanting to know that particular information. Anything else?'

Josie nodded. 'We had dinin' room etiquette. You must never say, "Pass the cruet, please." I got that right cos I've never even heard of cruet. You say, "I *wonder* if you could pass the salt, pepper, mustard." And do you know that a lady or gentleman never puts vinegar on fish or bacon and eggs?'

'I didn't, but I'll keep that in mind for future reference. Now, tell me what's upsetting you?' her aunt said, looking Josie directly in the eye.

Josie could see that it was no use attempting to keep the meeting with the headmistress to herself.

'Miss Dagleish isn't going to put me up for any auditions this term because of my hair.'

'Ah. So asking that young woman to finish you off with the clippers hasn't helped?'

'No.'

'But you can play boys' parts. Elsie did at your age.'

'That's what I told her,' said Josie.

'And?'

'Boys only.'

'Really?'

Josie gave a dismal nod.

'But you're so good at playing them,' said her aunt.

Josie attempted to smile.

'Never mind, you can audition for parts next term. Although why you have to go away and work in some of these companies beats me. Why can't they rehearse plays at the school and perform them there? And anyway, what's the rush?'

'I think Miss Dagleish is worried I might grow too tall and there'll be less parts I can play.'

'You're hardly likely to be a giant, are you? Elsie's twenty-four and she's a titch. She still sometimes gets cast as a child. Don't you fret. You've got plenty of time. Anyway, it'll give you more of a chance to make friends. How are those two comic ones, Derek and John?'

'There'll be rehearsin' in a Shakespeare Company from Monday. They're sharin' the same part.'

'So you won't be seeing so much of them then?'

'Not for three months. They're tourin'.'

'And you're still not making friends with the girls.'

''ow did you know that?' asked Josie, surprised.

'I guessed. Years of being in charge of young women,' she added.

'There is one girl,' said Josie slowly, 'but she's always readin' books.'

'Look who's talking! You're Arthur Ransome mad.'

'I know. But hers are always ballet stories and the girls in them are always prancin' around and bein' . . .'

'Girlish?'

Josie forced herself to smile.

'So what else are you upset about?' pressed her aunt.

'If I don't get any acting work, I won't be able to earn any money to pay you back.'

'I don't want you to pay me back. As long as they see what a talented young niece I have and help her to use that talent then I'm happy. I'm sorry I can't afford to send you to one of those top notch stage schools like Italia Conti or Corona but I was told that your school is the best of the cheaper ones.' She gave a broad smile. 'You wait till they see you in full flood. There's none of that namby-pamby little Miss Helpless about you. You've got spirit.'

Josie lowered her nose into her cup and said nothing. Unfortunately, she did feel helpless. It was because of the comments Miss Dagleish had made about her face. Josie knew she could improve her voice and her dancing, but what could she do about her freckles?

'And?' said Auntie Win, picking up the dismal expression on her face.

'Remember when you told the man who was in charge of sellin' this flat that you were buying it without a husband or a father's permission and that you had the money?'

'Yes.'

'And that he was so shocked it looked as though he had sucked a lemon and been smacked across the face with a wet fish?'

'I do indeed. I treasure the memory.'

'Well, when I told Miss Dagleish that Ralph was in the Theatre Workshop Company . . .'

'Ah. Same reaction.'

'Yeah.'

'I wouldn't mention that to your mum. You know how proud she is of him, especially now he's playing in a London theatre and not gallivanting all over England.'

'So why won't she let me see him in *The Hostage*? Is it because there's a swear word in it?'

Auntie Win nodded.

'More than one I'm afraid.'

'Miss Dagleish said that the Theatre Workshop Company had no style.'

'That's true. They take your breath away instead.' Auntie Win smiled. 'And make you laugh.'

*Sounds more fun than what we're doing at school*, Josie thought.

'You look exhausted,' said her aunt. 'Early night, I think.'

'But I don't want to be asleep when Mum and Dad call.'

'You don't have to go to sleep. You can read that book Molly's lent you.'

Josie was still sharing Auntie Win's double bed. The other bedroom in the flat was filled halfway to its high ceiling with suitcases, boxes, books, dining-room chairs, a table, stacks of light brown wood in assorted shapes and sizes, and what her dad called *men's tools*. Her aunt's plan had been to put all the bits of furniture and the shelf units together in the sitting room before Josie moved in. Unfortunately, all that stood on the white carpet was a modern, red high-backed settee, a matching armchair and footstool, a low coffee table with a shelf underneath, a radiogram which housed a wireless and record player, and a television set hidden behind wooden shutters.

Stacked in a box in an alcove by the fireplace were her aunt's records, and under the window in the unfurnished dining room area was a pile of new curtains with black and white geometric designs. What her aunt needed was a second pair of hands but when any of the husbands of the women from the neighbouring flats had come round to help her, they had bolted out of the door as soon as they had spotted her wielding her Black and Decker drill.

'I'm not going to shoot you with it!' Josie had heard her aunt yell late one afternoon when she had returned from school to witness another well-meaning man scurry out onto the landing and run down the stairs. But Josie didn't mind sharing her aunt's room. It was cosy and she liked watching the flickering gas flames jiggering up the lines of jagged white bony-looking things in the tiny fireplace.

Climbing into bed, she settled back against the pillows and opened *Winter Holiday*. Since she had begun reading it she and Henry's half sister, Molly, had been copying two of the characters' way of sending messages to one another by drawing stick people with their arms placed in the alphabet positions of the semaphore code. The sisters, Nancy and Peggy Blackett, then drew the legs to look as though they were dancing to take attention away from any would-be spies who might be tempted to read their weekly letters and guess they were using the code. But she found it impossible to concentrate. Instead, she stared at the two photographs on her bedside table.

One was of her brother Harry and his young wife in the Australian outback. The other was of Josie in a bathing suit, taken with her mum and dad on the pebbly beach in Sternsea with Elsie, her older brother Ralph and his red-headed wife, Jessica. Josie was much younger than her brothers and sister. Ralph was seventeen when she was born, Elsie, twelve and Harry, fourteen. Elsie's fiancé, Henry, wasn't in the beach picture because he had been taking the photograph. It had been a special family picnic to celebrate Josie being offered a place at the stage school.

On the wall above the fireplace was the picture that made it all possible, a framed photograph of Auntie Win in her uniform receiving her premium bond cheque.

Josie shut her book and glanced across at the pile of library books on her aunt's bedside table. Ever since Auntie Win had seen Jack Hawkins playing a detective in the film *Gideon's Day*, she had been reading the Gideon novels. Three of them were stacked on top of each other along with another of the author's books, *Let's Kill Uncle Lionel*. Mum said she didn't know how Auntie Win could sleep after reading her crime books. Josie wondered too.

Some nights, just thinking about the titles of the books had her imagining a masked intruder creeping up the fire escape, slipping into the kitchen and through the sitting room. Within seconds he would be advancing down the passage, ready to crash into their bedroom, a revolver blazing in his gnarled and withered hand. It didn't help that her aunt often forgot to bolt the kitchen door. If Josie woke up during the night she would creep down the passage to check that it was locked.

On the far side of the room was a bookcase filled with green and white paperbacks with grisly titles, many of them written by women: *Dancers in Mourning*, *More Work For the Undertaker*, *Police at the Funeral*, *Death of a Ghost*, *Hide My Eyes*.

How could someone with a nice name like Margery or Dorothy write about murders? There was even one called *Spotted Hemlock* written by a woman called Gladys Mitchell, and hemlock, Josie knew, was a quick-acting poison. But then Mrs Hale, the owner of the house where the Carpenters lived, wrote detective novels too and her name was Henrietta.

*Enter a Murderer* and *Bullets for the Bridegroom* had just caught Josie's eye when the telephone rang in the hall. As she thrust the blankets aside and leaped out of bed, she heard a wave of laughter from the radiogram in the sitting room.

Her aunt was already standing by a small table in the hall holding the receiver.

'She's fine, Ellen. She's poking her head out of the bedroom door in her striped pyjamas as I speak,' Auntie Win said. She handed the receiver to Josie and returned to her comedy programme.

'Hello, Mum,' said Josie.

'Hello, love. How was school?'

Josie hesitated. It was so lovely to hear her mother's cheerful voice that she didn't want to upset her by telling her how lonely she felt.

'I'm being put up to Form III on Mondee.'

'What?!'

She heard her mum talking excitedly to her dad. Within seconds he was on the phone.

'Yer mum's told me. That's a turn up for the books. Promotion again, eh? You take after yer mum in the brains department, you do.'

Josie didn't like to tell him that it was because the work was too easy and that it had nothing to do with her being brainy.

'Is everythin' packed fer tomorrow night?' It was her mother back on the phone again.

'Yeah.'

'Elsie told me you're off to Winford on Saturday morning to see her and Larry in the run-through.'

'Yeah.'

'Can you give Henry a message at the Carpenters tomorrow tonight?'

'I can't,' said Josie. 'He's still in Scotland filmin' the documentary. I can give Elsie the message, though.'

'Thanks, love. Can you tell her that this solicitor man came round while we were out and spoke to one of the Dawson daughters from the upstairs flat. Sounded urgent. He needs to find Henry. It's about some legal business. Henry's old school didn't know that the Carpenters left this address nine years ago. And she couldn't give him his London address because she don't know it. Instead, she told him about little Larry working at Winford rep because she overheard us talkin' about it in the hall when she was leaving for school one mornin'. The solicitor's going to send a letter addressed to Henry at the theatre, care of Larry. Can you ask Elsie to pick it up?'

'Yeah. Larry would only lose it.'

'Or draw Sputniks on it and shove it with all his other drawin's,' said her mum.

Josie laughed. 'Has his mum got the parcel . . . ?'

'With your Guide uniform in it? Yeah. She rang to tell me it arrived this morning. But, Josie, you've only been to three meetings. You can't be enrolled unless you've been to at least four, and then there's all them tests to pass.'

'I've done most of them already. I want to pass the rest tomorrow.'

'What's the rush?'

'I'm still only a tenderfoot. Unless I'm a proper Guide I can't go campin' in the summer.'

'You don't want to go sleepin' on the ground,' interrupted her dad down the receiver. 'It ain't very comfortable, I can tell you. I 'ad enuff of it in the army.'

'I still want to go,' said Josie.

Ever since she had read the first of the Arthur Ransome books, *Swallows and Amazons*, her dream had been to go camping and sailing. Her parents had no interest in that sort of thing. Being a Girl Guide was the only way she would be able to find out what it was like to sleep under canvas and cook out in the open, and if she passed certain tests as a Guide, she could be a Sea Ranger when she was older and learn to sail. She had it all planned.

'How's Auntie Win's cookin'?' asked her mum.

Josie was about to tell her about the incinerated beans but suspected that her mother might not think it was so funny.

'Delicious,' she said.

'Mm,' said her mother in disbelief. 'Now you get to bed. We'll ring you again when you're at the Carpenters.'

Josie had hardly replaced the receiver when the doorbell rang.

'That'll be Mrs Jenkins!' her aunt yelled from the sitting room.

Josie padded barefoot down the hall and opened the door. Peering at Josie through spectacle lenses as thick as marbles stood a tiny elderly woman. In one hand she held up one of Auntie Win's cardigans, in the other, a long, grey, woolly sock.

'All done,' she announced, waving them.

Josie was staggered. It was only yesterday she had torn a hole in her sock on a large splinter on the floor of the school cloakroom. She observed that the elbow of her aunt's cardigan had also been darned.

'Kettle's on!' her aunt sang out, 'and I've just put out the custard creams.'

'That's what I like to hear,' said Mrs Jenkins excitedly, and she pushed her way past Josie and headed rapidly for the sitting room.

It was a weekly routine. On certain nights, Mrs Jenkins and Josie's aunt would watch television together. Mrs Jenkins didn't own one and she enjoyed a lot of the programmes Josie's aunt liked, especially if they had detectives in them.

Taking the mended sock into the bedroom, Josie hopped back into bed.

'I knew it was him! The brute!'

Josie woke with a start. Her aunt was sitting in bed next to her gazing in triumph at the last page of a *Gideon* book.

'Who did what?' Josie asked sleepily.

'Never you mind. It's far too gruesome for me to tell you. Oh, I do like this Gideon chap.'

'Is he like Sherlock Holmes?' yawned Josie.

'Nothing like. Sherlock Holmes is a private detective. Gideon is part of the police force. High up. And he's married with children. Quite ordinary, yet sharp and determined.'

'I thought you didn't like men,' said Josie.

'There are a few decent ones. Not many, I grant you, but a few.' Her aunt leaned back on her pillow and stared gravely at Josie. 'When you get married, make sure you marry a man who's had a bit of an education and who'll buy you carpets and a refrigerator.'

Josie had heard this piece of advice so many times she knew it by heart.

'Yes, Auntie Win,' she sighed.

What she didn't say was that she had decided she was going to be like her aunt. She would never marry. Marriage was being stuck at home baking cakes while your husband went out, did exciting work and had cake waiting for him as a reward when he returned home.

'Auntie Win, is that why you've never married anyone? Because you've bought your own carpets and refrigerator?'

But there was no answer. Having discovered the identity of the murderer, her aunt had sunk into a deep and satisfied sleep.

Josie leaned across the bed and switched off her lamp.

# 3

# In and Out of the Fray

'PLAY OUT TO THE AUDIENCE, JOSEPHINE,' demanded Mrs Havilland. 'Nice sweeping gestures, and remember to gaze up at the dress circle. You never know who's going to be up there watching. And keep smiling!'

The acting mistress, Mrs Havilland, was a big lady, in every way. If Josie's father had stood next to her he would have looked like a gnome. Her stout body resembled a giant egg timer, and Josie suspected that she wore a corset with bones in it. Upright, with a commanding voice, she barked out instructions.

Acting lessons were the ones Josie should have enjoyed the most but she dreaded them On her first day she had been informed that everything she had done in her school plays had been incorrect and had been instructed to *erase all memory of it* from her mind. At Miss Dagleish's establishment she would learn about the art of acting from scratch. Unfortunately, Josie was finding it so difficult that she had begun to wonder if she could act at all. What made her feel even more uncomfortable were the three mothers sitting at the side of the room in their hats, coats and gloves who kept making comments or gazing rapturously or sternly at their offspring. The other pupils thought it odd that no relative ever came to watch her.

'Smile? But I'm givin' the King some bad news,' Josie explained politely.

There was a disapproving tutting from Trixie's mother, a tall, sophisticated woman Josie had heard Esmeralda and her friends refer to as *chic*.

'I think I know better than you, young lady!' snapped Mrs Havilland.

'Lady!' spluttered Trixie from behind Josie.

'Quite,' Mrs Havilland muttered. 'Not perhaps the appropriate noun to use since we now know with whom your brother has been working.'

Josie watched as Mrs Havilland taught them gestures that would convey feelings: clasped hands and eyes upwards for overwhelming sadness with extra marks if you could produce a tear, palm of the hand on the chest for sincerity, both hands slapped to the cheeks for shock, and finger wagging with a smile for anger.

The previous week, when Josie had been playing someone who was furious at being treated unjustly, the acting mistress had stopped her.

'An angry girl is an ugly girl. Anger with a laugh, remember? Otherwise the audience won't like you. Even in a fury, be elegant. Observe the other girls. With any luck you might learn something.'

And Josie had sat at the side, watching them throw their arms out at the invisible stalls, smiling through their tears, forever stretching their lips and exposing their teeth at every opportunity. If they could do it, why couldn't she?

It was then that she had remembered Elsie's words: 'Are you sure you want to go to a stage school? You might pick up bad habits.' Josie hadn't understood what her sister had meant and still didn't. How could she tell the difference between a bad habit and a good one?

Also, most of the pupils at the stage school wanted to be stars. She didn't. She just wanted to act. Maybe it was because working in the theatre felt more down to earth to her. By Josie's sixth birthday, Elsie was already a drama student and her older brother, Ralph, an actor, and whenever she had been taken to see them perform, she had forgotten they were her brother or sister. On stage they were completely different people and they did not keep gazing out at the audience with an enormous grin all the time.

Just when she was beginning to think it couldn't get any worse, there was an elocution lesson.

'Today,' announced Mrs Havilland, 'we will be addressing the "y" sound. Hands up who can tell me how "y" should sound at the end of a word?'

Doris flung up an arm.

'Yes, Doris?'

'"I" as in "bit",' she said smugly.

'Correct. And how should it *not* be pronounced? Yes, Thelma?'

'"Ee" as in "bee".'

'Well done, Thelma. Now I'd like you to repeat after me: *orfli*. I'm *orfli* pleased to meet you, your lordship.'

And everyone chanted the sentence after her.

'I'm *frahtfli* sorry, madam,' she said.

And so it went on. *Jolli* good. *Terribli* cold. *Splendidli* arranged. *Prettili* decorated.

And the mothers clapped.

'Now, before the class is dismissed, I want to bring an extremely serious matter to your attention.' Mrs Havilland clasped her hands and held them firmly under her ample bosom. 'ITV!' she said dramatically. 'Now we all know what the school policy is regarding ITV, don't we?'

The mothers nodded in unison.

'We do not approve of ITV. In fact, it is forbidden for pupils from this establishment to watch such common, working-class, cheap entertainment, besides which, there are far too many American programmes on that channel.'

*But there are American programmes on the BBC too,* thought Josie.

'Which I firmly believe will destroy our British traditions if they are allowed to keep being shown. As you know,' she said, looking directly at the mothers, 'I am in complete agreement with Lord Reith on this matter. The influence of commercial television is like . . .' Here she paused. 'Like what?' she demanded.

Thelma raised her arm.

'Yes, Thelma?'

'Smallpox and Black Death.'

'Correct. And . . .' she added, swinging her head back to the mothers who were now sitting to attention, their gloved hands resting on their handbags.

'Bubonic plague,' they chorused. 'And juvenile delinquency.'

'I don't know how they have the gall to show those vulgar quiz shows and those dreadful men wrestling one another in boxing rings,' Mrs Havilland continued. 'Why the government doesn't close it down defies belief.'

Josie was sorely tempted to ask Mrs Havilland how she knew so much about ITV if she never watched it.

'Which is why we never put pupils up for auditions for that . . .' She paused as though the letters ITV were too distasteful to utter. '. . . establishment. The BBC, however, is quite a different kettle of fish.' She glared at the class. 'That *other* channel is not for the intelligent and cultured viewer so I hope that *none* of you are ever tempted to stray in that direction.'

They all dutifully shook their heads but Josie had her fingers crossed.

In the break between the acting and dance class, the girls in her form declared that she was too lower class to join them at the tea house. This was accompanied by whispering about Josie's brother working with *that Joan Littlewood*. Secretly relieved, Josie nipped upstairs to the empty classroom and examined the fourth-form display board. There were tips on appearance and grooming, advice about what colours to wear if you were a brunette, a blonde or a redhead, and how you had to finish off your outfit by either wearing a knitted beret or gloves.

Pinned on the middle of a board was a picture of a young

woman in a grey suit. 'A grey flannel suit is an investment for any girl,' she had heard the deportment teacher announce repeatedly to visiting mothers. 'Tailored, of course.' The jacket must be fitted to emphasise the waist, and the skirt had to fall in box pleats. This information was followed by a list of accessories a young girl needed to acquire.

With a sinking heart, Josie realised that she would be hearing more about the wonders of the grey suit the following year. By the time she had reached the words at the bottom of the display (*NEATNESS, CLEANLINESS, PATIENCE AND CALMNESS*) she had had enough. She nipped over to her desk and took out *Winter Holiday*. Returning to it was bliss. Lost in a scene where two characters, Dick and Dorothea, were 'sailing' at night on a sledge on a frozen lake in a swirling blizzard, she was interrupted by a loud cough. She glanced up to find Miss Dagleish standing in the doorway glaring at her. Josie sprung to her feet and curtsied.

'Are you not required in Grade IV Ballet?'

'After the break, madam. Yes.'

'The break finished ten minutes ago. If you spent less time burying yourself in books and more time concentrating on eliminating the bad habits you have acquired, you might be fortunate enough to be given a role in a production before the school year is out. Now off you go and get changed.'

Later that afternoon, Josie hauled her case and duffle bag up the stone steps to a tiled porch, and pulled the iron chain by the Carpenters' heavy front door. A bell clanged in the distance. She pressed her nose against the stained-glass window and stepped back as a shadowy figure approached. The door swung open and a slim middle-aged woman with dark wavy hair smiled down at her.

'Hello, Josie,' she said, taking her luggage.

'Hello, Mrs Carpenter.'

As Josie removed her school hat in the vast hall, revealing her shorn hair, Mrs Carpenter gave a sharp intake of breath.

'I thought I'd be put up for boys' parts if I had it cut even shorter,' Josie explained, 'but it didn't work.'

'Oh, well never mind,' said Mrs Carpenter. 'We all make mistakes.'

Josie noticed that the door to her left was ajar. It led to the room where Mr Carpenter marked books and prepared lessons, and Mrs Carpenter typed up manuscripts for a publisher. Molly would be in there attempting to rid herself of most of her weekend homework before Guides. It was the usual Friday night routine but she was still disappointed that she couldn't stick her head round the door and have a chat.

'Go away, Larry!' she heard Molly shout. 'I can't think when you keep interrupting me.'

'Larry!' called out Mrs Carpenter. 'Come out of there!'

A tiny boy with red hair shot out into the hall. Unlike Josie's hair, which was a dark mahogany red, Larry's hair was a light ginger. Though he was nine, he resembled a six year old, which was why he had been given a role in *Life With Father*.

'Molly won't help. Can you teach me, Mummy?'

'I'm sorry, but I've washing and ironing to do.'

'But if I don't know how to do it by tomorrow Mr King will be angry with me.'

'Tiddle-de-winks,' explained Mrs Carpenter catching Josie's eye. 'Larry needs to be able to play it on stage with Michael Bailey.'

'Can't Michael show you?' Josie asked.

'I never see him after rehearsal. He has to go back to your school for lessons. Do you know how to play it?'

'No. But what about the other lodgers?'

There were footsteps coming down the staircase. A tall, lean man with a neat beard and a sheaf of manuscript paper in his hand was heading for the hall. He was over from France and staying in Henry's room while he was filming in Scotland. Josie stared at him in awe. His name was Mr Philip Hart. Molly had told her all about him. He was in a jazz quartet and wrote music for films. He smiled at them and opened the door into a massive room on the other side of the hall. Larry tugged at her arm but she was too shy to ask him and he looked too busy to help them. Within minutes they could hear him playing the piano.

'What am I going to do?' Larry wailed. 'There's only Miss Partridge left.'

They looked at each other in dismay. Miss Partridge kept herself to herself at the top of the house. Molly nicknamed her 'the angry mouse'.

'I heard your dad say her bark is worse than her bite,' said Josie reassuringly.

'But I don't like her bark.'

'I'll go with you.'

'Not until you're out of that uniform,' said Mrs Carpenter. 'I need to put your blouse in the wash and sponge down your gymslip and tie.'

Josie tiptoed through the study, glancing briefly at Molly who was sitting hunched over a table at the bay window surrounded by books and paper. She folded back the two dividing doors between the study and Molly's book-lined bedroom. A pair of Josie's pyjamas lay folded at the end of a neatly made camp bed. All her pyjamas were boy's ones with the flies sewn up. She hated frilly nighties and girls' pyjamas, especially if they were pink or had flowers on them.

She flung off her uniform, throwing it into a scrambled heap on the bed. Peering through the high windows overlooking the walled garden and tree-filled graveyard beyond, she pulled on her corduroy trousers, shirt and jersey.

Back in the hall, she found Larry sitting at the foot of the stairs waiting impatiently for her.

'I'll do the talkin',' she told him.

They walked slowly up the stairs, past the rooms on the first floor, the one on the second floor and up to the landing between the two attic bedrooms where they could hear muffled voices coming from Miss Partridge's wireless. Larry clutched her hand. She knocked politely on the door, forcing her mouth sideways into a stage-school smile. There was no response and the smile began to develop into a nervous tic.

'A fiery horse with the speed of light, a cloud of dust and a hearty Hi Ho Silver!' whispered Larry urgently. 'That's what the Lone Ranger says when he rides away with Tonto.'

'So why are you sayin' it?' asked Josie, puzzled.

'Because I wish we were doing that.'

'I'll try again.'

By now the smile had lost its fight to remain stretched across her teeth. This time Josie knocked so hard that she hurt her knuckles. She was vigorously blowing on them when the door was flung open and she found herself staring up at a disgruntled Miss Partridge. Tall with untidy hair and flushed cheeks, she glowered down at them.

'Yes!' she snapped.

Josie swallowed.

'I wouldn't *normally* interrupt you, Miss Partridge, as I know you've got *lots* of readin' to do,' she began politely, 'but this is an emergency of the *utmost* importance and we have no one else to turn to and the deadline is tomorrow and there will be all *hell* to pay and plenty of fireworks if we don't find out soon.'

'An emergency?' she said, frowning. 'What kind of emergency?'

'Life and death,' said Larry.

'Well, it ain't that bad,' said Josie.

'You don't know Mr King,' added Larry.

'Anyway, it's *extremely* serious,' Josie stated emphatically. 'So we're keepin' our fingers crossed that you know all about it cos we don't and no one else does.'

'I'm sorry, but I have been unable to understand a single word you've uttered. Now if you don't mind . . .'

'Do you know how to play Tiddle-de-winks?' Larry cried out in despair.

'Tiddle-de-winks?'

And then to Josie's astonishment, she smiled.

'Oh, *Tiddlywinks*!' she exclaimed. 'Yes, I know how to play. I happen to be the Withercombe Heath's 1954 Tiddlywinks champion.'

Josie and Larry glanced at each other in amazement.

'Miss Partridge, if you show Larry how to play it, you'll save his bacon,' said Josie.

'In that case you had better come in,' said Miss Partridge regally.

'Not on my own,' whispered Larry, dragging Josie in after him.

Miss Partridge had her own set of Tiddlywinks, and by the time Molly had finished her Latin homework downstairs, the Withercombe Heath's 1954 champion had taught Larry and Josie the rudiments of the game. Because it was usually played between four players, Josie and Larry had to pretend to be two people. Miss Partridge gave the small, flat, red and blue discs called winks to Josie, and the green and yellow ones to Larry. She drew back one side of her rug and set out her Tiddlywinks mat on the bare floorboards.

Most of the time was spent trying to make their winks fly into a small pot by pressing a bigger disc firmly down at the edges of the smaller ones or making them land on each other's winks.

By this time Larry was laughing.

'Do you *have* to go to Guides tonight?' he asked later through a mouthful of toast in the warmth of the basement kitchen.

'Yes,' Josie told him. 'I'm hopin' to get enrolled tonight.'

Mrs Carpenter had just finished ironing her red neckerchief.

'Over to you,' she said, standing to one side. Armed with a tape measure, Josie folded the neckerchief several times until it was two and a half inches wide, refolded it in half and made a knot. Two pieces were left on either side, ready to tie at the back of her collar.

A navy blue skirt, blue blouse with two folded, buttoned-down pockets and new leather belt with the trefoil in the metal buckle were hanging over a nearby chair.

'But I need more Tiddlywinks practice,' he implored.

'I'm sure Miss Partridge won't mind playing a game with you,' said Josie.

'Now, don't you go bothering her,' said his mother.

'She likes it,' said Larry.

'Really?'

Footsteps began descending the stairs to the kitchen and Molly peered round the door, dressed in her Guide uniform.

'Hurry up, or we'll be late.'

'Have you brushed your hair?' asked her mother, glancing at the tangle of sandy curls sticking out from under Molly's beret.

'Yes!'

'You could have fooled me.'

Josie grabbed her uniform, ran up to Molly's bedroom and undressed. As she did up her Guide blouse, skirt and belt, she felt a rush of nerves. With trembling fingers, she pulled on her fawn socks and stepped into her polished lace-up shoes. She raised her collar and carefully tied the red neckerchief in a reef knot at the back.

'Right over left and left over right,' she chanted to herself. She mustn't tie a Granny knot tonight of all nights.

She checked that both buttons on the two front pockets were done up, walked over to Molly's dressing table and placed a navy blue beret on her head. Facing the mirror, she raised her right hand, enfolding her little finger with her thumb and gave the threefold salute.

Half an hour later, she and Molly were striding along the pavement towards the school where the Friday meetings were held, while Josie continued thinking about the knots she would be asked to tie that night. On her first week, her patrol leader, Sheila, had explained the meaning of the good turn, as well as the Guide salute and handshake. By the second week, Josie had arrived with the Guide promise and the ten parts of the Guide law learned by heart and had quickly picked up the whistle, hand signals and tracking signs.

On the third week she turned up with a letter from Mrs Carpenter stating that she had watched Josie strip and make a bed correctly. Josie then learned the three flags that made up the Union Jack, the correct way to fly it, and how to prevent the end of a rope from fraying by winding a piece of string tightly round the end. Whipping, they called it.

Stepping into the school passage, Josie could hear girls chatting loudly at breakneck speed. As they walked into the brightly lit school gym, the Guide lieutenant – Lefty, a tall woman in her thirties with large white teeth who was prone to sudden outbursts of laughter – gaped at her in astonishment when she spotted Josie wearing a uniform. She glanced in the direction of Captain, a middle-aged upright woman who treated the meetings with a certain amount of gravitas. Fortunately she had her back to them.

Molly and Josie separated and headed in the direction of their respective patrol corners. Each patrol had a screen with a picture of a bird and a motto. The Skylarks patrol's was *Always Aim High*. The Robin patrol's was *Brave and Friendly*. The Wren patrol's was *Keep Trying*. Molly was in the Skylarks. Josie was in the Bullfinch patrol. Its motto was *Never Say Die*.

'When someone says, *"Never say die"*,' Josie had asked Sheila on her first night, 'does that mean that there are some people who go around saying "Die" all the time when they shouldn't?'

'No. It means never giving up when the going gets tough,' she had explained. 'And that there's usually always an answer to a problem.'

Sheila was an upright, confident, fourteen year old in her last year at the local secondary modern school. A First Class Guide with a trail of badges sewn onto her long sleeves, she was working towards her Queen's Guide badge.

Once everyone had arrived in the gym, the sound of a whistle indicated it was time for each patrol to stand in line for roll call and inspection. For the last three meetings, Josie, as the only tenderfoot, had been at the end of the line but that evening, a nervous, slightly built girl wearing a mauve mohair cardigan was there instead. Her name was Carol.

Sheila examined each member of her patrol, straightening their ties and berets.

'You know you shouldn't be wearing your uniform yet,' she said to Josie.

'I've been practising my knots,' said Josie. 'I'm sure I know them well enough to pass tonight.'

Everyone stood to attention as Captain left the Robin patrol and headed in their direction. Her eyebrows shot up as she approached Josie. Josie lifted her chin and stared straight ahead. Auntie Win would have been proud of her.

'We'll see,' Captain said quietly, and then gave a welcome smile to the new girl.

After the inspection, the patrols returned to their corners and Sheila asked Josie to tie a reef knot, a double overknot, a round turn and two half hitches.

From the expression on the patrol leader's face, Josie was convinced she had done a good job. Behind her, from the Skylarks, Molly was giving her a thumbs up sign. Josie watched Sheila hand the knots to Captain where they were examined solemnly. And then she gave a nod. When Sheila returned she was smiling.

'I've passed, haven't I?' shouted Josie and she leaped in the air.

Sheila laughed.

'You're going to be enrolled at the end of the meeting.'

The rest of the evening was filled with games and work towards badges while Sheila instructed Josie as to what she would need to say at the enrolment.

And then it was time for the patrol leaders to be called

up by Captain, who had now pulled on a pair of leather gauntlets. The colours were raised, the four patrols spread themselves in a horseshoe formation, and Josie stood with her arms by her side. Two Guides, who were carrying the colours – the Union Jack and the Guide flag – marched slowly through the open part of the horseshoe and up to the front where they stood one on either side. Sheila gave Josie a nod and together they walked towards Captain.

'This is Josie Hollis,' announced Sheila solemnly, 'and she wishes to become a Guide.'

Captain looked gravely down at her.

'Do you know what *on your honour* means?' she asked.

'Yes,' answered Josie. 'It means I am to be trusted.'

'Can I trust you on your honour to do your best? To do your duty to God and the Queen? To help other people at all times? And to obey the Guide Law?'

Josie looked directly at Captain. Making the Guide sign level with her shoulder, she made the promise. Captain held the trefoil badge in her hand. The three leaves symbolised the three parts of the promise. In the leaf at the top there was a star. On either side there was the letter 'G' in the two leaves The words *Girl Guides* were engraved in what looked like a metal ribbon below.

Captain walked over to Josie and pinned the badge onto her tie. From now on she would need to polish the badge every week. Then it was time for the handshake, which had to be done with the left hand.

'Josie Hollis, welcome to the great Guide family,' said Captain. 'As a member of this family I trust you to keep the promise and to try to do a good turn every day.'

Josie saluted Captain, took a step forward and faced the colours. First she saluted the Union Jack to show her loyalty to her country and then to the Guide Flag to show her loyalty to the Guides.

Captain then indicated to Josie that she should face the Company.

'St Bartholomew's thirty-second Girl Guides, I present you with our new member, Josie Hollis of the Bullfinch patrol.'

Josie saluted again and everyone saluted back.

'You may now return to your patrol and you are entitled to all the privileges of our worldwide movement.'

Josie walked over to her patrol beaming, the company sang *God Save the Queen* and the colours were taken down.

The ceremony was over.

The evening was rounded off with a talk from Captain and some songs, including a strange one called *Ging Gang Gooli* and a lovely slow one called *Kumbaya*. They finished with a tune Josie had heard in a film being played on a militairy bugle at the end of a day. It was called *Taps*.

'Day is done,' they all sang softly.

'*Gone the sun.*

'*From the sea*

'*From the hills*

'*From the sky.*

'*All is well*

'*Safely rest*

'*God is nigh.*'

With overwhelming relief, Josie now knew she had

something good to hang on to if things grew worse at the stage school.

Once back at the house, she and Molly raced up two flights of stairs to the sitting room on the first floor where Mrs Carpenter had laid out plates to warm in front of the fire. Molly's father arrived soon after with the fish and chips.

'Everything ready?' he asked as he stepped into the warmth.

Friday night was fish and chip night, as it was with Josie's family. Mr Carpenter handed the bundles of hot newspaper over to Mrs Carpenter and turned on the twelve-inch TV in the corner. While he moved the aerial around, concentrating on the reception, the food was served onto the plates. Josie and Molly pulled out the little tables and handed out the cutlery. Finally the zig-zaggy lines on the screen disappeared and the picture came into focus. Balancing the aerial precariously on a stack of books, Mr Carpenter walked gingerly backwards towards the settee while everyone kept their eyes on it, willing it not to fall.

'This is Ada from Bradford,' said the glamorous hostess on the screen, introducing Ada to the quizmaster, Michael Miles.

A short man with heavy glasses, holding what looked like a flat brass drum and a stick with a knob on the end, hovered beside a stout, bespectacled housewife.

'Ada,' said Michael Miles jovially. 'How nice to meet you. Are you well?'

'Yes,' said Ada.

'Out!' yelled Molly and Josie, as the audience groaned above the sound of the gong being struck.

It was the Yes / No interlude part of *Take Your Pick*. Each contestant had to answer questions for sixty seconds without saying Yes or No in order to reach the next round.

Josie fingered the trefoil-shaped Girl Guide badge that Captain had pinned onto her tie that evening.

Molly caught her eye and smiled. They both knew what the trefoil badge meant. It meant Josie would be going camping with her in the summer, a fully fledged member of the Bullfinch patrol.

# 4

# Winford

'SHE AND DAD USED TO ARGUE ALL THE TIME,' said Elsie. 'I suppose she was used to being the the boss and when Dad came back he wasn't going to have it.'

They were sitting in a railway carriage with Larry on the way to Winford, a half hour journey from London, and talking about the time when Auntie Win and cousin Joan shared a small house in a bombed street with Josie's mother, Elsie and her brothers. After her father had returned home from the army, they had all tended to get under each other's feet.

'But they don't quarrel now,' said Josie.

'That's because they don't live together. And once she joined the Women's Army Corps, she became happier, less argumentative.'

'Women's *Royal* Army Corps,' Josie corrected her.

'Beg pardon, your highness. Women's *Royal* Army Corps.' Elsie gave a mock salute. 'And then when she became an officer she could boss people to her heart's content.'

'She told me that she left the WRAC so she could see more of us.'

'That's nice.' Then Elsie frowned. 'Let's hope she finds a job where she can rule the roost a bit otherwise she'll be bossing us again.'

'She doesn't boss me around.'

'That's true. But I think you two are quite similar.'

'Really?' said Josie brightly.

'Now let's get on with helping Larry with his lines.'

'Yes. Hurry up or it'll be too late,' urged Larry impatiently.

'Yes, boss,' said Josie, teasing him.

'The three act play is set in New York in the eighteen eighties,' said Elsie, peering over her round tortoise-shell-rimmed glasses. 'Would you read Whitney's lines, Josie?'

'In an American accent,' interrupted Larry. 'Like Michael does.'

Larry was playing a boy called Harlan. Although he had three older brothers, most of his scenes were with nine-year-old Whitney.

'I play two parts,' explained Elsie. 'A young, nervous maid who is frightened out of the house at the beginning of the play by Mr Clare Day, the father of the red-headed boys. And later I play a middle-aged maid who stays.'

'Clare?' said Josie. 'But that's not a man's name.'

'It is in America,' Elsie said. 'Right. Let's begin.'

For the remainder of the train journey, Elsie and Josie helped Larry with his lines. As the play progressed and he had less to say, Elsie talked him through the scenes he didn't know so that he would be able to respond to what was happening when they came to rehearse them on stage. Being silent during them, he hadn't been called to the earlier rehearsals and it worried him because he was meant to follow Michael, the boy playing Whitney.

'Once we're in the theatre, we'll go over your moves on stage,' Elsie reassured him. 'Just keep remembering that Harlan is a happy little boy who loves playing board games.'

'Like Whitney and his baseball?' asked Larry.

'That's right.'

'But Whitney is good at baseball which means I have to be good at Tiddlywinks,' he said anxiously.

'You will be. Remember we have a week until opening night.'

The train began to slow down.

'Quick! We're here,' said Elsie, opening the door, and she and Josie grabbed Larry's tiny hands and helped him leap across the wide gap onto the platform.

It had been six years since Josie and her parents had paid a farewell visit to the Palace Theatre before moving to Sternsea, but as soon as they stepped through the stage door she felt instantly at home. But then she always felt at home whenever she set foot into a theatre and she had been inside many because of the roles her brother and sister had played.

'Hello, Elsie,' said a cheery voice from the wooden cubicle. A man in his eighties, sitting by a paraffin heater, was peering out at them.

'Hello, Wilfred,' said Elsie.

Next to him stood a younger version of him in his sixties.

'Any post for me, Samuel?' she asked.

He shook his head.

'Is there a letter for my fiancé, Henry Carpenter?'

'The C box is empty. Is he joining the company then?'

'No. He's not an actor. He's a camera operator. But there's a solicitor who's trying to reach him. He doesn't know his address but he knows Larry is working here . . .'

'Ah. So you want me and Dad to keep our eyes peeled for a letter addressed to him.'

'If you would. It'll say *Care of Larry*.'

'Right-ho.'

She nudged Josie forward. 'Wilfred, do you know who this is?'

'No. Should I?'

'Remember a certain night twelve years ago when my very pregnant mother came backstage after a show?'

He nodded his head vigorously.

'Don't think anyone who were 'ere would forget that night. There were no time for her to get to the hospital, were there?'

'And the entire company, including my father, were hovering in the corridor while she gave birth in one of the dressing rooms.'

'And we had a party afterwards,' he said, beaming.

'This is the baby who was born in that dressing room. This is Jo.'

Josie shoved her hands awkwardly into the pockets of her duffle coat.

Wilfred looked confused. 'But it were a girl who were born 'ere.'

'Jo *is* a girl.'

Josie beamed.

'She likes being mistaken for a boy,' explained Elsie.

'Except when I get told off for bein' in the Ladies,' Josie said.

'Oh well,' murmured Wilfred. 'Takes all sorts.'

'Samuel, can we go on stage?'

'I should think so. Fiona's already there, marking up.'

Josie knew from both Elsie and Ralph that *marking up* meant measuring different areas on the stage and drawing chalk marks on the floor so that the cast would know where the doors and furniture would be set, and could time their moves and dialogue in exactly the same place at every rehearsal.

'Come on, Jo,' said Elsie.

Josie followed her sister and Larry up the steps to the door that led backstage.

'Fiona is the ASM,' Elsie explained to Josie.

'Assistant stage manager,' said Larry.

'I know that,' said Josie.

They stepped into a corridor.

'That's where the kitchen and the sitting room for the cast is,' said Elsie, pointing to the left. 'It's called the green room. There are two dressing rooms on this floor. Number one and number two.'

'And I was born in number two.'

'That's right.' Elsie tried the door but it was locked, as was the green room. 'It's because we're early,' she said.

'How many characters are there in the play?' asked Josie, trying to imagine how many actors and actresses would be getting into their costumes in each room.

'Fourteen. But because I play two of them, there are thirteen in the cast plus the other two boys who take turns playing Harlan and Whitney.'

'What about the older brothers?'

'They're played by two adult actors who look young. Clarence is supposed to be seventeen and his brother John is supposed to be . . .' She glanced at Larry.

'Fifteen!' said Larry.

'Well done. Michael and Larry and the other two boys are the only children in the cast. You might meet Michael's matron later.'

'But she isn't like the school matron who looks for nits,' Larry explained.

'No,' said Elsie, smiling. 'She's a theatre matron, a chaperone. She and Michael are staying in lodgings in Winford at the moment. The other Whitney and Harlan rehearse on alternate days.'

They carried on down the corridor and pushed open a door into the stage left wings. A young woman in slacks and a jersey was on stage pushing furniture from the set of *Gigi* to one side.

'Do you mind if I go through Larry's moves with him?' Elsie asked her from the wings. 'I can give you a hand with the furniture.'

'Being bribed is my weakness,' Fiona said, throwing aside a clump of fringe off one eye. There were shadows under her eyes, Josie observed, yet she seemed to have the stamina of three people. 'Help yourself. Though you'll have to put up with me marking up around you.' She glanced at Josie. 'And who's this?'

'Jo,' said Elsie.

'I'm helping out,' said Josie, quickly.

'And sneaking into the auditorium to watch the run through?' Fiona added suspiciously.

Elsie laughed.

'I've met professional actors and actresses backstage, but I've never seen them rehearse before,' Josie added. 'Please can I –?'

'I have heard nuzzink,' interrupted Fiona in a foreign accent. 'I 'ave seen nuzzink. I say nuzzink.'

Half an hour later, Fiona was sitting with Elsie downstage watching Larry and Josie with the prompt book, their backs to the auditorium, and as Josie acted Whitney's part with her sister's copy of the play, Larry began to relax and laugh.

It was when they came to the Tiddlywinks section that Fiona let out a whoop of delight.

'You can play it!' she exclaimed. 'I've been having sleepless nights over that. Michael always has to dash off after rehearsals and I haven't had time to learn how to play it so that I can teach you both. Oh, that's made my day!'

It was during the next scene that Josie became aware of noises in the wings as the other members of the cast began to arrive. By the time they reached the final scene, the two cast members who were playing Harlan and Whitney's mother and father, Vinnie and Clare, had joined in. Josie didn't understand a lot of what was going on because she hadn't read the whole play, but she picked up that Mr Clare Day was being rushed off to be baptised, having never got round to it as a baby.

There was a moment when Larry suddenly stopped. 'Josie looks at me,' he said.

'Yes?' said Elsie 'What's wrong with that?'

'Michael doesn't. He acts as though I'm not there.'

'I expect it's because he's had to rehearse without you and had to imagine you,' she said. 'Once you spend more time together I'm sure he'll look at you then.'

It was only when Larry and Josie were running off stage holding hands that they heard someone clapping in the auditorium.

'Well done, Larry,' boomed the voice of Ben King, the director.

Fiona whirled round. 'Jo came in early to help Larry out,' she explained swiftly.

'Thank you, Joseph. Now I think we'd better start the run-through. Everyone on stage.'

Josie nipped into the wings and headed for the stage door. Elsie had already asked Samuel if she could watch from the dress circle and he had agreed to let her sneak through a side entrance by the foyer at the front of the theatre.

'And keep quiet,' he said, as she slipped in, 'or Mr King will have my guts for garters. And remember, no sneezing, no coughing and no laughing!'

By the time Josie had sprinted along red and white corridors with their framed photographs of past productions on the walls, had leaped up several flights of wide, ornate stairways and crawled backwards on hands and knees down the carpeted stairs and into a seat, she realised from the tone of Mr King's voice that he was not in the best of moods. The cast were standing on stage looking lost and Fiona was being sent off to make an urgent phone call.

Elsie had explained earlier that until the cast had run through the entire play without stopping, Mr King wouldn't be able to see if it hung together or be able to pinpoint its strengths and weaknesses. But no one was moving. Instead, they were all gazing hopefully into the wings.

'Where the dickens is he?' yelled the director. 'If she doesn't bring him soon we'll have to start without him. She knows we have a matinee of *Gigi* after lunch. Really, this is too bad!'

Josie scanned the stage but she didn't know the play well enough to guess who might be missing. And then she remembered that Elsie had said that there were two children in the cast. Of course! There was no other small boy. No Michael.

Fiona reappeared and walked down to the front of the stage. She looked uneasy.

'Well?' said the director impatiently. 'Is he on his way?'

'Not yet, I'm afraid.'

'Please don't tell me he's overslept.'

'No . . .' began Fiona awkwardly.

'Then why hasn't the matron brought him here?'

'He's refused to leave his lodgings. He's terrified he might be run over and go to hell. The theatre matron forced him to eat the lamb chops the landlady had cooked last night.'

'Oh,' said the young actor playing Clarence. 'He's a Catholic. They're not allowed to eat meat on a Friday. It's a mortal sin.'

'A priest is on his way to the lodgings to hear his confession,' added Fiona. 'He's in a terrible state. He'll be along later.'

'Well, we can't wait to start the run till he arrives. Pity that other little feller's gone.'

'I haven't,' said Josie loudly from the dress circle.

The director peered up to her hiding place. 'And what are you doing up there, sonny?'

'Watching. I'm from the same stage school as Michael.'

'How fortuitous. Did you audition for me too? Because if you did, you didn't make much impression.'

'No,' said Josie and she crossed her fingers. 'I was rehearsing for an advert for . . . um . . . Virol.' She remembered her mother made her take a spoonful of it with Minadex every morning in the winter. 'It keeps you healthy,' she added. 'And it's a wonderful tonic.'

'You don't need to try to sell me the stuff. Get yourself down here. I take it you have a rough idea of what you're doing.'

'In the scenes with Larry,' said Josie.

'We'll push him around,' said Hugh, the middle-aged actor playing Clare Dale, 'until Michael turns up.'

'Someone get him a copy of the play,' said Mr King.

Elsie was gazing up at her open-mouthed and Larry was beaming.

'Right, let's start,' roared the director. 'Act One, Scene One.'

Josie savoured every moment of the run-through. By now she had an idea of what Whitney was like – a boy who wanted to be out playing baseball, who was so good at the game that he had been chosen to pitch with the city boys and that he desperately needed to be out of the house and with them as soon as possible. Breakfast was a barrier between being stuck indoors and experiencing the thrill of pitching, and he must remove it as quickly as possible before someone else took his place.

There was no time to be nervous about the scenes that were unfamiliar to her because the rest of the cast were so keen to do the run-through that they swept her along with them. It was during the scene while she was kneeling on the floor playing Tiddlywinks that Samuel appeared.

'I'm sorry to interrupt, Mr King, but Michael Bailey's parents have rung the stage door and left a message. They're very upset at the way their son has been treated by the matron and are travelling down from Manchester to take him home.'

There was a stunned silence. The director shook his head.

'You'd think a grown woman would understand that you don't force a Catholic child to eat meat on a Friday. It's as bad as forcing a Jewish child to eat pork!' He came up the steps at the side of the auditorium and onto the stage, tugging frantically at his thick white hair. And then he stopped and looked down at Josie.

'How old are you, Joe?'

'Twelve.'

'Splendid. We can get a licence for you. And you look nine, which is even better.'

'It runs in the family, sir,' said Josie politely, thinking of Elsie.

He looked at her curiously for a moment.

'Does it? Mm. Well, I must say, your stage school may employ the most inept theatre matron I've ever had the misfortune to come across but they seem pretty well organised on the understudy front. Did Miss Dagleish send you?'

'No. I came with my sister,' said Josie slowly.

'Me,' said Elsie.

'Ah! To watch her in the run-through. Not very professional, Elsie.' He turned back to Josie. 'Why have I never seen you at any auditions then? And please! No more extolling the virtues of Virol.'

'I've only been at the stage school for a few weeks, Mr King.'

She was about to drop into a curtsy and stretch her mouth into a winning smile when she suddenly couldn't be bothered. It felt too silly.

'Good,' he said. 'You'll play Whitney in our production then.'

Josie gasped.

'You have no objections to your brother being in the cast I take it, Elsie?'

Elsie shook her head wildly.

'Fine. Carry on with the scene.'

At the end of the run-through, Mr King gave notes to the cast in the auditorium so that Fiona could put back the *Gigi* furniture ready for the matinee. After he had dismissed everyone, he asked Elsie to stay behind with Larry and Josie.

'This afternoon, I'd like you and Joe to go through the Whitney scenes that are new to him and then again tomorrow with Fiona. Can you do that in your London digs?'

'Yes. There's an enormous room on the ground floor,' replied Elsie. 'I'll ask Larry's parents.'

'Good. Concentrate on Act One.'

'Ben, there's something I think you ought to know,' said Elsie. 'Jo is not short for Joseph.'

'Is this relevant?'

'It's short for Josephine.'

Josie's heart sank. Her one chance to work in a professional company playing a wonderful part would now be taken from her. Why oh why had Elsie spilled the beans?

Mr King stared at Josie in astonishment.

'Jo's my sister not my brother,' continued Elsie.

To Josie's relief, Mr King threw back his head and laughed.

'So what shall we call you in the programme? Walter Plinge?'

To Josie's bewilderment her sister collapsed into laughter.

'Walter Plinge,' Elsie explained, 'is the name used on a theatre programme when a member of the cast doesn't want anyone to know that they're playing a role. Sometimes people use it to disguise the fact that they're playing several roles.'

'No need for anonymity in this case,' said Mr King. 'She can use her own name, or a masculine form of it.'

But Josie didn't care what she was called. She didn't care if a bucketful of sausages fell on her head or it rained mud. Miss Dagleish had said it would be impossible for Josie to get an acting job and she had been given one without even auditioning for it.

# 5

# Lines

'AND THAT'S THE CUE FOR THE CURTAIN TO come down on Act One,' said Elsie.

Aside from a few chairs, a couple of small tables and a piano, the room on the ground floor was empty. She and Josie had shifted the furniture round to create the sitting room in the New York house and had methodically worked through every scene, move by move, line by line. Elsie explained that Mr King was one of the 'learn your lines and don't bump into the furniture' kind of director. It was left to members of the cast to make sense of what he was asking them to do.

After she had talked Josie through her scenes for the rest of the play, Elsie suggested that she use her bedroom to learn her Act One lines while she was out visiting a friend.

'What about, Miss Partridge?' Josie asked.

'She's not in. She goes to theatre matinees on Saturdays and has tea somewhere afterwards.'

'Elsie,' said Josie anxiously, 'Miss Dagleish doesn't know I'll be at rehearsals on Monday morning. If I don't turn up at school she'll be angry with me.'

'Mr King will ring the school and explain but remember, you still have to go to classes in the afternoon.'

Like Molly's bedroom, Elsie's window also overlooked the back garden and graveyard but from such a great height it made you feel dizzy. Inside her room were two alcoves on either side of a tiny arched black fireplace. One had shelves stacked with books, the other housed clothes hanging on a wooden rail. Stockings were drying over a piece of string under the window.

It was only when Josie found herself squinting to read her lines that she became aware it had grown dark. As she turned on the light, there were footsteps on the landing. She hesitated for a moment.

'Just one more time through this scene,' she told herself. 'Then I'll go downstairs.'

She had hardly begun when there was a gentle tapping on the door. She opened it to find Miss Partridge standing outside.

'I'm sorry,' said Josie. 'Was I making too much noise?'

'Not at all. I was just wondering how Larry got on with his Tiddlywinks.'

Within seconds Josie began to pour out the events of the morning and was ushered into Miss Partridge's room, where they ended up chatting over tea and flat biscuits with currants in them. *Squashed flies*, she called them.

'You must tell me more,' insisted Miss Partridge.

And Josie revelled in doing just that in minute detail, complete with impersonations.

'What a wonderful story!' said Miss Partridge, beaming.

'Fiona's comin' round tomorrow afternoon to go over Act One.'

'Including the Tiddlywinks scene?'

'Yeah.'

'Well, I'll be up here. I always catch up with my darning on Sunday afternoons. Just give me a call if you need me.'

Josie had just left Miss Partridge's room when she heard jazz coming from the ground floor room where she and Elsie had been rehearsing. She raced down the stairs and discovered Larry seated on the bottom step, listening. The music suddenly stopped and they could hear voices.

'They're packing up,' said Larry sadly.

Josie froze. 'One of them is American! Listen!'

As the door swung open, there were waves of laughter. A wiry man in his thirties wearing a cap stepped out into the hall. He was carrying what appeared to be a gigantic floor-length violin case.

'Hey, Pip! We 'ave an audience,' he exclaimed in a cockney accent and he grinned at them. 'How d'you like it?'

'A lot,' said Larry. 'Is that a double bass?'

'Yeah. You play anythin'?'

Larry shook his head. 'I want to play the saxophone.'

'Jerry!' the man yelled. 'There's a saxophone lover 'ere.'

A short stubby man with a battered trilby on his head peered round the door.

'Where?' he said.

Larry rose to his feet.

'Hi there, buddy! So you want to play a sax, eh?'

Larry nodded sadly. 'Yeah, but I have to wait till I'm bigger.'

'So play a clarinet.'

'But I like the saxophone better.'

'The clarinet is smaller. Learn to play that. Then when you're bigger, if you still want to play sax, you can pick it up easy. Especially if you play tenor sax.'

'Really?'

'Yup. You want me to have a word with yer dad?'

'Yes, please!'

'Can you play baseball?' Josie asked the American.

'Sure I can.'

'Would you show me how to pitch? Now?'

He laughed. 'Ah, the impatience of youth!'

'It's for a play called *Living With Father*.'

'I know it. I seen the film.'

'I'm playing Whitney and Larry is playing –'

'Harlan,' the man finished for her. 'That figures.'

'And we have a rehearsal tomorrow. I just want to show Whitney pretending to pitch because he's excited by the game.'

The man smiled. 'Come right in, little feller!'

As soon as the musicians had left the house Mrs Carpenter insisted that Josie ring her parents immediately to let them know about the acting job before their Saturday routine of settling down to watch *Dixon of Dock Green* with hot buttered crumpets. Her father cheered when he heard. Her mum said she would leave a message for Ralph at his digs and ring Auntie Win, which meant that Mrs Jenkins would hear the news five minutes later.

The following afternoon, Josie ran through Act One with Elsie and without the book. There had even been time to rehearse the scenes in Act Two. By the end of the day all she needed to learn were the lines for Act Three, and there weren't many since she didn't appear in the first scene and only had a few sentences to say in the last one. What would be more difficult to remember was what she had to do at the meal table, and she could only to do that with the props.

To her relief, Fiona and Elsie had liked Josie's mime of pitching an invisible baseball, which she occasionally put in when she was talking. It was while Larry and Josie were halfway through a game of Tiddlywinks that Mrs Carpenter appeared with blackcurrant squash, tea and homemade lemon cake on a tray.

'I do feel sorry for Michael having to leave the company,' she remarked. 'But if he had stayed, Larry and Josie wouldn't have had all this extra rehearsal.' She smiled. 'They're even beginning to look like brothers now.'

It was a little unnerving rehearsing with the cast on Monday morning but once Josie forgot she was speaking lines, it was as though she was flying.

There was one scene when Whitney's father was testing him on his catechism questions just after the doctor had told his father that his mother was very ill. When Elsie had rehearsed the scene with Josie the previous day she had said,

'Remember that although you're answering your father's questions, you're thinking of your mother all the time and wondering if she's going to die.'

When Hugh Burton, the actor playing Whitney's father was testing her, she could see that he was thinking of her too. There was a pause as they gazed at one another, until he snapped out, *'You don't know it well, Whitney,'* and sent him off. As Josie ran into the wings, she found Elsie standing there.

'Well done!' she whispered.

After rehearsals were over, Josie headed for the stage door where she found three boys from her school. The two youngest were in Form I, the older boy, Jim Eliot, was in Form III.

'Hello, Jim!' she said, surprised. 'What you doin' 'ere?'

'Audition,' he said. 'We're all going up for the same part.'

'Oh, what part's that?'

But before he could answer Elsie appeared to take her back to school.

'Good luck!' Josie said, quickly picking up her attaché case.

Jim stared awkwardly at her as she and Elsie stepped out into the street. It was a good job Elsie had turned up when she did, otherwise he might have had to answer her question.

# 6

# School Versus Whitney

JOSIE WAS HURRYING TOWARDS THE BASEMENT
to change for her dance class when she heard Miss
Dagleish calling out to her from the top of the stairway.
Josie was startled to see that the expression on her face was
far from friendly.

'In my study, young lady! Now!'

In an instant, Josie realised that Mr King must have
forgotten to phone the school and she was about to be
reprimanded for arriving late. She watched the headmistress
descend the stairs and followed her along the corridor. Once
inside her study, Miss Dagleish swung round and glared at
her. Josie quickly dropped into a curtsy.

'Look at you!' she barked. 'You're an absolute disgrace!
You cannot represent the school dressed in brown corduroy
trousers.'

'Mr King –' Josie began.

'Rang me at nine o'clock this morning and explained
everything.'

'Oh,' said Josie, confused.

'That is not how we behave in this school. I make the

decisions as to which pupils are selected for auditions. Not you. And it appears you had already rehearsed scenes from *Life With Father* before you even stepped foot in the theatre. Is that true?'

'Sort of. I was helpin' Larry out. He's the boy playing Harlan. The cast have been rehearsing without him and –'

'That is quite enough. I am ending this nonsense post haste and have sent three boys to Winford to audition for the role of Whitney.'

It was as though Josie had been slapped across the face.

*So that's why those boys were at the stage door*, she thought.

With shock it began to sink in that she wouldn't be playing Whitney after all.

There now followed a torrent of anger from the headmistress. Josie was called an amateur and a disgrace to the school. She was informed that turning up to any theatre not in uniform was bordering on criminal behaviour, and that she lacked the social graces. Miss Dagleish was only prevented from adding another damning remark when the telephone rang. Josie observed her pulling herself to her full height, switch on a smile and raise the receiver.

'Speaking,' she said.

By now Josie was shaking. After all the terrible things that had been said to her she wondered why she had been offered a place at the school. It was then that she grew aware that Miss Dagleish's face had changed from flushed to ashen. She was obviously receiving bad news; the death of a relative, Josie guessed by her expression. She knew she should retreat politely from the room but found herself unable to move.

'If that is what you have decided, Mr King,' Miss Dagleish said with gritted teeth. 'Well, we always try to aim high, Mr King. I'll organise a matron and . . .'

Josie watched Miss Dagleish's lips twitch.

'We've had no previous complaints about our matrons before but I'll . . .Yes. Indeed. But doesn't the boy have a mother who can –? Oh, I see. Well, if I can find a matron who is willing to look after *two* children . . .Yes, Mr King. I'll see what I can do. Goodbye.'

Josie stared, riveted as the headmistress slowly replaced the receiver. One of the boys at the school had obviously been offered the role. One of the juniors, she guessed because Jim Eliot was far too big. But why was Miss Dagleish so unhappy about it?

'Mr King has insisted you play Whitney,' she stated, her voice taut with disapproval, 'and has asked if one of our theatre matrons can look after this boy Larry as well. He also made a comment, which he seemed to find highly amusing. He said that watching you on stage was like taking Virol. Perhaps you could enlighten me.'

Josie gazed at her blankly, sensing it was better to remain silent.

'You do realise this was pure luck, my girl. You just happened to be at the right place at the right time. So don't let it go to your head.'

'No, madam.'

'The next rehearsal is at ten-thirty on Wednesday. When you return to school in the afternoon I shall expect to see you in uniform.'

'Yes, madam.'

'You may go.'

'Yes, madam,' said Josie, curtsying. 'Thank you, madam.'

She retreated hurriedly out of the study, fighting down a desire to yell with excitement. She was working! Now that she had a job perhaps the Form III and IV pupils would allow her join them in the tea house.

At the mid-afternoon break, instead of burying herself in a book in the classroom, she raced out into the rain, across the square to the tea house. As she flung open the door the third- and fourth-formers who were sitting at the tables turned their backs on her.

'Have you noticed there's a nasty pong in here?' Esmeralda remarked.

'I suppose when people do dreadful things,' said her friend Nesta, 'it makes them smell revolting.'

Josie was utterly bewildered. It was obvious they were talking about her but she had no idea why they were being so cruel.

'Poor Michael,' said Esmeralda. 'He must be broken-hearted.'

Josie strode over to her.

'His parents took him away. It had nothing to do with me.'

'But if you hadn't stepped in, it would have forced them to let him stay,' interrupted Merle.

'It's a boy's part, anyway. You had no right to steal it,' said Esmeralda.

'But I didn't.'

'Yes, you did. You learned his part off by heart and sneaked in hoping you could take over.'

'I bet you couldn't believe your luck,' joined in a girl called Ursula.

'Can't you see you're not welcome?' said Esmeralda haughtily. 'Go away!'

Josie dragged herself into Auntie Win's flat. The day had begun with her feeling happier than she had felt in weeks but it had all been shattered on her return to school. None of it made any sense. It was as though she had made people angry by doing her best.

The strains of *I Could Have Danced All Night* came from the sitting room against the background of heavy rain. She hung up her wet duffle coat and was standing with her arms hanging limply by her side when Auntie Win strode down the passage. Before she could open her mouth, her aunt had put her arms round her and Josie burst into tears.

'It feels as if I've been stabbed all over,' she sobbed. 'How am I going to rehearse tomorrow with everyone hating me?'

Auntie Win said nothing. She let her cry on and on. When Josie seemed to have emptied herself, her aunt pressed a handkerchief into her hand.

'I'll make you a nice cup of hot chocolate,' she said.

Josie stared anxiously up at her. Boiling milk and Auntie Win were a dangerous combination.

'Do you think that's a good idea?' she asked croakily.

They gazed at each other for a moment and then her

aunt's mouth quivered.

'I'm not that bad, am I?'

But Josie was nodding apologetically, and they burst out laughing.

'Come on. You can be in charge of the milk in the pan while I hunt for the chocolate powder,' she said and grabbed Josie's hand, pulling her towards the kitchen.

Once the hot chocolate was safely in two cups and they were sitting by the electric fire with the artificial logs, her aunt said, 'I presume Elsie doesn't know about this business at the school.'

'No,' sniffed Josie.

'Phone her tonight so you don't have to tell her tomorrow at the theatre in front of other people. She might be able to help you. The same thing happened to her when she was your age.'

'But she loved it at her grammar school,' said Josie.

'She wasn't bullied there. She was bullied outside.'

'But I haven't been bullied.'

'Oh, yes you have. I've seen this on occasion in the army and I won't tolerate it. I've heard about theatre people behaving like this.'

'But it isn't the theatre people,' exclaimed Josie. 'They did their best to help me. And Mr King said watching me made him feel as though he'd taken Virol.'

'Well, I suppose that's better than cod liver oil. It least it tastes nice. Which reminds me, now that the weather's getting colder, I'd better buy some.'

'Are you sure you won't accidentally put it in a stew, Auntie Win?'

'Ah, I see we're getting our old Josie back,' she said, smiling. 'Now drink up, and while I cook something easy, you can talk to Elsie.'

'It's jealousy,' said her sister over the phone, 'but I'm surprised Miss Dagleish was angry about you being given the role.'

'It's because I'm a little rough round the edges.'

'She didn't say that, did she?'

'No. But I overheard her talkin' about me to Mrs Havilland. She said I was so boisterous and had so little poise that I would make Noel Coward turn in his grave.'

'I'm not sure he'd like to hear that since he's very much alive.'

Josie giggled.

'That's better.'

'Elsie, she told me I have to wear my uniform to the rehearsal.'

'Oh. And it's not quite the right attire for flinging yourself on the floor and playing Tiddlywinks.'

'No. And I also don't want to remind Mr King that I'm a girl.'

'Wear it *to* the theatre and then change into the clothes you wore yesterday. You can bring them in your attaché case. Then after rehearsal . . .'

'I can change back into my uniform for school,' finished Josie for her. 'Elsie, I can't imagine anyone wanting to bully you.'

Josie heard her sigh.

'Seeing another person happy can cause so much pain for certain people that they have to try to remove it. But you know what helped me get through it? Concentrating on something else. That and good friends. Auntie Win's the best person to be with.'

'Don't tell Larry, will you?' said Josie.

'Of course not. Are you feeling a bit better now?'

'Much.'

'Supper's ready,' called her aunt.


Josie moved her books from the Form II row into one of the empty twin desks in the Form III row. At the first break-time, she walked hesitantly towards the boys but they told her to go away. Jim called her a thief because she had taken a boy's role, one that he could have played.

'But you auditioned for it,' she had pointed out.

'I don't have a sister in the cast,' he snapped.

They kicked the football away from her, making it clear she was no longer welcome. The girls huddled in their usual place by the wall, staring at her and jeering. She was just wondering how she was going to survive the rest of the break when Hilda stepped out of the back door, and glanced in her direction. To Josie's relief she seemed genuinely pleased to see her and ran over to join her. Like Josie, she too had begun rehearsals that week as a fairy in *A Midsummer Night's Dream*.

'How were your rehearsals?' Josie began quickly, steering any conversation away from *Life With Father*.

Hilda frowned.

'The person directing the movement wants the chorus of fairies to look identical. I keep being told off for moving too balletically.'

'But I thought they wanted girls who had studied ballet? Miss Dagleish said she would have put me up for it if it hadn't been for my hair.'

'Look, I know this sounds as though I'm big-headed,' said Hilda awkwardly, 'but I might be chucked out for being too good.'

'What?!'

'The director keeps saying that I'm not blending in. I really do try to dance less well but there's no mirror to check what I'm doing, so not only do I have to pretend to be a fairy but I also need to pretend it's not me playing a fairy.'

'Hilda,' said Josie slowly, 'have you seen *My Fair Lady*?'

'No. Why?'

'You ought to. It's not ballet, but the dancing is a lot more exciting than . . .'

'Tum-te-tum-te-tum?' said Hilda, prancing up and down on the spot with flapping wrists.

Josie laughed. She had never realised how funny Hilda could be.

'I was really looking forward to learning tap as well,' said Josie, 'but it's nothing like Gene Kelly and Fred Astaire here, is it?'

Hilda shook her head.

'Have you told your mum and dad?' Josie asked.

'No. They both work so hard to send me here.'

'Your mother works as well?' asked Josie, surprised.

'Yes.'

'You tell them the good bits and leave out the bad bits, don't you?'

Hilda nodded.

'Me too,' said Josie. They fell silent for a moment. 'Still, there's one good thing. At least we're both working, which means . . .'

'We don't have to be here so much,' finished Hilda for her. 'Want a Murray Mint?' she said, taking out a tube of sweets.

'Yeah! Murray Mint! Murray Mint!' she sang. 'Too good to hurry mint.'

'Shh,' warned Hilda. 'If Mrs Havilland hears you, she'll know you've been watching ITV.'

The next morning, Josie decided to wear trousers and a jersey to rehearsals and pack her uniform into the attaché case. There was no room for her blazer but because her duffle coat was so enormous she was easily able to wear it underneath.

It wasn't until later, while heading from Winford station towards the high street that she remembered she would be meeting the new matron at the theatre and would be in trouble for not arriving properly dressed. And then she recalled a piece of advice Elsie had given her. 'Once an actor or actress walks through a stage door,' Elsie had said, 'it's important that they don't take the outside world in with them.' And that was what Josie had to do. She was to forget about stage school. She must be Whitney, a nine-year-old boy who lived in a big house in New York with three lively red-headed brothers, a dizzy mother, and a father who barked loudly at one maid after another so that they all kept resigning.

Wilfred and Samuel were sitting in their usual places in the cubicle when she arrived.

"Ello there, Jo,' Samuel said, smiling. 'They're doing Act Two. Go on up.'

She leaped up the steps, slipped along the corridor and crept into the stage left wings. Not wanting to interrupt the scene between Vinnie and Clare, she stood motionless, observing them, aware that they were looking at each other. At school they were always being told to say *everything* out front to the audience. Could the teachers be wrong?

'Thank you,' she heard Mr King say loudly. 'Act Two, Scene Two next. Breakfast scene. Any sign of our Jo?'

*Our* Jo!

She really was one of the company! She poked her head round the proscenium arch.

'I'm here, Mr King.'

'Splendid!' he said. 'Stay up there.'

Fiona emerged from the auditorium to set up props for the breakfast table, with Elsie following, the lights from the stage catching the glass in her spectacles. She would be playing Nora, the newly employed dumpy middle-aged maid. She was beaming.

'Guess what?' she said to Josie. 'I'm to be your chaperone for this week's rehearsal period. It's to give your school more time to find a new one for the two performance weeks. It means we can travel together in the mornings but you'll have to travel back on your own after lunch.'

'Oh, good!' said Josie, relieved. 'I can keep wearing whatever I like to rehearsals.'

'We're ready,' yelled Fiona.

After the morning rehearsals were over, Josie changed into her uniform and waited for Elsie by the stage door. A young actress called Desiree was standing nearby, deep in conversation with the young actor who played the seventeen-year-old red-headed brother, Clarence.

She envied them for being able to stay. She had loved every second of the rehearsals and had even been allowed to sit in the auditorium to watch the scenes she didn't appear in.

'Cheer up,' said her sister when she arrived and spotted the expression on Josie's face. 'You're not leaving yet. I'm taking you to a café with us. I expect you don't get too many cooked meals with Auntie Win.'

'I do,' said Josie. 'It's just that they're *very* well cooked.'

As they began walking, Lionel – a portly, elderly actor who was playing a clergyman – joined them. Striding energetically alongside him was a woman in her thirties, Daphne Driscoll, who played Cora. Anthony and Desiree followed on behind.

Within minutes they were diving down a small back street into a warm, snug café. A thin, bespectacled man behind the counter nodded at them and smiled. It was obvious they were regulars.

'Do you still go to that tea house near your school for cheese on toast at midday?' asked Elsie, sliding two tables together.

'Yeah. I'd much prefer baked beans but with all the dancin' in the afternoon, it's a bit risky,' Josie said and pointed in the direction of her bottom.

'Jo!' laughed her sister.

'*Where e'er you be, let the wind blow free*,' Lionel recited gravely. '*I held it in and t'was the death of me*. That was written on a gravestone,' he explained. 'Someone had died because they hadn't allowed themselves to fart.'

Josie burst out laughing. It wasn't just because he had said the word 'fart' but because he had said it in such a booming Shakespearian manner.

'Could you say that a shade louder, Lionel?' interrupted Daphne dryly. 'I do believe someone in the next county didn't quite hear it.'

As Josie tucked into the sausage, mashed potato, cabbage and gravy that Elsie had ordered for her, the others savoured their eggs on toast, discussing who was in what play, who was casting and when. Anthony and Desiree were almost hidden from view behind a newspaper called *The Stage*, nodding and muttering, 'Hear, hear!' between mouthfuls of food.

The conversation turned to television. None of them earned enough money to rent a set but they knew people who did, and would occasionally drop round to watch a programme, rather like Mrs Jenkins did with Auntie Win.

'Anthony, did you manage to see the first episode of *Interpol Calling*?' asked Daphne.

'Yes,' said Anthony. 'What did you think?'

'Not much. I hope it improves.'

'I'm sure it will,' he said. 'It still has thirty-nine episodes to prove itself.'

'Having one blessed television channel is bad enough,' snorted Lionel. 'Without this other IT whatchamacallit channel.'

'V,' said Anthony. 'ITV.'

'Lionel, you're not one of these people who can't find one good thing to say about ITV are you?' said Daphne.

'I most certainly am. I absolutely loathe it. I don't know how you can waste your time watching it. The BBC aren't much better, so I've heard.'

'You've got *anti* ITVitis, Lionel' said Anthony, grinning.

'Well, I hope there's no cure.'

'Don't worry, Jo,' Elsie reassured her quietly. 'They always argue like this.'

'Our actin' mistress doesn't like ITV either,' said Josie.

'Good for her,' said Lionel. 'A woman after my own heart.'

'But my Auntie Win has it,' Josie added, tentatively, wondering if Lionel would ever speak to her again. 'Last Wednesday, Mrs Jenkins – she's one of our neighbours – came round to watch a detective programme with her on *BBC*,' she emphasised, hoping that would improve matters.

'*No Hiding Place?*' asked Desiree.

'Yeah. Auntie Win said it was like watching a film at the cinema.'

'I saw it too,' Desiree said excitedly. 'Lionel, instead of it being the usual thirty minutes it was a whole hour!'

'You didn't stay up for it, I hope,' said Elsie, frowning at Josie.

'No, I wasn't allowed to.'

'That's good. I don't think Mum would approve.'

'But Auntie Win told me about it when she came to bed,' said Josie. 'There was something about a man who was going to get married and this other man was planning to kill him and hide his body in the boot of a car.'

'Jo!' exclaimed Elsie. 'Didn't that give you nightmares?'

'No. I read a bit more of *Coot Club* and then I felt all right.'

'Arthur Ransome!' exclaimed Anthony. 'I liked his books too. I read all of them when I was a boy.'

'When was that then?' laughed Lionel. 'Last week?'

'Anyone want to share pudding and split the cost?' said Anthony hurriedly, glancing awkwardly at Desiree. 'There's spotted dick and custard on the menu.'

He looked badly in need of rescuing, Josie thought.

'Auntie Win watched another crime programme on Friday night,' she added. 'I expect it was because she was hoping there'd be a murder in that one too.'

Desiree laughed. And Anthony looked happy again.

After lunch, when she and Elsie were standing on the railway platform waiting for the train, Josie noticed her sister frowning.

'There's no need to worry about me,' said Josie. 'I can wait here on my own.'

'I know you can,' Elsie said, smiling. 'I wasn't thinking about you. I was thinking of that solicitor who called at Mum and Dad's flat asking for Henry's address. I phoned Henry in Scotland and because no letter has arrived at the theatre for him, he rang his old school. They told him no solicitor had been round to ask for his old Sternsea address.'

'You mean the solicitor lied?'

'Seems so. What's puzzling is how he found out that Henry's family used to live there. He's a little worried and so am I.'

'Why?'

'Because nine years ago his real father and his gran ran away to Australia. They're not nice people. Henry's concerned it might be his dad trying to find him and he's the last person on earth he'd like turning up at our wedding.'

'But if he *is* his dad, why hasn't he sent a letter to the theatre?'

'Maybe he forgot the name of it.'

'Elsie,' began Josie hesitantly, 'about this wedding . . . When I'm a bridesmaid, I won't have to wear one of those frilly dresses with a bow, will I?'

'Not with that prison haircut,' she remarked. 'I'll try to persuade Mum to let you wear a kilt. She'll never let you wear trousers, so you can give up trying.'

In the distance, a train was steaming towards them. As she watched it draw nearer, it felt as though an iron weight had dropped into the pit of Josie's stomach. She wished she were returning to the theatre with Elsie.

* * *

The afternoon lessons were with the six pupils from different forms who had also missed the morning lessons because of rehearsals. Their first lesson was English with Mr Bennett, a disgruntled young man who had a cigarette permanently glued to his lower lip. The only thing that made the lesson bearable was Hilda moving her books into the empty desk beside Josie.

'This is so boring,' Hilda whispered. 'Do you think he'd notice us reading a book?'

'I don't think he'd notice if we stood upside down on our desks and yodelled,' said Josie.

Hilda flung her hand across her mouth, shaking with supressed laughter. Josie beamed at her and pulled out *Coot Club* from her attaché case. As she returned to the world of the Norfolk Broads, with its gang of children protecting nesting water birds from the selfish antics of tourists in their noisy and destructive motorboats, Hilda opened *Dancing Star*.

Later that afternoon, Josie used every spare moment to go through her lines. Unfortunately Esmeralda Havilland overheard her in the cloakroom and spilled the beans to her mother, Mrs Havilland, who then called Josie and informed her that she would be taking her through the entire play to give her a demonstration as to how she should play her part. Josie pretended she was late for a class and dashed off.

The following morning, Elsie brought Larry to the rehearsals with them. When they weren't needed on stage she took Josie and him to a dressing room at the top of the theatre to go through their scenes. Elsie was so patient with him. If he became cross with himself for forgetting his lines or his moves, she would praise him and tell him how well he was doing for someone who hadn't had much rehearsal. It didn't take Josie long to realise that the more she became Whitney, the more he became Harlan and forgot about the nervous Larry.

Around midday, Fiona put her head round the door to bring them down for the final scene.

'Mr King has decided which four performances you'll be doing each week,' she said as they clattered down the stairs.

Josie held her breath.

'Rather than two different pairs sharing a matinee and an evening performance on the same day, he is going to have them do two shows on the same day. You and Larry,' she said, glancing at Josie, 'will be performing on Tuesday and Thursday nights and be in both performances on Saturday.'

Josie could have sung.

'That means Mum and Dad can come up to see the show on a Saturday afternoon and I can go to Guides on Friday.'

'I shouldn't mention the Guide meetings at your school,' Elsie warned her.

'Why?' said Josie, surprised.

'They might not approve.'

On Friday night, walking swiftly across the gym towards the Bullfinch screen with its *Never Say Die* motto, Josie was relieved to find that she hadn't frightened off the new tenderfoot, Carol, who was now standing shyly by their nature table. When she had spotted Josie's scalp the previous week, she had protectively touched her shoulder-length fair hair and stammered, 'I-I won't be made to have my hair cut like you, will I?'

She gave Carol a hearty wave, and Carol, in her pale blue mohair cardigan gave her a delicate one in return.

There were seven girls in Josie's patrol: their patrol leader, Sheila; her second in command, a cheerful girl called Dolly who was working towards her First Class badge; quiet, well-spoken Penelope, who had received her Second Class badge on Josie's first Guide meeting; a dreamy-looking girl called Lydia and a very earnest girl called Geraldine, who were both working for their Second Class badges. Aside from Josie and Carol, all of them were working towards badges to sew on their sleeves.

Josie had already spotted the badges she would avoid like the plague: needlework and embroidery.

'I want to start workin' for my Second Class,' she announced.

'But you've only just passed your tenderfoot test,' exclaimed Carol when Dolly went off to gather information.

'I passed that so I can go campin' but one day I want to go sailin' as well. The only way I can do that is to get me First Class badge so I can join the Sea Rangers when I'm older, and the only way I'll be able to take my First Class is if I've got my Second Class.'

'Can you swim?'

'Not yet. I have to learn how to do that too.'

'Have a look at this,' said Dolly, handing her a book.

'*How To Become a Second Class Guide,*' Josie read.

There were a series of intelligence, handicraft, health and service tests to pass, which included more knots and first aid.

Josie immediately spotted the two she would enjoy most: stalking, and having to light a fire outdoors using only two matches.

Dolly placed a tray on the floor. 'You can begin by learning Kim's Game.'

On the tray was a penknife, a comb, a small saucepan, a comic, a plastic cowboy, a knitting pattern and some groceries.

'You need to remember at least nine of the twelve objects. Geraldine will be doing it too. I'm starting you with twelve so that you can gradually work up to thirty.'

'Why is it called Kim's Game?' asked Josie.

'It's from a Rudyard Kipling story about a boy called Kim who trained himself to *observe carefully*, so he could remember everything he had seen and pass it on.'

'So it's training us to be a spy?' Josie said.

'It's training you to be observant. If there was an accident, it's vital that you can give as much information as possible to the police *and* it must be correct. In the Great War, Guides were taken on as messengers at the Foreign Office because they always repeated their messages accurately.'

'Really?' said Josie, impressed.

'Spread out all the objects and study each one carefully. Is it big, small, broad or thin? Is it old or new? What shape is it? Notice any markings or patterns or writing,' said Dolly. 'Test each other by writing down how many you can remember, or do it out loud. Play the game outside as well. See how many things you can observe on railway platforms, in shop windows, queues . . .'

'Sounds like my mum,' said Josie. 'She does that all the time.'

Dolly left them to it, and Josie and Geraldine took it in turns to look at all the objects for two minutes before covering them up with a tea towel.

'It's like that quiz game on telly,' commented Geraldine. '*Beat the Clock*. When all those objects go floating by, and the person watching them has to remember as many as possible, and they get to take home the ones they remember, and there's that quiz master who gives the audience funny looks and helps them out. You know, that tall, thin man who keeps saying "I'm in charge," and making people laugh when he does peculiar things with his legs.'

'Something Forsyth,' said Josie, concentrating.

'*Bruce* Forsyth,' said Geraldine.

A whistle blew. It was time for all the patrols to gather together and share news.

After the meeting, Josie and Molly stepped out of the comforting warmth of the school hall into a rainswept night. Molly's father was waiting for them with an umbrella, the fish and chips wrapped up in newspaper under his arm.

'See you next week,' Dolly yelled.

Josie turned and waved back to her.

'Don't forget your good turn a day, girls,' Captain called after them regally.

Through the crowd of chattering girls, Josie spotted Lefty glancing at Captain with such a look of mirth in her eyes that she appeared close to exploding. Josie tugged Molly's arm and pointed in her direction. They looked at each other and grinned.

'Come on, you two,' said Mollie's father. 'You'll get soaked.'

They clung tightly to him, one on either side.

'What's the joke?' he asked.

'It's Lefty,' squealed Molly hysterically. 'I think she finds Captain funny.'

'I think she finds all of us funny,' said Josie.

As they walked along the London streets, Josie could hear the rain pattering loudly on Mr Carpenter's large umbrella, feel the warmth of his arm through his coat, and smell the fish and chips sprinkled with salt and vinegar. She smiled. This was the life, and it was a million miles away from Miss Dagleish's stage school.

The following morning, instead of rehearsing one curtain call where the cast would bow to the audience, they had to rehearse the six curtain calls, requested by the authors of the play. These had to resemble stiffly posed photographs. The first was a family group, the second was to be Desiree and Anthony as a newly married couple, the third photograph was to be Elsie and the other maids standing in a line, looking over their shoulder at an imaginary camera, the fourth was of the four red-headed brothers wearing their straw hats and the fifth was their mother and father standing centre stage.

'Last curtain call!' Mr King yelled. 'I want everyone standing in two diagonal lines from Mother and Father who will be upstage centre. Take your bows from "Maggie" at the front. All together! Now!'

'Then it's the National Anthem,' said Mr King, glancing down at Larry. 'That's *God Save the Queen,*' he explained. 'And the curtain falls for the last time. Your opening night will be Tuesday. The other Whitney and Harlan will have their one on Monday. Jo, you will meet Larry and the theatre matron at the stage door at one o'clock on that day so that you can watch their dress rehearsal. It'll give you some idea of what the stage will be like with all the furniture and props. Now off you go to see the wardrobe mistress.'

The wardrobe mistress, a jolly red-faced woman in her fifties with grips in her hair and pins sticking out of a pinafore, resembled a hedgehog. Her 'wardrobe' was one of the dressing rooms. She flicked a tape measure across them, grunted and pulled out various brown knickerbockers and jackets, holding them up against them. She glanced at Josie's lace-up shoes.

'Those'll do,' she said, and she gave Josie a smile. 'You look like the cat that got the cream.'

'I *have* got the cream,' Josie said, beaming.

# 7

# The Tech

TO AVOID SCHOOL ON MONDAY MORNING, Josie convinced herself she was needed for the technical rehearsal.

'It'll only be the setting up of lights and props,' Elsie repeated in the corridor backstage. 'And you'll be on your own.'

Josie smiled. Being on her own, she would have the freedom to do what she liked.

They found Fiona and a young man in the stage right wings counting plates, bowls and cutlery. *Enough for a restaurant*, Josie thought. Fiona leaned back, resting the palms of her hands on the base of her spine.

'Have you washed and dried all this lot?' asked Elsie.

Fiona gave a weary nod. 'Eighteen service plates, twelve smaller ones, twelve glass plates for fruit, and eighteen coffee cups and saucers.'

'And then there's the cutlery,' added the young props man. 'Twelve butter pats, twelve sets of knives, forks and teaspoons, six fruit spoons, a serving spoon and a fork.'

'Fancy cleaning the silver, Jo?' asked Fiona jokily, and

she pointed to a tray of assorted grey objects including a tall coffee pot that towered above a toast rack, napkin rings and salt and peppershakers.

'Yeah!' said Josie. 'It can be my good turn for the day. I'm a Girl Guide. I'm in the Bullfinch patrol.'

The props man laughed. 'Don't look a gift horse in the mouth, Fiona,' he said.

Fiona scooped up the tray. 'Follow me then.'

She dumped the tray on a small table in the green room in front of one of the old sofas. There were a dozen or more teacups and saucers stacked on the draining board by a tottering pile of napkins.

'Twenty-four breakfast napkins,' yawned Fiona. 'Twelve tea napkins and four breakfast tablecloths.' She handed Josie a bottle of cleaning liquid and a couple of rags.

Josie sat happily amongst the silverware, smoothing it on. Through the open door she observed people carrying vases, armfuls of photographs in brass frames and boxes of ornaments. Fiona explained that they were *dressing the set*. Sensing the urgency of the props being ready on time, Josie rubbed the drab grey objects with gusto, turning them into gleaming silver, her hands growing blacker as she polished.

'Do you usually have so many things in a play?' she asked when Fiona popped her head round the door to see how she was progressing.

'No. It's just that there are quite a few meals in this one. And remember, there are six people in the family.'

'So will you and the props man be changing the cutlery all the time?'

'There isn't time. We have a false tabletop already laid in the stage right wings. I'll show you later if you like.'

Josie held up the silver coffee pot. 'What do you think?'

'Beautiful.'

Josie beamed.

The props man appeared and took the china away while Fiona piled food onto the draining board.

'Oh,' said Josie. 'We won't be miming eating food at the table any more?'

'No. And some of the cast have to eat kippers.'

'Does that mean you have to cook them every night?'

'No,' said Fiona. 'I have to fry bananas and put cinnamon on them. Makes them look like kippers from the auditorium. Easier to eat. And less smelly.'

Josie grimaced.

'Don't worry. You and Larry will be eating porridge.'

The deputy stage manager peered in. 'Hello, Jo,' he said, surprised. 'You're far too early. You're not needed till this afternoon.'

'She's helping me,' said Fiona cheerily. 'Then she can watch from the front, can't she?'

'If she makes herself invisible.' He turned to Josie. 'Mr King can get a mite fractious during a tech,' he explained.

'Does that mean bad tempered?' asked Josie.

'Yes,' they chorused.

The props man collected the tray with the silverware and Josie followed him and Fiona back into the wings.

'See that hinge?' Fiona said, indicating a metal contraption on the side of one of the flats. Josie glanced at the flat she was pointing at, a high, rectangular wooden frame which was a section of one of the walls on the set. 'We unlock that and swing it back, then two ASMs carry the false tabletop on stage and put it on the empty table.' She pointed to a tabletop on which china, cutlery and napkins were neatly laid out on a tablecloth. It was at that moment that Mr King could be heard calling Fiona from the auditorium.

'Nip round to the stage left wings,' she whispered. 'Go through the side door into the auditorium and watch from the dress circle.'

Josie slipped out into the corridor. Two dressing room doors were open. Inside one Eleanor West was standing in front of a mirror examining her long green and blue plaid dress with its narrow waist. Josie's eyes rested on a huge lump of material over her bottom.

Eleanor turned.

'It's a bustle,' she explained. 'Very fashionable in the eighteen eighties.' She smiled. 'I didn't know you were here for the tech.'

'I'm watching it so that I can explain things to Larry later.'

She was about to add, 'I was born in this dressing room,' but at that moment Hugh Burton peered out from the dressing room on the other side of the green room.

'Eleanor, can I borrow your number twenty?' he yelled.

Josie used this opportunity to disappear before Eleanor could ask her any awkward questions as to her presence in the theatre. She had planned to walk straight through the stage left wings but was stopped in her tracks at the sight of three long tables filled with the props for the three-act play, including, she noticed, a Tiddlywinks set. She smiled.

A male voice called out to someone above her head in the flies. Time to make herself scarce.

She darted swiftly down the side aisle while Mr King was shouting about some coloured gel he wanted for a particular lighting effect. As soon as she reached a door at the back of the auditorium, she leaped up several flights of stairs to the dress circle door, crawled down the stairs backwards so that she wouldn't be spotted, and crept into the first row. She gently lowered a seat, praying that it wouldn't squeak, and peered down at the stage. Gone were the bits of white marking tape and rehearsal furniture. Instead, she found herself gazing at a vast living room filled with huge tables and bureaus, long green curtains at the high windows and armchairs and sofas upholstered in the same colour.

'Whitney's home,' she whispered.

Through an upstage window, she could see a street.

*Madison Avenue.*

She spotted the panel in the wall that would swing open, allowing the false top to be carried to the large table where she and Larry would be sitting for their meals. Nearby stood a rubber plant in a brass pot. Something to watch out for, she thought, especially with Larry. He would probably walk into it.

A sumptuous velvet bell pull with a large tassel on it was hanging beside an enormous fireplace, stage left. The mantelpiece was draped in plum velvet on which stood the two silver candelabras Josie had polished so vigorously. Above it was an ornately carved mirror.

Lamps were everywhere. Josie watched the props man placing ornaments and books and a silver-topped jar filled with cigars onto tiny tables. Now she understood what dressing a set meant. It was making a room look as though real people actually lived in it. And she would be one of them.

Eleanor West swept in and stood motionless under a massive chandelier that was hanging from the false ceiling. Behind her, Fiona was placing candles into the two curved candleholders on the back wall.

'Right, Donald,' yelled Mr King. 'Let's start.'

Moving swiftly through the arch, Eleanor hitched up the skirt of her dress and glided up the stairs as the curtain fell.

'Curtain up!' shouted Mr King.

It rose to reveal Elsie as the nervous maid laying the table. Eleanor swept down the stairs.

'*Good morning, Annie,*' she said.

'*Good morning, ma'am,*' answered Elsie.

'Hold it!' shouted Mr King. 'There needs to be more light on that table!'

The technical rehearsal was a slow, painstaking process and the cast were often left to stand patiently and wait. Josie noticed that the two other boys who were playing Whitney and Harlan were showing signs of boredom. She couldn't understand it. She loved all the business of lighting the set. She also became aware that when they had to walk around the furniture, it made them forget their lines and she realised that she and Larry would need to know the living room as thoroughly as if it was their own home, otherwise they would do the same.

Suddenly she remembered she was supposed to be meeting him and the new theatre matron at the stage door. She dropped to her knees and began to crawl past the other seats and up the stairs at breakneck speed.

# 8

# Enter the Matron

LARRY WAS SITTING ON A HUGE WICKER SKIP by the wall opposite Wilfred and Samuel's cubbyhole. He did not look happy.

'Where is she?' Josie asked.

'In the Ladies, powdering her nose.' He looked puzzled. 'Why does she have to go to the Ladies to do that to her nose?'

'It's a secret code,' whispered Josie. 'For going to the toilet.'

'Do men have a secret nose code too?' he whispered back.

'No.' Josie sensed that the subject needed to be changed swiftly. 'What's she like?'

'Horrible. She looks like Olive Oyl in the Popeye cartoons. And she told me that I wasn't to speak unless I was spoken to, and that she would brook no nonsense. What does that mean?'

'I think it means she won't let us have any fun.'

'She won't shout if I do, will she?' asked Larry. 'I don't like being shouted at.'

'If she does, pretend she has a cow pat on her head.'

'What's a cow pat?'

'It's a plate-shaped piece of cow poo.'

Larry giggled.

'Dog poo is better,' he said. 'I know what dog poo looks like.'

At that moment, two spindly legs in thick brown stockings could be seen descending the stairs. Larry gave Josie an almighty nudge.

'Here she is!' he mouthed.

The theatre matron's name was Miss Merryweather but there was nothing merry about her. Miss Glum would have suited her better, thought Josie. Tall and thin, she wore beige from head to foot: beige shoes, matching beige bag, beige coat, beige scarf, beige gloves and beige hat. Even her face seemed beige.

By now other members of the cast had gathered nearby. Lionel glanced in Josie's direction and gave her a wink. To Josie's relief, Elsie appeared. She swept over to Miss Merryweather and shook her hand.

'I'm Elsie Hollis,' she said. 'Jo's sister. You must be the theatre matron.'

'That is correct,' said Miss Merryweather.

'We'll be having a bite to eat in a nearby café. Will you join us?'

'If you could just give me the directions, that will suffice. I've had strict instructions to sit on my own with the children.'

Josie was about to protest but the expression on Larry's face shut her up. His eyes seemed to say, 'Please don't leave me alone with her!' So, pretending to be meek, which had

Elsie nearly collapsing with laughter, Josie dutifully followed the tight-lipped Miss Merryweather through the door.

They stepped out into the street, the breath rising from their mouths like dragons due to the sudden drop in temperature. As they walked, Anthony and Lionel began to have one of their arguments.

Josie and Elsie caught one another's eye.

'Mollycoddling, that's what it is,' Lionel was declaring. 'A week's rehearsal is quite sufficient.'

'It is if you're happy to reel off your lines parrot fashion and move where you're told,' said Anthony.

'And what's wrong with that?' asked Lionel. 'As long as you tell the story . . .'

'It doesn't make for very exciting theatre, Lionel. That's probably why so many are closing down. If the productions were better they wouldn't be losing the audiences.'

'It's television that's taking the audiences away,' said Lionel.

Josie slipped closer to her sister.

'Is it true?' she asked Elsie. 'Are lots of theatres closing down?'

'I'm afraid so.'

'And it's television's fault?'

'That's what they say.'

'If more of the West End and TV stars were performing in theatres up and down the country,' continued Lionel, 'they would bring in more audiences, and then people wouldn't have to fight to stop theatres like the Golders Green Hippodrome from being pulled down.'

'That's not fair, Lionel' said Anthony.

'Arguing in front of children, really!' muttered Miss Merryweather.

But Josie loved hearing them argue. It made her feel part of their world.

'They say they're too tired to tour after all their film work,' said Lionel, 'but really they want to earn more money.'

'Well, wouldn't you?' said Daphne.

'As I said, if there *has* to be a star system, then we need to use it to attract more audiences.'

'There are no stars in Joan Littlewood's company,' said Elsie. 'And people come in droves to see them.'

'But her company live on beans,' said Daphne. 'Your brother Ralph must have told you that. They earn less money than we do. I've heard they have to do odd jobs at the Theatre Royal between rehearsals and performances. Even on Sundays.'

'Is that true, Elsie?' asked Josie.

Elsie nodded. 'Yes. They have no funding from the Arts Council.'

'Money!' murmured Miss Merryweather, disapprovingly. 'Really! Not a fit subject to air in public.'

'The café is around the next corner,' said Elsie, politely.

'Thank you, Miss Hollis,' she muttered, her nose in the air.

Once the café door was in sight, Josie's heart sank. It meant she would soon be separated from the cast.

'We'll see you soon,' Elsie said and she gave her hand a squeeze.

Miss Merryweather led her and Larry to a small table near the counter.

'What vegetables do you offer?' she asked the proprietor.

'Cabbage, carrots . . .' he began.

'That will do.' She ordered a chop with mashed potato to go with them and smaller portions of the same for Josie and Larry.

'And a large pot of tea,' she added.

The café door swung open. A slim, smartly dressed man in his forties wearing a raincoat and a dark trilby stepped inside, a leather briefcase and an umbrella with a cane handle in his hands. He sat at a nearby table.

'Excuse me, madam,' he said, leaning towards Miss Merryweather. 'Being somewhat of a stranger in this area, would you be so kind as to give me some advice as to –?'

Miss Merryweather stiffened.

'There's a menu,' she interrupted curtly, and she indicated the blackboard.

'Thank you. That is most kind. I must say it's a pleasure to see such well-behaved children. They're a credit to you.'

Miss Merryweather flushed.

'They aren't mine,' she snapped. 'I'm in charge of them.'

'Oh,' he said. 'Please forgive my impertinence. I should have guessed from your lady-like demeanour that you are their governess.'

Miss Merryweather's mouth twitched slightly.

'In a manner of speaking. I am what is called a theatre matron. A chaperone.'

'But I mustn't disturb you a moment longer. Thank you

again.' At which point the man brought out a newspaper. It was *The Times*. Miss Merryweather glanced quickly at it and Josie could see that she approved.

When it was time to leave, the man rose swiftly and held the door open for her. Miss Merryweather gave him a regal nod and sailed through.

Back at the theatre, good luck cards were already arriving for the opening night, and members of the cast in dressing gowns and make-up were running up and down the stairs. Josie knew that in the top dressing room the two children who were also playing Whitney and Harlan would now be in their costumes.

'Josie,' said Larry, 'I won't have to wear make-up, will I?'

'Of course you will,' interrupted Miss Merryweather.

'No one told me that,' he exclaimed, horrified.

'You'll look ill if you don't,' said Josie. 'The footlights take the colour out of everyone's faces. It won't look like make-up to the audience.'

'Will the men be wearing it?'

'Yes.'

'Even Lionel?' asked Larry.

'Did I hear my name mentioned?' boomed a voice above them.

'You've got reddy brown stuff on your face,' Larry gasped.

'Greasepaint. It's called greasepaint.'

'I won't have to wear lipstick, will I?'

'Certainly not,' snapped Miss Merryweather. 'And as I will be putting on your make-up, you can put the subject right out of your head. Now, we'd better find a seat in the auditorium.'

'Yes, I'll need you out there to prompt me in case I forget my lines,' said Lionel, beaming at Larry.

To Josie's relief, Larry laughed. 'You're funny,' he said

'Why thank you, kind sir.'

Miss Merryweather turned on her heel, indicating they should follow. They were stepping out of the stage door and into the street so that they could enter the theatre through the foyer when they almost collided into the man they had seen at the café. He raised his hat politely.

'Good afternoon, madam,' he said.

'Oh,' she said, flustered. 'Good afternoon.'

The play was too long for Larry and he grew restless. Josie asked Miss Merryweather if she could stay on her own to watch the rest of the dress rehearsal when they reached the end of Act Two, but Whitney and Harlan weren't in Act Three, Scene One, and since they spent most of the following scene sitting at a table, Miss Merryweather didn't think it was worth it.

'Can I wish Elsie good luck before we leave?' Josie begged.

'If you're quick.'

They hopped down the stairs and were about to push open a door into the foyer when it was opened for them. To Josie's astonishment, it was the smartly dressed man again.

'What a fortuitous coincidence,' he said. 'I was about to buy a ticket for the new play.'

'Do you mean *Life With Father*?' asked Larry.

'I do indeed.'

'We're in it,' said Larry.

'Ah, I understand now, madam!' he exclaimed. 'It is for this production that you have been engaged.'

'That is correct,' said Miss Merryweather,

'But we're not on every night,' said Larry. 'We're only allowed to be in the play four times a week. Tuesdays, Thursdays and twice on Saturdays.'

Miss Merryweather bustled them down the foyer steps and round the corner to the street that led to the stage door. A delivery boy was walking ahead of them, carrying a large bouquet. Once through the door, Josie ran up to Elsie's dressing room where she found her seated between two of the other actresses in the cast.

'Enjoying it?' Elsie asked.

'Yes, but we have to leave now. I just wanted to say good luck.'

Elsie gave her a hug. Josie was surprised to find that she had to stretch her arms to hug her back. Her sister felt enormous encased in the padding she wore as the second maid. Her hair was covered in talcum powder to make it look grey and there were wrinkles and shadows over her face.

She spotted a card from her mum and dad, and a telegram stuck to the mirror. It was from Henry, wishing Elsie good luck and sending lots of love.

By the time they had reached London, Josie was determined that the next time she and Larry travelled with Miss Merryweather, she would bring something with her to entertain him. It had been a miserable journey. Being in the matron's company was like sitting beneath a dark, oppressive cloud. Miss Merryweather was to take Larry home, leaving Josie to make her own way back to Auntie Win's flat. Running beside her striding figure, Josie began to feel an overwhelming sense of relief. Soon she would be separated from this gloomy woman and be gliding away from her on a bus to freedom. She didn't dare look at Larry because she felt so sorry for him having to remain with her.

They were heading for the exit when who should walk briskly past them but the smartly dressed man. He stopped, raised his hat and gave a slight bow.

'What a delight to see you again, madam,' he said. 'You didn't arrive on that train from Winford just now, did you?'

'Indeed we did, sir,' said Miss Merryweather.

'Extraordinary,' he said. 'Perhaps we'll have the pleasure of bumping into each other again at the café.' And with that he was gone.

Miss Merryweather looked as though she had lost track of where she was for a moment. She gave herself a little shake and they briskly strode towards their respective bus stops.

# 9

# The Opening Night

'AND WHAT EXPLANATION DO YOU HAVE FOR your absence yesterday?'

'Mr King asked us to be in the theatre to watch the dress rehearsal with the other Whitney and Harlan, madam,' Josie murmured, standing in front of Miss Dagleish's desk.

'Which was in the afternoon. So where were you in the morning?'

'At the technical rehearsal, madam.'

'Why?'

'The other boys have a chance to find out where everything is before their dress rehearsal. Larry and me – I mean, Larry and *I* – don't.'

'So Larry was there too?'

'No. He couldn't be there that early and I wanted to find out as much as possible so I can help him, see.'

Miss Dagleish gave an impatient sigh.

'As this is your first professional engagement I will say no more. In future, you need to remember that if you have to attend rehearsals in the afternoon you must do your four hours of school work in the morning.'

'Yes, madam.'

'Now, I understand you need to be at the theatre earlier this afternoon to run through scenes with Larry and the other members of the cast before tonight's performance. Naturally, it will not have the frisson of the opening night but then you will have all the excitement of the last performance, won't you?'

'Yes, madam.'

'I'm sure you'll be a credit to the school, though I would have been happier if you had been playing a girl. Will your parents be there this evening?'

'No, madam, but my Auntie Win will be. My parents are comin' on the matinee on the last Saturday.'

'Splendid.' Miss Dagleish gave a dismissive gesture with her hand. 'You may go.'

Josie curtsied. 'Thank you, madam.'

She shut the door behind her and hurried to the basement cloakroom. Safely out of sight, she danced around the hanging coats.

She had got away with it!

'. . . and last of all, I need to put blue liner along my eyelashes,' said Josie.

Elsie and Lionel glanced at one another.

'Who told you to do that?' asked Elsie.

'The make-up teacher at school.'

'A touch of *amateur night out*, I fear,' said Lionel.

They had congregated in the dressing room Lionel shared with Anthony and two other actors. Upstairs in dressing room seven, Larry had folded his arms and had refused to allow Miss Merryweather anywhere near his face. Elsie had taken him down to see Lionel so that they could talk man to man, along with Josie, as she was uncertain how much her sister had been taught in the few weeks she had attended the stage school. Before Josie could ask Lionel what he meant by 'amateur night out', Larry let out a yelp.

'Gosh! That's so big!'

He had spotted Lionel's large metal make-up box lying open. A tray at the top and the drawer underneath were divided into compartments filled with numerous stubby and slim cylindrical tubes in an array of colours.

'Greasepaint sticks,' said Lionel. 'You draw lines across your cheeks and forehead with them and then spread the colour evenly all over your face, under your chin and down your neck.'

At the bottom of the box were round orange and red tins with *Leichner* written on them, and clumps of hair.

'Why do you have so much?' asked Larry.

'Because over the years I have had to play many different characters. Take a look at Anthony's box.'

Anthony's smaller metal box had one tray with only a few sticks of make up in it. Some looked brand new.

'He'll collect more as he plays more roles.'

'What's all the hairy stuff for?' asked Larry.

'Moustaches and beards. I stick them on my face with a special glue called spirit gum.'

'But how do you know what greasepaint to put on?' interrupted Josie.

'Each stick of colour has a number. That thick white one,

for example, is number twenty.' He then pointed to a small, thin, black one. 'That is number sixteen. They have to have numbers because there are so many different shades for each colour.'

'So why hasn't Anthony got as many colours as you?'

'Because he hasn't played as many foreigners.' He picked up a pale pinky-orange stick and a rich orangey-brown one. 'These are five and nine, the combination most often used. If I were playing an Arab I would probably use number eight which is this one,' he said, indicating a stick that was a dark tan colour. 'If I were playing a Hindu, I would probably use number sixteen and for an African I'd use number eleven. That's what I put on my face when I played Othello. But if I were playing a black person from another region I would use number seven which is more of a brown colour, and if I were playing a Chinese person –'

'Have you ever played a Chinese person?' interrupted Larry.

'Oh, yes. An actor has to be able to play anyone.'

'Have you ever played a cowboy?'

'Not yet,' Lionel answered slowly.

'Have you ever had to wear lady's lipstick?'

'Only when I've played a pantomime dame.'

Larry sunk his fingers into a soft waxy clump in the box.

'That's putty,' said Lionel, 'for changing the shape of my nose before I put make-up over it. And in those round tins, one has face powder in it so that I don't appear greasy under the lights, and the other contains removing cream to take it all off afterwards.'

'What if I didn't wear this greasepaint stuff?' asked Larry.

'You'd be a different colour to everyone else on stage,' said Elsie.

Larry sighed.

'All right, I'll wear it, but only if you or Lionel put it on.'

'Agreed,' said Elsie. 'And Josie,' she added awkwardly, 'I think I'd better do yours as well and give you a make-up lesson. Your teacher sounds a bit . . .'

But she was lost for words.

Josie was puzzled. Did Elsie disapprove of what she had learned at the stage school?

After the dress rehearsal, they removed their costumes but left their make-up on ready for the evening's performance. Fiona dashed out with money and an order for sandwiches. Josie had to stay in dressing room seven with Larry and Miss Merryweather. From upstairs she could hear the others laughing in the green room and she longed to join them. She was rescued by a knock at the door. It was Samuel.

'Phone call for you, Miss Merryweather,' he announced.

'For me?' she said, astonished. 'But . . .'

She glanced at Larry and Josie with concern.

'I'll take him down to the green room,' said Josie quickly. 'Elsie's there.'

To her relief Miss Merryweather indicated with a nod that she was giving permission. Josie swiftly grabbed their sandwiches, and she and Larry trotted down the stairs behind her.

When they reached the corridor backstage, they followed

a young man and woman walking ahead of them. The woman was fashionably dressed in a red woollen jacket, hat, gloves and high heels, and was carrying a handful of envelopes. Her male companion had a clipped moustache and wore a long blue overcoat and a trilby cocked to one side of his head. They peered into the green room.

'Denys! Isobel! How lovely to see you!' cried a voice that sounded like Daphne.

Josie poked her head round after them.

'Hello, Jo!' everyone chorused. 'Come in too.'

'Ah ha! You've escaped,' said Lionel, giving her and Larry a mischievous smile, and he moved to one side so that they could squeeze in beside him.

'How did it go last night, Daphne?' asked the tall man they called Denys. 'Good reception?'

'Yes. They even enjoyed the six curtain calls. Are you in tonight?'

'Yes. Here are some late good luck cards. Sorry we couldn't be here last night but we had to go to the meeting at Golders Green Hippodrome.'

'And?'

'They've won the first round!' Denys said. 'The council have refused permission for it to be pulled down.'

'Oh, that is good news!' cried Daphne.

'They'd collected twenty-six thousand signatures,' said Isobel. 'And there were lots of big names there.'

'It's Bruce Forsyth's local theatre. He said he's with us all the way. They're going to keep collecting signatures and raising money. And they read out all these telegrams from famous people who couldn't get there,' added Denys.

'Like us?' said Lionel, and he gave Josie a wink.

'No, Lionel, not like you. As I was saying, there were telegrams from Laurence Olivier, Vivien Leigh, Gilbert Harding, Tommy Trinder, Richard Attenborough . . .'

'Who are they?' asked Larry.

Everyone fell apart laughing.

'Not so famous then,' Lionel quipped.

Miss Merryweather appeared at the door.

'Come on, you two. Time to get back into your costumes.'

As they left, Josie heard Lionel shouting after them, 'See you on the green.'

'What does that mean?' asked Larry.

'On stage,' said Josie.

Up in the dressing room there were good luck cards waiting for them from the cast, Josie's mum and dad, Auntie Win, Mrs Jenkins, Elsie and Henry, Ralph and Jessica, a telegram from Australia from her brother Harry and his wife, and a card from Larry's parents. There was even one from Miss Partridge wishing them good luck with their Tiddlywinks.

As Josie pulled on her long woollen socks and knee length breeches, she noticed that her hands were shaking.

There was a knock at the door. The call boy, a gangly teenage boy, poked his head round it to let them know there were thirty-five minutes till curtain up.

It seemed only a few moments later that he was back again giving them their beginners call, the one which warned them there were five minutes to go and that they must leave their dressing rooms to take their places either in the wings or onstage. Josie and Larry, accompanied by Miss Merryweather made their way downstairs.

Within minutes they were in the stage left wings, waiting at the foot of the steps leading to the platform where the staircase descended to the hall.

Josie's nerves had now been overtaken by excitement. As the low murmur from the audience faded into silence, there was the sound of a piano being played in the orchestra pit. This meant that the house lights would be going down. She heard the curtain being raised and squeezed Larry's hand.

High on the platform stood Eleanor West. She glanced down behind her and gave them a brief smile before turning back to look at the two light bulbs on the wooden frame on the flat beside her. One of them was red, the other green. The red one was on. It was the *stand by* signal.

Above them Anthony and David, who were playing the brothers Clarence and John, were hovering on the next step down poised to take her place. The green light flashed on and Eleanor made her way gracefully down the stairs and onstage.

'*Good morning, Annie,*' Josie heard her say.

Anthony and David had now moved onto the platform, and as they descended onto the set, Josie and Larry took their place.

*Me next*, she thought. She heard her cue – *a new suit* – and ran down the stairs into the living room, conscious of the bright lights in her eyes, the space beyond the stage a vast black hole. She couldn't see the audience but she could sense them.

'*Good morning, mother,*' she said, and kissed Eleanor on the cheek before running over to Anthony and David.

'*Good morning, dear,*' said Eleanor.

'*Who won?*' Josie asked brother 'John' excitedly.

'*The Giants. Seven to Three. Buck Ewing hit a home run.*'

And at that moment Larry came sliding down the banister to a wave of laughter.

'I've brought these,' said Larry, emptying his satchel onto the dressing room floor as they waited during the second interval. 'So we can play that game you showed me for training spies.'

There was a large Champion the Wonder Horse book filled with stories and comic strip adventures, a pale green and cream car, a red tractor, a plastic model of the Lone Ranger on his horse Silver, an olive-green tank, a *Swift* comic, a pale blue racing car, a yellowy-orange bear puppet called Sooty, a camouflage-patterned aeroplane and boxes with *Matchbox Series* and *Corgi Toys* printed on them. Larry opened one and drew out a smart white car.

'This is my best one,' he said and sent it speeding along the floor. It fell to one side. 'It moves better on lino. It shoots along then. That's because it's got glidematic suspension.'

'The only snag is you know all the objects already,' said Josie.

'Oh, I never thought of that.'

'Why don't we do a swap?' she suggested. 'You put out

xxx

your toys and I'll see how many I can remember and I'll . . .'
She paused. 'Well, I'll think of something.'

Only one more act to go, she thought, and it was flying
along. From the stairway she heard the call boy give the
beginner's call to the members of the cast who were in Act
Three, Scene One. The audience would now be back in their
seats.

'Time to put the game away, Larry,' she said scooping up
the toys.

It was the final scene and Miss Merryweather kept fussing
around them in the wings. It was *Josephine this* and *Josephine
that* when Josie was concentrating on being Whitney. She
wished the matron would go away.

*That is my seventeen-year-old brother and my mother*, she
told herself when Clarence and Vinnie were talking about
the ugly china pug dog. *They're putting the dog in the box now
and Father is coming down the stairs.*

There was the slam of a door.

'That's Clarence leaving with the pug dog in the box,' she
murmured to Larry.

Larry nodded.

There was now a mushy conversation between her
'parents' where her 'father' was telling her 'mother' that he
loved her and she began singing *Sweet Marie*.

'That's our cue,' whispered Larry.

There was the rush of the curtain falling. The flat was
unhinged and the false tabletop with breakfast laid out on it
was carried on and put on top of the table.

'Now,' said Josie, and she and Larry swiftly took their places at the table where two bowls of porridge were waiting for them.

'Time to prepare for the curtain call,' Miss Merryweather said curtly as they ran into the wings.

'Don't you worry about them,' said Daphne, grabbing their hands. 'You relax in the dressing room, Miss Merryweather. I'll bring them both up to you.'

'I really don't think –' she began.

But Daphne was already propelling Josie and Larry towards the prompt corner where they could watch what was happening on stage.

'Damn it!' they heard 'Father' cry.

A door slammed and the curtain slowly descended as 'Clarence' knelt at 'Mary's' feet to propose marriage. As soon as it hit the deck, Daphne drew Josie and Larry to where Fiona and the DSM were carrying the sofa. Once it was in position, 'Mother' and 'Father' sat in the centre, Larry ran to sit on the floor between them and Josie stood poised at their side. Within seconds the curtain rose to a round of applause.

'You have to rub it in hard,' said Josie in the dressing room as Larry gingerly pushed bits of removing cream round his face.

'But it's so horrible!'

'Do you want to go to your school tomorrow with bits of make-up on you?'

'No! The other boys will call me a sissie.' And with that

he began rubbing vigorously until his face had become a mess of colours.

Josie giggled. 'You look like a monster.'

Larry raised his arms and made a loud moaning sound.

'I am a Martian and I've landed on Planet Greasepaint.'

'Face me, young man,' said Miss Merryweather. 'We have a train to catch. Chin up and eyes shut.'

The door opened. It was Elsie holding two wet flannels and a towel.

'I thought these might come in handy,' she announced.

Elsie accompanied the three of them and Auntie Win to the station to wave them off.

'And did I look like a boy?' Josie asked her aunt.

'Had me and everyone else fooled.'

'What about me?' said Larry.

'You looked like a boy too,' Auntie Win said, smiling. 'And yes you were both wonderful. Your parents will be very proud of you. When are yours coming, Larry?'

'The last performance.'

'And I believe your parents are coming to the last matinee,' said Miss Merryweather to Elsie.

'Yes. They want to take Josie and Larry out to tea afterwards. Will that be allowed?'

Miss Merryweather gave a nod.

'I expect you'll be glad of the rest,' Auntie Win laughed.

'Not at all. They are, on the whole, very well-behaved children.'

*On the whole?* thought Josie. She had been doing a brilliant impersonation of sainthood and now all Miss Merryweather could say was 'On the whole'. She noticed that Larry was beaming at her. She knew what he was thinking. Slap up tea and no Miss Merryweather!

Minutes after they had arrived at the station, their train arrived. Without the wet flannels they would probably have missed it. Elsie kissed Josie and Larry good-bye and gave Auntie Win a hug. Once inside the carriage, Josie slid the window down.

'See you on Thursday!' she yelled at the top of her voice.

She pushed up the window and plonked back onto her seat. It was then that she realised she hadn't behaved in a very ladylike manner.

'On the whole,' muttered Miss Merryweather, giving her a penetrating glare.

For most of the journey there was a frosty silence broken only by Larry who was peering into the darkness, identifying the different trains. Finally, Miss Merryweather spoke.

'That phone call I received before the performance was from the gentleman in the café, Laurence. A Mr Lovatt-Pendlebury. He wanted me to inform you that he was going to watch the show tonight. I didn't tell you earlier because I didn't want to make you nervous.'

'What man?' said Larry.

'The man who spoke to you in the foyer.'

'Oh.' Larry looked puzzled. 'But I don't know him.'

'I think he was just being polite.'

Josie noticed that Miss Merryweather seemed flustered. There was another tense silence.

'I wish we could perform tomorrow night as well,' Josie blurted out.

'You may have to,' said Miss Merryweather. 'If the boy playing the other Whitney is ill, you will be expected to step into his shoes.'

'Is he expected to be ill?' asked Auntie Win.

'No. But I think Josie needs to know that one must always be prepared.'

'Be prepared! That's the Girl Guide motto,' said Josie. 'I'm a Guide, see. Bullfinch patrol.'

'In your home town?'

'Oh no. In London.'

'And is Miss Dagleish aware of this fact?' asked Miss Merryweather.

Josie suddenly felt uncomfortable. 'It's after school,' she said slowly.

'Nevertheless I think she should know, don't you?'

Suddenly, Josie remembered Elsie warning her to keep quiet about it. She could have kicked herself. To her relief Larry butted in.

'Will the boy playing Harlan be ill tomorrow, do you think?'

'I very much doubt it,' said Miss Merryweather, 'but if *you're* ill he will step into your shoes.'

'I promise I won't be,' he said with determination. 'I will eat all my horrible greens even if they make me sick.' He paused. 'But not sick enough to be ill.'

Josie hastily opened *Pigeon Post* before Miss Merryweather could ask her any more awkward questions about Guides.

Luckily, she and her aunt began to talk about the weather.

'So what do you think of her?' Josie asked her aunt when they went their separate ways at the London station.

'She reminds me of a sergeant major I used to know. Blunt. But I expect her heart is in the right place.'

As Larry walked away he suddenly peered round and gave Josie an envious look.

'See you on Thursday,' Josie yelled at him.

And then they disappeared into the crowd.

Josie was about to climb onto a bus with her aunt when something caught her eye, causing her to swing round sharply.

'What is it?' asked Auntie Win.

'I thought I saw the man who telephoned Miss Merryweather before the show,' said Josie. 'But it couldn't have been him.'

*Because being at the station at the same time as their arrival yet again would be too much of a coincidence.* Brushing aside her discomfort, she stepped quickly onto the bus, bursting to tell her aunt about the funny remarks members of the cast had been making in the green room.

# 10

# A Spanner in the Works

'BUT WHY?' ASKED JOSIE, FROM BEHIND THE raised lid of her desk.

'They said I was showing off,' said Hilda. 'But I really tried to do less.'

It was during the history lesson that Hilda told Josie she had been chucked out of *A Midsummer Night's Dream*.

'Esmeralda has taken my place.'

'But she's got two left feet!' whispered Josie.

'Yes, but they're obviously the right left feet, if you see what I mean.'

'Josephine Hollis!'

Josie peered over the lid to find Miss Dagleish standing at the door.

'Mrs Havilland wishes to see you,' she said, 'immediately.'

'That's not fair!' protested a tall spotty girl called Dorothy. 'Why doesn't she want any of us? We've been here much longer than Josie has.'

'It's not about a job,' Miss Dagleish said firmly.

There was no escaping Mrs Havilland this time, thought Josie, rising slowly from her chair.

Once she reached the corridor outside the acting room, she hovered for a moment, trying to come up with a plan of escape but was stumped. She was about to knock on the door when she heard Mrs Havilland and one of the mothers deep in conversation on the other side.

'And you think you might be able to find more work for James this term, Mrs Havilland?'

'With Christmas approaching, Mrs Eliot, I'm sure we shall.'

The door swung open, revealing the flushed face and enormous frame of Mrs Eliot. Draped around her neck under her lopsided hat was the fur of a dead fox, complete with head and glassy eyes.

'Ah, Josephine,' boomed Mrs Havilland.

'Josephine Hollis? The girl who was given the part James had been put up for?' She glared at Josie as though she had committed the crime of the century.

'That is correct,' she said, ushering Josie in and shutting the door behind her.

Mrs Havilland gazed down at Josie in silence and made a downward motion with her head. Josie waited for her to say something but she only bobbed her head again, this time with more vigour.

'Haven't we forgotten something?' she said eventually.

'Was I supposed to have brought somethin' with me?' asked Josie.

'A curtsy,' she reminded her.

'Oh, yeah,' said Josie and gave a quick bob.

'That's better. And such a nice one too,' she said. 'So

balletic, but then of course you did ballet before you came here, didn't you?'

'Yes, Mrs Havilland.'

'It's a pity you don't remember to curtsy more often, don't you think?'

'Yes, Mrs Havilland.'

'Now, my dear, your aunt has rather misled Miss Dagleish and me. We were both under the impression when she informed us that your brother was working in Stratford that she was referring to Stratford Upon Avon. Not atte Bow.'

'Atte Bow?'

'Stratford East. East London.'

'Oh. Aren't they the same?'

Mrs Havilland's eyebrows shot up.

'Indeed they are not. Stratford Upon Avon means the Royal Shakespeare Company, the crème de la crème of classical acting. Stratford East means *knees up* kind of acting.'

Josie was mystified.

'Knees up?' she repeated

'A lot of lower class nonsense under a certain Miss Littlewood. Sadly, I suspect a touch of her influence has had a deleterious effect on you due to your brother being in her company but rest assured it is not too late to nip that in the bud. Now, you may be wondering how I happen to be aware of this state of affairs. The answer lies in the fact that I was present at last night's performance in Winford.' She gave Josie a steady look. 'Let's examine that bowling, shall we?'

'I was taught how to pitch by an American musician,' began Josie enthusiastically.

'That's as may be,' interrupted Mrs Havilland. 'But real life and the artifice of the theatre are two quite different animals. You're too rough. A touch of elegance is what you require.'

The word *elegance* made Josie's heart sink.

'Now, there's no need to look so despondent. I am going to give you lots of help.'

*That's what I'm afraid of*, thought Josie.

'Observe the way I curve my arm and copy me.'

She then proceeded to make a movement that reminded Josie of a photograph she had seen of Margot Fonteyn dancing *Swan Lake*.

'Mrs Havilland,' began Josie. 'Whitney is a boy.'

'I know he's a boy,' she said sternly, 'but you're playing him as though he's a boy from the streets. You're too rough. This Whitney is a cultured, well-educated boy. This should show in his upright demeanour.'

*He has to be a bit rough*, thought Josie, *otherwise he wouldn't have been allowed to join in a game on the street.*

'Luckily I have Michael Bailey's script here which I previously marked for him.'

Over the next hour Mrs Havilland insisted on changing the way she stood, the way she moved and even told her that her American accent should not be so strong. The worst moment was when they came to the scene where Whitney's father was testing him with a series of questions.

'In this scene I noticed that you kept looking at your

father. Now, tell me what's wrong with that.'

Josie hadn't a clue.

'Don't worry. It's because you're a beginner. The answer is that we can't see your face, can we? You need to look at the audience over your shoulder as he speaks to you. In fact, I've a better idea. Turn your whole body to face the audience, place your hands on your hips and smile.'

'Smile!' exclaimed Josie, unable to contain herself any longer. 'But he thinks his mother might be dying.'

'Exactly. Smile through your pain. That would be more effective and would wring the audience's heartstrings.'

*And Mr King would wring my neck.*

'It will make you appear courageous in a tragic situation, do you see? Now, I won't allow you home until I am completely satisfied with every single scene you're in.' Mrs Havilland gave a light laugh. 'If you had come to me in the first place, we wouldn't have had to do this, would we?'

By the time Josie had returned to Auntie Win's flat that evening it was too late to ring Elsie at the theatre. She would already be on stage. Her aunt could see that her niece was worried about what she had been asked to do in the extra acting lesson and attempted to reassure her.

'They must know what they're doing,' Auntie Win said. 'I couldn't see anything wrong in the way you were playing Whitney but I'm as much a beginner as you are. Maybe she thinks she can help you be even better.'

But it felt totally wrong to Josie.

At school the next day she was tempted to pretend she

was ill but realised that if she did, the other Whitney would be asked to step into her shoes that night, and Larry would have to act with a boy who was a stranger. She longed to tell Hilda but each time she attempted to broach the subject, a huge lump rose up into her throat. Instead, Josie asked her more questions about *A Midsummer Night's Dream*.

It was during the deportment class, which involved walking up and down the stairs in the hall with yet another book on her head, that she decided to tell the teacher she had to be in the theatre much earlier because Mr King wanted to rehearse a scene with her and Larry in it. He needed more help, she explained, switching on a sickly smile, because *alas* he wasn't lucky enough to attend a good stage school. She just hoped the teacher wouldn't check up on her.

By midday everything was packed ready for a quick escape but as she was running through the hallway she heard her name being called out. It was Miss Dagleish. She felt her face burning.

'Gloves, Josephine!' she commanded.

Josie put down her attaché case and hastily dragged out her white gloves from the pockets of her duffle coat. With trembling hands she manoeuvred her fingers into them, grabbed her case and stumbled out of the door. As she jumped down the steps she could see her bus pulling away.

'Oh no!' she cried, breaking into a sprint. 'Please!' she yelled in desperation after it. 'Please stop!'

She heard the bell ring from inside and it shuddered to a halt. The tall West Indian bus conductor hauled her on.

'It's your lucky day, my girl,' he said.

'Thank you,' gasped Josie and almost curtsied.

Once she had reached the railway station, she weaved her way swiftly around the passengers. Her heart fell when she spotted the length of the ticket queues. She glanced at the railway clock.

'Seven minutes,' she whispered.

The instant she had a ticket in her hand she darted towards the platform. The railway guard had already raised his flag and blown his whistle and her train had begun to move. She dashed to the last carriage and swung the door open. As she hurled herself headfirst across the floor, the guard gave an angry yell and someone inside the carriage leaned across and slammed the door behind her.

The train juddered forward. Josie struggled to her feet and threw herself back with relief against one of the upholstered seats. Two smartly dressed middle-aged women on the other side of the compartment stared at her. She nodded her thanks to the woman who had closed the door for her. Perspiring profusely, she pulled off her gloves and hat. The women stared at her head in horror but Josie hadn't the energy to explain that she wasn't infectious, and that the reason she had such a short haircut wasn't because she had nits . She closed her eyes, hoping that she would reach the theatre before Elsie's rehearsals had finished.

By the time Josie had reached the stage door, having run without stopping from Winford station, she could hardly breathe. Wilfred and his son stared at her in alarm.

'What's the matter, Jo?' began Wilfred.

'Elsie,' she gasped.

'She's on stage,' said Samuel.

He threw open the door at the side of their little cubicle and leaped up the steps to the swing door. Within minutes he had returned with her sister.

'You look terrible,' she said. 'Are you ill?'

Josie shook her head.

'Is it something to do with the show?'

Josie nodded.

'Mrs Havilland has changed the moves,' Josie said, and to her embarrassment, her eyes began to sting.

'Don't worry,' said Elsie, disappearing back inside. 'I'll have a word with Mr King.'

Ten minutes later Fiona appeared at the top of the steps.

'Mr King wants to see you, Jo.'

Josie dragged herself up the stairs.


'Come closer,' Mr King said.

Out of the corner of her eye, Josie recognised some members of the cast. She walked downstage.

'I hear that your acting mistress has changed your moves. Is that correct?'

'Yes, Mr King,' she murmured. 'And she's coming again next Tuesday to see if I've improved.'

'I see.' He frowned. 'I've asked the people in some of your scenes to stay behind to see these new moves. Let's start, shall we?'

It wasn't until she was in the scene with Hugh Burton,

standing with her hands on her hips and smiling out at the audience that Mr King exploded.

'Enough!' he cried. 'You look like Peter Pan! And when you're pitching the ball it's like a scene from *Giselle*! We're now going to have to ask the other boy to play your role.'

'Wait a minute, Ben,' said Elsie. 'Her acting mistress refused to allow her to go home from school yesterday until she played Whitney as instructed.'

By now tears were rolling down Josie's face. She brushed them aside, furious with herself for being such a baby.

'I came early to tell you about it because I knew it was wrong!' Josie blurted out. 'And now you're angry with me! And if I don't do what she wants, she'll be angry with me too. And I'm trying to do my best and now everyone's angry with me!'

Within minutes the cast had their arms around her.

'We're not angry with you,' said Eleanor.

'In fact, we feel downright sorry for you,' said Hugh.

'Mind you,' said Daphne, 'I don't know what possessed the woman to have you doing all those poses. I'm sorry, Jo, but they are rather funny!'

Suddenly everyone began prancing around the stage, copying what Josie had been asked to do. Josie couldn't help laughing. To her relief Mr King was smiling too.

'Do you think you can return to playing it the way I directed you?' he asked.

Josie nodded.

'But what am I going to do about Mrs Havilland?'

'I will ring the school first thing and explain that because there are so many tables and pot plants on the set, not to mention members of the cast coming and going, that if your moves are changed it will mean that everyone else's moves will also have to be changed to prevent a series of collisions.' He glanced at Elsie. 'Do you think you can help her dispense with all the sugary musical comedy influences before Miss Merryweather arrives with Larry?'

*Larry?* In all her panic Josie had completely forgotten about him. If she didn't unlearn what Mrs Havilland had forced her to do, Larry would be all at sea. And then she remembered what he had said on that first Saturday, that Michael never looked him in the eye. Now she understood why. And Josie cared far more about Larry than Mrs Havilland.

'Elsie, when you marry Henry, Larry will be a kind of brother, won't he?'

'Yes. A brother-in-law and Molly will be your sister-in-law.'

And though Josie wasn't happy at the stage school, it suddenly occurred to her that if she hadn't been a pupil there, she wouldn't have stayed with the Carpenters at the weekends and got to know them better. Neither would she have been a member of the Bullfinch patrol, or be standing in the Palace Theatre with her sister.

'Let's start then, shall we?' said Elsie.


'So what did your friend think about *Fog* at Palmers Green?' Fiona asked Elsie in the green room.when they were taking a break.

They were gulping down hot cups of tea. This time some of the cast had brought sandwiches back with them from the café so that Elsie and Josie could join them.

Elsie gave a thumbs down sign.

'Really? I thought it was supposed to be a *hilarious* comedy,' said Fiona.

'It wasn't.'

'What was it about?' said Josie through a mouthful of sandwich.

'Ten people in a house haunted by a madman.'

Josie was giggling so much she almost choked.

Samuel poked his head round the door. 'Phone call for you at the stage door, Jo.'

'Ah,' said Lionel. 'Perhaps it's Pinewood film studios,'

Downstairs, Samuel held out the receiver for her to take.

'Hello?' she said shyly, pressing it to her ear.

'It's me,' said Auntie Win. 'I wanted to find out how you fared.'

'Elsie's sorted it all out. At first I couldn't think straight but as soon as she said, "Think baseball, that's the most important thing in your life," the old moves came back.'

'You mean Mr King didn't like Mrs Havilland's changes?'

'He hated them.'

'Oh dear. She won't be too happy about that, will she? Still, I'm glad Elsie's been helpful. The other reason I'm phoning is that I thought you might need cheering up, so I've booked tickets for us to see *West Side Story* on Wednesday.'

Josie gasped.

'And I've booked an extra ticket for Hilda. She can stay overnight and sleep in my bed.'

'But there isn't room for three.'

'I'll sleep on the settee. But I advise you both to keep it to yourself.'

'Can't I tell Elsie?'

'Of course. I mean at school. Just in case anyone is jealous.'

Josie thought that was a very good idea.

'Auntie Win?'

'Yes.'

'I love you.'

'Jolly good.'

# II

# The Gentleman

'*BANG! CRACK! TWICE IN QUICK SUCCESSION Mike's colt .44s speak,*' read Josie dramatically over the sound of the railway guard's whistle, '*and the burning brand is shot from one man's hand.*'

To prevent Miss Merryweather from constantly telling Larry to sit still on the return journey to London, Josie had packed her *Film Fun Annual* to read to him.

'*"Startin' a forest fire hereabouts can be mighty bad medicine!" cried Mike.*' The train had hardly begun to pull out of Winford station when a sharp gust of wind blew into their carriage. The door had been flung open. Miss Merryweather gave a startled jump as a man leaped in accompanied by a vociferous 'Oi!' from the platform guard. He seated himself by the window and removed his hat. To Josie's astonishment, it was the gentleman who had spoken to them in the café and theatre foyer. As soon as he spotted them his eyebrows shot upwards.

'Good gracious, Miss Merryweather,' he said apologetically. 'You obviously intended this carriage to be private for you and your charges. Please forgive this unwarranted intrusion. I am more than happy to change carriages at the next station if you would prefer.'

Miss Merryweather gave a little shake of her head.

'That is quite unnecessary, Mr Lovatt-Pendlebury,' she murmured.

'Go on, Josie,' urged Larry, impatiently. 'What happened next?'

Josie continued reading, acutely aware of the occasional rustle from the man's newspaper and the fact that Miss Merryweather kept staring at exactly the same page in *The Lady* magazine. As the cowboy story rose to crescendo, there was a *swift and decisive* battle, one of the villains fell *to a bullet from Mike's trusty six shooter*, the gang was rounded up and *there was no more opposition to the railroad*.

At which point the man cleared his throat.

'Miss Merryweather, I note that you read *The Lady*.'

'That is correct.'

'Then you may have chanced upon articles written by myself on the best art galleries in Europe for discerning holiday makers.'

Miss Merryweather blushed. 'Are you a writer?'

'Of sorts. I write the occasional piece when asked. I suppose I might be what is regarded as a . . .' He hesitated. 'A connoisseur.'

He then proceeded to tell her about his trips to Rome and Florence, Paris and Vienna. To Josie's surprise, Miss Merryweather appeared to be genuinely interested. Every now and then, when he wasn't regaling her with the splendours of Rome's antiquities, the joy of a Strauss concert in Vienna or the freshness of the air in the Swiss Alps, he would turn and ask Larry questions, but Larry was so interested in Josie's annual that he would only give a quick 'yes' or 'no' before returning swiftly to a particular picture. It was a rocket that resembled a metallic ball with four long thin spikes sticking out of it – a sputnik. Because the man ignored Josie, she was able to observe him unnoticed and play Kim's Game on him.

1. *Navy blue striped suit with matching waistcoat.*

2. *Shiny navy blue tie.*

3. *Slim silver tie-pin across the knot of the tie.*

Unlike her school tie, his knot was a short, slim tube.

4. *Silver chain hanging across his waistcoat leading into a tiny pocket low down.*

*He must have a pocket watch*, she thought.

5. *White handkerchief rising out of left breast pocket in a triangle.*

The train gave a sudden jolt, sending Josie and the *Film Fun Annual* flying across the carriage.

'Josephine!' Miss Merryweather exclaimed.

Mr Lovatt-Pendlebury retrieved the annual from the floor and handed it back to Larry. In so doing, his raincoat slid to the ground and a small book fell out of one of the pockets. He swiftly picked up the raincoat and tucked it back inside but not before Josie had a chance to read the title.

6. *A book about travelling in Europe.*

'Do you ever attend the opera, Miss Merryweather?' he asked before Josie had time to sit down again.

'I'm afraid it is somewhat beyond my means,' she

answered demurely. For some odd reason, the more Mr Lovatt-Pendlebury talked, the more uncomfortable Josie felt.

'Trust your instincts,' Auntie Win was always saying. 'That's what the best detectives do.'

But later, back at the flat, when Josie told her aunt how he had given her the creeps, she had tried to reassure Josie that he was probably harmless.

'You read too many detective novels,' she had said.

'But Auntie Win,' Josie had protested, ' *you're* the one who's always reading detective novels, not me!'

On Saturday afternoon, Miss Merryweather was escorting Larry and Josie through the stage door when Samuel leaned over the counter.

'Phone message for you, Miss Merryweather,' he said. 'From a Mr Lovatt-Pendlebury. He's left a number for you to ring at your convenience.'

For a moment she seemed taken aback.

'Josephine, take Laurence up to the dressing room. I shall follow you in due course.'

'Yes, Miss Merryweather,' said Josie meekly.

As soon as they were upstairs, she flung a handful of objects onto the floor and made for the door. 'I have to go and, um . . . powder my nose,' she said, jumping up and down on the spot to convince Larry she was desperate. 'Take a look at those objects and when I come back I'll see how many you can remember.'

Larry knelt down and stared intently at them.

Josie crept swiftly down the stairs and halted when she

heard Miss Merryweather's voice.

'A concert? . . . Oh well, I'm not sure. My evenings are fully . . . Tomorrow? On a Sunday? . . . No. I haven't been to an afternoon concert for some time . . .Well, that is most kind . . . Afterwards? . . . Oh, yes I know of it. It's a very charming little tea house.'

This was followed by a gasp.

'But that is . . . I mean . . . Are you sure? . . . In a taxi? . . . That is most considerate . . . My address? Yes, of course . . .'

Having heard enough, Josie bolted back up to their dressing room.

By the time Miss Merryweather had returned, she found Josie seated innocently next to Larry on the floor as he called out the names of the objects he had remembered. Miss Merryweather, Josie observed, was humming.

The play had full houses for both performances. Because there were no rehearsals the following day, five members of the cast joined them in the train carriage on their way home to their London digs. Josie couldn't stop smiling. She always felt far more relaxed and at home in their company than she did with Miss Merryweather. If it hadn't been for her friendship with Hilda, she would have liked to stay in the theatre with them for ever and never go back to the stage school.

While they chatted among themselves, Josie put a cord around her waist and attempted the new knot Sheila had taught her the previous night at the Guide meeting.

'I say, that looks rather good,' said Lionel.

'It isn't,' said Josie, 'look.' And she slid the knot to her waist.

'What's wrong with that?'

'If I was hangin' from a building, the loop would shrink and destroy my stomach. A bowline knot mustn't slide, you see. My patrol leader says that the most important thing to remember is,' and she took a deep breath, *'that the loop must be on the standing part of the cord where the strain comes around the bend on the free end, otherwise it will not hold.'*

Lionel nodded solemnly.

'Yeah, I don't know what it means either,' said Josie.

'We've got the carriage all to ourselves,' interrupted Larry suddenly. 'And there isn't that man who keeps asking me questions.'

Immediately, Miss Merryweather drew herself up.

'I'll have you know, Master Carpenter, that Mr Lovatt-Pendlebury is a very cultured man. He has travelled all over Europe.'

*I know*, thought Josie. *I feel as though I've been there with him.*

'You could learn a lot by observing his manners, young man.'

When the theatre matron arrived on Tuesday evening in her usual beige outfit, Josie noticed she was wearing a pink scarf, and that there were traces of rouge and powder on her face. Josie suspected it had something to do with the Sunday afternoon concert with Mr Lovatt-Pendlebury.

That night's performance sped by at a lick. Hardly had

they put on their make-up than they were slapping removing cream on their faces and hastily wiping it off with wet flannels so that they wouldn't miss their train. Once inside the carriage Miss Merryweather stared out of the window. She didn't even complain when Josie read Larry a four-chapter space adventure story, *Voyage to Vulcania* while he drew happily in a sketchbook.

As they drew nearer to London, Josie quickened her pace.

*"'Nice to be home," grinned Joe Dillon, "even if it's only on the moon!"'*

The train began to slow down.

'Miss Merryweather,' Josie said, closing the annual. 'We're here.'

Miss Merrywather gave a violent start. Josie slid the window down and reached for the handle on the other side of the door. Glancing up, she was surprised to see a familiar figure in the crowd, bearing a single rose wrapped in tissue paper. She pretended not to notice and quickly withdrew her head.

They stepped down onto the platform with the other late night passengers.

'Look,' said Larry, tugging at Miss Merryweather's sleeve and pointing. 'It's that man again.'

'Laurence! It's rude to point. To whom are you referring?'

Larry pinned his arms to his side and jerked his head forward at Mr Lovatt-Pendlebury, who was now heading in their direction.

Josie observed Miss Merryweather's cheeks turn pink, as though she had stepped out of a hot bath.

'Mr Lovatt-Pendlebury!' she exclaimed. 'This is a surprise!'

'Well, when you told me yesterday about all this travelling you have to do after the evening performance, I thought I cannot allow you to remain on your own at such a late hour.' He bent down and smiled at Larry. 'And how are we, old chap?'

'Very well, thank you,' Larry replied.

The four of them walked to the end of the platform, Josie feeling invisible again as he chatted away to Miss Merryweather and bombarded Larry with questions. Miss Merryweather nodded, drinking in his every word while he continued to gaze at her as though she were the most interesting woman in the world. To Josie's surprise, he began to ask about Henry. But then Henry was Larry's half brother, she reminded herself. He was probably only being polite.

She was about to leave them when she spotted a familiar figure striding in her direction.

'Auntie Win!' she yelled.

'I've come to keep you company on the bus,' she announced.

Josie ran up and hugged her.

Mr Lovatt-Pendlebury stood politely to one side and lowered his head as they said their goodbyes to Larry and Miss Merryweather

'I assume that's the "man in the café",' her aunt commented as they walked away. 'Have you changed your mind about him?'

'No. I still don't like him,' Josie said, and shivered.

The following evening, seated between Hilda and her aunt in Her Majesty's Theatre, Josie had the sensation of being physically lifted by wave after wave of dance explosions as the music pounded across the footlights. *West Side Story* was the dramatic tale of two New York gangs of American and Puerto Rican teenagers who were at war with one another, the Jets and the Sharks. Constantly in trouble with the law, the New York police tried to encourage them to get on with one another, to no avail.

The songs in the new musical had the power of the back streets and yet Josie heard her aunt whisper, 'It's almost like opera.' One moment the songs had Josie laughing, the next they filled her with a happiness so intense it was as though she were about to burst, only to be shaken by ones about murder and despair. Scenes of the story were told through powerful dance sequences between the gangs. They slouched around being 'cool' and then shocked the audience with their physical violence. Had they leaped off the stage Josie was convinced they could have blitzed their way through the streets of London with their knives.

There was one particular character who caught Josie's attention, a tomboy called Anybodys who longed to be one of the Jets but who was continually being pushed away. Usually Josie cringed at anything 'romantic' but she found herself being drawn into the love story between Tony, a boy who had left the Jets to 'go straight' and Maria, a sweet-natured Puerto Rican girl.

'You two are very quiet,' said Auntie Win during the interval. 'I take it you're enjoying it.'

They nodded vigorously.

'It's the best musical I have ever seen in my whole life,' said Hilda.

Josie waited until Auntie Win had left them to join an ice-cream queue before she spoke.

'Hilda, what are you thinkin'?'

'I'm thinking I have to find someone to teach me that modern kind of ballet. That's how I want to dance.'

'Me too. But how?'

'It says in the programme that a man called Jerome Robbins is the choreographer. Perhaps we could write to him.'

'He probably lives in America. He won't know anything about dance lessons here.'

'There must be a way,' said Hilda quietly.

At the close of the musical all three of them were crying. The audience remained silent as though too stunned to clap. And then a man in the dress circle gave one almighty yell and in seconds there was a roar of voices. To Josie's amazement people rose to their feet and she and Hilda and her aunt stood up to join them.

As soon as the morning lessons were over the next day, Hilda and Josie ran into the dance room, spinning and flinging themselves in every direction. Instead of placing their arms in set positions, they tossed them aside, whirling and leaping into the air. The sensation was so exhilarating it was all Josie could do not to laugh with the sheer freedom of throwing her body in all directions.

Hilda dropped into a crouch, clicking her fingers rhythmically like the Jets did in the musical. Josie joined her.

'*Cool!*' they sang.

They were interrupted by one sharp clap. It was the dance mistress.

'Into line, please,' she ordered. 'And what kind of dancing was that?' she asked disapprovingly. 'Rock and roll?'

'It's from *West Side Story*,' said Hilda, beaming. 'We saw it last night!'

'Not what I call musical theatre,' said the dance mistress.

And it was back to step and point. And step and point.

'What are you planning to do, Hilda?' whispered Josie in the school cloakroom later that afternoon.

'When I get back home, I'll tell Mum I have to stay at school late tomorrow night. Then I'm going to wait at the stage door at Her Majesty's Theatre, and when the cast arrive I'll ask them where we can learn to dance like them.'

They said their goodbyes and Josie grabbed her attaché case. She had promised Larry she would travel on the train to Winford with him so that he wouldn't be left alone with Miss Merryweather. Yet again she had managed to convince Miss Dagleish that she was needed at the theatre earlier than the time she had been called. She was also desperate to get out of the building so that she could avoid Mrs Havilland who had taken to glaring at her with pursed lips ever since Mr King had explained to her over the phone that Josie needed to stick to the moves he had given her.

Luckily she was able to catch a bus sooner than planned. Seated on the top deck, she studied her notebook with the stalking information she had written down at the last Guide meeting. She wouldn't be able to take the test until she had a chance to go out into the countryside and stalk an animal or a bird but she had decided to practise on humans first at the railway station.

*Invisibility*, she read. *Blending with your background.*

'*When taking cover,*' she muttered, '*always look round a bush or boulder, not over the top or you will be seen by your quarry before you can see it.*'

There wouldn't be any bushes to hide behind at a railway station but she could look out for a tea urn or a porter's trolley piled up with luggage.

'*Do not take cover behind a scanty hedge with the sun behind you, or you will be seen silhouetted against the light.*'

After reading about crawling through a field on your stomach, she finally came across some useful information. It concerned the importance of remaining still and avoiding eye contact with an animal, although in her case it would be the eye of a person. She glanced out of the window and was startled to find that the bus was already at the station. She stuffed her notebook into her coat pocket and grabbed her case.

By the time Josie had bought her ticket she had an hour to kill before Miss Merryweather and Larry were due to arrive. She played Kim's Game on an old woman who was selling flowers, observing her mottled hands, her clothing, the colour of her hair and the kind of shoes she was wearing.

The person she chose to stalk was a young mother who was standing with two small children at the newsagent's shop. Listening intently to their conversation, she blended into the background by pretending to read a comic. It was one she usually avoided, convinced it would be too sissie. To her surprise, the stories were quite good and there were no boring tips on how to make an embroidered mat for your posh dressing table. The woman's chatty son reminded her of Larry. A couple of times she was aware of him staring at her but she deliberately avoided his eye.

As they moved away she overheard him say, 'That boy in a dress was reading *Bunty*! That's a girl's comic, isn't it?'

Josie slipped outside to check the railway clock. She still had plenty of time to stalk someone else. She was in the middle of studying the crowd of passengers when to her surprise she spotted Mr Lovatt-Pendlebury. And then she had an awful premonition. Perhaps he was going to travel to Winford with them. The thought of having to endure endless descriptions of 'sights of culture on the continent' made her heart sink. But why on earth had he arrived so early? And then she had a brainwave. She would stalk *him*!

Dawdling nonchalantly towards a massive pillar, she peered round it. He was striding towards the line of wooden cubicles that housed the public telephones. There was a handy little corner near the last cubicle. Unfortunately, he would be able to spot her easily if she tried to walk over to it, as there was nowhere to conceal herself between where she stood and the wall on the other side. She spotted a tall woman carrying a suitcase. Making sure she didn't look her in the eye, Josie strolled alongside her, headed calmly towards the wall, pulled the notebook out of her pocket and pretended to read.

*I must look round the corner*, she told herself firmly. She took a step forward. As he opened the door of the end cubicle, Mr Lovatt-Pendlebury glanced round. Josie quickly withdrew. She waited until she heard the folding door close and peered out again.

A screw on the hinges must have prevented it from closing properly because she could hear him shoving pennies in and dialling a number. She couldn't have wished for anything better, though she knew that eavesdropping on a telephone conversation wouldn't help her pass her stalking test. The A button was being pushed and there was the sound of money clattering, which meant he was connected to the person at the other end. Suddenly she felt awkward. He might be telephoning Miss Merryweather. But then she remembered that Miss Merryweather wouldn't be anywhere near a phone. She would be sitting with Larry on a bus on her way to the station.

She decided to find someone new to stalk and was about to leave when Mr Lovatt-Pendlebury used a word that caused her to whirl round.

*Larry.*

Why was he talking about Larry? And who could the person on the other end of the line be? She edged closer, struggling to hear what he was saying through the deafening announcements for train arrivals and departures.

'The little chap's last performance will be Saturday night. That's right. At the theatre in Winford.'

His voice was drowned out by yet another announcement.

'Don't be late,' she heard him say.

And then at last the penny dropped and it explained his interest in Larry. He wasn't just a writer of art exhibitions or operas. He was a talent scout! And he was obviously arranging for another talent scout or a director to come and see Larry perform on the last night.

She hurried for the exit, having heard more than enough. She now needed to keep a close eye on the time and re-enter the station to make it look as though she had only just arrived. Mr Lovatt-Pendlebury mustn't find out she had been hanging around earlier or he might suspect she had spotted him. She stood still for a moment to catch her breath, and it was only then that she realised she was shaking.

*Get yourself in the right mood*, she told herself firmly. *You've just jumped off the bus havin' come straight from school.*

She made for the entrance.

When Josie re-entered the station, she spotted him standing with Miss Merryweather and Larry by the platform gates. Slipping among the passengers she headed for a queue and then turned round so that she would be seen arriving from the ticket area. To make it look even more convincing, she strode towards Larry waving the ticket in her hand.

He was beaming with relief.

'I'm not late, am I?' she asked innocently. 'It took longer than I thought to buy a ticket.'

'Then I suggest you put it in your purse for safe keeping,'

said Miss Merryweather brightly. 'You don't want to lose it, do you?'

And she smiled! It was such an unusual sight it was almost frightening.

'Did you bring *Film Fun* with you?' Larry asked.

'Yeah. I mean, *yes*,' she added, correcting herself.

'Well done!' sung Miss Merryweather.

As soon as their train pulled in, Mr Lovatt-Pendlebury found an empty carriage.

'Did you remember to bring your sketchbook, Laurence?' Miss Merryweather asked as they settled in their seats. 'It's very kind of Josephine to read you stories from her annual but she needs to save her voice for tonight's performance.'

'Yes, Miss Merryweather.'

But Josie suspected that endless stories about cowboys and spacemen all the way to Winford might hinder any conversation between her and Mr Lovatt-Pendelbury. After Josie had finished reading a comic strip called *Trouble Trail*, Larry began his usual drawings of sputniks and Josie returned to *Pigeon Post*, which meant she could eavesdrop more easily.

And as she listened to Mr Lovatt-Pendlebury share more of the wonders of so and so's performance in *La Traviata* and the 'exquisite poetry' of some French bloke, and the delights of sitting outside drinking coffee amongst artists, watching boats floating by on the Bois de Boulogne, she observed him mowing down Miss Merryweather with flattery.

And the more she listened, the more she realised how impossible it would be to tell Miss Merryweather what she had overheard outside the telephone box. Josie suspected Mr Lovatt-Pendlebury would only deny it and that Miss Merryweather would believe him. And then there was Larry. If she mentioned the talent scout in front of him, it might make him feel self-conscious during the Saturday night performance or tempt him to show off, and if the scout wasn't interested in him, it would upset him.

She hated Mr Lovatt-Pendlebury. She suspected that the only reason he had paid Miss Merryweather so much attention was so that he could be near Larry. She was certain he was nothing but a big fat liar. Even if by some miracle Josie did manage to convince Miss Merryweather that Mr Lovatt-Pendlebury *had* been deceiving her she would be heartbroken, and their last days at the Palace Theatre would be terrible, not just for her but for all of them.

And then another thought occurred to her. Suppose Mr Lovatt-Pendlebury, after pretending to like Miss Merryweather, had then *really* fallen in love with her? It was all so complicated. Without realising it, she sighed.

'Is it the book?' Miss Merryweather asked.

'What?' said Josie, startled.

'The deep sigh. I wondered if it was caused by a passage in the book you're reading.'

'No, Miss Merryweather. It was . . .' Josie hesitated. 'It was because I was remembering there are only three performances to go.'

'Ah yes. But all good things must come to an end, isn't that so, Mr Lovatt-Pendlebury?'

'I hope not all good things, Moira,' he said gently and gazed at her with such tenderness that Josie felt embarrassed. Miss Merryweather, Josie observed, seemed dazed, as though she had forgotten that Larry and Josie existed.

For one horrible moment Josie thought they might actually kiss one another. For safety's sake she quickly returned to her book.

'This is just the beginning, my dear,' Josie heard him say.

There was a tiny intake of breath from Miss Merryweather.

'Oh, Cedric, do you mean it?'

'I have never been more serious in my life,' he murmured.

Instantly, Josie realised she had to keep her mouth shut. From a selfish point of view she and Larry were having a far better time since Miss Merryweather had gone all gooey over *Cedric*, and if Larry needed to give a good performance on Saturday night, the last thing he needed was Miss Merryweather screaming at him or weeping all over the place.

## 12

# SOS

'WHEN A GUIDE SENDS AN SOS SIGNAL USING a fire, it's the flames that send the message,' Sheila explained to Josie and Geraldine. 'Flames can be seen for miles, and that's when you use the blanket to help send the signal. You hold it in front of the fire to hide it and then take it away when you want to show the flames.'

'So is that what the Red Indians did?' Geraldine asked.

'No. They made smoke signals. You need to put leaves on some grass in front of the fire and then cover it every now and then with a wet blanket to make those kinds of signals.'

'Wouldn't it have been easier for them to dial 999?'

'Not if they were in the middle of nowhere.'

'And the telephone box hadn't been invented,' added Josie.

'And for signalling long distances there's also Semaphore,' Sheila added.

'I know semaphore,' said Josie.

'Do you?' she said, impressed.

'So does Molly. We learnt it so that . . .' She paused not wanting them to know that they used it as a secret code when writing letters. 'Er, for when we join the Sea Rangers.'

'It's a dying art,' said Sheila earnestly. 'Hang on a minute.'

Josie watched her nip over to Molly's patrol leader and exchange words. Within minutes she was waving Josie over to join them. Molly was already by their side.

'Show us,' Sheila said.

Josie and Molly lengthened their arms and crossed them in front of themselves.

'That's to show we're ready and about to begin,' explained Molly.

They slammed their left arm down at one side and placed their right arm on a low diagonal.

'That's A,' said Josie.

They brought it up so that it was level with their shoulders.

'B,' they chorused.

By the time they had reached Z, the entire hall had crowded round to watch them.

'Captain, could they try for the Signallers badge?' asked Lefty.

'Indeed they could,' said Captain, looking delighted. 'They're halfway there.'

Towards the end of the meeting the subject of a Christmas concert was announced. All the patrols had to come up with ideas that would show an audience what being a Girl Guide entailed.

'We could mime Bible stories,' said Penelope, 'like the one about the Good Samaritan. That could show them how we do a good turn every day.'

This was greeted with a thoughtful silence.

'How about demonstrating our emergency first aid skills?' said Geraldine. 'We could put someone's arm in a sling.'

'And I could have a sprained ankle,' added Carol.

'How about an aeroplane crash?' suggested Josie eagerly.

'Now that would be a real emergency,' said Dolly.

'But would we have to roll around the floor?' asked Carol.

Josie sprang to her feet. 'Let's start rehearsin' it now!'

But Carol was not the only one who didn't want to get her clothes dirty.

'Could I still just have a sprained ankle?' she pleaded.

Josie wracked her brains to work out how someone who was sitting in a plane could have a sprained ankle. She was also beginning to realise that they were all a bit shy about performing. There was only one thing for it; she would have to throw herself into the scene and hope they would join in. She was in the middle of writhing and screaming when she grew aware that Lefty was peering down at her.

'Captain sent me over,' said Lefty. 'You see –' Suddenly she broke off and gave one of her squeaks of laughter. 'Now, I really must be serious,' she admonished herself. 'Josie . . . you are giving a really good impression of someone who is being burned alive and dying in excruciating agony, but this is supposed to be a *Christmas* concert and, well, the thing is . . .it's not very Christmassy, is it?'

'Any other ideas?' said Sheila, after the lieutenant had re-joined Captain.

'How about if I sprain my ankle tripping over a paper chain?' suggested Carol.

'I don't think so,' said Sheila. 'Why don't we look at something we're good at?'

'I'm knitting a scarf at the moment,' said Geraldine.

'No,' they chorused.

'Josie?'

'How about a funny sketch?'

Suddenly, everyone began to get excited. Their discussions were interrupted by a game of Port Starboard before a singsong and a few parting words from Captain.

'Now I know you all might be tempted to do only funny turns at the concert.' Josie caught Sheila's eye.

'But I think you should try to do something . . .' She paused, as though profoundly moved. 'Beautiful.'

Josie spotted Lefty hurriedly studying her knees.

'*Beautiful* will give you a far deeper sense of satisfaction.'

She then proceeded to describe a scene at the court of the King of France. They could all wear lovely clothes for it she suggested, and demonstrate dances of that period or be in a Ye Olde Merrie England scene.

'Gracefulness and good speech. It is these arts which will help you grow into attractive young women.'

Josie gave a quiet groan.

'I don't like the idea of all that young lady business either,' whispered Sheila. 'Don't worry, we'll find a way round this.'

'Never say die,' said Josie.

'Exactly.'

'Congratulations, Miss Merryweather!' cried Daphne. 'Elsie has just told us your wonderful news!'

It was midday at the café, and Lionel, Denise, Anthony and Elsie crowded round Miss Merryweather's table.

'Can we see your engagement ring?' said Desiree, pulling up a chair.

Miss Merryweather removed her glove and stretched out her hand. Desiree leaned closer to admire the slender Victorian gold ring with its exquisitely set sparkling stone.

'And it's a diamond?"

Miss Merryweather nodded as though in a dream.

'I say!' Desiree breathed. 'But when did he propose? Oh, I'm so sorry. Am I being too nosy? Do tell us to go away if we're being a nuisance.'

Miss Merryweather flushed and smiled. 'No, that's quite all right.'

'Did he go down on one knee?'

'Yes,' said Miss Merryweather, her voice trembling.

'How romantic!'

Josie noticed Anthony gazing at Desiree as though taking notes.

'But when did it happen?'

'Last night.'

Miss Merryweather seemed unable to stop smiling, Josie noticed. She was smiling so hard there were tears in her eyes. So Mr Lovatt-Pendlebury *had* fallen in love with her. Thank goodness she hadn't spilled the beans. She could have ruined everything.

'But where –?' asked Desiree.

'Hampstead. We were on our way to a restaurant and he suggested we walk across the heath. I thought it was so that we could work up an appetite. It was a bit breezy, I can tell you.'

'And did you guess?' asked Desiree.

'I had no idea. I was too busy hanging on to my hat. And then we came to the pond. It's so lovely and secluded there. He put his hand in his pocket and the next thing I knew he was kneeling on the grass with a ring in his hand and he said . . .' She paused. 'He said, "I wonder if you would make me the happiest man in the universe."'

'How wonderful,' sighed Desiree.

'And he asked me if I would accept his hand in marriage.'

'And you said *yes*.'

Miss Merryweather nodded.

Within minutes, the café proprietor came over to the table to offer his congratulations.

'I'm afraid I don't have champagne but I think a cup of tea on the house for everyone would be the done thing.'

'Do you have a wedding date yet?' Desiree asked.

'Oh, Desiree, let her gather breath,' protested Daphne. 'She's been engaged less than twenty-four hours.'

'We're going to talk about it when he returns from Florence.'

'When is he leaving?'

'Monday. He wanted to propose to me before he left. He has to write an article about a sculpture exhibition there but he'll be back in a fortnight. He's taking me out between the two shows today.'

The tea arrived and everyone including the café owners raised their cups.

'To the enchanting Moira Merryweather,' said Lionel. 'May you have many years of love, health and happiness.'

'Hear, hear!' cried everyone. 'Love, health and happiness!' And they chinked their cups together.

Josie couldn't take her eyes off her. Miss Merryweather, she observed, looked beautiful.

As soon as the matinee was over, Josie whipped off her costume, threw on her clothes and removed her make-up. She had planned to meet her parents in front of the theatre but her hands were shaking so much that she kept making mistakes with her shoelaces.

'More haste less speed,' pointed out Miss Merryweather,

'Wait for me,' Larry implored.

'I'll come straight back when I've found Mum and Dad,' she said, grabbed her duffle coat and dashed through the door.

There was still quite a crowd coming through the foyer. She jumped up and down, attempting to peer over the theatregoers' heads. And then she caught sight of a stocky, black-haired man wearing a suit and a slim woman in a blue coat with a fake fur collar. Her matching hat had a feather pinned at the side. They were in their Sunday best clothes.

Josie had no time to call out to them. They had already pushed their way through the crowd and had flung their arms around her, laughing.

'We're so proud of you!' said her mother, kissing her cheek.

Her dad grinned down at her.

'I didn't believe it were you,' he said. 'I forgot you were our Josie.'

It was the best thing he could have said. Arms linked, they strolled to the stage door just as Miss Merryweather was coming down the stairs with Larry.

'We've come to pick up our little boy, Laurence Carpenter,' said a voice. Josie whirled round to find Mr and Mrs Carpenter and Molly peering over the counter at Samuel and Wilfred.

'Mummy!' yelled Larry.

Within seconds it was like two family reunions.

'I do hope it's all right if we take Larry off somewhere for tea, Miss Merryweather,' said Mrs Carpenter. 'I know you have to be responsible for him . . .'

'No, that's quite acceptable. But I suggest he doesn't eat too many cakes. We don't want him sick during his last performance. I too am off to tea.' She paused as though for effect. 'At the Royal Winford tea house.'

'Blimey!' commented Samuel, leaning over the counter. 'I hope someone else is payin' the bill.'

'Someone else *is* paying the bill, Samuel. My *fiancé*,' she announced, and with that she sailed out of the stage door.

'Now that's what I call an exit,' Samuel said, grinning.

'Samuel, can you suggest another tea house for us?' asked Mrs Carpenter. 'Somewhere a little less grand.'

'Table for six?' said a young girl in a black dress and a white apron.

'Two tables for three,' said Mrs Carpenter, and she turned to Josie. 'I think that's what you would prefer, wouldn't you?'

Josie nodded. She knew what mothers were like when

they got together. They forgot about everyone else and talked endlessly to one another, which was why Elsie had arranged to meet her parents at a later date. Her sister wanted Josie to have them all to herself. They were taken to a table in a corner by the window. Sitting with her parents for the first time in over six weeks, Josie felt as though everything that had happened to her since leaving home had all been a dream and that being with them in the tea house was real life. She kept touching her father's arm and leaning against him to remind herself of how he felt, breathing in the familiar smell of his hair cream.

The subject of Elsie's wedding came up.

'And yes, you can wear a kilt,' said her mother. 'Molly will be wearin' a long white ballerina style dress which will be covered in rose buds. Are you sure you wouldn't like to wear something pretty like that?'

'No, thank you,' said Josie firmly.

'And as Elsie said, Josie'd look daft in a long frock wiv that hair cut, wouldn't she?' said her dad.

'Oh Josie, you won't need to have it cut again before December, will you?'

'I don't think so,' said Josie carefully.

They were convinced she had been asked to have it cut for the part of Whitney.

'It depends what she gets offered next, I s'pose,' added her father.

Josie slipped her arms round him and buried her head in his chest.

'We're so pleased you're having a proper trainin', Josie,'

said her mother and she blew her nose hurriedly.

'Yeah,' said her dad. 'Though we miss you, gel.'

Josie struggled to ignore the lump in her throat. How could she tell them that the ballet classes in Sternsea were much better than the ones at the stage school? That the acting mistress now made her sit at the side of the room during acting lessons so that she could 'look and learn'? That, except for Hilda, the other pupils called her lower class? It was all she could do not to burst into tears and ask them to take her home.

'I can tie a bowline knot now,' she said hurriedly.

And then suddenly they were all dashing back to the stage door. After a hug and a kiss from her mother, her dad had held her so hard she thought he was never going to let go of her. Eventually, he had broken away, ruffling the little bit of hair she had left on her head. They had said their goodbyes and then they were gone.

Josie had hardly finished putting on her costume when Miss Merryweather took her aside.

'Josie, I have a rather important request,' she said. 'These last two weeks have been the most . . . well, let's just say, a time that one would not want to forget. Mr Lovatt-Pendlebury happened to discover that I didn't possess a programme and that I might like to have one as a keepsake. Unfortunately, he's mislaid his copy and has suggested that I ask you to pop round to the foyer after the performance to obtain one for me.'

Josie suspected this was more to do with the talent scout

coming round to talk to Larry in the dressing room. Perhaps Mr Lovatt-Pendlebury didn't want Josie around in case her feelings were hurt. But it couldn't be that, because he treated her as though she didn't exist. And why couldn't he get hold of a programme for her himself? But if it kept Miss Merryweather cheerful on their last night, she would do it.

'Of course, Miss Merryweather.'

And then she remembered how crowded the front of house had been when she searched for her parents. There would be a tidal wave of people leaving the theatre. It would take her ages to work her way through them and find one of the usherettes.

'Miss Merryweather, I could get one between Act Two and Act Three. I'm not needed in Act Three, Scene One, remember? I'll have loads of time to get a programme then.'

'Oh, I don't think that would be allowed.'

'But it'll take me ages after the show, especially with the stage hands taking down the set afterwards.'

'Oh my goodness! You're absolutely right,' she said. 'It'll be chaos.'

'It'll only take a minute to reach the foyer because the street at the side of the theatre will be deserted. And if I can't find anyone selling a programme, I can come straight back.'

'Well,' Miss Merryweather said slowly, 'if you promise you'll return immediately.'

'Course I will. I don't want to be late either.'

'Oh, Josephine,' she trilled, 'that is kind of you.'

* * *

'What you doin' in the foyer, Jo?' cried Gwyneth, a small, skinny usherette. 'You should be backstage!'

'Can I have a programme to keep?' she pleaded.

'Course you can, love. Have several. They're no good to us after tonight, are they?' She gave Josie a handful. 'Quick, you naughty girl. Get back!'

Josie shoved them in her coat pocket, dashed out of the theatre, nipped round to the lane at the side and sprinted towards the stage door. She was about to step inside when she heard Mr Lovatt-Pendlebury speaking. She whirled round but there was no sign of him. She stopped to listen. It sounded as though he was having a conversation with someone further down the road towards the river. It couldn't be the talent scout because he would be in the theatre watching the play. Thinking it a bit odd, she crept towards the corner and pressed herself against the wall.

'And that friend of mine's fixed up the telephone in your flat then?' she heard him say.

'Yeah,' answered a gravelly voice.

'Good.'

'So 'ow's it goin' wiv the old girl?' she heard another man ask.

'Like clockwork.' This was followed by raucous laughter. 'She swallowed it hook, line and sinker. She even thinks that bit of glass on her finger is a diamond!'

It was as though Josie had been kicked violently in the stomach. She was about to leap out and yell angrily at him for being a liar when she realised it was far more important to remain invisible.

'I'll make sure the boy will be in the dressing room on his own,' Mr Lovatt-Pendlebury added.

So the other two men *were* talent scouts . . . But they sounded like rough types. Something was very wrong.

'I've persuaded her to get rid of the other kid on an errand,' Mr Lovatt-Pendlebury was saying, 'which should keep her busy for a very long time.'

*Me*, Josie thought. *Well, that little plan hasn't worked, Mr Porkie-pie Lovatt- Pendlebury.*

'I'll ring Miss Ugly Mug at the stage door after the show, ask her to meet me for a brief farewell, and that'll leave the coast clear for you. Got your overalls?'

'Yeah,' they grunted in unison.

'There'll be other people in overalls hanging around too. As I told you, they hire extra hands to remove the set at the end of a play. They'll think you're one of them. You have the rug?'

'It's in the van,' said one of the men.

'Good. You can wrap him up in that.'

Josie nearly let out a cry.

'As soon as I give you the signal, move fast. His parents are in tonight and you do not want to bump into them. They might recognise you from the old mug shots of you in the papers all those years ago. They'll be collecting him at the stage door after the show. My *fiancé* . . .'

At this they all howled with laughter.

'. . . is supposed to be bringing him down to them. Only of course she won't be, because by that time he won't be in the building'

'And we takes the rug up to dressing room number seven?' Josie heard one of the men ask. 'And this Larry Carpenter, he'll be there on his own. Nine years old. Red hair.'

'That's right.'

'I dunno how you found him,' Josie heard his companion add hoarsely. 'We didn't even know he were born or that Henry had changed his last name to Carpenter.'

'I wouldn't have done if you hadn't remembered he used to live in that place in Sternsea.'

*Why were they talking about Henry?* Josie asked herself.

'The rest of the information I needed fell from the young neighbour's mouth,' Mr Lovatt-Pendlebury continued. 'Like a waterfall,'

*So Mr Lovatt-Pendlebury had visited their flat in Sternsea.* The thought of him being in the building where her parents lived made her shiver.

'Ta,' said one of the other men.

'Don't mention it. You've done me a favour. I've done one for you. That makes us quits. I'll keep my *fiancé* away from the theatre as long as I can. If anyone asks you why you're bringing the rug down again, say it's supposed to be for the upstairs bar and you'd been sent by mistake to the back of the theatre instead of the front. By the time she returns and discovers little Larry is missing, she'll assume he's running around the theatre and go looking for him. That'll give you a good half hour to get as much distance between you and Winford. And remember, don't go back to your place till tomorrow night. There'll be less people around on a Sunday to spot you. Once you have the little chap, his brother Henry will be eating out of the palm of your hand and he'll do whatever you ask. I'll pick up that stuff from you in a fortnight when I return from my little trip. It's in a safe place, I hope. Once my customers have paid for it, you'll receive your money.'

Josie heard them moving. She sprinted back down the street, darted through the stage door and flew past Wilfred and Samuel only to be met by Miss Merryweather and Larry coming down the stairs.

'Oh, thank goodness!' she exclaimed. 'Give me your coat and go on into the wings with Larry. Hurry!'

Dazed and trembling, Josie pulled it off and followed Larry up the steps.

Within seconds she was stumbling after him into the wings with the words *You are going to be kidnapped!* pounding inside her head. Larry, unaware of the danger he was in, was happily peering onto the set.

Josie had to tell someone what she had overheard – and soon – but it would be useless speaking to any of the cast before they went on stage because they would be thinking about the next scene. She glanced at Fiona waiting to carry on the false tabletop with the deputy stage manager. Close by was Elsie, dressed as the plump, newly hired maid. If Josie told either of them, Larry might overhear and panic. And at least on stage he would be safe. No one would kidnap him in front of a full house.

But what was she thinking? The plan was to take him from dressing room seven. Whatever happened, she must stop him being in that room. But his clothes were there.

And then she had an idea. She would persuade him to carry them to another dressing room.

Once he was safely hidden, she would leave a note for his mum and dad in dressing room seven telling them where they could find him. But what if the two men came into the dressing room and spotted her message?

She would have to write it in code. Semaphore code! And address the note to Molly. Larry tugged at her hand.

'Eleanor's singing,' he whispered.

The curtain fell. The tabletop with all the breakfast dishes and food was carried on stage and placed on the table. Elsie checked that the tablecloth was hanging over the sides and within seconds Hugh, David and Anthony were sitting round it. Josie and Larry walked onstage to join them.

As soon as the audience had stood for *God Save the Queen* and the curtain had fallen, Josie grabbed Larry's hand. 'There's something important I have to tell you,' she whispered. 'It's about the hide and seek game.'

'What hide and seek game?' asked Larry.

'Two of the actors will look for us. It's a tradition,' she told him. 'It's the last-night-last-found game. And there's a prize.'

She pulled back the swing door to the steps where Miss Merryweather was talking to Samuel at the stage door.

'Oh, there they are,' he said. 'You can tell Josie yourself.'

'Tell me what, Miss Merryweather?' asked Josie shakily.

'I've just received an urgent message from Mr Lovatt-

Pendlebury. I need to pop out for a few minutes. I won't be long.'

'But I need to talk to you first,' Josie said quickly. 'On yer own. In *private*,' she emphasised, glancing at Larry.

'Stay with him in the dressing room until I return,' Miss Merryweather instructed as she dashed out the door. 'You can tell me then.'

'But what about the game?' Larry blurted out.

'Quick!' urged Josie.

She dragged him up what now seemed like a million stairs. As soon as they burst into their dressing room, she picked up his clothes and shoes.

'I have to get changed,' protested Larry.

'No. The actors I told you about are comin' 'ere. You gotta get changed in another dressing room.'

They leaped down the stairs and peered into the two dressings rooms below. Three actors came flying out of dressing room four, leaving it empty. Josie swiftly pulled Larry inside. Behind a rail of clothes she spotted an old skip. She lifted the lid.

'This is a good hiding place. I'll help you.'

He pulled back. 'I'm not a baby. I can undress and dress myself.'

'I know. But we have to be quick.'

'See you Monday!' they heard someone yell.

'What about my make-up?' Larry said.

'You can clean it off after the game.'

It seemed to take forever to get him dressed. And then it occurred to Josie that when the two men couldn't find him in dressing room seven, they would come looking for him in the other dressing rooms, including dressing room four. For a moment she panicked.

'Larry,' she said hurriedly, 'the two actors will be pretending to be criminals or people coming to help strike the set and they'll speak in voices you won't recognise. But it's a trick. Even if they come in here and call out your name, don't answer them and don't laugh, or you'll lose the prize.'

'What's the prize?'

Josie thought quickly. 'A toy sputnik.'

She pulled out a handful of costumes and Larry climbed into the skip. She piled them back on top of him and pulled down the lid.

Now all she needed to do was to leave the coded note for Molly. She leaped up the stairs to room seven, tore off her costume, hauled on her shirt, sweater and corduroy trousers, laced up her walking shoes and pulled on her duffle coat. Ripping out a piece of paper from Larry's sketchpad she wrote MOLLY in big letters at the top, drew the first head and put the arms into the position for the first letter.

*Stop shaking*, she told her fingers. As soon as she had written LARRY IN THE SKIP IN DRESSING ROOM FOUR. JOSIE, she added legs to the figures and made them look as though they were skating. Swiftly, she drew a lake around them and a snowman with two pebble eyes, a pebble mouth and a carrot for a nose. Next to MOLLY she wrote WINTER HOLIDAY in large letters beside it, to remind her of the book that had made them start writing in the code so that Molly would realise there was a semaphore message in the figures' arms. She was about to dash out of the room to find Elsie when she spotted her made-up face in the mirror.

'Oh no!' she whispered.

Dunking her fingers in the removal cream, she rubbed it violently onto her skin, wiping it off in a frenzy. She grabbed the soaking wet flannel, slapped it onto her face, moving it in wild circles, then picked up the towel and swiftly dried herself.

*Elsie*, she thought. *I must find Elsie!*

She stood the picture next to Larry's sketchbook but it fell over. She was about to prop it up again when the door was flung open. Two pasty-faced middle-aged men in blue overalls were staring down at her. One was flabby and had a moustache tinged with grey. The other was bald, his square face frozen into a scowl. Under his arm was a rolled up floor rug. *Moustache* and *Scowler*, she nicknamed them inside her head.

'The strike is downstairs,' she said politely, praying that Larry was still sitting quietly in the skip and wouldn't suddenly appear from behind them.

This was the moment when they would realise that Larry was missing. And sure enough Moustache said the very word she had been dreading to hear.

'Larry,' he barked out.

'Larry?' Josie repeated innocently.

He was grinning like a hyena while the other man continued to glower at her. Speechless with fear, Josie switched on a smile that Mrs Havilland would have been proud of.

'Larry who?'

'Very funny,' said Scowler.

Josie shrugged as if to say, 'I dunno what you're talkin' about.'

To her alarm, they moved towards her.

*Please don't come up the stairs, Larry*, she thought. *Stay where you are.*

The bald-headed Scowler thrust a damp cloth into her face. It had a strangely sweet smell. The last thing Josie recalled as she slipped into unconsciousness was asking herself if she had remembered to set her alarm clock.

# Act Two

—◆—

## And Through Other
## Waiting Eyes

# I

# As If Into Thin Air

'AND YOU WERE WHERE, MISS MERRYWEATHER?' asked the police constable.

'In the high street, meeting my fiancé. He needed to leave for Florence sooner than expected and wished to say goodbye.'

She and Elsie, Molly and her parents had gathered in dressing room two to be away from the chaos and clutter of the set strike. Molly who was sitting bolt upright in an old armchair, a blank expression on her face, burst into tears. Her mother put her arms round her.

'I don't understand why they didn't stay in the dressing room,' she added. 'I assure you, Constable, this has never happened before. I have always put my charges' welfare before my own.'

'Until tonight,' said Mr Carpenter.

Miss Merryweather paled.

'But I can only have been absent a quarter of an hour at the most. Not very long at all.'

'Just long enough for them both to disappear,' Mr Carpenter muttered.

'Sir, this is not helping,' said the constable.

'They can't have just vanished into thin air,' Molly cried out.

'We'll find them,' said the policeman, gently and he glanced at Mr Carpenter. 'As soon as we hear anything we'll ring you immediately. Meanwhile, one of our police cars will take you home.'

'I am so sorry,' Miss Merryweather blurted out. 'I'll never forgive myself if anything has happened to them.'

Mr and Mrs Carpenter remained silent but it was clear to Elsie, from the expression on their faces, that if any harm had come to Josie and Larry, they would never forgive her either. Neither would she.

# 2

# Scowler and Moustache

THE PILLOW WAS AS HARD AS STONE AND IT refused to keep still, thought Josie groggily. She opened her eyes, but instead of seeing Molly's bedroom she found herself being hurled from side to side in a filthy old van. Bewildered, she struggled to make sense of what she was doing there but it was as though a cushion had been shoved inside her head, making it impossible to think. She could now hear men's voices coming from the cab.

'How much d'yer fink 'e'll give us fer 'im?' one of them was saying.

'Larry!' Josie whispered.

With horror it hit her that the two men who had pushed their way into the dressing room must have discovered his hiding place after all. But why had they taken her as well?

'You can identify them,' she could hear Auntie Win say inside her head. 'You weren't supposed to be there, were you? You know too much. You might tell the police.'

But where was he? There was no sign of him in the van. There was only one other place he could be. In the cab with them. She shivered.

'Don't matter, do it? A straight swap'll do nicely. Him in exchange for the boy. Or we can just bump the boy off. Whatever gives him the most pain.'

She became aware of a moaning sound and then realised it was coming from her mouth. She stopped and held her breath. With any luck, the van's engine would have drowned it out. At least some part of her brain must have begun functioning because she knew that she needed to find a way of protecting herself. On no account must they discover that she was awake and had heard them talking. Unless, of course, she was asleep and this was a bad dream. She shut her eyes and opened them. No. She was still in the oily van.

She had no memory of leaving the theatre. The last thing she remembered was the bald man with the scowl shoving a piece of damp cloth into her face. *Chloroform!* Of course! Her aunt had told her all about chloroform. It must have been put on the cloth to knock her out.

She struggled to sit up but slumped back exhausted. After a brief rest she manoeuvred herself upwards again, leaning on an elbow so that she could see through the back windows. Street light after street light flashed by. She felt helpless. Even if she had been strong enough to open the doors, it would have been too dangerous to throw herself out on the road at the speed they were going, besides which she was feeling so giddy she would have been run over by a car before she had managed to crawl onto the pavement.

As the van began to slow down, her fear turned into terror. There was a violent jolt and a sudden silence as the engine was turned off. The cab doors were now being opened. She began to panic. So much for the Guide motto *Be Prepared*! How could you be prepared for being kidnapped by two thugs? Learning how to tie reef knots and making slings for broken arms were of no use to her at all. And then she remembered something that might be.

*Kim's Game!* Hearing footsteps on the road she lay down again and shut her eyes. The doors squealed open.

'E's still sleepin' like a baby,' she heard one of them mutter. 'I 'ope you didn't put too much of that stuff on the rag.'

*He?* They must have given chloroform to Larry as well. She guessed that it was Moustache talking.

'If I did, I did. If I didn't, I didn't,' snapped the other voice. She recognised it as the voice that belonged to the bald-headed one with the square jaw. Scowler. A hand grabbed her ankles and dragged her across the floor of the van. It took all her concentration not to scream. Luckily her duffle coat cushioned her from being hurt too badly.

'Watch what yer doing!' hissed the one she guessed was Scowler. 'He ain't a sack of potatoes.'

So they thought she was a boy as well! And then she heard something that sickened her.

'I don't want him to wake up till I've put that stuff in his cocoa.'

'That'll keep him nicely knocked out, eh?' laughed Moustache.

'That is the idea, cloth head.'

She was thrown over one of the men's shoulders. She let herself go limp, as Elsie had taught her to do for a stage fall.

To her relief the other man walked on ahead, which meant that she could open her eyes without being seen.

*Narrow chipped pavement. Looks like an alley. Sound of cars coming from somewhere. A main road? A motorbike parked. A battered old pram lying on its side. Paper in the gutter. Sound of a door opening.*

She wondered why they weren't carrying both of them up the stairs. Larry, she realised must still be in the cab. Perhaps they were going to dump her in this building and take him off somewhere else. She felt herself stiffening. *Be like a rag doll*, she reminded herself firmly.

She longed to raise her head to take a better look but didn't dare. A sudden movement from her would give away the fact that she was awake and spying on them.

*Broken green tiles on a floor in a hall. Smell of cabbage and rotting fish. Piles of old paper on the stairs. Torn brown lino on the tiny landing past a rickety-looking lift that resembles a hanging cage. Another landing. A broken highchair outside a door and three mildewing cardboard boxes. Next landing. Wooden floorboards. Another flight. More floorboards. Almost black with dirt. Next landing. Old mattress, bicycle wheel with punctured tyre hanging down onto the floor. Another flight of stairs. Tiny landing. Sound of key in a door. Bit of old carpet. Smell of stale sweat.*

'Clear that, will yer?' grunted the man who was carrying her.

She was then thrown onto an old settee with such force that she had to hold her breath not to cry out.

'Gimme the number his lordship give us,' ordered

Scowler. 'And make the cocoa with that knockout drug in it. The stuff I shoved up 'is nose will be wearin' off by now. I'll wake him up. Then I make the phone call and get him to talk. We gives 'im the drink. And then our little Larry will be out for the count for twenty-four hours.'

*Larry!* Josie felt herself jump. They thought she was Larry! But how could they possibly have mistaken her for him?

And then it hit her. They had been told to grab a nine-year-old boy with red hair from dressing room seven, having no idea that Josie had red hair too and was small for her age.

She had to pretend she was Larry – not only to protect him but also to protect herself. If they found out they had taken the wrong child . . . She began to tremble. If she could just think more clearly and her head didn't feel as though porridge had been poured into it. But who were they planning to phone? And then she guessed. Larry's dad, of course! But Larry would be back home by now. It would be *she* who everyone thought was missing, not him. When Mr Carpenter talked to Scowler, he was bound to give the game away, and then what would they do to her?

She was tempted to make a dash for it, but she didn't even know if she was capable of standing, let alone putting one foot in front of the other. The floor near the sofa shook. She now had two choices: get a slap across the face or pretend she was already waking up. She gave a small groan and then felt herself being shaken.

'Wake up, sonny,' said a voice.

'Cornflakes,' she murmured, opening her eyes slightly.

It was the man with the moustache.

'He finks it's mornin',' he said to Scowler. 'Come on, sonny. We need to talk to yer dad.'

Josie nodded and pretended to yawn. To her relief it turned into a real one. By now she realised the less she said the better.

'And then after I've 'ad a little chat wiv 'im,' added Scowler, leaning towards her, 'you can 'ave a nice hot cuppa cocoa. You'd like that wouldn't you?'

Josie nodded dopily. She was just racking her brains as to how she was going to avoid drinking it when, to her astonishment she vomited violently all over him. The two men leaped backwards. Moustache gave a yell.

'I dunno why you're making such a racket,' Scowler complained. 'I'm the one who's covered in puke.'

'Water,' Josie slurred.

'Go on! Get 'im a mug of water!' commanded Scowler.

'Why me?'

'Cos I gotta git aht of this clobber, that's why.'

'But he might be sick over me,' said Moustache. 'What if 'e's got sumfin' catchy?'

'It ain't catchy. It's cos of the stuff I shoved in 'is mush.'

'You were only 'sposed to put a little on the rag.'

'I did!'

Josie kept her head lowered while they argued. Within a few minutes she had a dirty mug in her hand. Sipping the water slowly, she suspected that if she refused the cocoa they offered her later, Scowler would have no hesitation in forcing it down her throat. The thought of being unconscious for twenty-four hours petrified her.

She glanced around to see if there was anywhere she could dispose of a drugged cup of cocoa. If it had been a story in one of Auntie Win's green and white paperbacks, there would have been a leafy plant in an enormous brass pot in which she could have surreptitiously poured it. But there wasn't a plant to be seen.

In the corner of the room, Moustache was struggling to get a picture on the tiny screen of a television set and moving the aerial around.

'Not yet,' snapped Scowler. 'After the phone call.'

'But I don't want to miss *Sundee Night at the London Palladium*.'

*Sunday?* She must have been asleep all night and all day in the van. Her mum and dad would know she was missing by now and would be worried sick. She wished her dad would suddenly burst through the door, bang the two men's heads together and rescue her, but that was never going to happen. She had to escape from this nightmare all by herself.

'Make them think you haven't a clue where you are,' Auntie Win would say. 'It makes you less of a risk to them.'

That bit would be easy. It was then that Josie realised she was bursting for a wee.

'Toilet,' she murmured.

'You take 'im,' yelled Scowler from the kitchenette.

'On the station?' Josie added.

'Yeah, that's right, sonny,' said Moustache. 'I'm the station master and I'll show you where the little boy's room is.'

He took her hand and she pretended to stumble. It didn't

take much effort. Her head was so woozy all she needed to do was exaggerate what she was already feeling.

He led her to a small, grubby room on the landing below. Once inside, she bolted the door and leaned back against it, her heart pounding. She could of course refuse to come out but one look at Moustache and she knew the door would give way from the slightest blow from his shoulder, and causing him to lose his temper would not be a good plan. A wave of nausea swept through her and she was sick into the lavatory bowl. Once she had emptied herself, she held her head in her hands, dreading her return to the flat. She knew they would be watching her closely to make sure she drank the cocoa.

'As soon as they look away,' her aunt would say, 'get rid of it.'

But where?

Unless . . .

There was an episode in a Paul Temple detective story on the wireless where his wife, faced with the same problem, swapped drinks. But what if there weren't any other drinks?

'You all right in there?' yelled Moustache, hammering on the door.

'I just need to pull the chain,' she said, doing so.

Nervously, she unbolted the door.

Back inside the tiny flat, Scowler pointed to a chair by a table with the telephone on it.

'Sit there,' he commanded. 'I'm gonna ring yer dad.'

Shaking, Josie slid into it and watched him dial. After a few minutes he gave a malevolent smile.

'Mr Carpenter?' He paused. 'I'm callin' cos I 'appen to have a little someone 'ere who belongs to you.'

There was another pause.

'That's right. I ain't done nuffin to yer son yet. And I won't do nuffin if you do what I tells you and you don't call the coppers.'

And then it dawned on Josie that Larry must still be in the skip and that he had been locked all alone in the darkened theatre since Saturday night.

'Oh, yeah, he's right beside me. 'ere!'

He held out the receiver for Josie to take.

''ello, Dad,' said Josie, in the best Larry voice she could muster, aware that although the two men wouldn't be able to hear Mr Carpenter, they were listening to every single word *she* was saying.

'Larry! Are you all right?'

'Yes, Dad,' replied Josie hurriedly.

'What's happened to your voice? Have you been crying? Don't you worry, we'll get you away from that man.'

Josie remained silent.

'Larry? Can you hear me?'

'Yes, Dad.'

'Is Josie with you?' he asked.

She was about to say *Yes, Dad* but quickly stopped herself in case he gave her name away to Scowler after she had handed back the receiver to him.

'Did Molly see the *Winter Holiday* picture I drew for her in the dressing room?'

There was a sharp intake of breath at the other end.

'You're not Larry.'

'No, Dad.'

'Who are you? And how do you know Molly?' And then he gasped. 'Josie?'

'That's right, Dad,' said Josie carefully.

'You want him to think you're Larry.'

'Yes, Dad.'

'And the picture in the dressing room, it's important that Molly sees it, isn't it?'

'Yes, Dad.'

'Josie,' he said quietly. 'Is Larry still in the theatre?'

'What you two talkin' abaht?' interrupted Scowler suspiciously.

'That's right, Dad.'

'That's enough!' said Scowler, snatching the phone. 'You tell your step-son Henry we want to see him. Pronto . . . None of your business. Tell him I'll do a swap. Him for little Larry. I'll phone again tomorrer night. Same time.' There was a pause. 'Scotland ain't Timbuctoo. Tell him to git dahn 'ere and make it snappy. Or else.'

And he slammed down the receiver.

'I'm hungry,' said Josie.

'Got any of that Mother's Pride left?' said Scowler to Moustache.

'Yeah.'

'Give him a piece of that.'

Josie walked even more slowly to the settee. At least Mr and Mrs Carpenter would know that Larry was out of danger now. Unfortunately, they would have to tell her mum and dad she had been kidnapped. A picture of her mother crying came into her head. Swiftly Josie shut it out. She needed to use every ounce of concentration to escape before they discovered she wasn't Larry.

Moustache came in carrying a battered greasy tray. On it were three large mugs with steam coming off them. A slice of bread and marge was balanced on top of the one that had a chip on it.

'That's yours,' said Moustache, nodding at it. 'You git that dahn you.'

Josie took the bread and bit into it. Her plan of swapping mugs wouldn't work since the others had no chip. She picked it up.

The men turned away.

'What else is in the cupboard?' Scowler asked.

'Spaghetti 'oops,' said Moustache.

'That'll do. On toast. You git on wiv that and I'll keep an eye on him.'

''E's not goin' anywhere, is he? And I've only got two pairs of 'ands.'

Josie had to fight to stop herself from smiling. A picture of Moustache with four arms suddenly seemed very funny.

'You open a tin while I does the toast,' he whined. 'I ain't gonna slice off any more skin with that ruddy tin opener.'

Scowler gave an exasperated sigh.

'Don't you move!' he commanded, pointing at Josie.

Josie shook her head.

As Moustache and Scowler lumbered towards the kitchenette, Josie grabbed one of the other mugs, threw half the contents behind the settee, poured half her cocoa into it and hastily put it back on the tray.

Scowler glanced round the door.

'Drink up!' he ordered.

Josie buried her nose into the chipped mug. As soon as he drew his head back into the kitchenette, she grabbed the other full mug and repeated what she had done to the first one. She had hardly picked up her empty mug when Scowler re-appeared. She drew her sleeve across her mouth, curled up on the settee and put her head down.

'Looks like it's done the trick,' he murmured.

'Blimey!' she heard Moustache exclaim. 'Was it supposed to work that quick?'

'He's small and he ain't got much in his stomach.'

'You ain't given him too much, 'ave you?'

'Nah,'

'Ted?'

'What?'

'Are you really going to swap him for Henry? I mean, the little lad knows what we look like, don't 'e?'

'What d'you think?'

'But he's only a kid! Couldn't we just dump him up north or somefin'?'

'Anyway, who says we're goin' to swap? As long as we get our revenge for the nine years of hell he's put us through, that's all that matters.'

*Revenge?* thought Josie. *But what could Henry have done for nine years to make them so angry?'* He was a quiet sort of person who was happiest behind a camera lens.

'So I've been thinking . . .' said Scowler.

'Oh yeah?'

'He'd be pretty cut up if any harm came to the nipper, wouldn't he?'

Josie prayed she wouldn't be sick again.

'But he ain't done nuffin' wrong!' said Moustache.

'Keep yer voice down! I ain't decided yet. Now, where did you hide the snow? Once we get the dosh for keepin' it safe, that's our ticket out of 'ere.'

'A ticket? Whatcha mean?'

'We'll 'ave enuff smackers to move to where the cops don't know us, thickhead.'

'It's in a sugar bag. Behind the spaghetti 'oops.'

'Put it somewhere safer. I don't want you puttin' it in a cuppa by mistake. His nibs'll be pickin' it up in a fortnight, remember?'

'I know! I know!'

Josie was mystified. Why would grown men want imitation snow? And then she remembered Auntie Win telling her that some men played with trains and even made little villages around the railway tracks. Perhaps they put glue on the roofs of the model houses and sprinkled it onto them.

The floor near her shook and a hand grabbed one of her feet.

'What you doin?' she heard Moustache ask.

'Takin' his shoes off, ain't I? I ain't takin' no chances.'

Within minutes they were sitting on two battered armchairs with their spaghetti hoops, gulping down their drugged cocoa and watching the Tiller girls kicking up their long legs at the London Palladium. After yelling out the wrong answers at the quiz part of the show, they gradually fell silent.

Josie slowly raised her eyelids and stared across at the set. There was some sort of play on. People in northern accents were yelling at one another, and then there was the most wonderful sound. Snoring! And it was so loud it was a wonder they didn't wake each other up.

She lowered herself carefully onto the floor and crawled along the sticky lino hunting for her shoes. But there was no sign of them. Manoeuvring her way past the foul-smelling armchairs, she headed for the kitchenette.

They weren't on the floor in there either, and then she spotted them underneath the sink. The floor was so greasy that she almost skidded in their direction as though on an ice rink. She grabbed them and edged herself backwards. The door of the flat was only a foot away from where the two men were slumped asleep.

The man and woman on the television began yelling at each other again. She froze, willing them to get on with one another and keep the racket down. Very gently, she turned the doorknob until it gave a glorious click.

Still kneeling, she pushed the door open, eased herself out onto the pitch-dark landing and rose to her feet. To her alarm she felt so dizzy she nearly fell over. She leaned against a wall to steady herself and pulled the door to a close. She had hardly turned round when she nearly sent an empty bottle crashing to the floor. She quickly grabbed it before it went hurtling down the stairs.

Light music was coming from one of the rooms next to the kidnappers'. She hesitated. Should she knock on the door and tell whoever lived there she had been kidnapped? But what if they didn't believe her? And what if they were friends of the two men? No. She must concentrate on getting out of the building as fast as possible. She would put on her shoes later.

She shuffled backwards on her knees, feeling the steps with one hand while gripping her shoes with the other. The lift was on the landing below. As soon as she reached it, she eased the iron trellis to one side. It gave a loud squeak. She slipped in, hurriedly pulled the door across, and groped around for the bottom button. Within seconds of pressing it, she was juddering noisily downwards.

'Hurry! Hurry!' she whispered.

It hit the ground floor with such a crash that it caused her to cry out. A shaft of light spilled across the hall and a woman's voice yelled, 'Is that you?'

She squatted on the floor, motionless. After much muttering and complaining, there was the slam of a door and Josie was thrown back into darkness. She tried to open the lift door but it refused to budge. She jiggled it again.

By now her hands had begun to feel clammy. She pushed her shoes to one side and wiped a hand against her duffle coat.

'Please!' she begged.

This time it slid to one side and she stepped out. The front door was only a few feet away, the dim light from a street lamp struggling to fight its way through the greasy top window.

'Almost there!' she murmured.

Within seconds she was outside on the pavement. Never had a blast of cold air felt so sweet. She staggered across to a street lamp on the other side of a narrow road and knelt underneath it. Her fingers shaking, she put on her left shoe and tied the laces.

'One to go,' she said encouragingly to herself.

As she slipped her right foot into the other one, her toes hit a bulky object. She drew out what looked like a small bag of sugar.

'The snow!' she exclaimed.

Why on earth had they put it there? She shoved it into her coat pocket and pulled on her other shoe. She was in the middle of tying her laces when there was a loud 'Oi!' from above.

Hanging out of a top window was Scowler, and he was staring straight down at her.

'Stay there!' he screamed.

But Josie was already half running, half swaying down the alley and round the corner into a main street, the after-effects of the chloroform still muddying her brain. There were more street lights now so she was able to see more clearly, but then, she realised, so would her kidnappers. Being Sunday, the streets were deserted and there was no one to call out to for help. She had to get off the street and out of sight. A quick glance at the bus stops and she knew she was in London. She spotted an E sign on a wall. *East*, she thought. *East London*.

'Ralph,' she whispered. She remembered he did jobs on a Sunday with the other actors at that Joan woman's theatre in East London. If Josie could reach him, he would protect her.

She glanced backwards. To her horror, Scowler and Moustache were heading towards her and they looked apoplectic. She turned down the nearest road and stumbled past three small shops and a couple of pubs. Over her shoulder she spotted a dark alleyway. There had to be somewhere there she could hide. She could still hear them yelling behind her. Now she was running so fast she could hardly breathe. She dived into another alley. But it was hopeless. Her legs buckled underneath her.

Suddenly, out of the air it seemed, two strong hands gripped her powerfully from behind, lifted her off her feet and hauled her into the pitch darkness of a porch. Before she could cry out, a hand was placed firmly across her mouth. She lashed out with her arms but it was a waste of time. Whoever was holding her had a stillness and strength that was impossible to fight.

With despair she realised she had been hurled from the frying pan into the fire.

# 3

# The Stranger

A T LEAST HE HADN'T COVERED HER EYES, which meant that she had a good view of the alley. There were now voices she didn't recognise. The hand on her mouth relaxed.

'Don't be alarmed,' breathed a deep voice into her ear. 'I'm trying to help you.'

'Seen a red-headed nipper in a brown duffle coat?' she heard Scowler ask someone.

'Nah,' replied the voice of a young man.

Her two kidnappers were facing a gang of youths wearing blue knee-length coats with narrow black lapels and ties that looked like boot laces. The sort of clothes that Esmeralda and her fan club would condemn as being out of fashion. *Square*. But there was no mistaking them. They were Teddy boys, their hair sticking out from above their foreheads like duck's bills, and under their Edwardian-looking coats they wore ornate waistcoats, drainpipe trousers and thick-soled shoes.

'You seen a darkie?' asked the boy who had answered Scowler.

'Nah,' said Scowler.

They leaned towards each other in an animated discussion.

'You scratch my back, I'll scratch yours,' she heard Scowler say.

'Yeah! Instead of two pairs of eyes we'll have seven,' said the youth.

'So what does he look like?' said Scowler.

'Tall,' said a sharp-faced member of the gang, 'smartly dressed. Like a gent.'

'What did he do?'

'He was on our patch and tried to take the micky, that's what,' said the youth Josie guessed was their leader. 'So tell us about this nipper then.'

'He got somefin' which belongs to us,' said Moustache.

'Oh yeah?'

'Not worth much,' Scowler added, hurriedly. 'Sentimental value. Know what I mean?'

The youth nodded sagely. 'A thief, eh?'

Josie was furious. She hadn't stolen anything. They were the thieves. They had stolen her!

And then she remembered the package she had found in her shoe.

They began muttering about telephone boxes and times of phoning.

'If we see your darkie we'll tell you where he is,' said Scowler.

'And if we spot your nipper we'll nab him till you come and collect him.'

They ambled down the alley together. Once their voices

were out of earshot, the hand over Josie's mouth dropped. Glancing up at her rescuer, she was met by a pair of soft, friendly eyes. The owner of the eyes stepped out of the shadows and onto the pavement. He was black. He smiled down at her.

'Seems we're both on the run, old chap,' he murmured.

'I'm not a thief,' she protested. 'Honest. They kidnapped me and I escaped. Why is that gang after you?'

'Last Friday I was in an area they obviously think they own and they didn't appreciate my comments regarding their behaviour. They've been on the lookout for me ever since.'

'Why?'

'Because of the colour of my skin.'

Before Josie had moved up to London, Elsie had explained to her that people from all over the world lived there. She had already noticed that many West Indians were in charge of the buses. It was very different from Sternsea, but within a week of being in the city, Josie had grown used to seeing them about. She remembered overhearing Elsie talking to her mum and dad about riots in London the previous year in a place called Notting Hill Gate between black people and white gangs. But this man didn't have the same kind of accent as the bus conductors.

'You sound like a toff,' Josie said.

'So I've been told.'

'Like Paul Temple,' she added. 'He's a posh private detective.'

'Well, I can assure you I am not a detective, private or otherwise. I'm not even English. I'm French, though my ancestors came from Africa.' He smiled. 'It's a long story, and now I believe is not the time to tell it. My priority is to deliver you safely to your parents. Where do they reside?'

Josie was suddenly aware that she was swaying. Overwhelmed by a tidal wave of exhaustion, the thought of having to find the words to explain that her parents didn't live in London and that she was staying with her aunt was like being asked to climb Mount Everest backwards. And the last thing she wanted to do was to go back to her flat and to school and face being bombarded with a lot of angry questions from everyone. Not yet, anyway.

'Abroad,' she yawned. 'A woman was supposed to meet me off the boat but she never turned up and then I was kidnapped.'

The lies had slipped out so effortlessly it astonished her. But they were only tiny lies. Sternsea was far enough away to be 'abroad'. Having lied however, she realised she would now have to stick to her story.

And then she remembered where she had been heading. As if the man could read her thoughts, he asked, 'Have you another relative we can contact?'

'My older brother. He works with a woman called Miss Littlewood in Stratford.'

The relief from spilling those words out was so enormous she could have fallen asleep there and then on the pavement. She would tell Ralph everything and leave it to him to pass it on to her parents, her aunt, Elsie, the school, the police and Mr and Mrs Carpenter while she crawled underneath the nearest eiderdown and went to sleep.

'*Joan* Littlewood?'

'Yeah,' said Josie, surprised.

'He's in the Theatre Workshop Company?'

'Yeah,' she said, rubbing her face. 'In the Theatre Royal,'

'But this is extraordinary. The main purpose of my visit to England is to see her work! We must find him. And soon. Stay close and follow me!'

The gent turned quickly down the alley opposite the one where the men had been heading while Josie stumbled along beside him.

'My name is Mr Beauvoisin, by the way.'

'Bow–vwah-zahn,' she repeated slowly.

'And yours is?'

'Jo,' she said, hoping he would think she was a boy.

'Short for Joseph?'

She nodded.

'I'll call you that. And your brother's name?'

'Ralph,' she panted. 'Where are we going?'

'My lodgings.'

She stopped. Her mother had warned her not to speak to strangers or go off with them but there was no one else around to help her and this man knew about Miss Littlewood. She was sure Ralph would give him the thumbs up.

He glanced down at her.

'I promise you, I am not in the habit of picking up waifs and strays but I need to pick up the little English money I possess for our Tube fares. The only money I have on my person is French and, unfortunately, hardly had I caught sight of the bank on Friday to change it into English currency when that gang of Teddy boys waylaid me.' He smiled. 'There's a telephone you can use in the hall. But you need four pennies for it.'

'I have four pennies,' said Josie. She nearly added, *Girl Guides are told to carry them for emergencies*, before she realised that would give the game away.

'Splendid. Then you can ring Ralph from there while I go up to my room.'

*Useless*, thought Josie wearily. Her brother's telephone was shared by other lodgers in the hall of the house where he and his wife, Jessica lived, and anyway, she didn't know the number. Some Girl Guide she was. And then she remembered where she had been heading before Mr Beauvoisin rescued her.

'He'll be at the Theatre Royal.'

'Excellent. You can look up the number of the theatre in the telephone directory there.'

They walked past shabby, run-down lodging houses with signs outside saying *NO IRISH. NO BLACKS. NO COLOUREDS. NO DOGS*. Josie, who was struggling to keep up with him, couldn't take her eyes off them. She could understand why landlords and landladies might not want dogs. Dogs barking at night would keep other lodgers awake but she couldn't fathom out why they wouldn't want Irish or black people. In fact, she thought it was a nasty thing to write on a notice. And what on earth were coloureds? People who were orange and yellow and purple?

Mr Beauvoisin halted in front of a large, dingy house. The bulky front door had two long windows with red flowers and green leaves on the stained glass. He let himself in quietly with a key and pointed to a telephone on the wall above a low wooden table where there was a telephone directory.

'My room is on the first floor,' he whispered. 'I shall be back with you directly.'

While he crept up the stairs to a door on a tiny landing, she made her way to the table. She had just found the T section in the directory when a female voice from upstairs screeched, 'Is that you, Mr Bowvozzer?'

Mr Beauvoisin's door opened rapidly. Tiptoeing speedily down the stairs, he beckoned Josie towards the front door only to retreat rapidly when the outline of several figures with the tell-tale duck-bill haircuts appeared on the other side of the glass. He grabbed Josie's hand, dragged her past the telephone table, threw open the door under the stairs, pulled her into the cupboard and closed the door behind them. Josie stood panting in the dark amongst the smell of old boots and shoes, having just hit her shin on what she guessed must be a meter. From above, they could hear the pad of slippers accompanied by a rasping cough. By now the doorbell had been rung several times.

'All right! All right! I'm coming! Keep yer hair on!'

There was the sound of the front door being opened.

''ave you any idea what time it is?' a lady complained. 'What d'you want?'

'We was told you was the landlady who 'as black men staying 'ere,' said a young man's voice.

'This is the right 'ouse,' added another male voice. 'Ain't it?'

'If you mean, do I have gentlemen of a West Indian persuasion lodging 'ere, yeah. I do. What of it? Least they're clean and well behaved. So?'

'We're looking for one.'

'Oh yeah? Well, I've about twenty residin 'ere. What does he look like?'

'I dunno,' said another voice. 'I mean they all look the same, don't they?'

'Do they now?'

'He was wearin' a raincoat.'

'What sort of raincoat?' asked the woman.

'A waterproof raincoat.'

'A waterproof raincoat,' she repeated slowly. 'Well, you've had a wasted journey, my love, cos my lodgers only wear raincoats what leak like sieves.'

'What? Wiv 'oles in 'em?'

'She's 'aving you on,' said one of the gang.

'Aw, come on, Terry!' protested another. 'We're gonna miss the last Tube if we don't get a move on.'

There was a loud slam followed by ascending footsteps, but the dust was too much for Josie and she sneezed. Within seconds the door under the stairs was flung open and she found herself gazing up at an irate middle-aged woman with a cigarette wedged in-between her teeth and enough rollers on her head to flatten a road.

'Who the bleedin' 'ell are you?' she shrieked, glaring at Josie. 'And what you doin' under my . . . ?' It was then that she spotted Mr Beauvoisin.

'Out!' she yelled. 'The both of you!'

Josie jumped. She and Mr Beauvoisin stepped out into the hallway.

'What's this nipper doin' 'ere?'

'I was taking him to his brother,' began Mr Beauvoisin.

'Who 'appens to live in the cupboard under my stairs, I 'spose. His gran don't live there too, do she?' She folded her arms. 'I take it this 'idin' lark is all about the rent, Mr Bowvuzzer. You still ain't got it, 'ave you?'

'Yes and no . . .' And he took out a wad of notes.

'I want proper money,' she screamed. 'Wiv our Queen on it. Even the late King will do.'

'I assure you it is proper money. I tried to change it into English currency, but I was set upon by that gang of youths.'

'Oh, that just takes the biscuit. I ain't daft, you know. You overheard 'em and now I suppose you're gonna tell me they was after you?'

Josie was about to spring to his defence when Mr Beauvoisin squeezed her hand, warning her to stay out of the argument.

'I can change it tomorrow,' he said.

'Oh yeah? And I'm the ruddy Queen of Sheba! I want you out! I got a waiting list a mile long fer your room. Bag packed and out! Now!'

# 4

# Round the Corner from Angel Lane

JOSIE AND MR BEAUVOISIN, A PACKED SUITCASE in his hand, set out from Stratford station and down a road of railway cottages until they hit a deserted narrow street of shops called Angel Lane. Scattered shreds of newspapers were whirling past piles of fruit boxes and empty barrows that had been propped on one side. They hovered outside a small building called *Café L'Ange*.

'Angel cafe,' Mr Beauvoisin murmured.

They crossed over to the other side of the road and peered in through the window of a bakery.

'I wish that was open,' Josie said hungrily.

'On that I am in agreement with you.'

Behind a gate of criss-crossed webbed iron between the bakery and a haberdasher's shop there was a short passage leading to a heavy door with a wide arched window above it.

'I wonder what sort of shop that is,' said Josie.

'With this high locked gate and that solid door, I imagine it must be a jewellers,' said Mr Beauvoisin. 'Though this area doesn't look like the kind of place where people could afford such luxuries.'

At the end of the street they veered right. Narrow chimneys soared behind clusters of small houses in the distance, belching out columns of black smoke across the rooftops so that it was difficult to tell if the darkness was caused by the lateness of the evening or by the smoke drifting in their direction.

'Sulphur,' Mr Beauvoisin said, wrinkling his nose.

Josie could smell it too. 'Where's it comin' from?'

'The factories.'

They headed towards Salway Road. They had just passed a pub called The Red Lion and were about to cross the road to where a photographic shop stood when Mr Beauvoisin glanced upwards. High above them on a brick wall, written in large letters, was a poster with the words *Theatre Workshop*. It was an advertisement for a street market musical called *Make Me An Offer* by a man called Wolf Mankowitz.

'*Lyrics and music by Monty Norman and David Heneker,*' read Mr Beauvoisin aloud.

Josie spotted a long blue building ahead of them. 'It's a theatre!' she yelled.

They broke into a run. In the plain blue wall were three doors. Over an arched entrance above the one on the right were the words *Theatre Royal*. The same words were carved into the stone high above their heads.

'We have arrived in paradise, Joseph,' announced Mr Beauvoisin.

A van was parked near the middle door, which was open. From inside the theatre they could hear a man speaking.

'Ralph!' said Josie. 'He must be in there helpin' out.'

They slipped inside and found themselves standing at the back of the stalls in a darkened auditorium. Mr Beauvoisin hastily pulled her down behind a seat. At the far end was the stage where a man was painting a lectern on a raised platform. Another man was fiddling with what appeared to be thick electrical cables.

'Which one is your brother?' Mr Beauvoisin whispered.

'Neither of 'em,' she whispered back, disappointed.

'You've missed the last Tube,' she heard one of the men tell his companion. 'Do you want a lift home? Or are you sleeping in the wardrobe?'

'I'll take the lift,' replied his friend. 'I want something a little more comfortable than a camp bed tonight. By the way, did you remember to shut the door?'

Josie felt a tugging at her coat. Mr Beauvoisin was motioning her backwards. They retreated hurriedly through the door and onto the pavement.

'Where does Ralph live?' he asked.

'I dunno,' murmured Josie.

'Our only choice then is to go back inside the theatre ready for when he turns up tomorrow morning . . .'

He was interrupted by the clunking of the safety bar on the door followed by the sound of heavy chains.

'Too late,' he said. 'They're locking up. Quick!'

They raced towards the arched entrance, pushed their way through two pairs of double doors, past a small box-office window and through another set of doors into a dark corridor. As Mr Beauvoisin felt his way along the wall to his left, he let out a cry.

'Here!' he exclaimed in the dark. 'There's another door. We must be parallel to the stage by now.'

It squeaked as he pushed it open. He pulled her in and closed it behind them. Josie could hear him rootling around inside his suitcase.

'Splendid!' he exclaimed, snapping it shut.

Torch in hand, he switched it on and moved the light around them. It lit up what appeared to be a tiny room with a door at either side. Stuck on the back of the door they had entered were pieces of paper. Mr Beauvoisin aimed the torch at them.

'They're notes for the cast,' he said excitedly, 'written by Miss Littlewood.'

He pushed open the second door into the narrow stage left wings and swept the light towards the playing area, now unlit and deserted.

He gasped.

'What is it?' asked Josie, alarmed.

'I've never seen a stage this deep,' he said with enthusiasm. He swung the torch back to the wings, along the wall and onto a thin wooden ladder. 'That must lead up to the flies and gantry.'

Creeping out of the wings, they found themselves at the foot of a curved staircase and climbed upwards to where there were two doors. Men's voices were coming from the one that was open on the left. They sidled over towards it and peered around it. The two men they had seen on stage were standing in a tiny room in front of a wide stone sink.

'Someone's got to wash that pile of cups in here tomorrow

morning,' one of them said. 'They're not going to be happy when they see this paint all over it.'

'We have to wash the brushes out somewhere,' argued his companion.

Josie and Mr Beauvoisin returned quickly to the staircase and continued making their way upward until they could go no higher.

'The gods,' whispered Mr Beauvoisin as they reached the gallery. 'We'll need to feel our way with our hands. Too risky to use a torch with those two men still in the building. If they come through the auditorium they'll spot it. Gently does it.'

He grasped her hand and led her towards some wooden benches. 'We'll sleep here,' he said.

'On the benches?' asked Josie.

'No. Between them. Too dangerous *on* them. Who knows what might happen if we turned over in our sleep? I don't relish the thought of falling from a great height into the stalls.'

From somewhere in the theatre they could hear the two men calling out to one another. Then their voices faded away and there was silence.

'Mr Beauvoisin,' whispered Josie, 'we're locked in now, aren't we?'

'Well and truly.'

'So no one from outside can get in.'

'That's right. I'm sorry I can't offer you the camp bed one of those men was talking about. We're going to have to make do with this wooden floor, I'm afraid.'

But Josie didn't care. Scowler and Moustache couldn't reach her now. She was safe. Suddenly she began to shake uncontrollably.

'I'm so cold,' she stammered. *Ice cold*, she thought. To her alarm she heard scrabbling noises. 'What's that?' she cried.

'Me feeling around in my suitcase again. I'm keeping my torch switched off to save the batteries. I'm searching for some thick socks and a jersey you can wear. You can use your coat as a blanket and my towel for a pillow.'

'Mr Beauvoisin, I can't see you.'

'I can't see you either. But I can reassure you that we are both here. We'll sleep foot to foot. Then if you feel scared you can just kick the soles of my feet. Will that make you feel better?'

'Yeah.'

It was later when they had settled into their sleeping positions that Mr Beauvoisin began to ask her questions again.

'Joseph, do you know the men who kidnapped you?'

'No,' she said nervously.

'There's no need to be afraid. Now tell me about this woman who was supposed to meet you. You say she never turned up and they just grabbed you?'

'Yeah. They put a cloth on my face and I went to sleep.'

'You haven't yet told me how you managed to escape.'

'After I woke up, I heard them say they were going to put some stuff in my cocoa to knock me out so I put it in their cups when they were in the kitchen and it made them go to sleep instead.'

Out of the dark came the sound of laughter and she couldn't help smiling.

'But where did you put *their* cocoa?'

'On the floor behind their settee. But it didn't make them sleep for very long.'

'They probably gave you enough for a child but it wasn't a strong enough dose for an adult. Now, about your brother Ralph. You say he'll be here tomorrow?'

'Yeah.'

'And your parents are in which country?'

Josie was stumped. Geography was not one of her best subjects.

'Cyprus,' she said, remembering one of the places Auntie Win had been stationed, and she pretended to yawn. 'I'm tired.'

After they had said their goodnights, Josie lay staring into the blackness. Inside her head she could see Larry locked in the dark theatre, petrified and sobbing. By now his father would have told everyone how stupid she had been hiding him in the skip and her parents would be ashamed of her.

She had let Elsie down too. Once Larry had been hidden, he wouldn't have been able to hear what those men were planning to do to him and it was then that she should have gone straight to her sister and told her about the kidnappers' plans, before getting out of her costume. She would now be in trouble both with her school and the police for the same reason.

Desperate for some sleep, Josie closed her eyes, but every time she did she saw Scowler coming towards her with a dirty rag. The only way she could stop him hurting her was by staying awake.

She must have dropped off eventually because she was woken by Mr Beauvoisin calling her name.

'Yeah,' she answered sleepily. 'What is it?'

'You cried out,' he said. 'You must have been having a nightmare.'

# 5

# Casing the Joint

JOSIE WAS WOKEN BY THE WHIRRING OF AN industrial vacuum cleaner and lights on the stage. On opening her eyes, she was surprised to find that it was a much smaller theatre than the one in Winford. The gallery felt so close to the stage she was convinced she could have leaped down onto it with ease. Mr Beauvoisin was already gathering up his belongings. Josie swiftly removed the thick socks and put on her shoes. She slid her arms back into the sleeves of her duffle coat and crawled up the stairs behind him towards the left-hand side of the gallery. From behind a little wall, they cavesdropped on the women in the dress circle.

'The cleaners,' whispered Mr Beauvoisin.

The top of the wall came up to Josie's chest. Mr Beauvoisin knelt down beside her to stay out of sight. From their position they still had a good view of the stage, which was now bathed in a pool of pink light. Voices were coming from the wings.

'Quick, Meg! Let's get out of 'ere!' they heard one of the cleaners hiss urgently. 'Otherwise she'll have us joining in!'

There was a clatter of heavy footsteps as the women made what sounded like a hasty retreat.

A group of men and women of all shapes, sizes and ages walked onto the stage. Three of them took off their trousers, revealing black tights underneath. Some of them had bare feet.

*They must be freezing,* thought Josie.

A teacher was talking to them from somewhere in the stalls, a well-spoken woman with a deep voice. Josie was puzzled. They seemed a bit old for pupils. Some of the men looked the same age as her gran. There was an old man with a crinkly face and a young Italian-looking man with black hair who kept making her smile. Alongside them a tall woman was sharing a joke with an attractive blonde and a young woman with red hair.

They rose in unison onto the balls of their feet, stretching their arms high above their heads before sinking slowly to the floor. Josie leaned forward to take a closer look. Standing upright now, hands by their sides, they began to fall forwards, backwards and sideways. She wanted to shout, 'Look out!' but every time it appeared as though they were about to hit the ground, they put a foot out at the last minute. After these strange exercises, they shook their arms and legs and did an exercise where they knelt on one leg, and with one fluid motion moved slowly to their feet, stretching upwards again.

Transfixed, Josie observed them reaching out, punching the air, gliding in slow swooping circles or moving heavily as though there were weights attached to their ankles. It was a million miles away from standing frozen in a tableau in the dance classes at the stage school, or stepping and pointing with a straight back. One moment the class seemed to float, the next moment they were making flicking movements or walking with jumpy, almost nervous, gestures, only to suddenly hurl themselves forward with an energy so powerful that it made their silent bodies appear to roar. Just from watching them, Josie knew exactly what they were feeling.

This was followed by breathing exercises. Each time they breathed out they did a physical action on the breath and made a strange sound. Then they all began to sing, 'Diddy dum diddy dum diddy dum dum.'

'Mozart,' whispered Mr Beauvoisin. He glanced at Josie. 'The tune.'

This was followed by tongue-twisting rhymes similar to the ones Elsie recited to make sure her diction was up to scratch.

'Speak from your tummies!' the woman shouted. 'Not from your mouths!'

The pupils then began to invent scenes and the teacher talked about units and objectives. Josie couldn't make any sense of it.

'What does the teacher mean?' she whispered.

'Each character in a scene has an objective in each unit of a scene,' said Mr Beauvoisin.

Josie was no wiser.

'Each person is heading towards something in particular, in the different sections of each scene,' he added. 'They need to concentrate on where they're going.'

'Around the furniture?' Josie guessed.

Mr Beauvoisin seemed to find this extremely funny and bowed his head, his shoulders shaking.

'Emotionally,' he whispered to one side. 'And she's not a teacher. She's Miss Littlewood.'

And then the penny dropped. It was the Joan woman!

'What does he or she wish for right now?' they heard her ask them.

One glance at Mr Beauvoisin and Josie realised that he was determined not to miss a single second of what he was witnessing. Josie gazed around at the auditorium. In spite of the fusty mould smell of the plum-coloured bumpy paper on the walls there was something beautiful and magical about the place. It was strange how an old and shabby building could make her feel so completely at ease. It was as though the kidnappers had ceased to exist and someone had placed a hand on her shoulder to reassure her that she was safe. *I wish I could stay here*, she thought.

Ralph would be somewhere in the building, she knew that. A few minutes more of watching what was happening on stage before finding him and telling him what had happened wouldn't make much difference, she told herself.

The members of the class were now moving around, making noises and acting out the feelings that Joan shouted at them. Aside from the red-headed woman, there were only men on stage now. They had been asked to be sharks and vultures but to conceal it from one another. Suddenly, they were bidders at an auction while a man on a box was raising an imaginary object for sale and asking for offers.

'It's not a lesson,' she whispered.

'No,' murmured Mr Beauvoisin happily. 'It's a rehearsal!'

And then she twigged. It was the cast of *Make Me An Offer*, the show advertised on the poster outside, and they were doing the *knees up* kind of acting Mrs Havilland disapproved of so thoroughly.

The odd thing was that they didn't appear to be acting at all. They were real people at a sale, and the sale was happening right in front of her eyes, and although they spoke and moved naturally around one another, Miss Littlewood hadn't given them any moves. The cast did what they wanted! Witnessing the way they performed, it was as though Josie had walked out of a dark prison into the sunlight and had been filled with an energy so powerful that it made her want to leap into the air and push aside imaginary cobwebs.

The auctioneers disappeared and two of the actors walked on stage chatting to one another, carrying a park bench. As they dashed into the wings, two women followed. One was pushing an enormous black pram. To Josie's amazement, the Joan woman asked them to *dance* a conversation! Now she was as intrigued as Mr Beauvoisin. What on earth did she mean?

One of the actresses moved towards the other with a sideways sweeping movement and the other woman leaped and stretched an answer. By watching the way they danced around the park bench, she could tell that the tall actress playing someone called Gwen was off in a dream, as though talking about something romantic. Gwen was reaching upwards, as though trying to soar into the clouds, and Josie could see that it irritated the other woman, who was making low, heavy movements, as if trying to pull her back down to earth. And when Gwen danced a question, her friend answered by pushing her body forward with a jolt and then hurriedly twisting away with a toss of her head, as though she were lying.

From stage left, two other women ran on, spotted the pram in front of the bench and began leaping around it, making make a fuss of the baby inside it. Suddenly they were looking up and spinning and everyone was running and ducking.

*Rain*, thought Josie. They picked up the bench between them and carried it off into the wings while another woman appeared and wheeled the pram off, making kissing faces to the baby inside. No assistant stage managers, Josie observed. The cast moved the scenery and props themselves!

Miss Littlewood asked them to bring back the bench and pram and repeat the scene, only this time they were to speak. Again, she didn't tell them where to go. The two actresses moved around the bench naturally. What was even more extraordinary was that their accents sounded like her gran and her dad. They didn't talk the posh English that her dad referred to as 'speaking with a plum in yer mouth'.

'I'll watch that scene from the gallery,' Miss Littlewood announced.

Josie jumped back in alarm. Mr Beauvoisin tapped her on the shoulder and indicated the double doors by the foot of the steps next to a theatre box with seats in it. Together they ran down and dived swiftly through them.

The doors led to a small wardrobe where shelves were stacked high with lopsided boxes of costumes. In the centre of the room stood two sewing machines with foot treadles and ornate drawers. Scraps of material and a half-made hat were on the chairs behind them.

Mr Beauvoisin dropped his suitcase and they manoeuvred themselves gingerly around an ironing board, tables and two laden chairs, avoiding the tiny fragments of material scattered on the floor. On the narrow wall between two enormous sash windows – each with twelve framed squares of grubby, mottled glass – was a large black socket. A wire led from it to a heavy black iron, now resting upright on the ironing board.

'What's that?' asked Josie, pointing at an oval instrument hanging by the window on the right.

'A lute. I expect they use it for their Shakespeare plays.'

Josie pressed her nose against one of the glass squares. She could just make out the shape of the factories in the distance. It was strange not being able to see out properly but comforting to know that not even a pilot in a plane flying past could see in.

Under the window was a large cardboard box overflowing with more costumes, their sleeves hanging over the sides.

It was while they were absorbing the clutter of clothes, hats and shoes that a slim woman in her twenties, her black hair scooped up loosely under a colourful scarf, waltzed in carrying a bag.

'Hello!' she exclaimed.

Mr Beauvoisin glanced quickly at Josie and then at the

woman. Josie could guess exactly what he was thinking. *How am I going to explain what we're doing here?*

But the young woman didn't seem at all perturbed.

'Who are you?' she asked, smiling.

*Now we're for it*, thought Josie. But before she or Mr Beauvoisin could answer, she solved the problem for them.

'Are you volunteers?'

# 6

# Volunteers

'YES!' THEY BLURTED OUT.

Immediately the young woman pressed a finger to her lips.

'Keep your voices down,' she urged. 'If you speak normally up here you'll be heard on stage. By the way,' she added quietly, 'I'm Annette.'

'Mr Beauvoisin and Joseph,' said Mr Beauvoisin. 'Are you the wardrobe mistress?'

'No. I'm an actress. We look after our own costumes and sometimes sneak up her to do our own ironing,' she said, smiling. 'I don't have one at my digs.'

She dumped her bag at the end of the ironing board and proceeded to pull out a couple of flared skirts and a blouse. 'Gerry's given you permission to be in the theatre, has he?'

*Who's Gerry?* thought Josie.

'Oh yes,' said Mr Beauvoisin calmly. He glanced round. 'Tell me, how do you find anything in here?'

'Believe it or not there's a place for most things,' she said, and pointed to the labels on the boxes under the table saying *Gloves, Ties, Corsets.* 'But yes, I agree, it is rather a mess.'

'So we could help by tidying up in here.'

'Difficult to do. As you can see there's not much room to move.' She dropped her bag on the floor and slid one of the skirts over the ironing board. 'And if you shifted anything, people might not be able to find what they needed.'

'Are you in *Make Me An Offer*?' he asked.

'No.'

'Would you mind if I asked you about a matter which has been puzzling me?'

'Fire away,' said Annette, reaching for the iron.

'When I've seen the Theatre Workshop Company perform, they've always appeared so in tune with one another, very much an ensemble. Yet when I watched some of the cast warming up with those exercises . . .'

'Laban.'

'I beg your pardon?'

'They're based on the work of a man called Rudolph Laban. Sorry, I interrupted. What were you saying?' she said, easing the iron along the skirt.

'When I was watching, I noticed that a couple of the cast seemed to be a little impatient, as though finding the rehearsal games annoying. That surprises me. I know many actors in France who would love to work with Miss Littlewood.'

'Hang on a minute, how do you know what's been going on in the rehearsals?'

'We've been watching from the back of the gallery,' said Josie.

Annette let out a whistle.

'You'd better not let Joan find that out. You're either in or out.'

'What do you mean?' said Mr Beauvoisin.

'If she catches the cleaners in the theatre during a rehearsal, she makes them come onto the stage and join in the improvisations. She won't allow spectators. The cleaners are now very careful when they work.' She paused. 'Those cast members you mentioned, they're probably not used to her ways.'

'I don't understand.'

'Most of them have never worked with her before so she's having to train them quickly at the same time as rehearsing them. She only agreed to direct *Make Me An Offer* for some theatre bigwig if she had Harry Greene and Marjie Lawrence in the cast. They're the only two people from her old company. She needed them so that the other cast members could see how she worked. Most of the people she's already trained are performing in other plays.'

*Like Ralph*, thought Josie, whom she now realised wouldn't be arriving until after the *Make Me An Offer* rehearsals had finished.

'I thought I recognised a couple of them,' Mr Beauvoisin exclaimed. 'They were in the company which came to Paris in 1955.'

'How on earth can you remember them from four years ago?'

'Because until then I had never witnessed such powerful and versatile acting and at times they made me laugh so much I could hardly breathe. When someone does that to you, you don't forget.'

'But why don't some of them like her way of rehearsin'?' Josie interrupted. She envied them. They were far better off than the pupils at her stage school.

'Oh, most of them are fine about it now but we all get a bit frightened when we have to do things that are unfamiliar, don't we?' She laughed. 'Marjie told me that some of them had even turned up to the first rehearsal having learned all their lines.'

'But what's wrong with that?' asked Josie. *That's what we're told to do at school*, she thought.

'Joan doesn't like people to do that until they have become the person they're playing and can respond to the others as those people. And it's a waste of time if it's a new play because she has a tendency to throw the script aside and make the actors improvise around the writer's plot. Playwrights can come up with wonderful ideas but the dialogue can be a bit . . .' She paused as though struggling to find the right word.

'Literary?' suggested Mr Beauvoisin.

'Yes,' agreed the woman.

'What does that mean?' asked Josie.

'Speaking in a bookish way rather than speaking naturally,' he said.

'Wooden,' the woman added. 'She even encourages her casts to improvise during the performances, and that can be frightening for actors who aren't used to it.'

'So, does she want them to be frightened?' Josie asked.

'If it makes them a better actor or actress, yes. And I've seen them take off once they're past that fearful stage.

It can be quite exhilarating.'

Mr Beauvoisin gazed at her quizzically. 'But how have *you* managed to see all this if Miss Littlewood doesn't allow spectators?'

'Ah. If you promise to keep it a secret, I'll show you.'

The young woman set the iron to one side, and beckoned them to follow her. As they squeezed past racks and shelves of clothing, Josie noticed a couple of camp beds with a tartan rug and an army blanket thrown over them. The woman gently opened a door at the side and crept out. Josie and Mr Beauvoisin followed and found themselves high above stage right. Peering down, they could see the stage below. Josie glanced at Mr Beauvoisin who was smiling broadly. He didn't need to say anything. She knew exactly what he was thinking. *We can watch and listen to the rehearsals from here!*

They eased themselves back into the wardrobe. It wasn't until the young woman had closed the door that Josie asked about the beds.

'Do people live here?' she whispered.

'Not now, but a few years ago, when Joan first moved into this theatre, the cast didn't earn enough money to stay in lodgings, so when they had finished the day's rehearsals or painting sets or cleaning or carpentry, they would cook food over the gas rings dotted around the theatre and sleep in the dressing rooms.

'This was where the wardrobe mistress used to sleep. It was the only way she could finish making the costumes in time. Sometimes she would be sewing all night. Nothing's changed there,' she added, smiling. 'The company even used to have a cooking rota. Chef of the week, they called it. One actor's pièce de resistance was apple omelette.'

*Sounds like my Auntie Win*, Josie nearly blurted out.

'They had a few close shaves when the sanitary inspector made an unexpected call. Sleeping in a theatre is illegal, you see. But they managed to hide the gas rings and the other electrical devices they were using for cooking. Unfortunately they couldn't hide the beds.'

'So he found out?'

'No. He was told they were for the cast to have a rest before the rigours of the evening performances.'

Josie returned to squinting through the mottled glass. Even though it was freezing in the wardrobe, she loved it there. Suddenly, the thought of returning to the outside world filled her with dread. It wasn't only because those two men were still after her but it was also because her stupidity would have brought disgrace to the school. She would either be expelled and have to go to her local school in Sternsea, where she would have no chance of stepping foot inside a theatre for years, or be allowed to stay at the stage school and be glared at by the teachers and called names by Esmeralda and her gang. She knew her mum would be worried about her but she couldn't bear the thought of seeing the disappointment on her dad and Auntie Win's faces after having made such a mess of things, and it dawned on her that these could be the last few hours she would be able to spend inside a world where she felt most herself; a world where occasionally she had the chance to fly.

'How do the playwrights feel about actors improvising their play?' she heard Mr Beauvoisin ask.

'Some are used to it and end up being happy with the result. Some aren't. The writer of *Make Me An Offer* doesn't want anything changed. And that's not how Joan works. You'll probably hear him growling to himself in the upstairs bar or green room or having rows with Joan. That is, if you stay long enough, and I have to warn you,' she said, glancing at Josie, 'the air can get somewhat blue.'

'What's blue air?' asked Josie quickly, sensing something interesting.

'A maelstrom of swearing.'

'So,' said Annette, looking at them curiously, 'what sort of jobs are you going to be doing here?'

'Anything Gerry asks us to do,' Mr Beauvoisin replied.

'I'd go downstairs, if I were you, There are plenty of jobs in the foyer that need doing. And now is a good time to leave by the gallery. Joan isn't there any more. I can hear her on stage.'

They could hear her too. She was yelling. 'You're not supposed to be playing a part. You're supposed to be playing a human being! And don't *speak* the words. *Throw* them!'

As Mr Beauvoisin picked up his suitcase, the young woman glanced at it puzzled.

'Overalls and tools,' he explained.

They slipped out through the swing doors to the gallery. Josie expected Miss Littlewood to turn and yell, 'Who's up there?', but she needn't have worried. She was still too busy having an argument with someone on stage.

They dropped down to the floor and crawled between the wooden benches.

'There are no stars in this production, Wolf,' they heard her snap. 'And that includes playwrights!'

Moving in a semi-circle, they crept out through the door they had previously entered, nipped swiftly downstairs and made straight for the green room. It was deserted. Mr Beauvoisin marched towards the paint-splattered sink and picked up a bottle labelled *Polyclean*.

'We've found our first job,' he announced, dropping his case and unscrewing the lid. 'Time to take off our coats and roll up our sleeves, young Joseph.'

They had hardly finished cleaning and scrubbing it when a tall, lean young man strode into the room. He stared at them in astonishment.

'Hello! Who are you? And what are you doing up here?'

'Volunteers,' said Mr Beauvoisin quickly. 'We've cleaned the sink.'

The man's face broke into a smile.

'Wonderful! I can honestly say that is not one of my favourite jobs.'

'So is there anything else you would like us to do?'

As if the two men could read each other's minds, they swung round and glanced at the unwashed crockery heaped on a nearby table.

'You don't fancy washing sixteen cups while I nip out and buy some tea and milk, would you?'

'Consider it half done,' said Mr Beauvoisin gallantly.

'And if you're keen to learn another job the actors do, I

would be very happy to teach it to you later.'

'Pulling up the curtain?' Mr Beauvoisin asked.

'Nothing so easy. Getting the boiler in the basement going. From next week it needs to be lit one hour before the show starts, to warm up the auditorium.'

As soon as the young man had disappeared, Mr Beauvoisin lit the gas ring and placed a kettle of water on it.

After the cups had been washed in the newly scrubbed sink, he whipped the tea towel he had found hanging beside the gas ring and handed it to Josie. Together they worked with speed and precision. And then Mr Beauvoisin began to laugh.

'What's so funny?' she asked.

'I was thinking of my stepmother. She dissuaded me from joining the acting profession, which is why I ended up being a barrister. She warned me that if I became an actor I would end up always being given the role of a mindless servant, and here I am washing up and cleaning.'

'You've got a *stepmother*!'

'Yes.'

'Really?'

'Yes, really.'

'Is she a wicked stepmother?'

He threw back his head and laughed.

'Extremely wicked. Which is why my father married her.'

'Because she was evil?'

'No! Naughty wicked, not bad wicked. She was a rebel. Still is. She ran away to Paris where she met and fell in love with him.'

'But you're not being a servant. All the actors take turns helpin' out here. That's what Ralph told . . .' She was about to add, *my sister, Elsie.* 'Me.'

'I know. It just tickled my funny bone.' He peered down at her, an eyebrow raised. 'So, young Joseph, are you going to tell me why you're in this country without your parents?'

Josie looked hurriedly away.

'My last school in Cyprus had a few days off for half-term at the beginning of this week. My parents are sending me to a new school here in England but my new school has their half-term at the end of this week and . . .'

She trailed off and kept her eyes averted. He was such a kind man that she was ashamed of lying to him. Once Ralph arrived, he would explain everything to him and that would make it all right. Until then she did not want to bring the outside world into the theatre.

'So your parents will have no idea that you're missing?'

'No. They're still on a ship on their way here.' She began drying another cup vigorously, her hands shaking. 'You said you were going to tell me where you came from,' she added hurriedly.

'Ah, yes. My great-grandparents were African. They were kidnapped too. They were taken to America and sold as slaves.'

Josie was shocked. 'Did they escape?'

'No. One of their daughters, my grandmother, married a man who had gone out to America to settle. He was French.'

'Did they catch the kidnappers?'

'They didn't try. They were allowed to carry on

kidnapping people from Africa then. Lots of people did it.'

'They were *allowed* to do it?' she said in disbelief. 'But why?'

'Because they didn't think black people had the same rights as other human beings.'

'But that's not true!' protested Josie angrily.

'I know, but that's how people thought then.' He sighed. 'Sadly there are many who still think that way.'

'Are they still kidnapping African people now?'

'No. Later some people demanded that they stopped doing it and eventually the slaves were freed. Luckily for my grandmother, my grandfather was a good man. He treated her well. My father was their only child. My grandfather was a very cultured man and paid for him to have tutors as a boy. He was even taught to play the piano.'

'But I still don't understand how you got to England, Mr Beauvoisin.'

'It all started with segregation. Do you know what segregation means?'

'No.'

'It means the separation of black people and coloureds from the white people. Up until then my father was used to mixing with white people, especially at musical gatherings. But because he was coloured – that's a mixture of black and white. Not grey,' he added wryly. 'Brown.'

'Oh!' interrupted Josie. 'That's what it means!'

'Yes. So because he was brown, his parents had to move from their big house into a tiny place in the poorer area where the black people lived. My father wasn't allowed to mix with white people any more, including his friends. They even had whites-only buses for white people and separate buses for blacks and coloureds.'

'But that's silly,' Josie exclaimed.

'I agree and very sad. He was pretty upset but he had his music and gradually he and his other classical musician friends began to listen to the music the poorer black people were playing. It was called blues. And then they began to play together but without written music.'

'Why?'

'They couldn't get hold of any.'

'But how could they play without it?' asked Josie.

'They listened to one another and improvised. And out of these musical conversations came a new kind of music, jazz.'

'But how did you become French?'

'During the First World War, my father joined the army and was posted to France. The white soldiers had their own units and the blacks and coloureds had their units. When they were on leave, his unit went to Paris. The Parisians treated the men from his unit well and let him play the piano *anywhere*. My father was so impressed with the city that he vowed that somehow he would return and raise his children there. He didn't want them to grow up in a place where there was segregation. After he married my mother, who was black, he persuaded her to come with him to France. She wasn't too happy about it at first but they smuggled themselves onboard a ship . . . But that's another story.'

'And they managed to reach Paris?'

'Yes, and I was born there in 1929. My mother died ten months later. After a few years, my father met and married my stepmother, an upper class English girl.'

'Posh,' said Josie.

'Very posh.'

'Is that where you got your way of speaking?'

He laughed. 'I suppose so, and from her family too.'

'Did they live in Paris?'

'No. She took me away to England when I was eleven years old.'

'Why?'

'Because the Germans had marched into France. My father was concerned that, being English, my stepmother would be arrested. He asked her to take me with her. He was concerned for my safety too. We managed to get out of France on one of the last boats to leave'

'And your father?'

He shook his head.

'He was killed while I was in England. I stayed and was educated here but after the war my stepmother encouraged me to keep up my French. She used to try to take me to France every year. She loved it there. Eventually I moved back, did my National Service in the French Army, returned to Paris where I saw the Theatre Workshop Company perform and here I am.' He smiled. 'How are those cups coming along?'

By the time the young man returned, Josie and Mr Beauvoisin

had set out the pristine cups onto the tray and, like a dancer, he swept off with them filled with freshly brewed tea for the cast.

It was as Josie was staring, puzzled at a ladder on one of the walls, that a voice from behind her made her swing round. It was the young woman they had met in the wardrobe.

'It goes up to the prop room,' she explained. 'Mr Beauvoisin, have either of you eaten?'

'No. I have a minor problem.'

'Money?'

'I have a little in pounds, shillings and pence but the rest is in francs and I haven't been able to change them into English currency yet.'

'Oh. Pity you don't have a cheque book.'

'I do.'

'Why don't you cash a cheque in a shop then?'

'Because every time I've tried, the shopkeepers have found it impossible to believe that a person of my hue could possibly have a bank account.'

'That's ridiculous. Look, there's a café that we all use near her. Come with me and I'll ask Bert about it.'

'Bert?'

'Bert Scaqelli. He and his wife May run Café L'Ange.'

'Ah yes, I know it. He's Italian, then, not French?'

'No. Cockney. Why?'

'The sign above it.'

'Oh.' She shrugged. 'I don't know anything about that. Anyway Bert might know where you can change your francs. He's probably seen every kind of money in his café. He might even cash your cheque for you. It's worth a try.'

'The Angel café!' Josie whispered, remembering how she and Mr Beauvoisin had peered through its windows the night before. She wanted to ask him if he thought it would be safe for her to go there in daylight but he was too busy talking to Annette.

# 7

# Waiting for Ralph

WITH DAYLIGHT FILTERING IN, IT WAS A shock to discover that the corridor, with its sumptuous dark red walls and mirrors high above her head, was the same black tunnel she and Mr Beauvoisin had run down less than twenty-four hours earlier.

The three of them manoeuvred their way past a woman who was on her knees scrubbing cream, black and burgundy floor tiles and volunteers busily touching up corners and cracks in the walls with tiny paintbrushes. From the downstairs bar came the sound of laughter and hammering. Mr Beauvoisin and Annette strode on ahead, talking non-stop.

They passed the box office, pushed open the second pair of double doors and stepped out under the arched entrance. Josie glanced round swiftly. To her alarm, her knees suddenly felt weak. They headed for the corner that turned into Angel Lane, where they found the stalls still empty.

'Fruit and vegetable market,' announced the young woman, 'but not on a Monday. Wait till you see it tomorrow. That is, if you want to come back.'

A gust of wind caused Josie to lose her balance. She raised

her hood to hide her face and peered out from beneath it at the shoppers, checking that Scowler and Moustache weren't lurking amongst them, but all she saw were women and small children. Head bowed, she remained close to Mr Beauvoisin.

'Bert's home-cured ham and his roast beef are very popular round here,' said the young woman as they stepped into the smoky café. Josie glanced at the mottled-marble-topped tables, the mirrors on the walls, the piles of tiny tins and long, narrow jars neatly stacked on the shelves. Bert was a friendly man with white hair and black-rimmed glasses. He was handing large mugs of tea over a counter to two men in raincoats and caps. The young woman introduced Mr Beauvoisin to him.

'So you're one of them actors,' Bert said, giving him a nod. Before Mr Beauvoisin could deny it, Bert was explaining that the actors and actresses from the Theatre Royal often ate 'on tick' and paid him back a week later when they had received their wages.

'My money problems are temporarily solved,' said Mr Beauvoisin as they sat – in a corner away from any prying eyes from outside, Josie noted. 'He's cashed a cheque for me.'

In only minutes it seemed, poached eggs on toast were on their way to their table. Josie hurriedly began eating.

'Some of the cast are loving Joan's way of rehearsing,' said Annette as she and Mr Beauvoisin resumed their conversation. 'There's an old comedian called Wally Patch who's really throwing himself into it. Harry and Marjie give him lifts to and from the theatre in their car and he has them in fits with his stories about his years working in the Denham film studios.'

Josie remained silent. The more invisible she made herself, she thought, the more they wouldn't mind her being with them.

'And there's another comedian who plays an American dealer. Italian name. Spinetti or something. *Victor* Spinetti. And Sheila Hancock and Roy Kinnear. Marjie and Harry say they're really good.'

After they had finished eating, they stepped back into Angel Lane and into the rain. Josie noticed that the iron gate across the road was now unlocked. They said their goodbyes to the young woman as she swung her bag over her shoulder and headed for the Tube station. Josie began to feel sick. Outside in the open air, she felt cornered and it was difficult to breathe. She was sure that once they were inside the theatre she would be able to breathe more easily again.

Back in the green room they discovered a group of volunteers with tins of distemper, keen to finish redecorating it by the following week.

Mr Beauvoisin and Josie returned downstairs to help polish the brass on the door handles and the handrails on the red stairways. Josie stood on a chair to remove the grease and grime trapped in the corners of the windows at the top of the doors that led to the bar. Through the glass she could see a narrow room with a heavy door at one end. Mr Beauvoisin was cleaning the wide-arched windows above it. The windows looked oddly familiar. She watched him glance out through them and then he waved at her. She climbed down and poked her head into the bar.

'These windows,' he said, 'do you remember where else you saw them?'

She shook her head.

'The so-called jewellery shop.'

It was the door they had spotted through the locked gate next to the bakery.

Josie was alarmed.

'Does that mean that people can walk in from Angel Lane?'

'No. The door can only be opened from the inside. They can only walk *out* from here to the lane. It's to stop people from trying to get in after the pubs close at ten-thirty, when there are still people drinking in the theatre bar.'

*That's good*, Josie thought. It meant that the only way Scowler and Moustache could get to her would be through the double doors near the box office, and only if she was in the foyer.

'Once they leave, the iron grating is pulled across and locked,' Mr Beauvoisin said.

Josie also learned from eavesdropping on conversations amongst the helpers that it was a private bar where the actors and members of the audience would often hang around after a performance and have a drink together. This was useful information for Mr Beauvoisin if he planned to stay the night again. It meant that after the show there would still be people in the theatre. The last Tube for the West End, she had overheard, left at eleven-fifteen so he would need to stay out of sight until after they had left the theatre and it had been locked up.

She also began to pick up the names of the people who worked regularly in the building as they called out to one another.

'He'll be in tonight,' she had repeated to Mr Beauvoisin when one of the actors came in to help and she had to explain yet again that he wasn't Ralph. She knew he would arrive for the evening's performance of *The Hostage* after the *Make Me An Offer* rehearsals were over. She would then tell him everything and after he had made a few phone calls, she guessed she would be picked up by the police during his performance and taken to a police station to face the music. Until that moment, she was determined to make the most of being with friendly people. She remembered Elsie telling her that when an actor or actress stepped through a stage door into a theatre, they had to leave their other life outside. It worked during her rehearsals in Winford and it was working inside the Theatre Royal. She began to envy Mr Beauvoisin for being able to stay.

As the evening drew nearer, the *Make Me An Offer* cast didn't appear to be leaving and it was then that she realised that *The Hostage* must have ended, and that Elsie had forgotten to tell her. That explained why a new production was being rehearsed. Eventually, Mr Beauvoisin spoke the words she had been dreading to hear.

'It doesn't look as though Ralph is going to turn up, does it?' he said. 'You'd better phone him after I've bought some bread, eggs and soup.'

'Do we have to go outside again?' she asked.

'I'm afraid so.'

There was a telephone box near the Underground station. Mr Beauvoisin waited outside, his hands filled with groceries while Josie stood numbly inside its walls. She bowed her head. It was all over. Once Mr Beauvoisin saw that she wasn't dialling he would call the police and she would have to face her parents, the school and her patrol. 'You have disgraced everyone,' she could hear them yelling at her. Larry, by now, would have been told she had lied to him, she would be chucked out of the Guides and never be able to go camping or sailing and . . .

At which point Mr Beauvoisin opened the door.

'You don't know his number, do you?'

She shook her head.

'Then we need to contact the police.'

'But my parents' ship will be here on Sunday,' she protested. 'Can't I stay with you until then?'

'No. This woman who was supposed to have met you might be in danger.'

Josie remembered her mother telling her that life was far less complicated if you were honest and told the truth. Once you had told one lie it would only lead to another and then you would have to keep telling more lies until you wouldn't be able to remember the lies you had told at the beginning. Josie now understood what she had meant.

'Oh, her. She's always wanderin' off. And I'm used to lookin' after meself. Please don't phone the police.'

'I was thinking *you* should do that.'

She shook her head wildly. She was finding it difficult to breathe again and it scared her. *Please let's go back to the theatre*, she begged him inside her head. *I'll be safer there.*

'The police would lock me up till my mum and dad got here.'

'No they wouldn't. They'd find somewhere for you to stay until they found Ralph.'

'But what if they can't find him and he turns up at the theatre and I'm not there? Please let me stay with you.'

Mr Beauvoisin gave her a piercing look.

'There's something else that's frightening you, isn't there?'

Josie remained silent.

'And you'd rather tell your parents than the police, is that it?'

She nodded.

'I see.' He paused. 'In that case, I shall continue to be your guardian until Ralph turns up, or failing that, your parents when they return on Sunday. Where are they to meet you?'

'At the school where I was supposed to be taken to by this woman.'

'On a Sunday?'

Josie could have kicked herself for telling such a stupid lie.

'Ah. It's a boarding school,' Mr Beauvoisin said.

'Yeah,' said Josie with relief.

'But I can take you there myself, tomorrow.'

'There won't be anyone there. It's half-term,' Josie added quickly.

'Oh yes. Of course it is. But we can't stay at the theatre. I need to find some temporary lodgings, which I'm afraid will necessitate many telephone enquiries and I doubt we have that many pennies between us.'

'There's a phone in the office upstairs in the theatre. I 'eard these people talkin' about it. It's on the same floor as the green room.'

'Mm. Not the sort of behaviour I would usually condone,' he said quietly. 'But in this instance I'm afraid it's a case of *Needs Must*.'

After Mr Beauvoisin had taken down details of landlords and landladies who advertised rooms to let on cards stuck on the windows of local shops, they returned to the theatre, nipped upstairs, ran past the green room and turned the corner into another corridor on their right. The door to the office was open.

They were in luck. It was empty. Josie stood on guard at the corner. She was to whistle a tune if she spotted anyone approaching. Occasionally, she ran back to eavesdrop but could tell from the expression on Mr Beauvoisin's face that all the places he had phoned were full. And then the tone of his voice changed and he was smiling at her and waving.

'That sounds most accommodating,' he was saying into the receiver. 'Why thank you, Mrs Nelson. Mrs Nelson, before we have the pleasure of introducing ourselves to one another, I think I ought to point out that in addition to the gentlemanly demeanour you have so kindly referred to, it might be prudent of me to mention that both my mother's parents were African. And they weren't white settlers. They were in fact . . .' He paused. 'That is correct, Mrs Nelson . . . I beg your pardon? Do you mean am I more Cadbury's Milk than dark Mint Choc? More Nestlé's Milky Bar than a sophisticated . . . ?' Josie watched him replace the receiver. 'She hung up,' he explained.

'Why were you talking about chocolate?' asked Josie.

'She wanted to know how dark I was. I suppose if I were more brown than black it would have made me a more desirable lodger, or vice-versa. She made up her own mind before I could discover her preference.'

Josie laughed.

'It's no laughing matter, young Joseph, we've lost yet another place. This evening's accommodation will have to be here again, I'm afraid.'

'Turn that light off,' they heard a man yell. 'We're not made of money.'

'Sorry, Gerry,' came a voice from the green room. 'It gets a bit dark in here sometimes.'

'Footsteps,' said Josie suddenly. 'Quick!'

They moved swiftly down the corridor. Turning the corner, they came face to face with a handsome bear-like man with dark, wavy hair, and a pipe stuck in his mouth. He was so big, observed Josie that she reckoned he could have picked her up in one hand and dangled her in the air.

'Hello! What are you doing here?'

'We've just come from the office,' explained Mr Beauvoisin. 'We're looking for someone called Gerry.'

'Well, you've found him.'

'Splendid,' said Mr Beauvoisin, smiling. 'We would like

your permission to be volunteers. I hope you don't mind, but while we've been waiting for an opportunity to meet you we've helped out a little already. My name is Mr Beauvoisin and this is a neighbour's son, Joseph.'

'Why aren't you at school?' asked Gerry.

'Half-term,' said Josie.

He took a few puffs on his pipe while scrutinising them and then nodded.

'Thank you,' said Mr Beauvoisin. 'You won't regret it, I assure you.'

He gave them a brief wave. As soon as he headed for the office, Josie and Mr Beauvoisin darted past the green room and headed for the gallery.

Crawling between the benches, they stopped and glanced down at the stage. The two women who played Gwen and Sally were standing by the park bench and peering out into the stalls.

'Monty!' they heard Miss Littlewood yell from somewhere in the theatre. 'Sheila needs a song here during the scene change!'

They quickly made for the wardrobe. Once there, they shoved the food and milk beside one of the sewing machines and tiptoed to the door that led to the stage right flies. Beneath them they could hear a private conversation between Miss Littlewood and the man called Wally.

'It's this line. I can't make sense of it,' they could hear him say.

'Well, change it, Wally.'

'Change what?' cried a male voice from the auditorium.

There was the sound of approaching footsteps.

'I suspect that's the writer Wolf Mankowitz speaking,' said Mr Beauvoisin.

'A line,' answered Miss Littlewood.

'Mine?' the voice from the auditorium asked.

'Who knows?' she said.

'Well, he's not changing it,' he protested angrily.

'I think they're about to have an argument,' whispered Mr Beauvoisin.

It was at this juncture that he placed the palms of his hands firmly over Josie's ears. Josie guessed that the air was turning blue. Eventually he removed them just as Miss Littlewood stepped out centre stage. Now Josie could see her clearly. She was wearing a pleated skirt that reached her calves, a matching jacket, a white blouse done up to the collar and a woolly hat. It was difficult for Josie to believe that this woman, who was now throwing back her head and laughing between taking drags from the cigarette she was holding between her long, slim fingers, was the same woman who only minutes previously had been yelling angrily at the playwright.

'She looks as though she has enough energy for the entire company,' Josie heard Mr Beauvoisin murmur.

# 8

# Into the Shadows
# and Into the Light

W HILE JOSIE WAS SPYING ON THE CAST OF *Make Me An Offer*, two plainclothes detectives and her aunt were seated in Mr and Mrs Carpenter's sitting room.

'It's important this kidnapper still believes he has Larry,' the detective sergeant emphasised. 'If he should discover he's kidnapped the wrong child . . .'

'He might hurt Josie,' Auntie Win finished for him.

'Exactly.'

'Her parents are desperate to come up to London. You can imagine what a state they're in.'

'That really wouldn't help their daughter.'

'Are you going to tell the newspapers?' asked Mr Carpenter.

'No. That might anger the kidnapper. We must wait until he calls back tonight. We also need to find out how he obtained your phone number.'

'He probably looked it up,' said Mr Carpenter.

'There are rather a lot of Carpenters in the telephone directory. He would need to know your address.'

Mrs Carpenter looked alarmed.

'As I said,' continued the detective sergeant, 'it's important we let him still believe he's kidnapped Larry. The heads at both Larry and Molly's schools must be told that they are unable to attend lessons because they have mumps. And Larry and Molly must be led to believe that they have to stay at home because a pupil at both their schools has the same illness. We'll inform Miss Merryweather not to let Larry's school know what's happened.'

'But what about Miss Dagleish?' asked Auntie Win. 'Miss Merryweather telephoned her yesterday and told her that both Larry and Josie had gone missing. Should we let Miss Merryweather know that Larry has been found?'

'No. The fewer people who know, the better,' said the detective sergeant. 'We'll continue to let her think that it's just Larry that's missing. Miss Dagleish is to tell Miss Merryweather and her staff that Josie's parents decided to take her home for the weekend after the show without informing Miss Merryweather. Once Josie arrived home, her mother was taken seriously ill and she now needs to look after her while her father is at work. We have emphasised that we do not want Miss Merryweather to discover the truth. We can't risk her giving anything away.' He paused. 'As we know, she's one of several people who know this address, as does Miss Dagleish and the ASM called Fiona who visited here. And of course there's the theatre management in Winford who have employed Elsie. Any one of them could have inadvertently given the address to this man, or been followed.'

'It's too horrible to think about,' said Mrs Carpenter. 'He

might be watching the house at this very moment.'

'I can assure you, Mrs Carpenter, that the only man watching this house is one of ours.'

The rehearsals had continued late into the evening. Miss Littlewood had worked for three hours with two of the actresses who were playing tiny parts. Josie couldn't understand why she was encouraging them to improvise and play strange games when they had hardly anything to say until Mr Beauvoisin reminded her that Miss Littlewood treated each role with equal importance.

Finally they overheard someone offering the actresses a lift home. Mr Beauvoisin closed the door above the stage and they backed into the wardrobe.

'What time is it now?' she whispered.

'Half past twelve. You'll have to clean your teeth in the Gents.'

'But that's right on the other side of the theatre,' she protested. *And I'm a girl*, she added inside her head. But of course she didn't say that. She had managed to get away with sneaking into the Ladies all day.

'Can't I use the sink in the green room?'

'I think there are people still in there.'

'Don't they ever go home?' asked Josie crossly.

'You can talk!' he exclaimed. He sighed. 'I'll put toothpaste on one of your fingers and you'll have to rub it on dry.'

Josie held out her forefinger.

Later, tucked up in one of the camp beds, she listened to

voices coming from the stage accompanied by the sounds of sawing, and found it strangely comforting.

'It doesn't look as though the kidnapper is going to call tonight,' said the detective sergeant. 'I suggest you go to bed.'

Mr Carpenter nodded. 'I still think you should warn Henry,' he said. 'This kidnapper might go after him next.'

'The police in Scotland are keeping a close eye on him.'

'But why hasn't this man rung back?' Mrs Carpenter asked.

The detective sergeant said nothing.

After he had been seen to the door, Bill Carpenter turned to his wife.

'Do you think we should have told him about that photograph Henry took nine years ago?'

'But that can't have anything to do with this man,' she said. 'There were two of them, remember? And they're both safely locked up.'

'Perhaps you're right. But I wish we didn't have to lie about Josie to Larry and Molly.'

'Me too, but I think it's for the best.' She took him gently by the arm. 'Let's try and get *some* sleep.'

Over the next few days, Josie would only venture out when she and Mr Beauvoisin visited the café. The rest of the time she helped the volunteers downstairs. One of them, a stout red-faced woman called Mrs P, who lived locally, was always popping in to give a helping hand but was really there because she was dying to know what was going on. On spotting the two of them cleaning and polishing, she had assumed they had met one another at the theatre, had taken a shine to them and brought them home-made cakes and cups of tea.

Everyone was growing more excited as the opening night of *Make Me An Offer* approached. There were to be some important people attending it and they wanted to be sure that the old theatre looked spick and span.

When she wasn't helping, Josie would sneak up to the wardrobe and nose around. Underneath piles of boots she discovered an enormous basket filled with Elizabethan costumes, khaki uniforms, waistcoats and huge cloaks made from dyed blankets. She draped one of the cloaks over her camp bed. There were boxes filled with hats, velvet caps with large feathers for women, flat caps, straw hats and trilbies for men, and in one particular box, a lion suit.

'*Androcles and the Lion*,' she said, reading the label.

She closed the lid and collected every scrap of material that littered the floor. It was an oddly soothing occupation and amongst the mess she recovered lost pairs of scissors and reels of cotton. When the floor was clear, an actor appeared out of the blue and swept it through. With all the mess gone it made her feel light-headed, as though, in the act of getting rid of all the tiny bits and pieces, it had removed a weight from her shoulders.

Mr Beauvoisin popped his head round the door, donned a pair of overalls he had hauled out from one of the boxes and produced a large plunger.

'Where are you going with that?' she asked as he strode towards the door.

'I'm setting out to remove whatever it is that has expired in the gents' lavatory. I would invite you to join me but I think you would need a gas mask.'

'Do you really think there's something dead in there?' asked Josie in alarm.

'No. But if I don't attend to whatever is causing the overpowering stench in the immediate and foreseeable future, I fear it could result in a death. Anything else you'd like to say to me before I venture into the unknown with my trusty weapon?'

'No,' she said, smiling.

'Yes. It's not a very enhancing subject for a conversation. Here goes!' He held the plunger high above his head and swooped out of the room. 'I may be gone for some time!'

The following day there was still no sign of Ralph but Josie was determined to stay put, even though she knew that the longer she remained in hiding, the more trouble she would be in when he finally did appear. The Theatre Royal was a safe cocoon where the happiness of the inhabitants enveloped her like a warm hug. She knew it was only temporary but she wanted to make the most of it while it lasted before being at the receiving end of so many people's anger.

She preferred to spy on the rehearsals from the gallery but it was too risky because she never knew when Miss Littlewood might suddenly appear there. At times the music was so jaunty that she had to retreat hurriedly to the wardrobe so that she could dance around the sewing machines. A new song, *It's Sort of Romantic*, had been given to the actress called Sheila. It wasn't a very long one but it was her favourite because of the way she sang it. The actress was so funny that Josie had to put her hand over her mouth to stop herself from laughing.

It was a wonderful world to hide in. If this was what Mrs Havilland called picking up bad habits, then she would pick up as many as she could before she had to return to school. Even Miss Littlewood's occasional angry outbursts ceased to shake Josie so badly because one moment she would explode in a flash and the next she would be chatting cheerily to the very person she had earlier been insulting.

It was on her fourth day of hiding, when she and Mr Beauvoisin had been sitting in the café, that she was flung violently back into the world she had so successfully shut out. Seated at another table were Harry, Marjie, Sheila, Roy and four members of the cast pouring over the latest *Stage*, much like Anthony and Desiree used to do. They had become quite heated over an article concerning performers who took over roles in the West End but who were neither mentioned in the programmes nor by the critics.

'It's disgraceful!' Sheila was saying. 'They did that in *West Side Story*, didn't they?'

And suddenly Josie was in Her Majesty's Theatre with Auntie Win and Hilda.

'Joseph? Are you all right?' asked Mr Beauvoisin.

'Yeah,' she said hurriedly. 'I just got somethin' sharp in my eye.'

\* \* \*

Auntie Win held the door open for Mrs Jenkins and forced herself to smile.

'Thanks for lending me another *Maigret* story, Winifred. I'll see you again for *No Hiding Place*.' She gave her a sympathetic look. 'You're missing young Josie, aren't you?'

'I'm afraid so.'

'Me too. Cheer up. I'm sure your sister will recover soon and she'll be back with us in no time.'

Auntie Win nodded. She hated having to deceive her friend.

Hardly had she closed the door when the telephone rang. She ran down the hallway and snatched up the receiver.

'Hello,' said a young voice at the other end.

'Oh, hello, Hilda,' said Auntie Win, attempting to hide her disappointment.

'Is Josie back yet?'

'I'm afraid not.'

'She hasn't answered my letter.'

'I don't expect she's had time.'

'Could you give me her parents' phone number? I won't keep her talking for very long, I promise.'

'Nothing has changed, I'm afraid. I've been given strict instructions not to give it to anyone. I'm so sorry, Hilda.'

'She will be coming back, won't she?'

Auntie Win could detect the anxiety in her voice.

'Of course she will,' she said firmly.

'Oh good. I've so much to tell her.'

As Winifred replaced the receiver she whispered to herself, 'Please don't let her be hurt.'

The telephone rang again. This time it was Josie's mother, and she was crying.

'Oh, Ellen,' Win murmured. 'I'm so sorry. There's still no news.'

Mrs P handed Mr Beauvoisin two tiny pieces of card.

'For October nineteenth, ducks,' she said.

'Tickets!' he exclaimed. 'For the opening night!'

'I knew you'd wanna be there. One of the cleaners spotted you two watchin' from the gallery. Don't worry,' she added, tapping the side of her nose, 'she 'asn't told Joan. There'd be fireworks from her if she ever found out. But I wouldn't risk watchin' it from there any longer, what wiv the show openin' on Mondee.' She leaned over Josie. 'Which is a good fing because by then, young man, you will have had your Sundee barf. Your ears and neck are beginnin' to look like you've been wrestling with a mud pie.' She glanced at Mr Beauvoisin. ''ave a word with his mum, will you?'

Josie felt herself reddening.

'But how on earth did you manage to obtain these?' he asked.

'I knows the box office lady. And that's all I'm sayin'. Ask me no questions and I'll tell you no lies.'

Heartbroken, Josie waited for Mr Beauvoisin to tell Mrs P that she wouldn't be around on Monday but to her surprise he said nothing.

As soon as they were out of earshot on the stairs leading up to the dress circle, she blurted out, 'Are you going to let me stay?'

'It's not up to me, Joseph. It's up to your parents.'

'But they're at sea,' said Josie, examining her feet.

'Are they now?' he said quietly. 'I thought you said they would be here on Sunday.'

'If they arrive on time. Those ships are always being held up.'

This was followed by an awkward silence

'And I've just remembered something,' she said suddenly. 'There's this *boy* whose going to be startin' at the school, same time as me and his parents know mine. I can talk to him and then his parents can tell my parents where I am when they get to the dock.'

Mr Beauvoisin's eyebrows shot up.

'Are you telling me there's someone you could have called earlier this week?'

Josie nodded.

'Joseph!' he exclaimed. 'You need to phone them instantly.'

But back inside the telephone box Josie was racking her brains for a number she could ring. And then it hit her. Hilda!

Slowly she began to dial, her hands shaking.

It was Hilda's mother who answered the phone. Josie pressed button A and the money jangled inside the telephone box. She turned her back to the door.

'Can I speak to Hilda, please, Mrs Martin?' she asked shakily.

'Yes, of course. Is that Josie speaking?'

'Yes, Mrs Martin.'

'Hilda will be so pleased you've called. She's just been speaking to your aunt. How's your mum?'

'Very well, thank you, Mrs Martin. I'm speaking from a telephone box so can Hilda come quickly please before the money runs out?'

Josie listened impatiently to her calling out to her.

'Hurry!' Josie whispered to herself.

'Josie!' yelled a familiar voice.

'H-hello, Hilda,' she stammered. 'Can you tell Auntie Win –?'

'Did you get my letter?' she interrupted.

'No. Hilda, could you –?'

'It must have got lost in the post. I knew there was a reason you hadn't answered it.'

'Hilda, this is very important –'

'Guess what!' she cried. 'I've been allowed to join some of the dance warm-ups before *West Side Story*! And two people in the cast are going to try to find out about dance classes for us. Jazz, they call it. I've got heaps to tell you –'

'Hilda,' said Josie in desperation, 'I've escaped!'

'I know. Lucky you. I wish I could. Mr Bennett is worse than ever. When do you think you're –?'

'Can you ring Auntie Win back and tell her?'

And then the money ran out and she was cut off. She held on to the receiver, pretending to listen while she made a quick calculation. She had to find a way of staying in the theatre a little longer. One more week of people being friendly to her would give her the will power to ask Mr

Beauvoisin to take her to a police station to face a ticking off, if Ralph still hadn't turned up.

It was only when she stepped out of the telephone box that it suddenly occurred to her that Hilda hadn't been angry with her for making Larry stay all night alone in a skip. Was it possible that she didn't know? She had even sounded pleased to hear from Josie. What was even odder was that she hadn't asked Josie why she wasn't at school.

'Well?' said Mr Beauvoisin.

'My parents have been held up. Their ship hasn't arrived in England yet. They'll be back the Tuesday after next. They sent a telegram to my friend's parents. Good job I phoned 'em, eh? They're going to telegram my parents and tell 'em to come and pick me up at the theatre.'

'Joseph, why can't these people look after you?'

'They don't know me very well and anyway they're going away. But they've already let the school know I'm going to be a week late.'

'Do your parents usually send you ahead of them without any money?' asked Mr Beauvoisin.

'They gave it to the woman I was supposed to meet.'

'Perhaps that's why she disappeared.'

This was beginning to be even more complicated, thought Josie. The non-existent woman was now a thief!

She noticed that Mr Beauvoisin was staring at her.

'Why are you looking at me like that?' she asked nervously.

'Mrs P is right. I don't know why I didn't spot it before. You're filthy. It's soap and hot water for you. And I'll wash those trousers, shirt and jersey as well.'

'But what am I going to wear?'

'I noticed there are costumes for *A Christmas Carol* in the wardrobe. There are bound to be clothes for Tiny Tim. You can wear those while your clothes are drying on the boiler under the theatre.'

'All right. But not my underwear.'

'I'll second that. You've been wearing it so long that your school matron will probably have to burn it!'

'Can we leave now?' Josie asked, desperate to be back inside the safety of the theatre walls.

# 9

# The Opening

'HOW COME YOU CAN IRON CLOTHES, MR Beauvoisin?'

He had piled her shirt and jersey at the end of the ironing board and was pressing her trousers. It had taken two days for them to dry.

'In the army you're taught how to look after yourself. In all circumstances.'

She thought of her aunt, who had no patience when it came to ironing. Her dad was very rude about her domestic skills. He said that if it were possible to burn a salad, Auntie Win would find a way of doing it.

Mr Beauvoisin held up the pressed trousers.

'One garment down, two to go, *monsieur*,' he said, tossing them to her. 'I must say,' he said, surveying her scalp, 'I still can't get over the lighter shade of your hair. It's Titian now instead of mahogany.'

Josie wasn't going to ask him what he meant. The memory of standing by torchlight beside a steaming kettle while her scalp had been vigorously rubbed with a giant block of soap over the green room sink still lingered.

Once they had changed, they nipped downstairs to the foyer. Mr Beauvoisin had taken evening clothes from his suitcase and was looking like a proper gent with his white silk scarf, cuff links, waistcoat and a bow-tie under the stiff collar he had attached to his shirt. Josie spotted Mrs P waving to them at the end of the corridor, and they headed in her direction. She beamed at them, looking suitably impressed.

''aven't you both scrubbed up loverly,' she said, giving Mr Beauvoisin the once over. 'Borrowed from the wardrobe?' she asked, giving him a wink.

Josie was about to deny it when she felt Mr Beauvoisin's foot slowly pressing down on her toes.

'You have sharp eyes, Mrs P,' he said.

'Oh, I know. My Arthur says I'm like that lady what Agatha Christie writes abaht, that Miss Marbles. And you, Master Joseph! Your mum's done you proud. I 'ardly recognise you. Now I must love you and leave you, Mr B, cos I've brought a friend wiv me tonight and she ain't never bin to a theatre so she's a bit nervous. TTFN!'

Josie watched her approach a small, dumpy woman dressed to the nines in her Sunday best.

'Stick close to me,' said Mr Beauvoisin. 'I think there's going to be quite a crowd tonight.'

It was at that moment that Josie became aware of the outside world invading her sanctuary – and possibly bringing in danger. She grabbed one of his sleeves as they headed towards a group gathering outside the door to the stalls. Mrs P and her timid friend were now a little way ahead of them.

As Josie eavesdropped on the conversations in the queue

she was surprised to discover how many people sounded like her dad's family. The last time she had heard so many cockney accents in one place was when she was little. She used to stay with Gran in the holidays and pop round to see her aunts and uncles and cousins. That was before all the houses in their street were boarded up and the residents had moved to a new town and into newly built houses with indoor bathrooms.

'I dunno,' she heard Mrs P's friend whisper. 'This ain't for the likes of us.'

'I beg to differ, Mrs T,' said Mrs P. 'This is our theatre, this is. We got every right to be 'ere, same as anyone.'

'But take a look at that posh lot over there!' She jerked her head towards a group of men and women in evening dress.

'Oh, it's cos it's the first night, and some blokes from the newspapers are gonna write up stuff abaht it. I know fer a fact there's someone from the Stratford Express comin' tonight.'

'"ere,' she heard Mrs T say excitedly. 'Is that who I think it is?'

She was staring at a tall, handsome man in a long black coat.

'Yeah.'

'But 'e's famous!'

'So's she,' said Mrs P, pointing to a young woman with blond hair and a mink stole draped round her shoulders.

'She's never . . . ?'

'She is.'

'Mrs P, I don't think we should be 'ere.'

'Oh yes, we should,' she said, firmly linking arms with her friend.

Josie could feel the excitement bubbling up around her. Luckily, it was so crowded that she was completely hidden from anyone who might be on the look out for her.

'Why are them people carryin' rugs and hot water bottles?' she heard Mrs P's friend ask anxiously. 'Were we supposed to bring 'em wiv us?'

'Nah. I expect it's cos they're sitting dahn the front. The boiler only heats the auditorium when the safety curtain's dahn. As soon as it goes up, the poor so and sos sittin' close up gets hit by a blast from the stage that's as cold as flippin' Alaska.'

Once inside the stalls, Mr Beauvoisin and Josie followed the crowd up the main staircase. They passed the circle and carried on up the stairs towards the gallery, walked past the tiny gallery box office and took their place on the fourth bench from the front. There was no mistaking the identity of the woman with the woolly cap who sat in the middle of the front row with a notebook and pen.

'Miss Littlewood,' whispered Mr Beauvoisin to Josie. Josie nodded.

Sitting on the other side of Mr Beauvoisin were Mrs P and her friend, now engrossed in the programme.

'Look at this!' Josie heard her exclaim. 'Mrs Chambers, Mrs Parham, Mrs Snell and Mrs Woolmer. They're the cleaners 'ere and I know 'em all! I knows everyone 'ere. I knows the people behind the bar and Monica in box office and . . .'

Mr Beauvoisin winked at Josie. *Thank you, Monica*, he mouthed and Josie smiled. They now knew who had given Mrs P the tickets.

'But I better warn you,' Mrs P was saying, 'you won't be standing to attention at the end. They don't play the National Anthem 'ere.'

'You're jokin' ain't you? No *God Save the Queen*! That's shockin'!'

'No it ain't. It's only played for Her Majesty when she pops round.'

'Does she pop round 'ere?'

'Not regular like. But she's always very welcome. Anyways I 'ope you like it. It'll take you back to the Portobello Road without you havin' to take the tube.'

Josie peered down at the stage. All she could see was the safety curtain and the heads of the musicians as they tuned up their instruments. Since the conversation with Mrs P she hadn't dared watch any more of the rehearsals, what with people hanging lights, and painting pieces of the set in the stage right wings, and musicians attending the rehearsals. Instead, she had to make do with peering through a window in one of the doors into the stalls or sitting on the stairways, eavesdropping. This would be the first time she would see the whole story instead of bits of it in odd scenes. She sat forward and peered over the heads of the people in front of her, impatient for the show to begin.

The lights in the auditorium faded and the safety curtain rose. Josie gasped. There were no footlights!

She whispered frantically to Mr Beauvoisin who, from

the smile on his face, appeared not to have noticed.

'Watch carefully,' he whispered back. 'The Theatre Workshop Company have a completely different way of lighting their productions. I spotted it when they came to Paris.'

A light came up on a small, raised platform where a young couple in their nightclothes, Charlie and Sally, were having a heated conversation in the early hours of the morning. Josie guessed that the screen behind them was supposed to be the bedroom of their flat where their baby was sleeping. They argued and sang about how the large black pram filled their kitchen like a lodger. Josie was able to see their faces clearly because of the angle of the lights above and around them.

'*Charlie, ask Abe Sparta if we can keep the pram in his shed. Maybe that's a solution,*' said Sally.

The lights on their flat dimmed while other lights came up on areas of the stage where shoppers and dealers were now moving with energy across and around one another, shouting and singing about their wares. It was as though Josie was watching a film, with one scene melting into another.

'*Come'n have a gander*

'*At the Portobello Road,*' they sang, flooding across the stage.

'*Buy yourself a bargain*

'*In the Portobello Road.*'

A man was pushing an ancient pram from which saucepan lids and jewellery were hanging. He parked it firmly in a spot downstage as though it were his regular pitch. A big, tubby man was following him with a suitcase that appeared to be stuck to a small table.

*'Here's a classy load of gear*
*'It's just your cup of tea.'*

The man unfolded the table and opened the suitcase, pulling out fluffy toys and balloons. The shoppers moved around to take a look, the dealers lifting up china pots for them to examine. There were no stagehands, Josie observed. The cast, as they had done in rehearsal, moved everything themselves.

One dealer put a colander, filled with flowers on his head and posed for a customer. It was whisked from person to person until it reached the tall actress at the end of a line who played Gwen. She stuck a broom in it and held it aloft. The dealers gesticulated and did comic turns singing, *'Make me an offer,'* as the shoppers milled round them, feeling and examining their wares, some peering with concentration, others mildly inquisitive or shiftily, as though they were up to no good, while a couple of American tourists seemed overwhelmed by it all.

Charlie appeared, pushing a barrow with pieces of ornate blue and white pottery on it.

Gwen looked straight out at the audience. *'Here's Charlie,'* she said. *'I'm mad about him. He's a dish, look at them curls.'* And she began sweeping the ground near him, making unsuccessful attempts at catching his eye.

It was as though, in seconds, Portobello Market was in front of Josie's eyes, but not because there was fancy scenery, but because of the way the actors moved around one another.

It was the final number of the last act. Sally and Charlie, the dealers and the rest of the cast were pouring onto the stage to cheers from the stalls to the gallery.

'*Pinch the opera glasses, dear,*' sang out one of the dealers to the audience, '*but leave the seats behind.*'

'*Make me an offer!*' they sang lustily, throwing their arms with punching gestures into the air.

Josie grinned up at Mr Beauvoisin who was laughing.

'*Magnifique!*' he exclaimed.

'So what d'you think, Mrs T?' they heard Mrs P say to her friend.

'I ain't seen nuffin' like it! Oh, can't we see it again?'

Josie and Mr Beauvoisin followed the audience downstairs, where they found the bar tightly packed, the locals squashed up together with the upper classes from the West End.

The remaining theatre-goers were sweeping down the foyer, out through the main doors and heading for the Tube station. Mr Beauvoisin beckoned Josie to follow him. Outside, they walked briskly along the pavement to the door that led into the long corridor where the flats were painted: the scene dock. Moving swiftly down it, they stumbled into the stage right wings. Mr Beauvoisin gripped Josie's hand and guided her onto the stage. The safety curtain was down again and it was pitch black. Eventually, they reached the stage left wings and peered out to check that the coast was clear. The lights were ablaze and there was laughter coming from the green room.

They leaped up the stairs and headed for the now empty gallery.

Stumbling into the wardrobe, tripping over boxes and colliding into hanging garments, Josie felt a peace as powerful as coming home.

They squinted through the mottled windows, listening to the members of the audience that were still milling about in the street.

'Isn't it strange how things happen?' murmured Mr Beauvoisin. 'If I hadn't chosen that particular bank to try to change my money, I wouldn't have been chased by those Teddy boys and I wouldn't have been in that alley and seen you running away from those men.'

'Why did you pull me into that porch?' Josie asked.

'They would have caught you otherwise. And you looked terrified.' He smiled. 'Never for one moment did I dream that it would lead me to this theatre and I would be present at the opening night of one of Joan Littlewood's productions!'

The people who worked in the downstairs bar were delighted to see them again the next morning. Mr Beauvoisin picked up the glasses and washed them up while Josie emptied the ashtrays and picked up cigarette butts off the floor. Local people kept putting their noses round the door, full of talk about the new show.

The cast returned for notes, voice and movement warm-ups and improvisations in preparation for the evening show. Mr Beauvoisin, Josie noticed, no longer mentioned Ralph. She suspected it was because he didn't believe he existed.

It was a few days later, when they were sitting hidden away in their usual corner in the café, that she remembered the package in her coat pocket. She pulled it out.

'What's that?' Mr Beauvoisin asked.

'It's stuff to stick on models to make it look like winter.'

'But that's a sugar bag.'

Josie shrugged. 'Well, it's not sugar.'

As she shoved it back into her pocket, she heard Marjie Lawrence reading from *The Stage*.

'*A triumph of imagination and ingenuity,*' she announced.

'It's a review,' whispered Mr Beauvoisin. 'And it sounds like a good one.'

'Sheila has a good mention,' they heard Harry Greene say. '*Extremely amusing as a woman left on the shelf.*'

Josie remembered how the audience had loved her new song, how they made her sing it again and again, shouting, '*Encore! More!*' until eventually she had yelled back, '*There bloody well isn't any more!*' before Mr Beauvoisin had been able to slap the palms of his hands over Josie's ears. '*He hasn't written any more! Shove off! We've got to get on with the show!*' Which had caused the whole house, including Josie to collapse with laughter.

'Wally's got a good one too and Dilys and . . .'

In an instant, Josie was flung back to dressing room seven after her first performance in *Life With Father*. Larry's face was covered in a mess of make-up and removing cream with his arms outstretched, pretending to be a Martian visiting Planet Greasepaint. But it was like a dream. She knew she was still Josie, but when she looked back at the girl who had played a boy called Whitney who loved baseball, it was as though it had happened to a completely different person.

# 10

# Half-truths

IT WAS ODD THAT JOSIE HADN'T MENTIONED her mother's illness, thought Hilda, and that she was calling from a telephone box. Maybe she was out shopping for her mum and was in a hurry to get back home. Hilda had been meaning to pass on Josie's message to her aunt for days but what with reading her library books coupled with the excitement of being allowed to join the back row of the pre-show warm-up of *West Side Story*, it went clean out of her head. It was a week later that an incident at school jogged her memory.

She had been changing into her dance tights when she overheard Mrs Havilland speaking in hushed tones on the stairs and had crept towards the door to eavesdrop.

'Trust her to get involved in something criminal,' she had heard her whisper angrily. 'She's too rebellious by half. It was bad enough her having her hair shaved off and pinching that boy's part! Now not a word about this to anyone, Esmeralda, or I'll be in trouble with the police.'

Hilda was startled. The police! By now she had guessed that Mrs Havilland had been talking about Josie. But why on earth would Mrs Havilland be in trouble with the police if Esmeralda blabbed? Blabbed about what? It was bad luck that Josie's mother had been taken poorly and that Josie had to stay at home to take care of her but it was hardly criminal. It was at that moment that Hilda remembered the message.

She heard footsteps descending and leaped back to the bench.

'Oh!' said a sharp voice. 'Hilda!'

Hilda gazed up innocently as she slipped one of her feet into a ballet shoe.

Mrs Havilland's face was scarlet.

'How long have you been here?' she asked abruptly.

*Long enough*, thought Hilda.

'Sorry, Mrs Havilland,' said Hilda brightly. 'Am I late?'

'Indeed you are. Now hurry along please!'

Surrounded by boxes of costumes, Josie lay on her camp bed absorbing the silence. It had been another day of working in the theatre, happily cleaning and listening to the chatter of the other helpers and sneaking upstairs to spy from the wardrobe door as the cast went through their warm up before the show. Miss Littlewood wanted it to be a first night every night. She expected the cast to act differently each evening. Josie liked to spot the changes.

The last members of the audience had now left the bar and Mr Beauvoisin had climbed into the other camp bed. She had been so busy thinking about the show that when his voice suddenly boomed out of the darkness, it made her jump. She had assumed he was asleep.

'Isn't it about time you told me what you're really running away from, Joseph?' he asked.

Josie remained silent.

'I know you're awake,' he said. 'I can hear you moving.'

'The kidnappers,' she murmured.

'If that is the case, why have you resisted calling the police? Are you in some kind of trouble? Have those men threatened you? If so, you can help the police catch them . . . unless of course you don't want them to be caught. Is that it?'

'I do. But if they can't catch them and they find out I've squealed, it might make them so angry they'll come after me again.'

*Doesn't he understand*, thought Josie, *that while I'm in the theatre no one can touch me?*

'The truth, please,' said Mr Beauvoisin. 'Are you running away from your parents?'

'No!'

'That only leaves school.'

There was an awkward silence.

'Ah,' she heard him say.

*It's not that*, thought Josie. *It's just I don't want to leave here and go back to everyone being angry with me. I want to stay here for ever.*

'You didn't like it at your old school, I take it. Were you bullied?'

'No,' said Josie slowly. 'It's just that most people don't, I mean, *didn't* want to have anything to do with me. And the teachers don't, I mean, *didn't* seem to like me either.'

'Really? You seem a likeable chap to me. Why do you

think the pupils didn't like you?'

'Wrong colour hair. Wrong *attitude*. Wrong number of freckles.'

'I was bullied at school too. Physically as well.'

Josie was astounded. Mr Beauvoisin was such a kind man. She couldn't imagine anyone being nasty to him.

'Why?'

'Wrong colour. Wrong attitude. Wrong number of brain cells. So, tell me, what is the wrong number of freckles?'

'Too many.'

'Snap.'

'Too many brain cells?' she exclaimed.

'Correct. Apparently a person who is black is not supposed to excel in academic subjects, especially if he achieves higher marks than a white boy.'

'Was it horrible?'

'It was horrible.'

'Were you lonely?' she asked.

'Very lonely.'

'Did you tell your stepmother?'

'No.'

'Why?'

'Because she would have removed me and I might have ended up somewhere worse. And if I had left the school, the bullies would have won, wouldn't they?'

Josie thought of Esmeralda Havilland. She didn't like the idea of her winning.

'I suppose so.'

'And anyway, I grew to like some of the teachers. And

I made a couple of friends by the time I reached the sixth form.'

'I have too, I mean, *did*. One friend.'

*Hilda*, she thought. And outside school there was Molly. But Molly would have nothing more to do with her now. Poor Larry must have been in a terrible state after spending all night in a skip in the theatre.

'Joseph, whatever it is you're running away from, you'll have to face it eventually, however frightening it is. And people here are beginning to ask me why you're still hanging around with me instead of attending school. It's time for us to come to an agreement. If your parents still haven't collected you by Tuesday, then you must contact the police. Agreed?'

'Agreed,' she murmured in the dark.

But she had no intention of keeping her word.


Auntie Win was returning to the kitchen after an episode of *The Invisible Man* to contemplate whether to have baked beans on toast or tomato soup when the telephone rang. She darted through the sitting room into the hall and grabbed the receiver. But it wasn't Josie.

'Hello, Hilda,' she said, disappointed.

'Is Josie's mother still ill?' she asked.

'I'm afraid so.'

'Only she didn't say anything about it when she rang.'

'Rang?' For a moment she was speechless. 'Hilda, what do you mean when she rang? When was this?'

'Last week.'

'Last week!'

'Yes. She asked me to phone you and give you a message. I tried but you were out and then I forgot. Sorry.'

'Never mind,' said Auntie Win, fighting to control her voice. 'Just tell me what she said, Hilda.'

'I don't understand why she wanted *me* to tell you.'

'Hilda, I'm sorry to rush you but I would really like you to give me her message.'

'It was something about how pleased she was to be away from school. Oh no, I'm going to get her into trouble now. I'd better let her tell you that herself. She didn't want you to know that she didn't like being at the stage school.'

'Hilda, please continue.'

'I ought to let her tell you properly when she comes back.'

'Well, she isn't back yet and she did ask you to give me a message, so if you could do that, please. What exactly did she say?'

'Not much really. Her money ran out. I'd been doing most of the talking.'

'I would be grateful for anything, Hilda.'

She was now finding it almost impossible to suppress her impatience. *For goodness' sake, girl*, she wanted to yell, *will you please tell me what she said!*

'It was something about getting away. No, it wasn't that. Oh yes! She said she'd escaped.'

'*Escaped?* She actually used the word *escaped*, Hilda? This is very important. You're absolutely certain she used that word?'

'Yes. And then her money ran out.'

'And that's all?'

'No,' said Hilda hesitantly. 'Is she in trouble with the police?'

Auntie Win took a deep breath.

'The police?' she answered carefully. 'No. Why would you think that?'

'It was something one of the teachers said at school.'

'Really? You'd better tell me.'

Hilda poured out every word she had heard and who had said it.

'Mrs Havilland must have been talking about someone else,' said Auntie Win. 'You haven't mentioned it to anybody, aside from me, have you? Your mother, for instance?'

'No.'

'That's good. You know how these false rumours start and it wouldn't be very nice for Josie to discover people had been telling lies about her behind her back when she returns to school, would it?'

'No.'

'But thank you for letting me know, Hilda. We'll keep it between ourselves, eh?'

'Yes,' said Hilda, sounding relieved. 'I'm so glad it's not true. I've a good mind to tell Mrs Havilland what I think of her.'

'No need,' said Auntie Win quickly, 'especially as they're not talking about Josie. And Hilda?'

'Yes.'

'If you hear any more of these stories, you will tell me first, won't you?'

'Yes. I'm sorry I left it so late to phone you.'

'Never mind. Now I must hang up so that I can phone her at her parents' flat. She'll probably be wondering why it's taken me so long to return her call.'

'Oh, yes, of course.'

But Auntie Win didn't dial the Sternsea number. She dialled 999.

By Tuesday morning, Josie knew she was beaten. In desperation she had tried to invent some convincing lies to tell Mr Beauvoisin so that she could continue to remain inside the Theatre Royal walls, but she was stumped. She dreaded him finding out that she had deceived him. It would make yet another person angry with her. She had thought of running away but didn't want to be alone in unfamiliar streets with those men after her. And even if she could find her way to Auntie Win's flat, she couldn't go back there after having let her aunt down so badly. At least her aunt must have been told by Hilda she had escaped by now, which would mean that her mother would know too.

Downstairs, in the foyer, she hovered by the entrance and peered out into the street. She spotted Mr Beauvoisin walking towards her with bread rolls and a bottle of milk. She waved to him but he seemed not to have seen her. There was a folded newspaper under his arm. He looked serious. She waved again but he still made no response. This wasn't like him at all. And then she had a horrible thought. Maybe someone was watching him and he didn't want to draw attention to her. Quickly, she retreated out of sight.

As soon as they met in the corridor, all he said was, 'Wardrobe.'

They went through their usual preamble of sneaking up into the gallery and through the double doors. Once inside the wardrobe, he silently indicated a chair by one of the sewing machines. Josie was alarmed by his manner.

'What is it?' she asked nervously.

'I think you should sit down.'

As Josie did so, he unfolded the newspaper and placed it on her lap. Spread across the front page in large letters were the words *NINE-YEAR-OLD GINGER-HAIRED BOY, LARRY CARPENTER, KIDNAPPED FROM WINFORD PALACE THEATRE!*

Josie gave a cry, the full horror of what she had caused staring her in the face. Because of her stupidity, Larry was now in the hands of those horrible men. Somehow they must have found out that he was still in the theatre and had gone back to grab him before Mr Carpenter could reach him.

'Your name isn't Joseph, is it?' said Mr Beauvoisin softly.

She shook her head. They must have mentioned in the newspaper that she had been kidnapped too. It meant he now knew she was a girl. She stared up at him, unable to stop the tears streaming down her face.

'You're Larry, aren't you?'

# II

# The Game's Up

'I THOUGHT YOU WERE SMALL FOR A TWELVE
year old. Your parents aren't abroad at all, are they?'

'No. But I'm not Larry. And I *am* twelve years old.
We were in the same play together and they took me by
mistake. But now they must've got him and it's all my
fault! I should have gone straight to Elsie instead of hiding
him in the skip.'

'Elsie?'

'My sister.'

'Your sister!' Mr Beauvoisin frowned at her. 'You've
been telling me quite a few lies, young man.'

'I know. I'm sorry. I was so scared.'

'Of those men?'

'Of everybody.'

He drew up a chair beside her and looked her squarely
in the eyes.

'Let's have the truth now, shall we?'

She took a deep breath.

'I overheard these men plannin' to kidnap Larry but I
couldn't tell anyone straight away because Larry was with

me and I didn't want him to know, so I hid him so he would be safe. That's when I should have told my sister but I wasted time gettin' out of my costume and my make-up. Those men I call Scowler and Moustache found me in the dressing room, thought I was him and nabbed me. I was so stupid! And there's another thing,' she added, reddening. 'I go to a stage school. My parents live in Sternsea.'

'So this school is a boarding school?'

'No,' said Josie, shamefaced. 'I've been stayin' with my aunt.'

'What!'

'She lives in London. She used to be in the army, like you.'

'Joseph, she must be worried sick, and your parents must be distraught. Why didn't you tell me all this before? Why on earth don't you want them to know where you are?'

'Because they'll all be so angry with me for not telling anyone and I don't want them shouting at me. I don't want anyone shouting at me!' And then she told him about the telephone conversation between one of the kidnappers and Larry's dad. 'He must have said somethin' that made them twig they'd got the wrong person and that Larry was still at the theatre.' Her hands were shaking as she gripped the newspaper. 'They must have gone back there and grabbed him!'

Mr Beauvoisin looked thoughtful.

'That doesn't make sense to me.'

'How else could they have got hold of him?' she blurted out angrily.

'Joseph, kidnappers usually threaten to harm the person they've taken if the police are informed. And I doubt that Larry's parents would have talked. If this newspaper knows about it, so do the police.' He shook his head. 'It doesn't add up.' He gave her a steady look. 'You know what you have to do, don't you?'

She shook her head miserably.

'Oh yes you do. What you should have done two weeks ago. Phone the police.'

'But it's too late now! Those men have got Larry. And the police will say that's my fault too and be even angrier with me!'

'If those men have Larry you *must* speak to the police. You're the one person who can identify them.'

'But you've seen them too. Couldn't you tell the police instead of me?'

'I saw them in the dark. You've seen them at close quarters. The police have many photographs of criminals. They may have pictures of these men. You could help catch them.'

She nodded. She knew he was right. And then she noticed him staring at her.

'And the other secret you're holding back?'

'You won't like me when I tell you. I don't like it either. You'll think I'm a sissie.'

He looked thoughtfully at her. 'You've won a flower arranging competition?'

'It's worse than that.'

'You've murdered someone?'

'No! That's silly!'

'So is this conversation. Now, out with it!'

'I'm a girl.'

Mr Beauvosin stared at her in amazement and then he hit his forehead with the heel of his hand.

'Of course!' he exclaimed. 'Now that I look at you, it's obvious. I need my head examined.'

It was all over now, thought Josie. He would look down his nose at her and treat her as though she was stupid and weak and he would immediately hand her over to a lady who would probably throw her clothes into a dustbin and hand her a dress to wear. And there would be no more pitching in and helping out with mucky jobs at the theatre any more.

'But this is terrible!'

'I knew you wouldn't like it,' she muttered crossly.

'I don't mean that. I mean, it's terrible that you don't like being a girl.'

'It's not a very nice thing to be.'

'Nonsense. Is it your parents who don't like it?'

'No. They even let me wear trousers and boy's shirts.'

'Why do you wear boy's shirts?'

'Because girls blouses are frilly and I hate them. I hate all girls' clothes. All those horrible puffed sleeves and bows and taffeta dresses and hair slides and petticoats and necklaces and –'

'My stepmother never wears frilly clothes. It's not compulsory, you know. Does your aunt mind you being a girl?'

'No.'

'And does she wear those kinds of clothes?'

'No. I think she likes it that I don't wear frills.'

'There you are then. And she doesn't sound like the sort of person who would be angry with you either.' He gazed at her for a moment. 'Tell me, would you be happier if you went to a police station with her?'

'Yeah. I think Mum might get too upset.'

'And that would make you upset?'

She nodded. 'But Auntie Win . . .'

'Would keep a cool head?'

'Yeah. But I still can't remember her phone number.'

'Let's put our thinking caps on. Now, what was the name of the boy you phoned?'

'Hilda.'

'Ah. Will her mother have it?'

Josie suddenly sat up straight.

'Yeah! Hilda stayed with me one night and her mum phoned her to say goodnight. Mr Beauvoisin, can you ring and ask her?'

'No. She wouldn't give your aunt's number to a stranger. By the way, I can't call you Joseph any more. What's your real name? Boadicea? Pandora? Cleopatra?'

Josie smiled.

'Josie, but you can call me Jo.'

'Jo it is then.' He rose quickly. '*Allons-y,*' he added, beckoning her up to her feet. 'We must make haste. The telephone!'

\* \* \*

285

Josie pressed button A.

'Josie!' said Mrs Martin. 'How lovely to hear you. How's your mother, dear?'

'She's very well thank you.'

'Oh, that is good news! I'll just call Hilda.'

'Not yet. See, I need to ring Auntie Win and I can't find her number. Can you give it to me, please?'

'Doesn't your mother have it?'

'Er . . .' said Josie, floundering.

'Oh my goodness! You don't want her to know you're phoning her, do you? She's got worse, hasn't she? Hilda told me she was seriously ill but we hoped –'

Josie gave a cry.

'Don't you worry, love. Here's your aunt's number.'

Josie scribbled it down.

'Thank you, Mrs Milton.'

'Oh, Josie! You poor girl. I'm so sorry.'

'Goodbye,' said Josie hurriedly, and she slammed the receiver down and looked up at Mr Beauvoisin who was squashed in the telephone box beside her. 'I've made my mum ill!' she cried. 'Very ill!'

'Ring your aunt,' he said gently and handed the receiver back to her.

With shaking hands, she shoved in the pennies and began dialling.

'Hello?' It was her aunt's voice.

She pressed button A again.

'Auntie Win,' she began hesitantly.

'Josie!' she cried. 'Where are you?'

'In Stratford. I'm calling from a telephone box.'

'Give me your number. Quick! When the money runs out I'll call you back.' Josie did so.

'What are you doing in Stratford?'

'Looking for Ralph. Elsie said he did jobs at the theatre there when he wasn't working but he didn't turn up and they'd started rehearsing the next show and he wasn't in it and I didn't want to talk to anyone else. I didn't know that his play had finished and then –'

'It hasn't,' she interrupted. 'It transferred to Wyndham's theatre. I thought you knew. Didn't anyone at the theatre tell you that?'

'I didn't ask because I thought it had . . .' And then she burst into tears. 'Is Mum dying?'

'Dying? No, love. Whatever gave you that idea?'

'Hilda's mum said she was really ill! That's how I got your number. She gave it to me.'

'She's as fit as a fiddle aside from having had no sleep for a fortnight worrying about you. Why on earth didn't you ring me sooner?'

'I told Hilda last week to tell you I'd escaped.'

'She only told me two days ago.'

'Two days! Why didn't she tell you sooner?'

'She forgot. She had no idea you had been kidnapped. The police asked Miss Dagleish to tell the teachers and Miss Merryweather you had to stay home because your mother was ill. Oh, Josie, why didn't you call the police?'

'Because they'll be angry with me. It's my fault Larry's got kidnapped –'

Suddenly she was cut off. As Josie replaced the receiver, a dumpy woman who had been waiting outside with a bag of groceries opened the door.

'Out you come!' she said impatiently.

'I'm being phoned back,' Josie explained.

'Stop larkin' around,' said the woman crossly. 'Out!'

'It's true, madam,' said Mr Beauvoisin.

The woman looked him up and down, pursing her lips in disapproval.

The phone rang. Josie snatched up the receiver.

'Auntie Win!'

'Larry's safe.'

'No, he's not. I've seen it in the newspaper.'

'You got a nerve!' the woman shouted at Josie. 'You come out of there or I'll give you a clip rahnd the ear! This ain't a private phone, yer know? And *you* can git aht an' all,' she added, glaring at Mr Beauvoisin.

Josie pressed the receiver hard against her ear. The woman was making it impossible for her to hear her aunt's voice.

'Say that again,' Josie pleaded.

'That was to fool the kidnapper into thinking he had taken and lost *Larry* so that he wouldn't try to find out where he lived and try to kidnap him again. As soon as we knew you were safely out of his hands, the police asked the newspaper to put it on their front page in the hope that you would see it and come forward.'

By now the tears had begun to stream down Josie's face.

The woman who had been making loud tutting noises leaned in closer.

''ere, sonny, I didn't mean to upset you.'

But Josie just stared up at her, unable to speak.

'I'll make my phone call later, ducks. Don't you fret,' she said, and closed the door.

'I was so stupid!' Josie gulped.

'Stupid! It was your quick thinking that saved Larry from being snatched. As soon as Mr Carpenter had finished speaking to you, he dialled 999 and the Winford constabulary were at the Palace Theatre like a shot. The picture you'd drawn was still there. They called out Larry's name but he didn't answer. It wasn't until Molly arrived and read the message in your drawing that they found him in dressing room four in the skip.'

'But he must have been scared stiff.'

'If it had been any other night he would have been, but there were people working all through the night on Saturday and all Sunday putting the new set up and dressing it and hanging the lights. He was hungry and had to keep sneaking out to the lavatory but aside from that, the first thing he asked was had he won the sputnik? And was thrilled to bits when his dad told him he had.'

Josie burst out laughing.

'That's better,' said her aunt. 'Now where have you been sleeping?'

'In the Theatre Royal.'

'Now, listen carefully. Stay there. I'm going to phone the police so they can pick you up.'

'No! I don't want to speak to them on my own.'

'You won't have to. You have to have a relative with you.'

'I'd rather wait till the morning.'

'The morning? Josie!'

'I want to see *Make Me An Offer* one more time. After tonight I won't have a chance to see it ever again.'

'That's not possible, Josie. While you're running about, you're in danger. The kidnapper will still be looking for you because he still thinks you're Larry.'

Josie was about to tell her aunt that there were two kidnappers but then realised that if she did, there would be even less chance of getting what she wanted when she asked the next question. She would tell her later.

'Please. Just one more performance. It's the best musical I've ever seen.'

'I thought *My Fair Lady* and *West Side Story* were.'

'This is different. It's about people like Dad and Gran. Really like them, Auntie Win.'

Josie could hear her sigh.

'How about if I buy us both tickets for tonight so we can watch it together?'

'Oh, thanks! Can you get one for a friend of mine?'

'All right, but you're coming straight back with me afterwards and then we're going to the police station first thing in the morning. Is that clear?'

'Can my friend come too?' asked Josie. 'He can sleep on the couch.'

'We'll talk about it when I see you. I'll meet you in the foyer half an hour before the show.'

Josie replaced the receiver and glanced at Mr Beauvoisin who was beaming down at her.

'She wasn't angry with you at all, was she?' he said.

'No,' said Josie, and she smiled. 'I think she's a bit proud of me.'

# Behind the Scenes

'MISS DAGLEISH?'

'Speaking.'

'It's Mrs Carpenter.'

'You've had some news about young Josephine Hollis?' she asked quickly.

'Yes. And it's wonderful news. She's safe. She's been hiding in the Theatre Royal in Stratford. She escaped from her kidnapper and went there to find her brother Ralph. Her aunt is on her way there now. She'll be with Josie when she talks to the police tomorrow morning. As soon as I have more news, I'll let you know. It means you can tell the teachers that her mother is *recovering from her illness*. She's a very courageous little girl, Miss Dagleish.'

'Yes, indeed,' said Miss Dagleish politely, though she wished the child had chosen a more salubrious theatre to hide in.

'If it hadn't been for her . . . Well, it's too horrible to think about,' said Mrs Carpenter.

'Quite. Thank you for letting me know.'

'But you mustn't say a word to anyone. Not until she's

spoken to the police.'

'Of course not, I quite understand.'

As soon as they had said their goodbyes, Miss Dagleish pressed one of the silver buttons on the top of the telephone to disconnect them, looked up a number in her notebook and dialled.

'Hello! This is Miss Dagleish speaking. I wish to speak to Miss Merryweather. Could you please knock on her door? Thank you.' She waited for a moment. 'Miss Merryweather? . . . Speaking. I have some very good news for you. . . .Yes. Safe and sound . . . Escaped from . . .' She paused, suddenly remembering that Miss Merryweather believed that it was Larry who had been kidnapped. '. . . *his* kidnapper . . .' she added hastily. 'This is strictly between you and me. I shouldn't really be telling you this at all but I know how worried you've been, and this is such good news and you're one of our best chaperones. I don't want to lose you. . . .Of course not. No one blames you, Miss Merryweather. No, not at all . . . Oh, hiding in a theatre, would you believe? Stratford atte Bow. Theatre Royal . . .The police will be talking to . . .' She paused. '. . . *him* tomorrow. . . Now perhaps you can enjoy a good night's sleep . . . Not at all. It's my pleasure . . . And remember, not a word to anyone. Goodbye, Miss Merryweather.'

Later that afternoon, one of the lodgers knocked on Miss Merryweather's door to tell her that a Mr Lovatt-Pendlebury was on the telephone.

'Oh, Cedric!' Miss Merryweather cried, as soon as she was on her own. 'I'm so relieved you're back. The most awful thing has happened while you've been away! But it's all right now, thank goodness.' And she burst into tears.

'Oh my dear. Not an illness in the family, I hope,' he murmured.

'It's young Larry,' she began. 'I can't talk about it in the hallway.'

'I shall be with you post haste,' he said soothingly. 'We can go somewhere private and you can tell me everything.'

An hour later, a telephone rang in a grubby attic flat in a back street of London. Two men were sitting staring by it.

They glanced fearfully at one another.

'Right on time,' said Moustache. ''Ow we gonna break it to him?'

'We ain't. You wanna live, don't you?'

'If you don't talk to him, he'll smell a rat and be rahnd 'ere like a shot.'

Scowler picked up the receiver.

''Ello,' he growled.

'I'm back from my trip to *Florence*,' said the voice at the other end, 'and I've had a very interesting conversation with my *fiancée*, a very interesting conversation indeed. I hear you've mislaid something.'

Scowler threw Moustache a frightened look.

'Mislaid somefin'?' he repeated slowly.

'Small red-headed nine-year-old boy. Ring any bells?'

'Oh, yeah,' he said, fighting to remain nonchalant.

'I happen to know where you'll find him.'

Scowler sat bolt upright.

'Oh yeah?' he said, eyeing Moustache. 'Where?'

'Theatre Royal. Stratford. I should get over there, pretty sharpish. He's paying a call to our friendly boys in blue tomorrow and they just might get out their lovely scrapbooks of photographs for him to take a gander at.'

'Thanks, mate!'

'My pleasure. My *fiancée* has been spilling more beans than Heinz.' He roared with laughter. 'I'll see you on Friday when I pick up the snow.'

'Yeah. Fine,' said Scowler, his throat suddenly feeling bone dry. 'See you Fridee then.' He slammed the receiver down and sprang towards the door. 'Move!' he ordered Moustache. 'We're off to Angel Lane.'

'What for?'

'To pay a visit to a little theatre rahnd the corner. We're gonna git back some property plus teach a little tyke a lesson he ain't never gonna forget. He won't give us the slip again, even if I 'ave to chain 'im to Big Ben.'

'Yes?' said the police sergeant behind the counter.

In front of him stood half a dozen handbag-carrying middle-aged women in their Sunday best coats, hats and gloves. He groaned inwardly. More complaints about youngsters playing their rock and roll music too loudly, too late at night, he suspected. They were staring expectantly at one particular woman who had a newspaper under her arm.

'Go on, Mrs Briggs, show 'im!' urged a tiny woman with more wrinkles than a sun-dried prune.

The woman with the newspaper stepped forward and

slammed it dramatically onto the counter, the headlines facing the sergeant.

'I knows who kidnapped this boy! I were the kidnapper's landlady, I was. I chucked him out a couple o' weeks ago. The boy with him had red hair, brown duffle coat and looked scared stiff. I thought he were up to no good hidin' him under my stairs. Tall gent. Of a dark persuasion. Funny name. Mr Bowvuzzer.'

'You're certain about this?' said the sergeant, looking alert.

'If me muvver were dead I'd swear on her grave. *And* he were on the run. Said it were from a gang of Teddy boys but I knows he were lying. He give me some cock and bull story about his rent money too. He were late wiv it cos he said he couldn't get to the bank to change the money he had. Tried to fob me off with it sayin' I could get it changed meself. It was toy money, if you know what I mean. I told him to clear off sharpish.'

'On his own?'

'Nah! The boy went wiv him. If only I'd known. I could 'ave stopped him.'

The sergeant swiftly picked up the phone and began dialling.

'Guv, Sergeant Herbert speaking. I have a Mrs Briggs here. She's seen the missing nipper with the red hair. And she knows the kidnapper. She was his landlady. She chucked him out a fortnight ago but he can't have got very far because the only money he has is funny money. So it looks as if chummy is up to his ears in more than one kind of crime . . . Right, guv.' He replaced the receiver. 'Mrs Briggs, you're to wait here.'

'I told you so,' she announced triumphantly to her group of friends, and she sat down with a self-satisfied smirk. 'A nice cuppa cha would go down nicely, Sergeant,' she added.

'Where do you think you are?' he said, leaning over the counter, an eyebrow raised. 'The Ritz?'

# 13

# Danger!

JOSIE STARED ANXIOUSLY OUT AT THE STREET from the theatre entrance.

'Where is she?' she muttered, glancing at Mr Beauvoisin.

It was now raining so heavily it resembled a monsoon. She wondered if the Underground stations had been flooded, and that was what had delayed her aunt. Or maybe she hadn't yet left the flat. But she and Mr Beauvoisin couldn't leave the theatre to call her from a phone box because if no one answered, it would mean that she was on her way, and there would be no one to meet her should she arrive in their absence. And if Josie stayed at the theatre and Mr Beauvoisin phoned her aunt's flat and she *was* there, she would wonder why she was being called by a man she didn't know. Added to which, Josie did not want to be left on her own – by now she had begun to worry that her aunt had been involved in an accident or had gone to the wrong theatre.

Act One had been and gone. Her last night in the theatre and she couldn't even listen to the show from behind the wardrobe door.

'What shall we do?' she asked, shivering.

'Let's sit in the foyer for a while,' he suggested. 'It'll be warmer there.'

They had hardly been there five minutes when Mr Beauvoisin leaned towards her.

'Josie,' he murmured. 'There's a man peering through the glass from outside. Do you think you could take a surreptitious look at him out of the corner of your eye? He looks like one of the men.'

Josie turned her head slightly and gave a frightened gasp.

'He's the one I call Scowler!' she exclaimed.

Within seconds Scowler was yelling to someone across the road.

'Move!' said Mr Beauvoisin, grabbing her arm. 'Door into the wings.'

'But there'll be people there,' she protested.

'No choice.'

He hauled her into the small space between the two doors and dragged her into the stage left wings. She could hear the auction scene in full swing on stage.

*Where now?* she asked herself in desperation.

As though he could read her mind, he whispered, 'Underneath.' He pulled her down some steps. 'They'll be in the building by now. We need to get outside and head for the telephone box down by the Underground station. And then it's 999, Auntie Win or no Auntie Win.'

'But how can we get out?'

'Through the door from the stage right wings to the corridor where the flats are painted. We walked down it after the opening night, remember?' They were now in what appeared to be a long black tunnel. Above them they could hear feet moving about. 'Ouch!' he cried.

'What's the matter?' whispered Josie.

'I hit my head.'

They moved tentatively forwards. On their left were curtains, the entrance to the orchestra pit where the sounds of an accordion and a trombone were coming from.

The actors playing the dealers would be above them by now. She and Mr Beauvoisin stood motionless, listening. It was nearly the end of the scene.

'We need to stay put,' he whispered.

Josie understood why. The last thing the cast needed was to have them colliding into them when they came running through the door on their way to the dressing rooms.

'*Make me an offer,*' they could hear the auctioneer demand. '*Make me an offer. Let's keep the bidding alive. Come on now, let's say five?*'

The bids were coming fast and furious and as the red-headed woman sung '*Eighty-five*' seemingly for ever. They could hear one of the men say, '*Okay. Drop it, lady,*' and there was the sound of her voice dropping lower, and the audience laughing.

And still the bidding continued.

'As soon as they've all gone through,' murmured Mr Beauvoisin. 'We'll head for the wings and hide until we have a chance to make our way to the scene dock door. Once we're outside, we run like blazes to the telephone box.'

The auctioneer was now singing to Charlie, '*Six fifty for the very last time.*'

And as he held on to the last note they could hear everyone singing,

'*A bit for me*

'*A bit for you*

'*A bit for us*

'*A bit for me.*'

'*SOLD!*' yelled the auctioneer.

'*SOLD!*' they could hear the others yell.

At any moment a backcloth with a park painted on it would be flown in and a bench would be carried on for the next scene.

'*SOLD!*' yelled everyone again.

Mr Beauvoisin led her to the steps and they edged slowly upwards.

'What if we meet someone coming this way under the stage?' asked Josie.

'I'll pretend I'm a musician,' said Mr Beauvoisin.

Luckily, no one did. They listened to the actors heading for the dressing rooms. Once it was quiet, they headed for the wings. The voices of the two actresses who were playing Gwen and Sally seemed as loud as if she and Mr Beauvoisin were on stage with them. Mr Beauvoisin took Josie's hand and guided her between a pile of tall, painted flats. There was a wave of laughter from the auditorium.

They peered out. Near the door, costumes were hanging on a rail near a prop table. They dashed past them, pushed open the scene dock door and ran down the corridor to the door at the end.

'Almost there!' whispered Mr Beauvoisin.

He flung it open and they stumbled out onto the pavement into a deluge of rain. 'And keep an eye out for a policeman!' said Mr Beauvoisin.

They were about to sprint towards Angel Lane when the double doors at the theatre entrance opened and out strode Scowler and Moustache. All four of them froze for a moment, gaping at each other as the rain continued to pour mercilessly down on them, and then the two men began running at them.

Josie and Mr Beauvoisin had no choice but to retrace their steps. Mr Beauvoisin yanked her backwards through the open door and they fled back down the corridor. They pushed their way through the inner door to the stage right wings and Josie was dragged swiftly behind a couple of flats upstage. Mr Beauvoisin didn't have to explain. Moustache and Scowler had followed them and were standing in the wings. They were now trapped between the kidnappers and the stage.

Sodden with rain, they remained motionless, while yards away, Sally and Gwen were chatting about the pictures.

'*I think he's got the most wonderful teeth of any film star,*' Gwen was saying.

'*Sounds like a horse,*' said Sally. '*Go on, what happened next?*'

It was the moment when Gwen avidly described a scene where a man and a woman were running from a refinery that was about to explode, and how the two of them were trapped in rising treacle. And Sally, who was in a bad mood, was growing more and more annoyed with Gwen every time she swooned about anything romantic.

'*For you everything has a romantic side,*' she complained.

Josie and Mr Beauvoisin glanced at one another. They both loved the next song.

'*Yes, it has really,*' sighed Gwen, played by the actress with the long legs and the wide smile. '*It's sort of romantic,*' she sang. '*Being in love.*

'*Sort of romantic. With stars up above.*'

And for a fraction of a moment, Josie forgot about the two kidnappers as Gwen's friend Sally tried to bring her down to earth by interrupting her with, '*Bye Baby Bunting. Daddy's gone a-hunting.*'

Two more actors joined them behind the flats hauling up their collars ready to run across the park. To her astonishment, they gave them a friendly nod. Mr Beauvoisin pulled his squashed trilby out of his pocket, pulled it firmly down on his head and raised the collar of his raincoat, beckoning Josie to pull up her hood.

Of course! They could run across the stage with the others. And then she had a brainwave. Rain sometimes turned to sleet. She pulled out the packet from her pocket, prized it apart, poured some of the powder into her hand and sprinkled it over her shoulders and over her head making shivering movements.

'Sleet,' she whispered.

Mr Beavoisin and the others nodded enthusiastically. She emptied more of the white powder into their outstretched hands and they shook it over each others' shoulders and onto an umbrella someone was holding. Mr Beauvoisin lowered his head and Josie sprinkled some onto his hat. Once the packet was empty she shoved it back into her pocket.

Sally and Gwen were now talking about men and marriage. Josie bowed her head.

'*If friends can't talk about things then I don't know what friendship's for,*' Josie heard Gwen declare.

'This is it!' Mr Beauvoisin whispered.

'*It's starting to rain,*' they heard Sally say.

This received a tremendous laugh as the rain from outside could already be heard drumming on the theatre roof.

They dashed across the stage past the backcloth with the park painted on it and into the wings on the other side. Suddenly Mr Beauvoisin disappeared.

'Where are you?' Josie whispered.

'By the wall. Ah! I've found it!'

'Found what?'

'The wall ladder the flyman uses. We need to get out of sight in case those two decide to run under the stage to catch you. There's no need to be scared. It'll be too dark to see how high up you are.'

Josie stretched out her arm into the dark void and stumbled in the direction of his voice. He pulled her towards him, placing her hand on one of the rungs.

'Start climbing.'

The advantage of learning ballet, thought Josie, was that it made your legs strong, making her ascent pretty easy. Once she had reached the top, she groped around the floor and crawled over the last rung. Within seconds, Mr

Beauvoisin was beside her. He pointed upwards to where pieces of scenery were hanging.

'The flies,' he muttered urgently.

They fumbled through the semi-darkness and stood to one side. In front of them, above two waist-high wooden beams built at right angles, thick, heavy ropes were hanging coiled into loops as though on an old sailing ship ready to be used to haul up or lower scenery. Retreating into the inky darkness, they could hear the flyman handling the ropes round the corner. They glanced over the wooden bar down to the stage right wings. Scowler and Moustache were still standing there. Mr Beauvoisin swiftly pulled her back into the darkest part of the flies as the flyman walked round to where they had been hiding.

Before Josie had time to take a breath, Mr Beauvoisin whisked her round the corner to the area behind the other section of the flies. There it was deeper and even darker. In seconds, he lifted her onto a wooden wall ladder and stood on the rung below her. The flyman had already moved back round again and was now only yards away. Half-lit from the lights drifting upwards from the noisy stage, he seemed completely unaware of their presence, totally absorbed in what was happening beneath him.

From the stage came the sounds of whoops and catcalls as the dealers, followed by the rest of the company, ran into the Portobello Road for the last number.

'*Make me an offer!*' she heard them sing to the rooftops.

And it was obvious from the audience's response that they were loving it. As Josie clung on to the rungs, she had to use all her self-control not to sob her heart out. The one place where she had felt safe was no longer a refuge. Near the heavy wooden bar Josie could see the outline of the flyman stepping over the mess of unknotted ropes lying all over the platform. He was gathering them and hanging them up in loops when he suddenly gave a loud hiss.

'Oi!' he whispered. 'What you two doin' up 'ere? Get the bloody 'ell out of 'ere or I'll call the police!'

Josie was about to climb down when Mr Beauvoisin gripped her firmly, at which point she realised that the flyman wasn't talking to them. He was talking to someone else and it didn't take a genius to figure out who. The next thing she heard was the thundering footsteps of the flyman running after the intruders down the ladder to the stage left wings.

'Now!' whispered Mr Beauvoisin, pushing her upwards.

Josie wondered why he wanted them to hide even higher when there was only a ceiling above her. Her head had hardly touched it when Mr Beauvoisin reached out and pushed it off her head. It was a trapdoor! He gave her a gentle push and she scrabbled up onto the roof. Already they could hear footsteps returning to the flies, accompanied by voices. Mr Beauvoisin silently closed the trapdoor, leaving the two of them staring out through the rain at the rows of houses and street lights below.

'Let's move out of sight in case anyone else has the same idea. Over there!' He pointed at a chimney.

They stumbled over broken tiles and grey smutty ash, and crouched down behind it. Leaning back against the bricks they almost laughed with relief.

'I believe that is what is called a close shave,' murmured Mr Beauvoisin.

Minutes later they heard the slow tread of shoes crunching on the roof's rough surface. Mr Beauvoisin pressed a finger to his lips. The footsteps were drawing closer.

'What's that smell?' Josie whispered in his ear.

'Gauloise,' he whispered back.

'What's Gauloise?'

'A French cigarette.'

'You might as well come out,' said a deep, commanding voice that Josie instantly recognised.

'I am afraid the game's up, Josie,' he sighed.

They both rose from their hiding place. Standing in front of them was a woman wearing a woolly hat, holding a large black umbrella in one hand and a cigarette in the other. Josie waited in trepidation for her to shout at them, having heard her yelling at the cast and writers of *Make Me An Offer* for the last fortnight.

It was Joan Littlewood.

Josie glanced quickly at her hat, remembering having heard one of the actors in the café say that if it was shoved to the back of her head, it meant she was about to give you a basinful. And from the way he had said 'basinful', she guessed that it was 'of trouble'. But if the hat was on straight you knew you were going to be all right. To Josie's relief it was on straight.

Miss Littlewood smiled, a stream of cigarette smoke drifting out through the tiny gap between her front teeth. Josie found herself riveted to her eyes, which were now scrutinizing her with such intensity that she felt as though she were being hypnotised.

'Wonderful!' Miss Littlewood said eventually. 'Don't bother with the trapdoor. I have the window of the prop room open. You can make your way down the ladder to the green room from there. Follow me. And then you can explain your unexpected début to me.'

# 14

# Discovered

'PRICELESS! A FRENCHMAN WHO SOUNDS AS though he's walked out of an Evelyn Waugh novel and a Girl Guide who looks like a boy! I couldn't make it up! So a gang of Teddy boys were after you, Mr Beauvoisin, because you have black skin?'

'I'm afraid so.'

'It's like me and my freckles,' explained Josie.

Miss Littlewood stared at her mystified.

'I have too many of them, see. I'm only supposed to have a few over my nose and the tops of my cheeks.'

'Who says?'

'Miss Dagleish. She's the headmistress of the stage school I go to.'

Miss Littlewood grimaced.

'Oh. And how long have you been a pupil there?'

'Not very long. I only began this term but I'm not very good at the actin' lessons, though I did get a job at Winford rep.'

'Tell me more,' Miss Littlewood said, taking another drag at her cigarette.

'Well, it's Mrs Havilland, you see . . .'

'Mrs Havilland?'

'She's the actin' mistress and she always wants us to –'

Miss Littlewood raised her arm.

'Take off that dripping coat and show me.' She gestured Josie to get up onto her feet.

'I am now going to demonstrate *shock*,' said Josie, and she opened her mouth like a demented goldfish and slammed the palms of her hands against her cheeks.

Miss Littlewood smiled.

'Keep going!'

So Josie did, exaggerating everything Mrs Havilland had insisted they do. Mr Beauvoisin and Miss Littlewood howled with laughter. Spurred on, she threw herself into every pose she hated, always remembering to turn her head out front and smile.

'Smiling through pain!' she yelled. 'Smiling through your tears! Smiling through your fears! Smiling through your ears!' And then something snapped. 'Smiling through your teeth! Smiling through your knees,' she cried, thrusting a leg out. 'Smiling through your feet, your elbow, your head and,' she added, turning her back on them and bowing, 'smiling through your bum!'

Mr Beauvoisin and Miss Littlewood applauded.

'And now for my audition speech.' Josie clasped her hands and gazed painfully into the distance. 'Oh Miss *Highli*-nose, I'm so *terribli sorri* but it pains my heart to have to break the most *ghastli* news to you . . .'

'Enough!' cried Miss Littlewood.

'But this is deadly serious,' said Josie earnestly. 'I mean, *deadli* serious.'

'Deadly's the word! Presumably you have to return to this establishment after your visit to the police?' asked Joan.

Josie nodded.

'Why?'

'Because I want to act.'

'Then go to an ordinary school and invent plays with your friends.'

'But I'd have to sit behind a desk all day.'

Miss Littlewood gazed thoughtfully at her.

'How long did you work at the rep?'

'Two weeks.'

'How about I offer you both two weeks' work in *Make Me An Offer*? You would be people in the market scenes. You would need to spend enough time in the theatre so that I can train you, though it would be a drop in the ocean. But it would be a taste of a different kind of acting.'

Mr Beauvoisin and Josie stared at her open mouthed.

'You'd have to chip in with other jobs too. Everyone rolls up their sleeves in my company. You'd also be responsible for taking care of your costume. I once sacked an actor for chucking his one on the floor of the dressing room after a performance. Tools of the trade, you see.'

By now Mr Beauvoisin and Josie were slowly nodding.

'Yes, please,' said Josie. 'There's only one snag.'

'Which is?'

'I'd need a tutor and a chaperone.'

'Oh we can fix that. And now Mr Beauvoisin,' she said,

turning to him, 'what's your first name? I can't keep calling you Mr Beauvoisin.'

'Bertram.'

'Tell me about yourself. I know you're not from the West Indies.'

'I'm part French, part African, part American and culturally part British.'

'But what brings you here?'

'You, Miss Littlewood. I first saw your company perform at the Paris International Festival four years ago.'

'Ah yes. We're always made to feel so welcome in Paris,' she said. 'I'm afraid we're not given such a warm welcome in England.'

'I find that extraordinary! You should have an arts centre of your own.'

'The Arts Council give us next to nothing, which is why we need so many volunteers.'

'But then if they did, might they not impose what they wanted you to do? I imagine they would elect a board, vote you off it, and change it to something that bore no resemblance to the Theatre Workshop Company you have created.'

'The actors have created,' she corrected him. 'But you still haven't answered my question.'

'It's a long story.'

'I'm not going anywhere.'

Miss Littlewood listened attentively, observing him closely and occasionally nodding her head. Suddenly she gave a laugh.

'Well, your school won't need to find a tutor, will they?' said Miss Littlewood to Josie. 'He's standing here. All we need now is a chaperone. But whoever she is, she will have to join in. I don't have observers.'

At that moment, Gerry, the bear-like man with the black wavy hair, strode in accompanied by a very anxious looking Auntie Win. Josie gave a loud yell, ran across the room and flung her arms round her. Auntie Win held on to her tightly.

'What happened to you?' asked Josie.

'I foolishly decided to travel by taxi and we had to take all these detours because . . .' She suddenly stopped and stared at Mr Beauvoisin. 'Who is this?' she asked briskly.

'Mr Beauvoisin. He's been looking after me.'

Her aunt merely nodded at him. To Josie's surprise, she didn't even say thank you.

'And this is Miss Littlewood,' said Josie.

'Pleased to meet you,' she said.

'And guess what! I'm going to work here!'

'You're not working anywhere until we've been to the police station,' her aunt said firmly. 'I had a long conversation with them before coming here and they're expecting to hear from me again this evening. We're not wasting any more time. We're going tonight.'

'There won't be any transport now,' said Miss Littlewood. 'But Gerry will drive you there.'

Josie noticed her aunt observing Mr Beauvoisin in a manner that was far from friendly.

'Mr Beauvoisin rescued me,' Josie told her.

'Thank you,' she said stiffly.

'You're angry with me!' she cried.

'No, I'm not. I'm angry at you being kidnapped.' She turned to Gerry. 'Is there a telephone I can use? I need to let the police know we're on our way.'

As soon as she had left the green room, Mr Beauvoisin caught Josie's eye.

'I don't think it would be a good idea to ask your aunt if I can sleep on her couch. She has enough to cope with.'

But Josie had her mind on other things. She realised that if she wasn't allowed to work with Miss Littlewood, this might be her only chance to ask her questions about acting before she was whisked away.

'Miss Littlewood, about that training you said we would be doing – why do you make people do all those exercises before they can pretend to be another person?'

'What if an actor had to play a bricklayer?' she replied.

Josie thought of Ralph. 'Yeah?' said Josie slowly.

'He not only needs to observe how bricklayers work but he also needs to have the flexibility in his body to be able to move like one.'

'Is that what my brother had to do in *You Won't Always Be On Top*?'

'Your brother?'

'Yes. He's in your company. He said he had to learn bricklayin' for one of your plays. He's in *The Hostage*.'

'Is he now?' And she smiled. 'Well, yes you're right. During the play you mention, the actors had to build a wall. They were playing the kind of men who spend most of their day outside in all weathers, mixing cement and carrying heavy loads. Now a bricklayer is not going to move in the same way as, say, a librarian is he?'

'No,' said Josie.

'And that would affect the way he speaks. Have you noticed that often the way a person moves affects their voice?'

'So the more ways an actor or actress can move their body, the more kinds of people they can play?'

'Yes.'

'Elsie says its shoes that help her.'

'Elsie?'

'My sister. She acts as well. See, the bricklayer would wear boots because of all the mud, wouldn't he? And the librarian would wear shoes with soft soles. Elsie says she always tries to rehearse in the kind of shoes her character would wear because that changes the way she walks.'

'I'd like to meet her,' said Joan. 'Is she working now?'

'She's been in a play at Winford Rep. It finished last Saturday. I don't know if she's in the next one or not.'

On hearing footsteps, she swung round to find Auntie Win standing in the doorway. Yet again, her eyes were fixed on Mr Beauvoisin.

'The police would like you to travel with us,' she said.

'Gerry and I are going to have a Chinese meal by the docks,' said Miss Littlewood. 'We'll take you to the police station, and after we've eaten we'll pick you up. Bertram, you can sleep at the theatre again.' She smiled at Josie. 'Then we'll take you and your aunt home.'

\* \* \*

Miss Littlewood and Gerry sat in the front of a large, ramshackle American car that bumped and spluttered its way along ill-lit streets with Josie wedged in the back between her aunt and Mr Beauvoisin. Her aunt squeezed her hand so tightly at one point that it hurt.

Miss Littlewood seemed to be a completely different person in the car. In the theatre, she was very talkative, while the man called Gerry would quietly puff away at his pipe. In the car it was the other way round. Miss Littlewood was quiet and he was the chatty one. He asked Mr Beauvoisin over his shoulder about haunts in Paris.

Josie's aunt didn't speak a word and whenever Josie tried to catch her attention, she looked away, as though hiding a secret. It was when they arrived at the police station that Josie began to feel nervous.

'Thank you, Miss Littlewood,' said her aunt. 'This is so kind of you.'

'Not at all. And it's Joan.' She beamed at Gerry. 'We're enjoying it, aren't we?'

'Yes,' he said, and laughed. 'It's not everyday we have criminals chasing fugitives round the theatre.'

Josie watched the car drive away. As she and her aunt and Mr Beauvoisin walked slowly up the steps to the police station, she couldn't understand why her aunt continued to be so unfriendly towards him. Her aunt pushed open the door and walked straight up to a counter where a desk sergeant and three policemen appeared to be waiting for them.

'This is Josie Hollis,' Auntie Win began. 'I rang earlier . . .'

To Josie's surprise, the sergeant glanced over her shoulder and said, 'Mr Bowvuzzer, I presume?'

Before Mr Beauvoisin could reply, the police sergeant indicated a door to his left.

'I think we need a little chat, don't you, sir?' He held it open for him.

Mr Beauvoisin nodded and walked through the doorway, looking far from happy.

'Will he be all right?' asked Josie.

'If you and your niece would like to come with me, Major Lindsay,' said one of the other policemen, 'Detective Inspector Gallaway from the Yard would like to speak with you.'

'The Yard!' exclaimed Auntie Win.

'He means Scotland Yard,' Josie whispered. 'Not their back yard.'

'I know that,' her aunt whispered back.

# 15

# The Wrong End of the Stick
# and Getting Back on the Horse

'WHY DO YOU KEEP ASKING QUESTIONS about me and Mr Beauvoisin hiding in the theatre?' Josie protested wearily. 'And why do you want to know about the other volunteers? I want to tell you about the kidnappers.'

She was seated next to her aunt in a chilly room by a tiny oil heater that gave out little warmth. Opposite them, on the other side of a table, sat a detective in his fifties who looked a bit like Jack Hawkins in the Gideon film. The detective sergeant sitting beside him was a younger man in his thirties with thin, sandy hair and bald patches.

'Would it be possible for her to do that, Detective Inspector Gallaway?' asked her aunt gently. 'It might lead us to . . . ?

He nodded.

By now Josie had had enough. She just wanted to go to bed.

'Like I told you,' she shivered, 'they thought I was Larry.'

'We know,' said the detective inspector gently. 'Larry's father gave the police that information. And we also know that they wanted to upset his half-brother, Henry.'

'Yeah, they talked about swappin' him with me or hurting me to get their revenge on him.'

Auntie Win squeezed her hand.

'And you're sure you have no idea why they're so angry with him?' asked the detective inspector.

'No.'

'Let's return to the Theatre Royal.'

Josie gave an impatient sigh.

'You were kept prisoner in the building . . .' he continued.

'No! I went there after I escaped.'

'If you're telling me the truth, why did you remain there?' asked the inspector.

'Because I could forget everything there.'

'That doesn't make any sense . . .' he began.

'That's because you're not a thespian,' said Auntie Win. 'A thespian is. . .'

'Yes, yes,' said the detective inspector. 'I do know what a thespian is.'

'I don't,' said Josie.

'Someone who's in the acting profession,' she answered. 'Detective inspector, I have a nephew and another niece who are also in the business. That's how I know how their minds work. Once they walk through the stage door into a theatre, the outside world ceases to exist. Bombs could fall around the building and they wouldn't notice a thing. They would carry on regardless. The show must go on and all that.' She was aware that he was frowning. 'Ah, yes. I'm not supposed to interrupt, am I?'

He shook his head slowly and returned to Josie.

'I'm a little confused. You say some other men discovered you at the theatre and then pursued you inside? So tell me, how did you get away from them?'

'Me and Mr Beauvoisin pretended to be in the cast. There's a bit in the musical where people run across a park in the rain, but I thought I'd make it look like it was sleet so I poured imitation snow over us and gave some to the other people standin' there so they could pour it over themselves as well.'

'And this stage snow was in the wings?' asked the inspector.

'No. It was in my pocket.'

'Which you just happened to have on you at the time.'

'It didn't belong to me. It belonged to the kidnappers. I found it in one of my shoes.'

The detectives leaned back in their chairs. The detective sergeant, Josie noted, was staring in exasperation at the ceiling. He didn't believe her!

'When I ran away, I had to grab my shoes and put them on later,' she said, frowning. 'That's when I found it.'

The detective sergeant lowered his head and stared at her.

'And you scooped it up in handfuls and put it in your pocket, is that it?'

'It wasn't loose,' said Josie irritably. 'It was in a sugar bag.'

'Ah,' said the detective inspector. 'I understand now. It was sugar.'

'No. One of them hid it in there to make it look like

sugar. I heard them talkin' about it.'

She turned to Auntie Win.

'Can we go home now? You said Mum and Dad'll be waiting up for me to ring 'em. They'll have gone to bed if we don't hurry.'

'They'll stay up, I promise you,' said Auntie Win.

'We've nearly finished,' said the detective inspector. 'There's one or two more questions I'd like to ask. But let's clear up this sugar business. You heard these men talking about the contents of this sugar packet.'

'Yeah. They called it snow but o' course they meant pretend snow. If it were real snow it would have melted.'

There was a sudden silence in the room.

'And you say you threw it over yourselves before you ran across the stage,' said the detective inspector eventually.

'Yeah.'

'And Mr Beauvoisin didn't mind having it chucked over him?' asked the stunned detective sergeant.

'No. I told you. He was running away too, from a gang,' she yawned. Now she was the one feeling confused. 'But they didn't find him.'

'A gang!' exclaimed Auntie Win. 'You never mentioned anything about a gang before.'

'Please!' warned the older detective quietly. 'You need to remain silent.'

'Oh yes, I'm sorry,' she murmured.

DI Gallaway took a deep breath.

'And this gang was after the snow too?'

'No. They didn't know anythin' about the snow and even

if they did, why would they want it?'

It was as though she were in a bad dream. They were making it all so complicated. Why didn't they just let her tell the story from the beginning?'

'Was it because of the counterfeit money?' suggested the detective inspector.

'You might have to explain what counterfeit means,' suggested Auntie Win.

'Forged money,' said Josie. 'I know what it means.'

'So, Mr Beauvoisin had the forged money . . .'

'No. It's not forged, it's French, but he couldn't spend it until he'd changed it into English money. And he couldn't get close enough to the bank where he wanted to change it because the gang didn't want him on their patch.'

'That's what he told you?'

'Yeah.'

'It's a pity you threw all the snow away,' said DS Mason quietly.

She drew the packet out of her duffle coat pocket and dumped it on the table.

DS Mason leaned forward excitedly.

'His fingerprints will be all over it,' he exclaimed.

'Only if he's been handling it recently,' said DI Gallaway.

Josie stared at them completely perplexed.

'But we might as well get the lab onto it in case he has,' he added.

DS Mason reached out to grab it.

'Gloves,' said DI Gallaway, reminding him. 'We'll need to take your fingerprints too,' he said to Josie.

'To eliminate me from your enquiries,' she said.

The detective inspector raised an eyebrow.

'My aunt reads a lot of detective stories,' she explained. 'That's how I know.'

'We've got him now!' said DS Mason excitedly.

'Got who?' said Josie.

'This man must be very big,' joined in Auntie Win, unable to contain herself. 'A kidnapper, a smuggler of . . .' She paused, glancing aside at Josie. 'Of something not very nice. And a forger!'

DI Gallaway nodded. 'So it appears.'

'But there are *two* of them,' Josie added insistently. 'Not one.'

'This other one,' said DI Gallaway, 'is he also black?'

Josie stared at him as though he were mad.

'Also?' she repeated. 'Neither of them are. They're both white.'

'Is that what Mr Beauvoisin told you to say?' said Gallaway.

'No. Mr Beauvoisin stopped them from catching me. They were the ones who were after me in the theatre.'

The two men glanced at one another and then at Auntie Win. DI Gallaway gave her a nod.

'Josie,' said Auntie Win, 'why are you trying to protect Mr Beauvoisin? Has he threatened to hurt you if you tell the truth?'

'Threaten me? He's looked after me. Got me food.'

'Yes, well, he needed to do that to keep you alive, I suppose,' said DS Mason.

And then it hit her.

'You think *Mr Beauvoisin* kidnapped me, don't you?'

'We know he did,' said DI Gallaway. 'So there's no use denying it. His landlady told us. He kidnapped you and kept you in the theatre.'

'No he didn't. I kept myself in the theatre. Ask Larry's dad what the kidnapper sounded like on the phone. His voice was nothing like Mr Beauvoisin's voice.'

'He disguised it, didn't he? Or was it the other kidnapper talking?'

'No! Mr Beauvoisin wasn't even there.'

'Where?'

'At the place where they took me after they'd nabbed me from Winford theatre.'

'What place?'

'A tiny flat at the top of this old building with the cabbage smell where they tried to put me to sleep with the cocoa.'

But she could see by the looks on their faces that they didn't believe a word she said.

*It's because I'm a girl,* she thought. *They think my brain is made up of frilly ribbons.* And then she remembered something else.

'Kim's Game!' she exclaimed. 'I played Kim's Game there!'

'It's a memory game,' explained her aunt.

'I learned it in the Girl Guides. I'm in the Bullfinch patrol.'

'The Bullfinch patrol,' DS Mason repeated slowly.

Josie shut her eyes and proceeded to describe everything she could remember from the time the kidnappers took her out of the van to when she left the building; how many stairs there were up to the room, what colour the tiles were, the objects scattered on the floor alongside the walls, the cranky lift in the middle with the lock that jammed and then everything she could remember about the attic flat down to the chipped mug and the stains on the settee, and finally, the street outside and the main road around the corner.

DS Mason suddenly perked up.

'I know where that is,' he said.

'So do I,' said DI Gallaway. 'And it isn't where Mrs Briggs' lodgings are. He must have been renting two places.'

'Not *he,*' said Josie in exasperation. '*They!*'

She shut her eyes again and described both men in detail.

'And they were both very pasty-looking,' she finished off.

'She's a bright girl,' said Auntie Win. 'She wouldn't make this up.'

There was a knock at the door.

'Come in,' said DI Gallaway.

A young policeman peered round the door.

'Important phone message, sir.'

DI Gallaway stood up slowly.

'Perhaps you can make some tea for young Josephine and her aunt,' he said to the young constable.

It was some time later when the two detectives returned. This time DI Gallaway was carrying a couple of cardboard folders. He sat down and clasped his hands.

'Josephine,' he began.

'Please call me Josie,' she pleaded.

'Josie it is then.' He gave her a smile. 'Since we last spoke, we've received some new information from one of our police stations. Your sister's fiancé, Henry Carpenter, has been in touch with them. It seems that when he was fifteen, he took a photograph of two men committing a crime. The photograph was used in evidence in court and it helped the police put them away in prison for nine years.'

'Really?' said Josie, astonished.

'But why didn't Mr and Mrs Carpenter mention this earlier?' Auntie Win blurted out.

'They believed there was only one kidnapper and assumed that the two men Henry had photographed were still behind bars. They had no idea they had been released.'

He spread some photographs across the table.

'There!' Josie yelled, immediately spotting the square-faced, bald Scowler. 'That's one of them! He's the one who spoke to Mr Carpenter on the telephone.'

The detective put the photograph to one side. Josie kept looking. In the end she shook her head.

'No,' she said, 'I've never seen any of the others.'

DI Gallaway opened the second folder and spread more pictures across the table. Josie looked through all of them carefully. One caught her eye. He did seem a bit familiar.

'This looks like the other man, only he hasn't got a moustache, but I'm almost sure it's him.'

The two detectives looked at one another knowingly.

'Well done, Josie,' said DI Gallaway.

'But what about Mr Beauvoisin?' asked Josie.

DI Gallaway smiled.

'You're a good friend, Josie.'

'We checked the money he was carrying,' said the younger detective, looking awkward.

'Oh my goodness!' said Auntie Win. 'It's French, isn't it?'

'That is correct, Major Lindsay.'

'And he's not a kidnapper at all.'

'That is also correct.'

'So, can he sleep on your couch, Auntie Win?' asked Josie.

'We've just walked in the door,' said Auntie Win into the receiver. 'Oh, yes, she's right beside me.' She handed it to Josie.

'Mum!'

'Oh Josie! You naughty girl!' cried her mother and she burst into tears.

'Josie?'

It was her dad now.

'Hello, Dad.'

'If I get my hands on those . . . !' He paused as though attempting to control his temper. 'That Miss Merryweather should be sacked. She should never have left you and Larry alone.'

And it was at that moment that Josie realised that in all the muddle of endless questioning she had forgotten to tell the police about Miss Merryweather's fiancé, Mr Lovatt-Pendlebury.

'Dad,' she began, 'there's something important I need to –'

'Josie?'

It was her mum again on the phone.

'I'm sorry I called you naughty.' Josie heard her blow her nose. 'You frightened us.'

'But I'm all right now, Mum. And I'm going to be in a musical!'

She gasped. 'Oh no, I don't think that's a good idea.'

'With Miss Littlewood!' Josie added excitedly.

'Oh my goodness, she'll have you gallivanting all over the country and we'll never see you!'

'Only for two weeks, Mum. In the Theatre Royal.'

'Oh no, you're not,' she said firmly. 'We're coming up there to pick you up. You're coming straight home where we can keep an eye on you.'

'Josie?' It was her dad again. 'I 'eard. Best thing for you, gel! Get back on the horse.'

'You and your getting back on the horse,' she could hear her mother exclaim. 'She's not running for the Derby!'

'Well, she don't want to be sitting 'ere thinkin' about it all, do she?'

'And Elsie's goin' to be in it too,' Josie interrupted. 'She's goin' to be my chaperone.'

'Elsie?' said her mother back on the phone. 'Really?'

'Well, she'll do a ruddy sight better than that other woman,' yelled her dad in the background.

'She'll be stayin' with Ralph and Jessica so she'll be near the theatre. And I helped the police. They had photos of the kidnappers and I pointed them out.'

She could hear her father cheering.

'I'm in the middle of talking to her,' her mother protested. 'You'll get your turn in a minute.'

'Atta girl, Josie!' he shouted down the phone.

'Thank you!' she heard her mother remark, having snatched back the receiver.

'It's a really good musical, Mum,' said Josie, willing her mother to be happy about it.

'I'm not sure,' she said anxiously.

'Well, at least everyone will know where she is,' said her father.

*And we're going to have a plain-clothes detective constable watching us in case Scowler and Moustache come back for me,* Josie was about to say but thought better of it. *And it'll be two more weeks away from Mrs Havilland!*

Her dad must have said something to cheer her up because she heard her mum suddenly burst out laughing, and after advice from her about eating properly and getting enough sleep, Josie returned to the sitting room where Mr Beauvoisin was sitting on Auntie Win's couch, nursing his nose in a handkerchief.

'Are you sure you don't want me to call a doctor, Mr Beauvoisin?' her aunt was asking.

'It looks worse than it is I assure you, Major Lindsay. If it was broken I think I would know about it.'

'That door you walked into at the police station must have been made of iron,' said Josie.

Mr Beauvoisin peered over his bloodstained handkerchief.

'Indeed it was. But I'm here now. And I'm enormously grateful to you, Major Lindsay, for allowing me to stay overnight.'

'Call me Winifred,' said Josie's aunt. 'After everything

you've done for our Josie, you're part of the family.'

'You're sure you'll be all right for rehearsals tomorrow, Mr Beauvoisin?' Josie asked anxiously.

'Josie!' cried her aunt.

'She's absolutely right to enquire. We don't want to waste any time. Tomorrow we will have our first Laban movement class.'

'But I thought you weren't starting until Monday,' said Auntie Win.

'Officially yes. But Joan wants us to begin as soon as possible.'

Mr Beauvoisin and Josie grinned at one another.

'I give up!' said Auntie Win, and she laughed.

It was later when Josie was drifting off to sleep that she remembered that there was something she needed to tell the police. Unfortunately, it had gone clean out of her head. The next thing she knew, her aunt was waking her up and all she could think about was that she would be spending the next two weeks doing what she loved doing most in the world.

# 16

# Looking Through the Body
# with Different Eyes

'MISS DAGLEISH? . . . IT'S JOAN LITTLEWOOD at the Theatre Royal . . . Oh yes. . . She's been very well behaved . . .' She beamed at Josie. 'I'm phoning you because I'm offering her two and a half week's work in our new production, *Make Me An Offer*. Starting today . . . Yes, I understand that and have organised a tutor and a chaperone for her . . . Her sister.' Joan glanced at Elsie, who was standing with her arm draped round Josie's shoulders.

'Her Aunt Winifred has offered to pick up the books she needs from your school and will bring them here . . . The tutor's a Frenchman. A Monsieur Beauvoisin . . . Oh yes, speaks English like a native,' she said, giving him a wink. 'Thank you, Miss Dagleish . . . A formal letter . . . Yes, of course . . . Thank you.'

As Joan replaced the receiver, a tall, lanky young man wearing a beige raincoat over a grey suit peered round the doorway into the office. His tangled scrub of dark hair was greased back above protruding ears and large doleful eyes.

'Ah, Detective Constable Timpson,' said Miss Littlewood, 'I explained to your superior that I don't have observers, and that the only way I'll allow you to keep watch on Josie in your capacity as a plain clothes officer while your colleagues hunt for these kidnappers is to join in'

The young man nodded.

'I am to take part in the rehearsals,' he said miserably.

'It means you will also be in the market scenes during the performances.'

'Yes,' he moaned. 'I've been warned.'

'Cheer up. It's not a death sentence. And you'll be called by your Christian name while you're working here undercover.'

'That is correct.'

'Which is?' she asked.

'Dickie.'

'You'll be doing a few exercises first, Dickie. Did you bring your shorts with you?'

For half an hour it seemed Josie had flicked her hands, her feet, her arms and head. She had flicked out every part of her body into the air. In her mind, she was flicking off a fly, flicking her feet as though attempting to flick chewing gum off her soles, flicking off imaginary people with her fingers as though she were Miss Dagleish letting you know that you could now leave her study. She even lay on her back and flicked her feet into the air.

*Flick! Flick! Flick!* Faster and faster. Secretly, she had earlier flicked away all the nasty remarks that had been made about her at school. Mr Beauvoisin was flicking his elbows above his head and below his knees. Elsie was flicking her hips to one side as if pushing someone away, and Dickie was flicking his entire body as though trying to flick a ball off his head.

Miss Littlewood then asked them to stand still and breathe.

'Ever wrung every drop of water out of a dishcloth?' she asked.

They all nodded, catching their breath.

'Imagine you are the dishcloth being twisted.'

And off they went, twisting their arms, legs, faces, and moving into tight circles, wrapping their arms around themselves.

Hardly had they moved one way than Miss Littlewood was encouraging them to stretch and move in ways Josie had never imagined were possible. One moment they were making dabbing movements, the next, sweeping movements. *Slashing*, she called it. Then they had to glide everywhere as though they were skating on a vast frozen lake. This was followed by punching movements with their feet and their legs and their arms, as hard and as energetically as they could.

'Now you are weightless,' Joan announced.

And they became balloons drifting into the sky, and as the air inside them was released, they had to descend in whirling movements, sweeping round each other.

And it felt wonderful.

After breathing low into their stomachs and moving as they breathed out on a word, they did exercises where they had to speak in a flicking, wringing, punchy or slashing way.

'Josie,' she announced. 'For *Make Me an Offer*, I want you to be a dabbing kind of girl.'

'A girl!' exclaimed Josie. 'Don't you mean a boy?'

'I do not.'

'But girls' parts are boring.'

'How many girls have you played?' asked Joan.

'None. I always played boys at me last school.'

'This will be a good experience for you then.' She turned to Elsie. 'You will be a gliding sort of person. You, Dickie,' she said, swinging round to the detective constable, 'you will be a punchy person. Bertram, you'll be a drifting kind of person.'

She set up scenes for them to improvise, scenes where they argued with one another or were on a crowded, bumpy bus in the rush hour. Finally, she asked them to tell her what they were like first thing in the morning.

Josie decided that the girl she was playing had to have everything organised for school the next day. Her satchel had to be tidy with no scraps of paper or pencil shavings scattered at the bottom. Her blotting paper would be folded neatly in an envelope to keep it clean. Before sitting on a chair, she would brush the seat. She liked her place at the breakfast table to be nicely laid out. Her sisters were loud and clumsy, thrusting their arms in front of her. This made her nervous, especially when she was eating a bowl of Cornflakes and they caused the milk to slop over the side of her bowl.

After these improvisations they were sent out into Angel Lane.

'Find someone who acts the way you've been behaving in the improvisations.'

Out in the market, Josie observed how the men behind

the stalls sold their fruit and vegetables. One man's voice and the way he moved was *punchy*. A woman who was examining some bananas very closely caught her attention. *Dabbing*, thought Josie, taking in how she held her fingers almost elegantly and prodded the fruit in quick movements. A young woman walked past Josie holding the hand of a two-year-old boy. She was pregnant but in spite of the jostling and shouting all around her, she seemed to drift through as though in another world. *Floating*.

Back in the theatre, they had to play one of the people they had seen and pretend they were in the market buying and selling.

'You are now in a different market,' Miss Littlewood said. 'Here the stalls sell a mixture of treasures and rubbish, pearls and tat, old clocks and ornaments and priceless antiques. Jo, tell me about the girl you're playing and why she might be there.'

'I'm very *particular*,' she said. 'I like to have my hair brushed to the side with an absolutely straight parting and the rim on my felt hat brushed. I like all my buttons done up. I like to be neat. But I also like very pretty objects, so I'm visiting the market to find a nice brooch to put on my cardigan or a pretty little box to keep my treasures in. I keep my treasures on the windowsill by my bed and I like to arrange them just so. *Dab. Dab. Dab.*'

'And what's your name?'

'Celia.'

It popped out from nowhere but it felt absolutely right. And it was then that Josie realised that she had been so absorbed in watching other people in the market that she hadn't felt frightened in Angel Lane and she had been able to breathe!

Miss Littlewood gathered the four of them together.

'Before Josie has to dash off to do her school work,' she announced, 'I need to have a word with you all before the cast of *Make Me An Offer* come in for their warm up.

'Usually, everyone in the cast works together before the show, but for the moment you are to be my surprise *keep-them-fresh-and-on-their-toes brigade*,' she told them with a mischievous smile. 'Your dressing room will be up in the wardrobe. Someone who knows the ins and outs of that room has very kindly agreed to help you find the right clothes for the people you're playing. She should be here any minute.'

'Hello!' yelled a voice from the stalls. It was Annette. 'Is someone talking about me?'

After lunch Mr Beauvoisin and Josie were given a small table in the corner of the cold office for lessons, where they sat with their overcoats on while Gerry's secretary, a young girl with black wavy hair and a shy smile tapped away on her typewriter. Mr Beauvoisin was concerned they would be in her way but she said she liked having their company. Apart from Gerry popping in occasionally, she often spent long periods of time in there on her own. Josie was certain she had also seen her tearing up tickets as an usherette and helping out behind the bar. The girl wore fingerless gloves and a scarf and was surrounded by typed scripts with pink blotches on them.

'Is that blood?' Josie asked, alarmed.

'No. Correcting ink. That's where the smell like nail varnish is coming from. Those are the mistakes I made,' she said, and sighed. 'I have to type up all those pages again.'

'*Poor you*, thought Josie. The thought of typing all day made schoolwork seem like a holiday.

'Come on,' said Mr Beauvoisin. 'Let's get started.'

# 17

# An Unexpected Intruder

BECAUSE JOSIE'S EVERY HOUR HAD BEEN FILLED with Laban exercises, improvisations and schoolwork, there had been no time for her to recall what it was she had forgotten to tell the police. It wasn't until Thursday night on their return journey to her aunt's flat on the bus that she remembered. She and Mr Beauvoisin had been talking about the auction scene.

'Why do people get so excited about auctions?' she had asked him.

'Because they're bidding against one another to buy an object for the best possible price so that later on they can sell it to someone else at an even higher price.'

'You mean it's like a competition? The one who bids the highest amount gets the object? So they're the winner?'

'In a sense,' said Mr Beauvoisin. 'But the more people who bid against each other, the higher the cost of the object becomes. That's why one of the bidders attending the auction pays Charlie *not* to bid, so that if that person is the highest bidder . . .'

'He won't have to pay so much.'

'Exactly.'

'But what if they pretend to be interested in something that they're *not* interested in, and pretend *not* to be interested in something they are interested in?'

'Ah. That's when the wheeling and dealing begins.'

'So no one knows exactly what everyone's up to?'

'Correct. Plus they're talking about each other behind their backs.'

'And that's why the audience finds it funny.'

'That's right, because they know what's going on even if the bidders don't. There's something else too. Because this is about antiques, some of the bidders will have accrued a hefty amount of knowledge. Charlie, for example, knows a lot about old vases.'

'Pots,' said Josie, smiling.

'Or pots as he calls them,' said Mr Beauvoisin. 'He's an expert at spotting the difference between a fake and an original. But the last thing he wants is for the other bidders to know that he knows the difference.'

'So lots of people could be fooling one another?'

'Yes.'

'So the bidders are like the fakes.'

Mr Beauvoisin laughed. 'That's one way of putting it!'

And it was at that moment that she remembered.

'Like Mr Lovatt-Pendlebury!'

'Mr Lovatt-Pendlebury?'

'Yeah. He's like those Wedgewood plaques on the panelling in that big house. He's a fake. He fooled Miss Merryweather, our theatre matron, into making her believe he was all mushy about her. Even the engagement ring he gave her was a fake. Everyone thought it was a diamond but it was made of glass.'

'Oh, so you're a diamond expert now.'

And that's when she remembered.

'No, I overheard him say so when he was talking to the kidnappers.' She reddened.

Mr Beauvoisin was puzzled.

'I don't remember you mentioning him. I assumed you had only overheard the kidnappers talking. Are you telling me that your chaperone's fiancé knew the kidnappers?'

'Yeah. The thing is –' she began awkwardly.

'Did he know where Larry lived?' Mr Beauvoisin interrupted.

'Not at first. But then he used to travel back to Larry's house with them. He said he wanted to chaperone *her* home after she had chaperoned Larry home! But I think he was just gettin' more information about where he and Henry lived. He was doin' it as a favour for Scowler and Moustache, and they were doin' one for him.'

'Which was?'

'Takin' care of somethin' for him.'

'I see. I take it you informed the police about this man.'

'That's what I'm tryin' to tell you.'

'Josie?' Mr Beauvoisin said quietly. 'You did, didn't you?'

Josie felt her face growing hot. 'I meant to but . . .'

'Are you telling me they know absolutely nothing about the conversation you overheard between this Mr Lovatt-Pendlebury and those two men?'

She shook her head.

'And there was the telephone call I overheard at the railway station too,' she added guiltily.

'How could you forget something so important?'

'I was tired and they kept interrupting me and asking questions about *you* all the time. And I couldn't think straight. Please don't be cross!'

'Josie, we have to let them know immediately.'

As soon as they hopped off the bus, Mr Beauvoisin strode briskly towards the nearest telephone box.

She groaned.

'Can't we wait till we get to Auntie Win's?'

'No time. We need to do it now!'

He opened the door and ushered her in.

'I'll warn your aunt first. She's probably in her night attire by now. She'll need to get dressed in case the police want to speak to you tonight.'

'Oh no,' wailed Josie. 'Can't it wait till the morning?'

'No, it can't. It's vital that the police have every piece of information about these men as soon as possible. If this man knows where Larry lives and he discovers that Larry's back home, he could pass on that information to the men who kidnapped you. They might hang around outside, find out that there's another Larry, put two and two together and grab him.'

'But Miss Merryweather doesn't have to chaperone Larry any more so he won't find out anything about him, will he?'

'The police still need to know.' He searched through his pockets. 'Dash it! You don't have any pennies, do you?'

Josie shook her head.

'Never mind.' He began dialling the operator. 'Hello,' he said, 'I'd like to make a reverse charge call, please.' He gave the operator her aunt's phone number.

It took a while for them to be connected. When Auntie Win's voice came through, it was so loud that Josie could hear everything, including a jaunty record that Josie recognised as *Caravan* playing on her radiogram.

'Winifred! It's Bertram.'

'Bertram? Why are you calling? Is anything the matter? Is Josie with you?'

'Yes. We're only a few minutes' walk from you.'

'I'll get the cocoa on then.'

'No. Get dressed. Josie didn't tell the police everything. I think you'll need to take her to the police station tonight. It's about a Mr Lovatt-Pendlebury.'

'Oh no, not him again. I've seen him. He seems perfectly all right to me.'

'Did Josie tell you about the phone call at the railway station and the conversation she overheard near the stage door in Winford?'

'What phone call?'

There was a strange pinging noise in the background.

'Bertram, can you hang on a minute? There's someone at my door.'

'At this hour?' he said, surprised.

'Just coming!' she sang out to whoever had rung the bell.

'Winifred! Don't answer it,' he yelled. But there was no reply. 'Hello? Hello?'

'I can hear her,' said Josie.

'So can I,' said Mr Beauvoisin, 'and she sounds angry.'

He slammed the receiver down and dialled 999.

'Police,' he said. 'I'm calling on behalf of a Major Lindsay.' He gave the address. 'No, she can't call you. Her phone is off the hook. I think she has an intruder . . .' He sighed. 'I don't have time to explain. Would you please let DI Gallaway know as soon as possible!'

He pushed the door open and they began running.

'Is there a neighbour you can stay with in the building?'

'Yeah,' panted Josie. 'Mrs Jenkins.'

'Ring her bell and stay with her while I go into the flat.'

They had just turned the corner into her road when Mr Beauvoisin instantly drew her back.

'Moustache!' she whispered.

He was standing outside the foyer door.

'I have a feeling I know who the caller is,' murmured Mr Beauvoisin.

'Scowler,' said Josie, and she found herself shivering.

'There's no time to wait for the police,' he muttered. 'Is your aunt good at locking the kitchen door?'

'Hopeless,' said Josie.

'Let's hope she hasn't improved.'

'The fire escape?' asked Josie.

'The fire escape,' he said.

They retreated to another road and headed for the one that backed onto the flats.

To their relief, the kitchen door was unlocked. As Mr Beauvoisin gently pushed it open, it they were met with the familiar smell of burned food.

'Stay here,' he whispered. 'And don't move!'

The door to the sitting room was ajar.

'If you don't tell me where the kid is, you won't be able to see for a week,' they heard Scowler yell at her. 'Do I make meself clear?'

'Crystal,' Josie heard her aunt say. 'You do realise the police are watching these flats.'

'Oh yeah? Well they must have gorn 'ome cos there ain't no cops rahnd 'ere, my love.'

This was followed by the sound of a slap.

Before Josie could cry out, Mr Beauvoisin leaped into the room, and after a series of loud thumps followed by a yell from Scowler, there was a triumphant cheer from both Mr Beauvoisin and her aunt.

Josie peered in. Mr Beauvoisin had one of Scowler's arms up behind his back. His eyes almost popped out of his head when he spotted her.

'I told you to stay in the kitchen,' said Mr Beauvosin.

'I want my property back,' he yelled. 'Gimme that packet and I'll never bovver you again.'

'How do I know you'll keep your promise?' Josie said crossly.

'Because I want nuffin' more to do wiv your bruvver's family. He's bad luck.'

'Which brother?' asked Auntie Win, bewildered. 'Ralph or Harry?'

'Henry!' yelled the man.

'Henry?'

'My brother *Henry,*' said Josie, staring at her aunt with a *we must protect Larry* gaze.

'Oh, yes of course!' she exclaimed, catching Josie's eye.

'*Larry*, he said to me the other day,' said Josie. '*Larry* don't you worry about a thing.'

'Indeed he did, *Larry*. Good old brother *Henry*,' Auntie Win added, not very convincingly. Acting, Josie noted, was not one of her aunt's talents.

'Sit down!' said Mr Beauvoisin, slamming him down on the settee.

A look of despair came over Scowler's face.

''And it over, sonny.'

'Couldn't you go back to the model shop and buy some more?' said Josie.

'Model shop?' repeated the man dully. 'What model shop?'

'Where you bought the artificial snow.'

'Snow?' said the man, looking decidedly on edge. 'What do you know about that?'

'I heard you talking about it at the flat.'

'And you think it's . . . ?' And then he laughed. 'Oh yeah! Course. The artificial snow for . . .' He hesitated.

'One of your models,' said Josie. 'I was trying to work out where you were going to glue it. Was it going to be on rooftops or a hill or model trees?'

'Was?' asked the man, his voice shaking. '*Am*, you mean. What *am* I going to put it on?' He gave a short high-pitched laugh. 'You got a clever head on your shoulders. 'Ow did you guess it was for stickin' on models?'

'It was easy really. I just put two and two together.'

The man began to make an impatient growling noise.

'Steady old chap,' said Bertram.

'Just give me the *artificial* snow and then I'll go.'

'Is it for a model competition?' asked Josie.

'That's right,' he said through gritted teeth. 'And it's *very very* soon. Tomorrer, as it 'appens.'

'Oh,' said Josie. 'I'm so sorry.'

'Don't be sorry! Just 'and it over!'

'I can't,' said Josie. 'When you were after us in the theatre and there was the bit in *Make Me An Offer* where it was raining in the park and we ran across the stage, we threw it over each other to make it look as though the rain had turned to sleet.'

The man's face now appeared to be charged with a series of electrical shocks.

'Threw?' he shrieked.

Josie nodded.

He flung back his head and gave a howl like a wild animal. Josie stared at him in disbelief. *What a baby*, she thought. Fancy making such a fuss about a bag of white powder.

'He'll kill me!' he whimpered. 'He'll string me up.'

'Steady, old man,' warned Mr Beauvoisin. 'There's a child present.'

'Oh. So is the artificial snow for your friend?' asked Josie. 'Is he the one entering the competition?'

The man nodded violently.

'But it wasn't your fault,' said Josie. 'Tell him I found it in my shoe and . . .'

Scowler sank his head into his big, stubby hands and began to make wild moaning noises.

To her surprise, Josie was beginning to feel quite sorry for him.

'Why don't you ask him to come upstairs and I'll explain what happened,' she suggested.

Scowler's head shot up.

'He's 'ere?' he said, looking terrified.

'Yes.'

'Where?' he yelled.

'He's standing at the front door downstairs.'

'But I left Percy down there.'

'The man with the moustache?' asked Josie.

'Yeah.'

'That's who I meant.'

The man gave a loud sigh of relief. Sweat was now pouring down his face.

'I gotta get out of 'ere, fast,' Scowler said. He pushed past them and made for the door.

Mr Beauvoisin tried to stop him but Scowler turned and gave him one almighty thump, sending him crashing into the bottle lamp. Then he grabbed Josie's aunt.

'If you don't want me to 'urt 'er you'd better not try and stop me!'

'Auntie Win!' yelled Josie.

He hauled her back along the passage, opened the door, and then pushed her to the floor while he escaped out onto the landing and down the stairs.

'Leave him, Bertram,' said Auntie Win. 'I'm fine, and I

think he's best out of the way,' she added, glancing at Josie.

'Might I suggest that after we phone the police we lock this flat up before anyone else pays us a visit?' he said.

'Detective Inspector Gallaway, I'm a grown woman!' Auntie Win bellowed down the receiver. 'Not an attention-seeking little shop girl! His name, I repeat, is Mr Lovatt-Pendlebury.'

'Major Lindsay, we have this all in hand,' he snapped.

'Then how do you account for the fact that one of the two men who kidnapped my niece has been in my flat, has been threatening me and . . .'

'What?! Why didn't you say so immediately instead of wasting my time talking about this man with the ridiculous name?'

'Because you were too busy telling me that I was an hysterical woman who read too many detective novels and was therefore suffering from an over-stimulated imagination.'

'I never said that.'

'You implied it.'

'I'll send two officers round –'

'Not until I tell you about the railway station telephone call and the conversation in Winford my niece forgot to mention when you questioned her, and the fact that those two men were extremely anxious to retrieve that very interesting packet of white powder before the end of this week. Aside from that, I want to know how they found out that she was staying here.'

'It seems we have a leakage in the plumbing,' he muttered.

'Hardly the metaphor I would have chosen, Detective

Inspector Gallaway, but not to put too fine a point on it, someone has not been keeping their mouth shut. I suggest you make Miss Dagleish's stage school –'

'My first port of call,' he finished for her. 'And I suggest you leave it to us, Major, and don't interfere.' He hung up.

'Typical man!' she snapped and slammed down the receiver.

# 18

# And Into Hiding Again

'SOMEONE IN THIS ROOM,' SAID DI GALLAWAY, 'has put the life of young Josephine Hollis in grave danger.'

It was the following evening. He and DS Mason were standing in Miss Dagleish's study. Seated opposite were Miss Dagleish, Miss Merryweather and Mrs Havilland.

'What has the girl been up to now?' complained Mrs Havilland.

'Miss Dagleish,' continued the detective inspector, ignoring her, 'I informed you that Larry Carpenter was safe and well but that Josie was still missing. I also instructed you to keep that information to yourself. Can you confirm that you did no such thing?'

Miss Dagleish paled.

'I did keep it within the strict confines of the school.'

DS Mason gave a sigh and opened his notebook

'And I only told Mrs Havilland, and of course much later, Miss Merryweather,' she added.

'Why, of course?' asked DI Gallaway.

'Because once I knew Josie's whereabouts, I felt it was

vital that she knew that Larry was safe. Not only had she been distraught over his disappearance but she also felt responsible. She was convinced it was he who had been kidnapped so I decided it would be perfectly acceptable to inform her that *Larry* had been found, even though it was really Josie. I never mentioned that it had been she who had been taken instead of him. Well,' she added awkwardly, 'not until this morning.'

'Did you at any time tell anyone where Josie had been hiding?'

'Well, naturally Mrs Havilland was cognisant of the full facts. And I might have told Miss Merryweather about the theatre where *Larry* had been hiding,' she answered stiffly.

'Where the kidnappers made a second attempt.'

Miss Dagleish pursed her lips.

'What else did you tell Miss Merryweather?' asked Gallaway.

'After I had allowed Josie to stay on at the Theatre Royal, I mentioned that *Larry* was now staying with Josie's aunt.'

D.I Gallaway looked astounded.

'Why?'

'It was an accident. I was about to let slip that Josie was back with her aunt before remembering that Miss Merryweather still thought that Josie was with her parents. As soon as I realised my mistake, I quickly said that *Larry* was staying with her instead.' She looked ruffled. 'In the circumstances I thought I had done rather well.'

'Didn't Miss Merryweather think that was rather odd?'

'Not at first,' she said slowly, glancing at Miss

Merryweather, 'but this morning when I was asked to explain why Larry was not staying with his parents, it was then that I told her the whole truth. And at lunchtime I let Mrs Havilland know that Miss Merryweather now knew as much as we did.'

'But by that time, the earlier information had been passed on.'

'I don't understand,' said Miss Dagleish.

'Last night, one of the kidnappers forced his way into Major Lindsay's flat and confronted Josie, still thinking she was Larry.'

'Oh my goodness!' cried Miss Merryweather. 'Has she been hurt?'

'No. Her tutor overpowered him. Unfortunately the criminal managed to escape, but without the tutor's intervention we could have been looking at a far more serious crime. Am I making myself clear?'

All three women nodded.

He next turned to Mrs Havilland, who had been growing more irritated by the second.

'I'd like to know why I have been summoned here, Detective Inspector,' she protested. 'All this has nothing to do with me.'

'Mrs Havilland, you knew that the kidnappers had taken Josie?'

'Yes,' she sighed wearily. 'And I also told no other member of staff.'

'You have three daughters, Mrs Havilland?'

'That is correct.'

'Your youngest daughter is called Esmeralda.'

Mrs Havilland stiffened.

'One of your pupils happened to overhear part of a conversation between you and Esmeralda concerning Josie and the police.'

'Whom?' she asked angrily.

'That is irrelevant. I need to know how many people your daughter has told. We will interview her at the police station and you will need to be present when we do.'

'But she's not a common criminal!'

'I would now like to speak to Miss Merryweather in private, so if you and Miss Dagleish could leave the room . . .'

'Me?' said Miss Merryweather. 'But I've already told you everything.'

'I'm sure you have, Miss Merryweather, but there might be some tiny, insignificant thing you have forgotten which might help us find these men.'

'Oh, I see. Yes, of course.'

Once Miss Dagleish and Mrs Havilland had left the study, DI Gallaway turned to DS Mason.

'Outside if you please, DS Mason.'

The detective sergeant gazed quizzically at him.

'Eavesdroppers,' he added quietly. The detective sergeant nodded, loped over to the door and swung it open. Outside, clustered together with Miss Dagleish and Mrs Havilland, were half a dozen girls.

'This way, everyone!' commanded Miss Dagleish, as though she had been in the act of ushering the pupils down the hall.

'Are you quite comfortable, Miss Merryweather?' DI Gallaway asked gently.

She nodded.

'I'm going to ask you again what I asked Miss Dagleish and Mrs Havilland. Did you at any time repeat the conversation between you and Miss Dagleish to another person?'

'No.'

'I see you're wearing an engagement ring, Miss Merryweather.'

'Yes,' she said, and smiled.

'How much did you tell your fiancé?'

Miss Merryweather looked startled.

'I a-assure you . . .' she stammered, and then she reddened.

'Let's start from the beginning, shall we, Miss Merryweather?'

'Why can't I stay here?' Josie protested. 'You heard what that Scowler said. He doesn't want anything more to do with me. He won't come back.'

It was early the following morning. Auntie Win was packing Josie's clothes into her attaché case.

'Josie, until he and his companion are under lock and key the police want your whereabouts to remain a secret. If you want to continue working at the Theatre Royal, you either do as you're told and stay somewhere else for your own safety, or you go back to Sternsea. What is it to be?'

'But where will I be staying?'

'At Ralph and Jessica's place. With Elsie. I'll buy you a sleeping bag, and drop it at the theatre.'

'But where will Mr Beauvoisin go?'

'He'll be staying here.'

'That's good. He can make sure you lock up properly.'

'Cheeky!' she said, snapping the case shut. 'Now hurry up. You and he have a bus to catch. You can't be late for Joan.'

'But will you be all right on your own?' Josie asked anxiously. 'He won't be back till very late.'

'I'll have Mrs Jenkins to protect me.'

Josie smiled.

'Atta girl!' said Auntie Win.

Being in the show on the Theatre Royal stage for the first time was a magical experience, yet for Josie it also felt completely natural.

In fact, she was no longer Josie but a girl called Celia who mingled with the market people, her savings in a small purse, searching intently for a brooch, while the stallholders caught her eye and showed her what they had on offer. It was like acting without wearing chains.

After it had ended, Dickie took her and Elsie to her brother's place on a motorbike with a sidecar. Josie's case was strapped onto the small luggage rack at the back. Elsie sat on the passenger seat wearing a crash helmet while Josie crouched in the sidecar hugging a cumbersome cylindrical bag containing a sleeping bag.

Fifteen minutes later, they pulled up in front of a tall, ramshackle Victorian house. Elsie unlocked the front door and stepped into a vast hall. They traipsed up endless wooden stairs sparsely covered with a threadbare carpet riddled with holes. There was a strong smell of floor polish, so that the house, although having the appearance of disintegration, smelled as though it were cared for.

Her sister tapped gently on one of the doors. Within seconds, it was flung open by a young woman with long, frizzy, flame-coloured hair. Dressed in black slacks with stirrups and a massive black sweater, she beamed at Josie. Before Josie could open her mouth, her sister-in-law had her arms wrapped around her.

'Oh, Josie!' she yelled, hugging her tightly 'I'm so glad you're safe!'

Dickie slammed a finger on his mouth.

'Of course,' she whispered, closing the door swiftly behind them.

Ralph and Jessica lived in a tiny bedsitter. Their bed was used as a settee during the day, and their two wooden chairs and table were the fold-away kind. Four people could sit at the table if two of them sat on the settee. Elsie had been sleeping on an army camp bed, now folded up by the table. Josie was to sleep in her sleeping bag on a blanket on the floor.

A kettle, which was attached to a small iron pipe, stood on the tiles in front of a tiny gas fire. At one end of the room, by a single gas ring on a stand, was a table with saucepans, china and cutlery on it. Josie glanced up at the peeling whitewashed wallpaper. Hanging over it were the framed portraits of men and women Jessica had painted. Dickie said his goodbyes and reminded Josie and Elsie that he would be picking them up in the morning.

'Am I being a nuisance?' Josie asked Elsie after he had gone.

'Quite the opposite. It means I won't have to stand squashed up next to people in the Tube in the morning.'

'That's all right then,' Josie yawned.

'Bed,' said her sister.

Once Josie was snuggled up in the sleeping bag, she felt as though she was in the wilds of America, lying by a fire to ward off prowling coyotes, her loaded repeater rifle by her side. She had just drifted off to sleep when she felt someone kiss her cheek and squeeze her.

'Ralph?' she murmured.

'Yes,' whispered her big brother. 'Now go back to sleep.'

'So how was tonight?' she heard Elsie ask him.

'Brendan was in again, shouting and swearing, and drunk as usual. He stood up and sang another verse of Howard's song. The audience loved it, of course. And then Howard said, "Now, Brendan, can we get on with this dreary play of yours?" which got another round of applause from the audience.'

'Are you sure he said *dreary*?' Jessica asked.

'Ah, now that would be tellin',' said Ralph in an Irish accent. 'We have a *child* present and she just might be eavesdroppin', don't you know.'

*Blue air*, guessed Josie as she drifted off.

She was woken again by Jessica talking urgently.

'Tell her, Ralph,' she heard her say.

Josie kept her eyes shut but her ears open.

'Is it bad news?' Elsie asked. There was a long silence.

'Ralph, you're worrying me. What is it?'

'I've decided to leave the Theatre Workshop Company.'

'What!' cried Elsie. 'But you love it, and I can't see you going back to plays where you have to wear a dinner jacket in the third act.'

'Once *The Hostage* comes off we could be thrown back to earning only pocket money and sleeping in the theatre again or on people's floors. I need more money. Not a lot. Just enough for us to live on.'

'I'll soon be thirty,' Josie heard Jessica tell Elsie. 'We knew that if we didn't have children soon, it would be too late.'

Josie heard her sister gasp.

'Yes, I'm pregnant,' said Jessica.

Josie was startled. *I'm going to be an auntie*, she thought.

'Oh,' cried Elsie. 'I'm so pleased for you!'

'We've been fighting to save every penny so that we can put down a month's deposit on a bigger flat,' she heard Ralph say. 'But until now it's been impossible, which brings us to our next piece of news, only you must promise not to let Joan know or I'll be relegated to the ranks of Public Enemy Number One.'

Josie pricked up her ears.

'Ralph is to receive three hundred and fifty pounds!' whispered Jessica. 'For a play!'

Josie nearly gave a yell. She slid her head deeper into the sleeping bag. It was enough of a shock finding out that her brother had actually written a play let alone hearing it had been accepted as well!

'Oh, Ralph, that's wonderful!' she heard Elsie exclaim.

'But why on earth don't you want Joan to know about it?'

'She hates it when people leave her company. You know how possessive she can be.'

'But she'd be delighted to know that one of her actors is writing. Is it because she throws playwright's scripts out of the window and says, "Let's improvise" to her casts, and you don't want her to do that with it?' asked Elsie.

'No. It's because it's for television and not for the stage. I have a feeling she might not be too happy about that.'

'BBC West had a competition for a ninety-minute play,' Jessica explained. 'Ralph was a runner up.'

'And then I received a letter to say that it's been scheduled for a production.'

'It's a very exciting time for writers,' added Jessica. 'The BBC and ITV are showing two hundred and fifty full-length TV plays a year.'

'So I've put down a deposit on a flat in Highgate. We'll have our own bathroom, a bedroom and a gas cooker.'

'It's in a terrible state,' said Jessica, 'but the landlord doesn't mind me redecorating it. In fact, he says that if I do a good job, he'll deduct money off our rent.'

'We're moving there in two weeks' time.'

*Two weeks?* thought Josie. If they were moving that soon, where would she be staying after then? *I must remember not to say anything to Joan*, she told herself and promptly fell asleep.


Auntie Win ushered Detective Inspector Gallaway and DS Mason into the hallway.

'Good news or bad?' she said, bringing them through to the sitting room.

'Both. We've apprehended the two men your niece calls Scowler and Moustache.'

'But that's splendid!'

The detective inspector looked grave.

'So what aren't you telling me?'

'Scowler is in hospital. He was found badly beaten. Moustache walked into a police station last night and confessed to the kidnapping. I've never seen a man so eager to be locked up.'

'He was frightened?'

'Terrified. But he won't tell us why. I suspect he's convinced he'll receive a similar punishment if he talks. We still can't be sure if Mr Lovatt-Pendlebury knows that Josie took the snow and disposed of it, or if in fact he was even the man who asked them to look after it for him, though it seems pretty likely.'

'And the man in hospital has refused to tell you?'

'He can't. He's still unconscious. One of our men is sitting at his bedside as we speak.'

'But if the owner of the drugs *is* Mr Lovatt-Pendlebury?'

DI Gallaway looked uneasy.

'Then we're dealing with a man who has no conscience and no morals. A man who lies effortlessly. He successfully pulled the wool over Miss Merryweather's eyes.'

'Does she know that?'

'She does now. She refused to believe it at first but once we told her the facts, she finally realised she had been duped to gain access to Larry, and she's keen to help. It was she who told Mr Lovatt-Pendlebury that "Larry" was staying here after Miss Dagleish phoned her with the information. She had the details of your flat in her address book.'

'Of course, having been Josie's theatre matron.'

'Mr Lovatt-Pendlebury obtained the information from her under the guise of offering to take her to visit Larry to reassure her he was in good health. Unfortunately . . .' He paused.

'Yes?'

'The following morning Miss Merryweather telephoned Miss Dagleish to ask why Larry was staying with *you* and not with his parents.'

'Don't tell me. Miss Dagleish let the cat out of the bag?'

He nodded. 'And Miss Merryweather passed it on to Mr Lovatt-Pendlebury.'

'So he now knows that the Larry who had been kidnapped was in fact Josie.'

'I'm afraid so. After our conversation, when Miss Merryweather realised she had been conned by this man, she wanted to hand in her resignation, but I reassured her that Miss Dagleish and her staff know nothing of this man and that if she could play innocent when next meeting him, she might be able to gain invaluable information.'

'And she's willing to do that?'

'Oh, yes.'

'She's a brave woman,' said Auntie Win.

'And an angry one. She might appear rather severe on the surface but her charges' welfare come first.'

'You think Josie's whereabouts must still be kept secret?'

'I do.'

'I accept that she can't return here but she can't stay much longer at her brother's place either,' said Win. 'He and his wife are about to move into a flat on the other side of London.'

'Do you know anyone who is not family who might be willing to put her up?'

'I'm afraid not. Do you think she ought to return to Sternsea?'

'No. Now that we know of the conversation Josie overheard, I suspect that the solicitor who chatted to your sister's neighbour and Mr Lovatt-Pendlebury . . .'

'Are one and the same person, which means he knows Josie's Sternsea address. I see what you mean.'

Just then the telephone rang.

'That could be from our station. I gave them your number in case there were any developments. May I?'

Auntie Win nodded.

The DI left the room.

'Do Larry Carpenter's parents have a landlord?' asked DS Mason.

'A landlady. Henrietta Hale. She doesn't live there but she owns the house. You might have heard of her. She writes detective novels.'

He shook his head.

'The house they rent used to be her home. She married a publisher called Hale. They live near that new building on the Thames, the National Film Theatre. Now that's a thought. I wonder . . .'

'More news,' interrupted DI Gallaway returning to the sitting room. 'Miss Merryweather has been in touch with the police. Mr Lovatt-Pendlebury has left the country for one of his European tours. Or so he says. He'd hardly win any prizes for telling the truth. But he's let her know he'll be contacting her on his return in ten days.'

'That gives us some breathing space,' said Auntie Win.

'Not necessarily. He might still be in the area. Until we know exactly where he is I think it wise that we continue to keep Josie's whereabouts under wraps.'

'Detective Inspector, do you really think he's responsible for that man being beaten up?'

'I never believe anything until I have all the evidence.'

'Then how do you account for the state of Mr Beauvoisin's nose after being questioned by your officers?'

There was an awkward silence.

'Those police officers have been severely reprimanded, Major,' he said quietly.

'I'm delighted to hear it,' she said. 'He only has one nose and I suspect he's rather attached to it.

'Aside from that,' he said brusquely, 'have you had any more thoughts concerning your niece's living arrangements?'

'The Carpenter's landlady. She's known Henry, Larry's half brother, since he was fourteen. His family even moved into her house in Sternsea for a while before she sold it and it was converted into flats. That's where Elsie's parents live now, in the bottom flat. She even helped Henry get his first job as a clapper-boy in the film industry. She was absolutely delighted when she heard of Henry and Elsie's engagement because she and Elsie get on like a house on fire. I have a feeling she might be willing to put Josie up.'

'Do you have her phone number?'

'No. But the Carpenters will have it. Do they know about the two arrests?'

He nodded. 'We visited them earlier this evening.'

'I take it you want Miss Dagleish to continue thinking she's staying here?'

'I do. I'm still not happy about trusting her school with confidential information. It would mean that if anyone from the school calls here, you would need to pass on messages to this Mrs Hale, if she agrees to take Josie in.'

'Naturally.'

'Major, can Mr Beauvoisin remain with you?

'Yes, of course, but he'll be at the Theatre Royal for another week which means I'll be on my own most evenings.'

'Is there any way you can contact each other should either of you need to?'

'There's a phone box near the theatre. We could arrange to have a regular telephone call at set times.'

'That could work. And if you don't answer, he can call us,' said DI Gallaway.

'Providing he can be assured that his nose is not in jeopardy again.'

'Point taken,' he grunted.

Josie gazed round the crowded café, wondering if and when she would ever see it again. For a month the Theatre Royal had been her whole world. After a few hours, she would no longer be slipping in and out of the market scenes and across the park in *Make Me An Offer*. There would be no more moving her body in different directions and throwing herself into improvisations. That morning, when their last Laban, voice and improvisation sessions were over, Josie had thought that Joan would say goodbye to them, but she treated them as she would on any ordinary day.

She gazed around the café knowing she had to make the most of every single second.

Mr Beauvoisin was standing at the till, settling up his bills, while Auntie Win sat beside her chatting to Dickie and Elsie. Huddled round the table beside them, with the latest copy of *The Stage*, were three of the cast. The writer of *Make Me An Offer*, Wolf Mankowitz had been on a TV discussion programme called *Monitor* about why British musicals weren't as successful as American ones and they were eager to know what the reviewer had written.

'It says,' said Harry Greene, smiling broadly, 'that Wolf was *naturally without a necktie* just to prove what a rebel he was.'

'Ouch!' said Marjie Lawrence, laughing. 'So what was their verdict on British musicals then?'

'Lack of good choreographers, lack of good dancers, lack of good actors and actresses, and bad promotion.'

'Oh. So nothing to worry about then,' she added dryly.

Their food arrived and the paper was thrust to one side. Josie picked it up and idly flicked over the pages. There was a photograph of a youth with his arm around a young woman who was wearing a cardigan buttoned up to the neck. She had just become his fiancé.

*Twenty-year-old rock and roller Marty Wilde*, the paper said, and then it went on about how they had met on an ITV programme called *Oh Boy*. She turned the page. *Sooty's Christmas Show*, she read. *Mornings and afternoons*.

Christmas? She wondered if she would be in a show by then. She noticed that pupils from one of the stage schools, Aida Foster, had been booked for Christmas already and that Gene Kelly was coming to London for a musical called *Flower Drum Song*.

As she closed the paper, the funny man called Wally who was sitting with Marjie and Harry gave her a wink. She smiled. The cast had cottoned on very quickly that the appearance of their mystery group of shoppers was one of Joan's ploys.

Josie tucked her arm into Auntie Win's and rested her head against her shoulder, just as Mr Beauvoisin appeared at their table with surprise bowls of spotted dick with custard.

'I thought we should have a farewell pudding,' he announced.

And then the last performance was over, *just like that* as Josie's mum's favourite comedian Tommy Cooper would say, followed by the dash to the wardrobe and the careful hanging up of their costumes.

'Dickie, don't tell me you've caught the acting bug,' said Elsie, observing his glum face.

'No, I haven't,' he replied. 'Although I've learned a lot

about observing people these last two weeks. I'm thinking it might be useful if I do undercover work.'

'You mean like a spy?' said Josie. 'Or a private eye?'

'Who knows, cheeky?' he said, beaming, and he tweaked her nose.

It was strange walking through the red foyer for the last time. So much had happened to Josie in the Theatre Royal that she had a feeling that a little bit of her would always be left within its walls.

She had said her goodbyes earlier to the volunteers and cleaners and Mrs P. She remembered how, a couple of weeks earlier, Mr Beauvoisin had taken her round to each of them so that she could confess that she was in fact a girl and not a boy, but instead of them being angry at her deception, they had laughed. They had all assumed that Miss Littlewood, or Joan as she preferred everyone to call her, had asked her to convince them she was a boy as one of her acting improvisations and they commended Josie on fooling them.

'Joan must be very chuffed wiv you,' Mrs P had said. 'Only she won't say nuffin'. She don't like to praise. She's afraid of people gettin' big headed.'

One of the many experiences that Josie had found invaluable was Joan's insistence that she play a girl. She had come to realise that she had avoided playing one not only because she thought girl's parts were soppy, but also because deep down she had believed she couldn't do it, having only played boys. Joan had encouraged her to play the kind of girl Josie would have found acutely uncomfortable pretending to be. She had made her feel as though she could play anyone if she put her mind to it, – and more importantly, if she put her body into it too.

Josie stood with Elsie, Mr Beauvoisin and Auntie Win at the arched entrance. Dickie pulled up on his motorbike and she clambered into the sidecar.

'I'll pop round to see you at Mr and Mrs Hale's tomorrow,' said her aunt, bending down to give her a hug.

'And I'll be travelling to school from there?'

'Yes.'

'And I'll be taking you,' said Dickie, handing Elsie the helmet.

'Josie, there's something I've been meaning to tell you,' her aunt began awkwardly. 'I wanted to wait until the show was over to avoid upsetting you.'

Josie's heart sank. 'Mrs Hale wants me to wear pretty frocks and pale pink cardigans?'

'No. It's about Guides. Until the police give their permission, I'm afraid you can't stay with the Carpenters at the weekend. It's just until they sort out all this business with the kidnappers,' she added hastily. She hated keeping their arrests a secret but that is what she had been instructed to do for Josie's safety.

'But I'm working towards my Second Class!'

And, how on earth was she going to get through a week of school without Guides to look forward to?

'And you're not to breathe a word about the kidnapping to Hilda until the police say you can. Neither are you to talk about Mr Lovatt-Pendlebury.'

'But I've already told her about him.'

'How much?'

'Oh, about him going all gooey over Miss Merryweather and about how he went on and on and on about his trips to Europe.'

'But that's all?'

'Yeah.'

'Good. Keep it that way,' said Auntie Win.

'But won't she think it's a bit strange that I'm not stayin' with you?'

'She doesn't need to know that.'

'But what if she rings me at your flat?'

'We'll arrange a regular time for you to ring her. And anyway, you'll be seeing each other every day so there's no need to talk to each other on the telephone much, is there?' She kissed Josie's cheek as Elsie climbed onto the back seat. 'You look after them both, young man,' she commanded Dickie.

The curved lid was closed over Josie's head.

'Goodbye, Theatre Royal,' she whispered, hugging her attaché case.

As the engine revved and the motorbike shot forward, she glanced through the little window on the off-chance that Joan might be standing on the pavement to wave goodbye to them but she was nowhere to be seen. She had probably forgotten about them already.

# Act Three

Comeuppances

# I

# Picking Up the Threads

MRS HALE USHERED JOSIE THROUGH A BOOK-
lined hall towards a telephone.

'Ring your parents straight away,' she said. 'They're staying
up late to talk to you. Tomorrow afternoon they're catching
a train to Waterloo and coming here for a lovely slap-up tea
round the fire.'

'With chocolate and ginger cake,' Mr Hale added with
relish. 'And then we'll take you for a little explore along the
South Bank – that's the south side of the Thames nearest to
us.'

Mr and Mrs Hale were a short, stocky couple in their
sixties. A friendly and talkative pair, they lived at the top of
an enormous Victorian building in a rambling flat full of big
rooms, high ceilings and old fireplaces. Unlike Auntie Win's
flat where the floors were covered in linoleum or carpet,
their dark wooden floorboards had oriental rugs thrown on
them, with comfy old settees and armchairs.

Every alcove was filled with books. There were even
books on shelves above the doors. Their dining room was
used as a study where papers and more books were stacked

on a long table. Mrs Hale wrote her detective novels at one end and Mr Hale read and edited authors' manuscripts at the other.

It was obvious that Mr Hale adored Mrs Hale, and they were always making each other laugh. They were delighted to see Elsie again, hear the latest news about Henry, and they beamed at Josie in such a manner that she had a strong desire to hug them.

'Hello, Mrs Hollis!' Mrs Hale sang out, minutes after dialling. 'Yes, she's here.' She handed Josie the receiver. 'Come on, Mr Hale. Cocoa.'

By the time Josie had chatted to her parents, drunk her cocoa and climbed into bed, she felt as though she had been there for months. She and Elsie had been given a bedroom beside the sitting room. There were hot water bottles in their beds, and laid out on top of the blankets were heavy eiderdowns in green and blue paisley. Even though the walls in the flat were thick, she could just hear Elsie chatting away with the Hales and Dickie.

Still too excited to sleep, she pulled a jersey over her pyjamas and slipped out of bed for the third time to make sure she hadn't imagined the view. Through the window, beyond the bomb sites and building sites, she could make out a glimmer of the Thames. In a few hours, hundreds of people would be crossing the bridges on their way to work, streaming up and down it in boats, or rehearsing music in the modern, concrete Royal Festival Hall.

As soon as Josie was awake the next morning, she slipped

on her socks and padded down the hall to the voices in the kitchen. Mrs Hale was spreading a damp jersey on top of a huge range. Josie immediately scuttled over to its warmth and leaned against it.

'Scrambled eggs on toast?' asked Mrs Hale.

'Yes, please!'

The doorbell rang.

'That'll be your parents. They couldn't wait till this afternoon to see you so they decided to come early. Like to –?'

But Josie was already flying down the hall.

'Do you think I'm a baby not going to school by myself?' Josie asked Dickie when he dropped her off at school the following morning.

'No. You went on your own before'

Dickie had parked his motorbike with the sidecar in a road off the square. He also had received instructions from DI Gallaway not to tell Josie that one kidnapper was safely in prison and the other was unconscious and handcuffed to a hospital bed. If she had known, she would have asked why she still needed to be under observation and why she had to stay at Mr and Mrs Hale's flat. Until the police had more information about Mr Lovatt-Pendlebury, the less she knew the better.

'And once we've got those crooks safely behind bars,' he told her, 'you'll be able to do it again.'

Josie dreaded going back. As she climbed out of the sidecar she felt as though the outer layer of her skin had been peeled off and that it would soon be scratched with cruel remarks. She walked alongside Dickie towards the square, glancing aside at the garden behind the padlocked gate and wishing she could unlock it and hide among the shrubs. Eventually, her feet took her round the corner and they headed towards the kerb opposite. Dickie knelt down and pretended to tie a shoelace.

'I'll wait here until you're through the door,' he said over his shoulder.

It was then that she spotted a familiar figure waiting for her on the steps.

'Hilda!' Josie yelled.

'I'll pick you up after school,' he added but Josie was already dashing across the road. Soon she and Hilda were linking arms and trotting up the steps.

'How's your Mum?' Hilda asked. 'Is she feeling better now?'

Josie hated the idea of lying to her friend. Somehow she had to find a way of telling her the truth without giving anything away.

She nodded.

Hilda gave her a squeeze.

'Oh, good.'

'She and Dad even came to London yesterday,' Josie said, and then she realised that she couldn't tell Hilda about the slap up tea around the Hales' kitchen table and how her parents, after having heard so much about Mrs Hale from Elsie and Henry, were delighted to meet her at long last. And how her dad had hugged her tightly on his lap while he and the Hales had made her and Mum laugh so much she thought she would be sick. And how relieved her parents were that Josie would be staying with the Hales for a bit.

'To see your Auntie Win?' asked Hilda.

'Yeah.'

Which was sort of true since Auntie Win had popped round in the afternoon.

By now Josie had picked up that her friend was bursting to tell her something.

'You started to say something about Her Majesty's Theatre . . .' Josie began.

And all the pent-up news Hilda had been holding back in secret for weeks came pouring out.

Hilda had waited outside the theatre armed with questions about where to find jazz ballet classes but the cast members of *West Side Story* had been unable to help her. However, one of them had asked the person in charge of their warm up if she could join in.

'I go as many times as I can after school, but don't breathe a word. If Esmeralda ever found out . . .'

'Her mother would arrange extra lessons for you so that you'd be too late to join in,' finished Josie for her.

Hilda nodded.

'And I couldn't bear that. It's wonderful, Josie. It's like a proper class. I've learned so much. I can ask if you can join in too.'

Josie said nothing. She couldn't tell Hilda that until the kidnappers had been caught, she wasn't even allowed out to attend Guide meetings.

But Hilda seemed not to notice and continued to talk

non-stop about the different exercises she was learning. They dumped their bags in the basement cloakroom and headed for the classroom. To Josie's relief, no one stopped her on the way to ask her where she had been. They assumed, like Hilda, that she had been looking after her mother and it was no different from being treated like one of the pupils who had returned after having been away on an acting job, which was half true. Everything was going to be fine she told herself.

And then it was French.

The teachers had been told that her aunt had picked up homework from the school to send to Sternsea for Josie to do while her mother was resting.

But having had at least ten lessons with Mr Beauvoisin, she was miles ahead of everyone. She kept her head down but eventually Miss Denton, the French mistress, asked her to hand over the work she had done while she had been away.

'Is this your own work?' she asked slowly.

Josie nodded.

'I'm afraid you will still have to do what the other pupils are doing. I can't make you an exception.'

'You'll have to keep up with us now,' said Trixie.

The teacher held the book out for Josie to take back to her desk. On the way back, Jim Eliot snatched it from her.

'Little Miss Dimwit!' he yelled.

Josie tried to grab it.

'Give it back to her,' Hilda shouted.

'Both of you! Sit down this minute!' commanded Miss Denton.

The other girls rallied round Jim turning the pages and shrieking with laughter, and then when they realised how well she had done they fell silent and stared at Josie as if she had landed from another planet.

Miss Denton strode towards Jim's desk, removed the book from him and handed it back to Josie. Sulkily, the girls returned to their desks.

'Your homework for Friday . . .' Miss Denton began.

And everyone groaned, including Josie.

She was ahead in maths too, but that was because Mr Beauvoisin had made it so easy to understand. By the time it was English composition, she ignored the racket in the class and drifted into writing about a world where howling blizzards and a snowstorm caused a girl to be lost. Rescued by a strange, silent man, the girl had been taken to a hut where there was a roaring fire and a hot drink. Later, wrapped in furs, she had been placed on a sledge drawn by husky dogs. The villagers greeted her with astonishment when the sledge arrived at their village and asked how she had managed to survive on her own. She told them about the man who had rescued her and had driven the sledge.

'What man?' they said. 'It was the dogs that brought you back.' The girl turned but there was no sign of her rescuer, not even a footstep in the snow. There was nothing except the sledge tracks. The man had been a ghost.

When Josie raised her head, she discovered that aside from Hilda, who was sitting quietly reading another ballet book, everyone else had already left the room.

Dance was the first lesson after break. Hilda was

impatient to show Josie the jazz ballet she had picked up but they were interrupted by the appearance of Miss Frobisher, accompanied by Miss Peabody carrying the gramophone player. Within seconds it was back to stepping and pointing to the strains of a soprano with a wobbly voice, followed by the familiar routine of gliding gracefully into pretty poses in the centre of the room.

It was when they had to tip their heads to one side, stick a finger under their chin and smile sweetly that Josie and Hilda glanced at one another in despair.

The next lesson Josie approached with caution. It was the acting class.

'Since this is your first lesson in four weeks you will be a little behind,' said Mrs Havilland with a smile that looked as though it had been taken out of the tiny freezer compartment at the top of Auntie Win's refrigerator. 'I suggest you sit and observe today.'

And Josie did observe. Very carefully. She was now acutely aware of the class sitting stiffly in a row while they took it in turns to do an audition speech; how Mrs Havilland instructed them to enter on the upstage leg – stepping out with their right foot if coming from stage left, and vice versa. She listened as Mrs Havilland demonstrated where to use a rising inflection and when to emphasise a word with a gesture, but also how she never asked the pupils any questions about the kind of person they were supposed to be or what they wished for or what was going on in the scene.

*This is all rubbish*, Josie murmured inside her head. 'You're not playing a part,' she remembered Joan yelling at someone. 'You're playing a human being!'

'And don't forget to give a little knowing smile when you say *your Lordship*, Thelma,' Mrs Havilland said.

*I can't do this any longer*, Josie thought.

Later, Josie dragged herself to a voice class with the fourth-formers. Esmeralda was already sitting in the front with three members of her fan club gazing at her.

'MGM studios!' she heard one of her hangers on cry. 'Really?'

'Yes, a new series called *Danger Man*,' said Esmeralda.

The voice teacher entered and it was back to everyone reciting 'How now brown cow'. It felt odd not to be moving around a room doing breathing exercises from the diaphragm.

At lunchtime, Hilda and Josie sat in a corner of the café while Esmeralda and her friends made snide comments about how ugly and diseased Josie looked with all her freckles. Josie left the tea house struggling to stay cheerful, while Hilda hooked her arm in hers and tried to make her laugh. They were just entering the hall when they spotted Miss Dagleish's secretary, who beckoned Josie to go over to the headmistress's office.

Nervously, Josie made her way down the corridor. She was about to tap hesitantly on the door when she changed her mind. *Punchy*, she decided and gave a hearty knock.

'Enter!' said a loud voice.

Head up high, Josie opened the door and bobbed into a curtsy.

Miss Dagleish was sitting solemnly behind her desk.

'I'll come straight to the point, Josephine. I have asked you here because of a certain matter that was brought to my attention by Miss Merryweather last month. She led me to understand that you are at present a member of a certain Girl Guide Company outside the school premises. From next term there will be no need for you to continue attending their meetings as there is to be a school Guide Company run by two of our teachers. Here you will be mixing with nicely spoken gels who all speak RP.'

Josie's heart sank. Her one means of escape taken away from her.

'And what does RP mean, Josephine?'

'Received pronunciation, madam,' Josie mumbled. 'Posh, like the BBC.'

'The Queen's English. That's what it means.'

'Yes, madam,' murmured Josie.

'You may go now,' she said with a flourish of her hand.

*Flick! Flick!* thought Josie as she backed miserably towards the door.

## 2

# Being Taught a Lesson

THE FOLLOWING MONDAY MRS HAVILLAND asked to see her.

'Next week, you are to attend your first audition for a film role,' she announced.

Josie was astounded.

'But Miss Dagleish told me she wouldn't put me up for one until next term,' said Josie.

'She's changed her mind.'

Josie beamed.

'What's the film about?' she asked eagerly.

'You don't need to know that, young lady. It's only a small part.'

'But what kind of person is this girl?'

'I think I've made it quite clear, Josephine, it's not an important role.'

'But every role is important. That's what Joan says.'

'*Joan!*'

'Er, Miss Littlewood.'

Mrs Havilland's jaw dropped.

'How dare you bring up that woman's name in front of me!

I've a good mind to report you to Miss Dagleish for insolence.'
She thrust a piece of paper at her. 'Here is the address with
directions. I'm afraid your aunt will have to escort you. Miss
Merryweather is otherwise engaged on that day chaperoning
a pupil who is auditioning for a far bigger role.'

At the midday break, Esmeralda's entourage had, as usual,
bagged the two tables near the counter at the tea house and
were gazing rapturously at her as she graced them with the
latest show business news. Josie and Hilda sat well away
from them by the window.

'What is it?' cried Thelma, hurriedly joining the group.

'You'll only understand what we're going through if you
listen to pop music,' Esmeralda declared.

'I do. Oh!' she gasped. 'It's something important, isn't it?
I can tell by the look in your eyes.'

'It's about Marty Wilde.' Esmeralda's fan club leaned
even closer. 'He's got engaged to one of the Vernon Girls.'

'How romantic!' Thelma exclaimed. 'But so sad.'

'You never thought he'd marry you, did you?' said Merle.
The others laughed.

'N-no, of course not,' stammered Thelma, blushing, but
Josie was surprised to see that she was upset.

'They met when they appeared in the *Oh Boy* series on
ITV,' continued Esmeralda. 'As you know, they're in the
*Boy Meets Girls* series now.'

Usually Josie switched off when Esmeralda was doing
her 'latest gossip' gatherings, but this time she was all ears
because she had the oddest feeling she already knew about

his engagement. She shook her head. *Impossible,* she thought. She didn't mix in the same glamorous circles as Esmeralda and her mother did.

A photograph of Marty Wilde with his arm across his fiancée's shoulder came into her head. But where could she have seen it? It couldn't have been in a magazine. She never read them. And then she remembered. It was in the Angel café. It had been in a copy of *The Stage.*

'Of course, I prefer more mature men myself,' said Esmeralda.

'But he is mature!' exclaimed Thelma. 'He's *twenty!*'

'Someone who's about twenty-five,' she added airily.

'And has a Mini,' added a girl called Barbara, significantly.

'Have you been in a Mini?' asked Doris, wide-eyed.

'I have actually,' said Esmeralda.

This was followed by squeals of excitement. Josie and Hilda looked at one another and raised their eyes to the ceiling.

'So what else has been happening since I've been away working?' chipped in a pretty blond girl called Sybil.

'One of our juniors is appearing at the Palace Theatre, performing mornings and nights in *Sooty's Christmas Show,*' said Esmeralda.

'A *London* show!' Barbara exclaimed.

'Yes! I tell you, this school is going up in the world. She's one of the Sooty Sweethearts. Sadly it's not all good news. Once again the Aida Foster babes will be in *Humpty Dumpty* at the Palladium. Makes me sick. They never take anyone from here. Favouritism. That's what it is.'

Hilda swung round.

'Maybe they're better dancers,' she said across the tea house.

There was an audible intake of breath from Esmeralda's fan club.

'Better than you perhaps, Hilda,' she quipped. 'Remember, it was I who came to the rescue in *Midsummer Night's Dream*. Without me, I doubt the play could have gone on.'

'You'd think she played Titania the way she goes on,' muttered Hilda to Josie.

'Putting that insolent interruption aside,' Esmeralda continued, 'I do have some rather splendid and up-to-date news. Gene Kelly is to direct *Flower Drum Song* in London!'

And then Josie twigged! Esmeralda wasn't mixing with the stars at all. *The Stage* was for adults but her mother probably bought weekly copies of it. Josie suspected she fed Esmeralda tit-bits from it about the world of entertainment.

Meanwhile the other girls continued to gaze awestruck at their idol while she lapped up their adulation. 'He's not looking for names, though,' she said. 'So we're in with a chance. He wants the right talent and the right people.' And here she glared across at Hilda and Josie. 'Which means *not* you!'

Josie glanced quickly at Hilda. She was just smiling and shrugging it off.

But Josie didn't find it at all funny. Hilda was so talented, yet Josie was certain that while Esmeralda was still a pupil at the school, Hilda would never be put up for that audition or any other dance auditions. To her surprise Josie found herself staring at her friend and thinking, *I have to get you out of here*.

Josie didn't mention the film audition to her aunt. With no chaperone to keep an eye on her, it was the perfect opportunity to put her escape plan for Hilda into action. On the morning of the audition, Hilda was to phone the school to say she was too sick to attend. She and Josie would meet outside the building where the audition was taking place and from there they would catch a bus.

Josie had told her that by an extraordinary coincidence, Hilda had been offered an audition on the same day, thanks to Elsie who had arranged it all. If Josie had told her the truth, Hilda would never have agreed to come with her.

All was going to plan, but when it was time to leave the school Josie found herself confronted in the hall by a tall, plump woman in a tweed suit and matching hat, carrying a dripping umbrella. Josie glanced briefly at the face beneath the hat. Early twenties, she thought, with an oddly familiar face.

'I am Mrs Ellington and I am to be your chaperone,' she stated. 'The school secretary, thinking it rather odd that your aunt hadn't been in touch with her decided to telephone her, only to discover that you had neglected to inform her of the audition.'

'I didn't want to bother her,' Josie said.

'Indeed. Well, you've been a bother to other people instead.'

'Sorry,' Josie mumbled.

With a heavy heart she followed the haughty young woman down the steps into torrential rain. This sudden appearance of a chaperone was going to scupper everything. Mrs Ellington would insist on accompanying her back to the school after the audition and it would be impossible to let Hilda know that she would be unable to meet her. Hilda would turn up and when Josie didn't appear, she would think she had gone to the wrong building.

Mrs Ellington opened her umbrella and Josie pulled the hood of her duffle coat over her school hat. They had hardly reached the bus stop when she began to give Josie a lecture.

'Fine feathers make fine birds,' she announced. 'You must be well groomed from your hair to your feet. That's advice from someone who knows,' she added meaningfully. '*Advice to a Player*. That will be your bible from the day you become a fourth-form pupil. A gentleman called Denys Blakelock has written it for drama students. My mother has obtained a copy for the benefit of the school.'

'*Jolli* good,' Josie was tempted to say but kept her mouth shut.

'Do you know how important a smile is on stage?'

'Yes,' said Josie slowly. 'We're taught that in our acting classes.'

'By my mother,' added the chaperone.

So that's why her face looked familiar! She was one of Mrs Havilland's daughters.

'Denys Blakelock says, and I quote, *If you can find a way of cultivating a sincere and natural smile, you will have acquired a prop worth having.* But I think it's useful to wear a smile off stage as well as on stage, don't you?'

She made a smile sound as though it were an overcoat, thought Josie.

'For example,' Mrs Ellington continued. 'Now.'

'Now?' repeated Josie.

'You are about to attend an audition, young Josephine. You should be practising your smile ready for making your first entrance.'

*With the correct foot*, Josie added internally. To her relief she spotted their bus approaching.

The only good thing about travelling with Mrs Ellington was that Miss Dagleish had given her money for their bus tickets. It meant that if by some miracle Josie could get rid of her, she wouldn't have to spend so much of her saved pocket money on fares later on. They sat downstairs, Josie by the window. Once Mrs Ellington had been given their tickets from a cheery young conductress, there was an uncomfortable silence.

'So did you go to Miss Dagleish's school?' Josie asked politely, desperate to break it.

'No. I went to a finishing school to prepare me for coming out as a deb.'

All this was double-dutch to Josie. 'A deb?'

'Debutante. Up until last year, young gels from good families were presented at very grand affairs where they would be introduced to cultured, eligible young men. That's what *coming out* means.'

Josie was none the wiser. 'What's a finishing school?' she asked.

'Let us suppose you are a man who makes antique tables. After you make one of these tables, you need to add the finishing touches. You need to sand it down, round off the corners and French polish it. Girls who go to a good finishing school are like newly made antique tables who have their rough corners smoothed.'

'Is that why we have French lessons?'

'What?' snapped Mrs Ellington

'Like the French polish.'

'Don't be absurd.'

'But if the tables have just been made, how can they be antique? An antique table is very old, isn't it? That would mean that only very old ladies would need to be sanded down and polished.'

'I mean one that *looks* like an antique table,' said Mrs Ellington in exasperation. 'A copy. Not the sort of furniture my family would ever dream of buying, of course – more the sort of item the nouveaux riches would buy. They're people who have made their money rather than inherited it but who desire to resemble people from the aristocracy.'

'Auntie Win won the premium bonds, but I don't think she's nouveau riche because she likes modern furniture.'

'More fool she.'

'And pays for my fees to go to Miss Dagleish's stage school.'

'Well, that shows she has some taste but, Josephine, however well your rough edges are smoothed, I'm afraid you will never be upper class.'

'But I don't want to be upper class. I want to act.'

'Well, yes of course. But most players are from the upper classes. I know because I was once an actress, but then I married.'

'So you aren't an actress any more?'

'Of course not. Married women don't go out to work. No respectable married woman, that is.'

Josie thought of Hilda's mother doing cleaning jobs to help pay for Hilda's fees and the idea of her being viewed as not being respectable made Josie very angry.

'But your mother works,' Josie said quietly.

Mrs Ellington looked as though she was about to explode. After making a series of strangled snorts, she eventually appeared to breathe normally again.

'My mother isn't *paid* for her contribution to the school! Daddy calls it her *little interest* but it's far more than that. She's an artistic philanthropist. It's her contribution to the arts. However, she realises that not everyone is fortunate enough to work in the hallowed portals of the theatre, which is why there is a secretarial course in the fourth form. The lucky ones go on to be stewardesses and wear tailored suits designed by Cecil Beaton.'

Far from impressing Josie, this revelation only filled her with dread.

'There's no need to worry,' said Mrs Ellington, noticing the look of despair on Josie's face. 'Next year in the etiquette lessons you'll learn how to make graceful entrances and exits through doorways, with handbags and umbrellas. It's a difficult profession to be accepted into but the good news is that stewardesses need to be replaced pretty often because they lose so many of them.'

'Is that because of aeroplane crashes?' asked Josie.

'No, you silly girl! It's just that during their training they learn how to prepare and present food well, and that makes them ideal wives. A lot of them have marriage proposals and leave the profession to get married. Often, they marry the pilots.'

'Do they leave too?'

'Of course not!' Mrs Ellington gave an exasperated sigh. 'All I'm saying is that if you don't acquire work as an actress, then being an air stewardess is an excellent training for being a good housewife.'

Josie had a sudden vision of Auntie Win as a stewardess; smoke billowing down the aisle of an aeroplane cabin. If her aunt were on a plane, it would be better if the pilot cooked the food and her aunt flew the plane.

'Why would a girl want to be a good housewife?'

'Every girl does.'

'I don't.'

'Well, you're peculiar then.'

Josie thought of Elsie. She couldn't imagine her never working in the theatre again after she was married. And then she remembered a married couple who were both still acting; Harry Greene and Marjie Lawrence in *Make Me An Offer*.

'Acting isn't that important anyway,' said Mrs Ellington grandly.

Josie was astonished. She was beginning to wonder if Mrs Ellington had ever acted at all. How could she think acting was unimportant? It was helping tell stories and making audiences laugh or think. Stories, Elsie had told her, were important. Everyone needed stories.

'What theatres did you act in?' Josie asked curiously.

'I performed in large church halls mostly, in drawing-room comedies. I never much liked being in theatres. Do you know what a drawing-room comedy is?'

'Yes. It's posh people being funny in a sitting room.'

Mrs Ellington reddened.

'Esmeralda warned me about your rudeness. I now see what she means.'

Josie was bewildered. 'I didn't mean –' she began.

'You've let the school down. You know that, don't you?'

Josie was stunned. 'But I've been put up into Form III.'

'Beauty is more highly regarded than brains in a girl.'

'You mean I've let the school down because I've done well in class?' Josie asked, now thoroughly confused.

'No. It's because you're an embarrassment. You've worked with that Joan Littlewood,' she snapped. 'A vulgar, foul-mouthed disgrace to womankind.'

Josie took a deep breath and counted to ten, before saying, 'If I've let the school down, why is Miss Dagleish sending me to an audition?'

'Because you need to learn that you can't have everything handed to you on a plate. This is one job you have absolutely no chance of being given.'

Josie felt as though she had been slapped across the face.

'But if there's no chance . . .' she began. 'Why –?'

'To teach you a lesson. It's to be your comeuppance.'

Josie pressed her lips together. Somehow she had to find a way of getting rid of this horrible woman.

'So I'll be humiliated?'

'Utterly.'

'But you're my chaperone, so you'll be humiliated too, won't you?'

Mrs Ellington gasped in horror.

'Unless you dump me at the audition place and scarper,' Josie added.

'What kind of language is that?'

Make Me An Offer *language*, thought Josie.

'And then you can leave me to get my comeuppance on my own, and go and have an upper class tea somewhere and say scone to rhyme with Ron and not scone to rhyme with bone.' She switched on the stage school smile, only it was more like the smile you might see on an aggressive chimpanzee. 'But don't eat 'em with one of them small forks or you'll look *silli*.'

By this time, Mrs Ellington's eyes had widened to such an extent that it was as though someone had stuck their fingers behind the lids and stretched them.

'I shall not forget this outrageous behaviour,' she spat out, shaking with anger. 'I will report you.'

It was obvious that she really wanted to shout at her but Josie knew she wouldn't because it was unladylike and undignified.

'If it hadn't been for the acting work you have been given this term, young lady, you would have been expelled long ago.'

'But you said I was to get my comeuppance by *not* getting this acting work,' said Josie puzzled. 'Does that mean I'll get my comeuppance *and* be expelled?'

'That's it!' Mrs Ellington spluttered, and she scrabbled round inside her crocodile-skin handbag, her hands shaking. 'Here is your ticket and money for your return fare. I will be alighting at the next stop. I won't bother wishing you luck, as it would be a complete waste of time. The verdict is a foregone conclusion.'

Josie bowed her head, fighting to stop herself from smiling. Once Mrs Ellington had stepped off the bus she sank back in her seat, almost laughing with relief. As soon as the conductress came down the aisle to take money from the new passengers, Josie called out to her.

'Excuse me, can you tell me where I have to get off?' Josie asked, holding out the piece of paper with the address on it.

'Course I can, love,' she said, beaming.

The large building where the auditions were to take place was a hundred yards from the bus stop. Ahead of Josie, she spotted boys and girls accompanied by women approaching a high door. The girls looked about the same age as her, all smartly dressed, all with long plaits. And at a glance it became clear why there was no chance of her being given the job. They were in pairs. They were all twins. Standing in the rain staring at them she felt bewildered that Miss Dagliesh and Mrs Havilland had set out to be so cruel to her, and she realised instantly that there was no point in turning up for the audition.

She had hardly turned away when she found herself thinking of Joan Littlewood. She could picture her vividly, leaning casually on one leg, her woollen hat pulled down straight, a cigarette in her outstretched hand. She wondered what Joan would have said if she had been there. And then she knew.

'Go on in there, my little clown, and improvise!'

Josie headed rapidly towards the entrance. At least it would be dry in there, she thought.

# 3

# Gatecrashing

JOSIE STRODE BOLDLY TOWARDS THE receptionist, a mousey-haired woman in a tweed suit seated behind a large desk.

'I've come to audition for Mr Clark and Mr Stanmore,' she announced in the manner she imagined Celia in *Make Me An Offer* might speak and she handed over the piece of paper Mrs Havilland had thrust at her. The receptionist peered over her glasses.

'I have you down as J Hollis. But this audition is for twins.'

'That is correct,' said Josie. 'Both our names begin with J. I'm Jane and my sister is Joy. My mother did it on purpose to save money on name tapes.'

'I see. But where is Joy?'

'On her way. She was so busy chatting to our chaperone that they missed the bus but they'll catch the next one.'

'Luckily Mr Clark and Mr Stanmore have several more people to see before your audition but your sister had better get a move on.' She beckoned a smartly dressed woman over to her. 'This is the production secretary. She'll escort you up to the waiting room.'

The waiting room was a bare room with chairs around the walls. As Josie sat down she observed there were boys of different ages and other pairs of girls. Half their chaperones, she guessed, were their mothers. Several of the children wore the bright green Corona stage school blazers with the yellow edging. Others wore grey or navy blue uniforms similar to her one, or were dressed up as though they were about to attend a première. Two girls in pink taffeta and lace dresses were having their hair combed and twirled into ringlets by their mother. Josie decided to keep her hat on, sensing that the appearance of her haircut might send a ripple of horror around the room.

'Film companies much prefer girls with long hair,' the mother with the comb told Josie, throwing her the kind of sympathetic look one might give if a member of Josie's family had recently been mown down by a lorry. She had obviously spotted the absence of plaits or, in fact, the absence of any sign of hair emerging from underneath Josie's school hat.

Noticing how most of the mothers fussed around their children, Josie appreciated how easy going her own mother was towards her. These mothers hardly allowed their sons and daughters to breathe between making them rehearse little speeches in the middle of the floor. Stage school pupils on the chairs lining the opposite wall were quietly muttering their set audition speeches in unison. Josie loathed the one she had been taught. It was from a play set in medieval times where a girl was pleading for her life, yet willing to die with a brave smile if that's what it took to save her brother from being executed and it had lots of *verily* this and *verily* thats in it.

The production secretary returned to escort one of the small boys to the next floor.

Josie concentrated on her body. She felt too self-conscious to move around the room doing Laban movements, so the next best thing was to think about them in her head. Jane, she decided was vertical, head aiming for the sky. Upright. Precise. Grammar school girl. Neat in movement. Alert. *Dab, dab, dab*. Joy was punchy.

Two of the girls were told to go upstairs. Hardly had they left the room when the receptionist put her head round the door.

'Jane, your sister still hasn't arrived. If she isn't here soon . . .'

'She'll be here any minute. I've never known her miss an audition yet,' Josie declared with as much gaiety as she could dredge up.

'But you're next.'

'Don't worry. I'll go on up, and when she arrives, do tell her to get a move on, will you?'

Ten minutes later Josie was hovering outside a door with a notice stuck on it.

'*AUDITIONS. RIVER ADVENTURE*,' she read. She threw her duffle coat onto the floor and knocked.

'Come in,' sang out a male voice.

'Vertical,' she murmured.

Josie opened the door, closing it carefully behind her and stood erect. Two men in tweed jackets and ties were sitting behind a table. A smartly dressed secretary with glasses like slanting pink wings sat between them taking notes. The man at the far end was holding sheets of paper with typed words on it. The script, Josie guessed. The man nearest the door was wearing round spectacles with tortoise-shell rims and was puffing away at a pipe. They gave each other a quick glance.

'You do know . . .' began the one with the pipe.

'That you wish to see my sister and me at the same time. Oh yes! But I couldn't wait. She's on her way so I thought I'd save you time . . .'

'And you are?'

'Jane Hollis.'

'Sit down, will you?'

Josie sat bolt upright at the edge of the seat.

'Now, tell us a little about you, Jane. Your hobbies . . .'

'I love reading, I attend ballet classes and I sing in a choir.'

'And you and your sister are at the same school?'

'No. I'm at a grammar school and Joy is at a stage school. That's how I heard about the audition. We're quite different.'

'But identical?'

'Like peas in a pod.'

'Well, Jane, we'd like you to read for us.'

'The twins are called Heidi and Bridie,' said the other man, handing her a page from the script.

'So what's just happened before this bit?' asked Josie in a perky, 'Jane' manner.

The two men smiled.

'You're the first girl to ask that question,' said the man wearing glasses.

'Oh dear,' said Josie brightly. 'I hope that hasn't put the kibosh on it.'

'Not at all. The twins have just escaped the clutches of two very nasty crooks . . .'

Josie very nearly fell off the chair. *Think 'Jane'*, she told herself sternly.

'And she's telling a policeman what's happened,' he continued.

'So it's vital that she gives him the correct facts?' said Josie.

'Indeed. Read it to yourself first,' he said. 'Then when you're ready . . .'

Josie nodded, indicating that she understood. Within seconds she knew it was a bit too jolly japes for her. But how would Jane read it? Being an intelligent and no-nonsense sort of person she wouldn't make a big thing out of the situation. She imagined herself standing in front of a police sergeant in a police station, giving an important statement. She stood up and took a deep breath.

'It was jolly *cold*. And the man had a jolly *enormous* nose,' she said matter of factly. 'We had to run awfully *quickly* to escape. But we have a jolly good *description* of the boss.'

'That will do,' said the man with the pipe after she had read some more. 'Well done. The problem is . . .'

'Hang on a mo,' Josie said, rising to her feet. 'I'll have a quick look outside.' She swung the door open, leaped out onto the landing and slung on her duffle coat. '*Joy,*' she muttered. '*Punchy, horizontal. East End.*'

'Joy!' she yelled as 'Jane' across the landing. 'Hurry up! They're waiting for you.'

Josie then flung open the door and left it banging against the wall.

'Sorry, I'm late!' she said with gusto. 'Bus conductor trouble.' And she leaped across the floor.

'You're Joy?'

'Yeah. That's me.'

'My goodness!' said the secretary. 'They do look alike.'

'I took a gander at yer notice so I knows the film is abaht a river adventure. So if you needs anyone who knows semaphore . . .'

'Semaphore?' commented the man with the pipe.

'Yeah. I'm workin' for me Signallers badge. I knows *all* the semaphore alphabet. SOS!' she yelled. And she threw her arms eagerly into the Save Our Souls semaphore positions.

'Joy,' said the man by the window, 'can you swim?'

'Like a fish,' she lied with enthusiasm. 'Breaststroke,' she added, giving a quick demonstration with her arms.

'And you're the one from the stage school?'

'Yeah. So I can speak posh if you need it.'

'And have you played any parts professionally?'

'Oh yeah. *Life Wiv Farver*. Jane and me played Whitney. We took turns and understudied one anuvver, and then we did a bit in *Make Me An Offer* at the Theatre Royal for a fortnight.'

The man with the pipe began to smile.

'You worked with Joan Littlewood?'

'Yeah.'

'Would you like to read a little from the script, Joy?'

'Yeah. Please!'

The secretary handed it over to her.

'You may want to read it through first,' he added.

It was the same piece she had read as Jane. *Over-enthusiastic and clumsy*, Josie decided.

'In a posh accent?' she asked.

The men nodded.

Josie decided that this twin had been running non-stop for a mile from the crooks and had to get the information to the policeman as quickly as possible, and that it was the most exciting thing that had ever happened to her in her entire life. She leaped over to the corner of the room and proceeded to stagger towards a copper on the street, breathlessly spilling everything out to him.

'It was *jolly* cold! And the man had a *jolly* enormous nose!' she gasped. 'We had to run *awfully* quickly to escape! But we have a *jolly good* description of the boss.'

'Thank you,' said the man with the pipe when she had finished, and he placed his hand over his mouth, as if trying to cover an oncoming sneeze. 'And where is Jane now?' he asked.

''Angin' abaht outside, I 'spect.'

'Ask her to join us again, will you?'

'O' course,' said Josie bouncily. ''Ang on a mo.' She threw open the door, ran round the corner, tore off her duffle coat, thought *vertical* and *dabby* and walked briskly back into the room.

'Hello again,' she said brightly.

By now the man by the door had laid his pipe down on

the table. He was resting his forehead into his hand and peering through his fingers. Josie suspected he was tired out from hearing so many twins read the *jolly* script.

'Where is Joy?' asked the other man.

'Oh, I thought you'd seen her,' said Josie primly.

'I'd like you to call her back.' He gave a sigh. 'I don't know. What a girl!'

'Indeed,' said the man with the glasses, beaming.

Josie peered out of the door.

'Joy!' she called. She whipped her head back in. 'Oh dear. She must have nipped back downstairs.'

'But we need to see you both together,' said the man by the window.

'Oh, but you have,' said his companion. And he picked up his pipe and pointed the stem directly at Josie. 'This is them!'

The secretary and the man by the window stared at Josie open mouthed.

'I am right, aren't I?' added the pipe owner.

Josie was about to deny it but one look at his eyes and she knew, as Auntie Win would say, that *the game was up*.

'How did you guess?' she asked.

'Joan Littlewood. *Make Me An Offer*. You are the only girl or should I say *girls* who have moved during the reading. Could you tell us why you turned up for this audition when you knew it was for twins?'

'I didn't until I got here,' said Josie.

'Explain, please.'

So she did. Everything. Including her real name.

'This is far more exciting than the script,' said the man by the window.

'This stage school,' said the pipe smoker, 'I've never even heard of it. Have we used anyone from there before?'

'No,' said the other man. 'We've another one of its pupils coming later for the part of the older child.'

*Esmeralda Havilland*, thought Josie.

'So you've done a bit of improvisation with Joan Littlewood then?' said the pipe smoker with interest.

'Only a fortnight, although me and Mr Beauvoisin watched lots of the rehearsals from the flies before that.'

'Beauvoisin! That sounds French. I don't suppose he speaks any, does he?'

'Oh yeah. He was born in France.'

'Pity he isn't African,' said the other man.

'Well, as a matter of fact . . .' said Josie slowly.


It turned out that there was a French African dockyard worker in the story. Josie remembered that when Miss Littlewood had given Mr Beauvoisin a part in *Make Me An Offer* she had encouraged him to join the Actors Union, Equity, which meant he could audition for the role. So although Josie wouldn't be in the film, Mr Beauvoisin had the chance of another acting job. As she gave them her aunt's phone number so that they could call him, she suddenly realised that if she hadn't turned up for the audition Mr Beauvoisin would never have known about it. And to her relief, far from the director being angry with her for wasting his time, he looked quite cheerful.

Downstairs, the receptionist gave her a strange look.

'Your sister never turned up,' she said.

'I know,' said Josie. She shrugged. 'Never mind.'

She was dashing out of the door when she bumped into a youth. She was about to apologise when she realised it was Jim Eliot. So he was the one going for the older part! There was no chance she would *pinch* this one.

'Good luck!' she said but all he did was scowl at her.

Outside in the rain, Josie scoured the street for Hilda. A heavy mist had begun to descend. 'Hurry up!' she muttered. And then she spotted her friend hanging on to her hat and running towards her with an attaché case. As Josie was gesticulating to her, she spotted a familiar motorbike with a sidecar approaching. It drew up in front of her. The rider pushed up his helmet and goggles, his ears popping out at right angles. It was Dickie.

'You were supposed to be with the chaperone,' he remonstrated.

'I was, but she'd had enough of me.'

'Which explains why I saw her returning without you.'

'But how did you know where to find me?'

'I'm a genius, that's how. I also recognise your friend. What's she doing here?'

'We're off to another audition.'

'Without a chaperone?'

'Miss Dagleish doesn't know. Please don't tell her. It's one for my friend.'

By now Hilda was a few feet away from her.

'Hello,' he said cheerfully. 'I'm a friend of Elsie, Josie's sister. I happened to be passing by and I thought you might like a lift.' He stared at Josie solemnly. 'Where is this audition taking place?' Josie handed him a scrap of paper with the address she had copied from Mr and Mrs Hale's telephone directory.

'Climb in,' he said, raising the roof of the sidecar for Hilda. He gave Josie the spare helmet. Hilda sat in the sidecar and stared up at Josie with an expression that said, *Where are we going?* But Dickie had pulled down the roof quickly to shelter her from the rain, and Josie was glad she didn't have to invent an answer. She climbed on the back, and within minutes they were roaring off, her arms wrapped round the detective constable's waist.

They drew up outside a large house. Over the red-bricked wall were the words, *The Aida Foster Theatrical School and Agency.* Josie jumped off the motorbike and Hilda climbed out of the sidecar.

'I'll be waiting for you here,' Dickie said firmly.

Josie nodded.

'Follow me!' Josie said urgently to her friend and began walking towards the building.

Hilda was standing on the pavement, gaping at the sign.

'Josie!' she cried. 'What are you doing? We can't just walk in there!'

'Yes, we can.' Josie turned back, grabbed her friend's hand and pulled her towards the door.

They stumbled into the main entrance only to find themselves facing a tall, thin man standing beside a camera on a tripod. His stocky companion was fiddling with a lamp.

'We shouldn't be here,' mouthed Hilda, panic stricken.

But Josie pretended she couldn't lip read. After a moment of eavesdropping, she cottoned on that the men were from a magazine and were taking photographs for an article about the school. The tall one smiled at them.

'Hello! Are you pupils here?'

'No!' Hilda burst out and proceeded to make a run for it.

Josie caught the sleeve of her coat and hauled her back.

'She's come for an audition,' said Josie. 'I'm here to keep her company.'

'I didn't know they were having auditions today, Sid,' said his friend.

'P-perhaps we've got the wrong day,' Hilda stammered.

'No, we haven't,' Josie said, beaming. 'She's a bit nervous.'

'Ah,' said Sid.

'But we're not sure where to go. You see, it's the first time we've been here.'

*At least that part is true*, Josie thought.

'The dance studio is down that corridor,' he said, and indicated a turning on the left.

'Thank you,' said Josie.

As soon as they had reached the corridor, Hilda began whispering in her ear but Josie continued to ignore her. She thrust a door open only to find herself gazing up at a group of tall, long-legged teenage girls wearing short blue tunics that only just covered their matching knickers. Josie took in their wide red belts, the black nylon dance tights and blue ballet pumps.

'Sorry!' she said, her face growing hot.

A girl with long, wavy blond hair and bright red lipstick ushered them out.

'The younger ones are along here,' she said and she led them round the corner, leaving them outside a door with a window in it. Josie and Hilda peered in.

It was a large studio with a wooden floor. Above the proper ballet barres that were fixed to the white walls were dozens of black and white photographs of the pupils, mainly girls. Instead of light bulbs there was a long bar of light along the ceiling. It was all very modern. Inside the studio were girls wearing the same blue tunics and red belts but with short white socks and blue dance shoes. They were having a class with a young woman with short brown hair, and it was clear from the way she moved that she had danced professionally.

Josie knew then that she had made the right decision. Observing the pupils doing their glissades from one corner of the studio to the other, she could see it was streets ahead of the ballet classes at Miss Dagleish's stage school.

They were so absorbed in spying on the girls that they didn't hear Sid and his companion approaching from behind. By the time Josie was aware of them, he had already leaned across and opened the door. The young teacher whirled round in surprise.

'Who are you?' she exclaimed, staring at Josie and Hilda.

'An auditionee and friend,' Sid said, cheerfully over their heads.

The teacher looked bewildered. 'But I'm not auditioning anyone today.'

'Oh no!' Josie blurted out. 'And my friend has come all the way from Nether Hopping with her leotard and tights!'

'There must be some mistake,' said the teacher. 'It's impossible for me to give you a dance audition now. These girls are about to have their photographs taken.'

'That's a pity,' said the photographer. 'Couldn't they join in while I take photos?'

'But you said the photographs will be in colour. They would stick out from the other pupils.'

'You're right.' And then he smiled. 'You don't have any spare tunics they could borrow? Then you could continue teaching and audition them at the same time.'

'Well, I don't know,' said the teacher uncertainly.

'We've some in locker five for emergencies,' said a girl in the front row.

Josie could have hugged her.


'We shouldn't be here,' protested Hilda in the changing room. 'We'll be in the most awful trouble if Miss Dagleish finds out!'

'Hilda, do you want to go back to *step and point* for the next three years?'

Hilda looked at her in alarm and slowly shook her head.

'And anyway it's an extra dance class, isn't it?'

At that Hilda brightened.

When they returned to the dance studio, there was an older woman standing next to the teacher. Her short, grey, wavy hair had been styled as though for a Paris catwalk. Elegant in her wine and cream dress with matching jacket, she gazed quizzically at them. It was obvious that while they had been changing, she had been informed about their unexpected arrival.

'This is Miss Aida Foster,' the teacher said. 'The school's headmistress.'

Without thinking, Hilda and Josie curtsied, to giggles from the class.

'And what school are you from?' she asked.

'Saint Christopher's,' said Josie hurriedly.

The teacher beckoned them to join the others, and so the class began, with the pianist in the corner playing music that actually made you want to dance to it. The photographer asked the class to stop and start again at intervals and Josie couldn't help noticing that his camera was aimed quite frequently in Hilda's direction. After the class was dismissed the headmistress asked them to stay behind.

'You are very good,' she said to Josie. 'And you,' she added, turning to Hilda, 'are exceptional. Good enough for ballet school, in fact. So why do you want to come here?'

Josie crossed her fingers behind her back, for Hilda had never said she wanted to come to the school. She looked tongue-tied and in need of rescuing.

'We've both seen *West Side Story*,' Josie began. 'Haven't we, Hilda?'

'Yes,' said Hilda hoarsely.

And then it all spilled out of her friend's mouth. How Hilda desperately wanted to learn how to dance like the dancers in the American musical and how she had been allowed to join in some of the warm ups with the company.

'I'd like you to sing something for me. Can you do that

without music?' asked the headmistress.

Josie suddenly remembered the sickly, sugary songs they had learned in their singing lessons.

'We could sing one of the songs from *West Side Story*,' she said hurriedly.

To Josie's relief, Hilda smiled, and they ran into the centre of the studio and did their version of *Cool*.

When they had finished, the woman looked at Josie and gave a wry smile.

'I take it you are the tomboy Anybodys?' she said.

Josie beamed and nodded.

'Now, Hilda, I'd like a ballad.'

Josie was stumped but before she could come up with a suggestion, her friend began to sing another song from *West Side Story* called *Somewhere*. And Josie was transfixed. This was a side of her friend that was rarely seen at school.

'Hilda, I don't suppose you would have an audition speech, would you?'

'No!' said Josie quickly. 'But we can improvise can't we, Hilda?'

'You certainly can,' said the woman, raising an eyebrow.

'It's Hilda, you see. I'm here to . . .'

She searched wildly for the right words but before she could say, *to give her a bit of courage*, the woman added, 'Do the talking for her?'

Josie smiled. 'It's just she goes a bit quiet when she's nervous.'

The woman nodded slowly and then gazed steadily at her friend.

'Do your parents know you're here, Hilda?'

Hilda went bright red. There was an awkward silence.

'Because I will need to contact your father, my dear.'

'Am I in trouble?' Hilda asked, nervously.

'No. But I need to know if he would agree to you attending a theatrical school.'

'Oh, he does,' Hilda blurted out. 'I mean he would. My mother is even working to send me to a . . .' And then she stopped. 'Oh dear.'

'I think you had better tell me the truth, don't you?' Miss Foster suggested.

Hilda glanced at Josie. Josie nodded.

When they had both spilled the beans, the headmistress seemed puzzled and turned to the dance teacher.

'I've never heard of this stage school,' she began.

'That's funny,' said Josie, 'someone else said that to me this –'

She stopped, realising from the woman's penetrating glare that she had been rude to interrupt.

'And from what you have both told me,' she continued, 'I'm not surprised.'

Miss Foster and the dance teacher walked away from them and spoke so quietly to one another that it was impossible to eavesdrop. The dance teacher left and the headmistress re-joined them.

'I will be sending a letter to your father, Hilda. And you are not to worry. I don't think he will be angry with you when he reads what I am suggesting. And now I think you had better return to . . .' She glanced at Josie. '. . . Nether

Hopping? Not the best place to choose, my dear. Other people watch *The Army Game* on ITV too, you know.'

Josie and Hilda burst out laughing.

'I need your parents' address too, young lady,' she said glancing at Josie.

'Well, I'm staying with . . .' And she paused because she remembered that Hilda didn't know that she was staying with Mr and Mrs Hale. 'My aunt.'

'And is this a real aunt or a fictitious aunt?'

# 4

# Double Trouble

ALL EYES IN FORM III WERE RIVETED TO JOSIE when she returned from Miss Dagleish's study the following Monday morning.

'What did she want to see you about?' mouthed Hilda from behind the lid of her desk.

'I'll tell you at breaktime,' Josie mouthed back.

When she did, Hilda almost wet herself laughing, but neither of them said a word to anyone. During the acting lesson, Mrs Havilland's refusal to acknowledge Josie's existence was so noticeable that after the class had ended, Trixie came scurrying up to her.

'Have you been expelled?' she asked.

'No.'

'So why did Miss Dagleish want to see you? You can't have been given a part.'

'I haven't,' said Josie.

'You'd better tell her, Josie,' said Hilda. 'It'll be out soon enough.'

'I've been given two.'

* * *

At midday, Hilda and Josie sat together in the tea house while Esmeralda and her cronies muttered at a nearby table.

Eventually, she raised her head and glared at Josie.

'Have you been telling lies again?'

'I haven't told lies before so how can I have told them again?' Josie said.

*It's your mum whose been telling porky pies*, thought Josie, *when she told me I was going up for one role.*

'Trixie says you've been offered two parts. That's impossible. You've only been to one audition and that was for twins.'

Her group went into a huddle and sniggered.

'That's who she's playing,' said Hilda slowly.

Esmeralda stared at Josie in disbelief.

'Don't be ridiculous! How can you play twins?'

Josie shrugged. 'I dunno. But that's what they want me to do.'

The door swung open and Jim Eliot marched up towards Josie's table. 'Is it true?' he yelled. 'You're playing the twins?'

'Yes. How did you know?'

He groaned.

'Miss Dagleish told me. I'm playing your older brother!'

'Yes, it's very sad,' said Miss Dagleish a week later, 'but all our chaperones and tutors are otherwise engaged which means, alas, you will be unable to play the two girls.'

'Please don't be sad, madam,' said Josie, 'just in case you couldn't find a chaperone, I asked Auntie Win if she would be one in an emergency and she said yes. And Mr

Beauvoisin's going to be my tutor again. He's been given a part too. He's going to teach me between his scenes. I learned so much French with him at the Theatre Royal. He even taught me some Latin.'

'Latin,' repeated Miss Dagleish slowly.

'Yeah,' said Josie. '*Amo, amas, amat, amamus, amatis, amant.*'

'Quite,' said Miss Dagleish dourly. 'I will give you your script on Wednesday. You realise you must be word perfect by the first day of rehearsal. You can't improvise your way through the story like Joan Littlewood asks her casts to do.'

'Yes, madam,' Josie said, and she bobbed into a quick curtsy and backed excitedly out of the room.

On Wednesday Josie waited to be called to Miss Dagleish's study but heard nothing. It was during the morning break that she noticed that Jim had a script.

'Is that for the *River Adventure* film?' she asked.

'It is,' he answered haughtily. 'Miss Dagleish handed it to me this morning.'

Josie dashed over to her study and knocked on the door.

'Enter,' said a voice.

She poked her head round the door and then remembered the curtsy.

'Yes?' said Miss Dagleish.

'I've come to pick up my script, madam.'

'It hasn't arrived yet.'

'Oh. But Jim has his script.'

'There was only one. I expect he's playing a more

important role and they wanted to make sure he had his in good time. I will let you know when your script has arrived. That is all.' And she gave a flick of her hand.

But by lunchtime the next day it still hadn't appeared.

'I don't like the sound of this,' said Hilda.

'Do you think Jim would let me borrow his script so that at least I can find out what the film's about?'

'Do you want an honest answer?' asked Hilda.

'No,' said Josie miserably.

'Miss one of the classes and read it,' Hilda suggested.

'How?'

'It's in his desk. I'll tell Miss Frobisher you've got diarrhoea and are in the lavatory.'

Josie nodded. While the others went to the dance class, she hid, counted to twenty, dashed back to the classroom and pulled the script from his desk. She lifted up her gymslip, stuffed the script into her knickers, and headed for the loos.

Sitting inside one of the cubicles, she took it out and opened it. To her surprise the words weren't typed like *Life With Father*. The scenes and moves were written on the left and numbered, and the dialogue was written from the middle of the page to the right. It took her a while to get used to it but once she got the hang of it, she could read it more rapidly.

It was an adventure story set in January of that year during the terrible smog. It began with fourteen-year-old Charles and his sister, ten-year-old Heidi, travelling from their school in Hampshire to meet their mother at a house near the Thames, where they were to meet the family of a man who had been courting her. When they catch a bus, the conductor informs them that although the bus has the correct number on it, it's travelling in the opposite direction. They jump out at the next stop and see the first signs of fog. Meanwhile, elsewhere in London, a ten-year-old girl called Bridie is attempting to find her friend Stan.

Heidi and Charles are enveloped by the mist and make for the Thames. Using the walls to guide them, they accidentally fall into a boat taking them further away from their destination. A couple of lightermen help them get back to a jetty where they find themselves near some bombed warehouses. In the basement of one of the warehouses they discover bags of ivory and a man who is unconscious, gagged and bound. Charles tells Heidi to phone for an ambulance, reminding her to keep touching the walls to guide her.

Bridie is doing the same but from the opposite direction. The two girls meet, their faces emerging through the smog and are shocked to discover that they are the spitting image of one another, although they talk differently. When Heidi tells the other girl what has happened, Bridie realises that Heidi's brother is in danger and needs to get away from the bombed basement before the criminals return. Because she knows the area, she volunteers to warn him and points Heidi in the direction of the nearest telephone box. Bridie disappears into the mist and finds Charles.

At first he can't understand why his sister is talking in such a strange way and wearing different clothes. They are about to make a run for it when the crooks return and capture them. Heidi meanwhile has followed Bridie and witnesses what has happened. Terrified, she feels her way back along the wall only to meet Stan, who is convinced that Heidi is Bridie putting on a posh accent. Eventually she convinces Stan that she is not Bridie. Both realise that they are in the same situation. Heidi wants to rescue Charles. Stan wants to rescue Bridie. They decide to work together. Stan knows his way around and Heidi is a quick thinker.

They discover that the two crooks are planning to smuggle the stolen ivory away in an old Thames sailing barge. With the help of an African dockyard worker, they rescue the other two, sail the barge with the crooks locked up below, and hand them over to the police. By now the two girls have realised they are twin sisters.

While they are taken off to a room to have cocoa, Bridie's dad turns up at the police station to report his daughter missing, as does Heidi's mother. On seeing Bridie's father, she faints. It turns out that Bridie's dad had been convinced that his son, his other daughter and his wife had been drowned during the terrible smog of 1952. And Heidi's mum had believed that her husband and other daughter had been drowned too, and it all ends happily with the family being reunited.

Josie liked the story. And it wasn't jolly japes at all. There were scary scenes in it but also comic moments and, unlike the audition script, the twins were very different. It was strange to think that at the beginning of the term she hadn't wanted to play any girls at all, and now she was pleased to be playing two of them!

She slipped the script back into her knickers, fled to the classroom, placed it carefully into Jim's desk and dashed down to the cloakroom where she found Hilda changing.

'How's your stomach?' asked her friend nonchalantly.

'Much better now,' said Josie, beaming.

Later that night, Hilda rang Auntie Win's flat in great excitement, desperate to speak to Josie.

'She's in the bath,' lied Auntie Win. 'Can't it wait until tomorrow morning?'

'I can't tell her at school. It'd be too risky. Someone might overhear.'

'I'll ask her to phone you when she's dried herself.'

After a swift goodbye, she dialled the Hales' number.

'Hilda?' said Josie, minutes later from their hallway.

'Oh, Josie,' cried Hilda, 'I've had the most wonderful news!'

'You've heard from Aida Foster, haven't you?' she guessed.

'Yes. The headmistress has been talking to Dad!' Here Hilda's voice went into a squeak. 'I've been offered a scholarship! No fees! They're even going to help me with the uniform. They want me to start next term. Dad's not going to tell Miss Dagleish until we've broken up. Thank you so much, Josie. You're my bestest friend!'

Josie swallowed.

*I'm going to miss you*, she thought.

'We've got to keep seeing one another,' Hilda added.

'Perhaps you can stay with me and Auntie Win sometimes,' said Josie.

'Yes! And you can stay with me. Mum won't have to go to work any more now. And there'll be no more Miss

Frobisher saying, "step and point" and "pose as though you are a fairy"!'

Josie laughed.

'Josie?' said her friend quietly. 'Don't you wish you were going there too?'

Josie decided not to tell Hilda that earlier in the evening she had been told that Miss Aida Foster had offered her a place too, but that there was only one scholarship and her aunt couldn't afford the fees.

'No. I wouldn't want to wear those black nylon tights when I'm older.'

At least that was the truth.

When Josie came off the phone, Mrs Hale popped her head round the door.

'While you're there, why don't you phone Elsie? It does seem strange that you still don't have a script. She might be able to advise you.'

'Don't worry,' her sister told her a few minutes later. 'She'll have to give it to you tomorrow so you can learn your lines over the weekend. Not everyone works like Joan, I'm afraid.'

'That's what Miss Dagleish said.'

'And you'll be working around the technicians. They'll need the correct cues. Although, having said that, it seems as though you were chosen because you had worked with Joan. After a good night's sleep, things will look better in the morning. At least you've read it and know what it's all about.'

'And there's to be a Billy Bunter show over Christmas,' said

Esmeralda airily to her tea-house audience.

It was midday on Friday and she was in full swing.

'Yesterday's *Stage*?' whispered Hilda.

'I'll ask Elsie,' said Josie.

Since Josie had discovered Esmeralda's little secret and had shared it with Hilda, they had both agreed that it might be wiser to keep it to themselves for the moment. Being Mrs Havilland's daughter, Esmeralda could take it out on Josie through her mother. Her revenge, Josie suspected, would probably be no more auditions for acting work.

Esmeralda then began talking about dance auditions and who had been picked to attend them. Hilda, Josie noticed, was not on the list.

Josie gave Hilda a conspiratorial smile. Unfortunately, Esmeralda spotted it.

'Smile all you like, Miss Hollis,' she snapped. 'But I can promise you it will soon be wiped from your face.'

'Take no notice,' muttered Hilda.

Later, when they had broken for lunch and Hilda and Josie were in the basement cloakroom, they heard Esmeralda coming down the stairs, whispering urgently to someone. Josie glanced at Hilda and pointed to their coats. Hilda nodded and they quickly sat on the benches, drew up their knees and hid underneath them.

'When she turns up on Monday and doesn't know her lines, she will be *out*. She won't be able to get away with her *improvising* this time.'

Josie nearly leaped out to ask Esmeralda what she meant,

for it was clear that she was talking about her, but then realised that Esmeralda would keep any further information close to her chest if she gave away her presence.

'Mother has it worked out to a T. You know Susan Bartholomew in Form I?'

'Yes,' said a voice Josie recognised as Merle.

'She has a sister in the top form of the juniors and they look alike. Mother has young Miss Josephine's script and has been working with them on it since Wednesday.'

Josie stiffened.

'Little Miss Big-head will arrive for rehearsal on Monday morning not knowing one single word, and my sister will turn up as the chaperone with the Bartholomew sisters and come to the rescue, so to speak.'

'So that's what you meant about the smile being wiped off her face,' murmured Merle. 'But don't you think that's a bit mean?'

Josie was startled. Merle had never shown her any sign of friendship.

'It'll be character building, Mother says. Now, not a word.'

'No, of course not.'

Josie listened to them running up the stairs. She clung to her knees, resting her forehead on them. To her embarrassment, she could feel tears streaming down her face. Hilda was whispering her name but she couldn't bring herself to answer. Her coat was pulled aside and she peered up at her friend.

'Why is Mrs Havilland being so nasty again?'

'Jealousy probably, because Esmeralda isn't working,' said Hilda. 'But don't worry, she'll never get away with it.'

Josie wasn't convinced.

'What am I going to do, Elsie?' Josie cried, clutching the phone that evening. 'When I told Mrs Hale, she said something about looking for the diamond in the dung heap.'

'Which is that they have no idea that you know what they're up to?'

'Yeah!' said Josie surprised. 'How did you know that?'

Elsie laughed.

'I guessed. Henry has told me all about her way of looking at problems.'

'But, Elsie, those sisters will know their lines off by heart.'

'In acting classes, when Mrs Havilland works with the pupils on speeches, do they know the whole play or does she just do their bits?'

'Their bits.'

'That's another advantage you have. You know the whole plot, which is even more important because films aren't shot in the right order.'

'What do you mean?'

'Some of the filming will be exterior, some interior. That means outdoor scenes and indoor scenes. If the weather is atrocious on a day when the company have scheduled to film scenes outside, they'll shoot indoor ones instead. They splice it all together in the correct order later. So it's very important to know what's happened in the scene before the one they're filming because you'll need to know what sort of mood Bridie or Heidi are in. If these two Bartholomew sisters only know the scenes they speak in . . .'

'I get it!' said Josie excitedly. 'There's this scene where Heidi has seen the crooks take her brother and Bridie away, and she meets this boy Stan. And he keeps interrupting her. If the Bartholomew sisters don't know what she's seen, they won't understand how urgent it is for her to fight to get a word in edgeways.'

'And there's another little diamond. If Mrs Havilland hadn't been so keen for you not to be in this film, she would have been coaching you instead.'

Josie gasped. 'Like she did in *Life With Father*.'

'Exactly. Feeling better?'

Josie laughed. It was one of those questions that didn't need an answer.

# 5

# Plotting the Plot

MR BEAUVOISIN WAS THE FIRST PERSON JOSIE spotted when she entered the church hall. He was deep in conversation with a bespectacled man who was smoking a pipe. Mr Stanmore.

'Don't worry, Bertram,' Josie heard the director say. 'My decision is final.'

Mr Beauvoisin turned and beamed at Josie.

She ran into his outstretched arms and as he swung her round he winked at her aunt over her head.

'Thank you,' Winifred mouthed.

He plonked her down on the floor. Already, members of the cast in their coats and scarves were gathering round a long trestle table. Josie guessed that the tall, burly man and the small, thin man with the enormous nose would be playing the crooks. A balding middle-aged man and a dumpy woman with a round, comical face joined them.

Opposite them, an elegantly dressed lady sat wearing matching earmuffs and gloves. A plump, friendly looking woman drew up a chair next to a small boy whose brown hair hung over his forehead. The boy had a copy of the script in front of him.

'He must be playing Stan,' whispered Josie to her aunt and they made for the chairs opposite them. It was at this moment that Jim Eliot entered with his mother, accompanied by Mrs Ellington and the pretty Bartholomew sisters with their long blond plaits. With a sinking heart, Josie watched Mrs Ellington stride towards Mr Stanmore. While Mrs Eliot seated herself next to the small boy, Jim joined her, placing his copy of the script on the table.

'My name is Winifred Lindsay,' said Auntie Win, introducing herself to the woman with the little boy. 'And this is Josie Hollis. She's playing the twins.'

'This is Terry Dawson,' said the woman. 'I'm Miss Cogan.'

'Oh. I assumed you were his mother.'

'No. Terry is at the Italia Conti stage school. Miss Conti prefers to use LCC licenced matrons. She's very strict about mothers not accompanying her pupils.'

'Really?' said Auntie Win, surprised.

'They're not even allowed backstage during a theatre production. Their mothers have to pick them up at the stage door.'

'That must seem odd when they've watched them in class or at rehearsals.'

Miss Cogan laughed. 'They're not allowed to sit in on classes.'

'Oh. Why is that?'

'It would only embarrass the children.'

Jim glanced awkwardly at his mother whose nose, Josie observed, had turned pink.

'And I think it very sensible that Terry is allowed to come

to rehearsal in mufti,' added her aunt.

'Mufti?' asked the boy, puzzled.

'Miss Lindsay means not in uniform,' said Miss Cogan.

'But we don't have a uniform,' said Terry. 'We just have a badge.'

*Lucky things*, thought Josie.

Mr Beauvoisin sat on the empty chair on the other side of Josie. By now a handsome man in his thirties had joined the pretty lady in the earmuffs. Josie guessed they would be playing her parents. Sitting opposite them, a white-haired man in his sixties was studying the script. There was a tap on her shoulder. It was a young woman she had heard being called Belinda. She gave Josie a friendly smile.

'You'll need to have your script out, Josie. We'll be starting the read-through in a minute.'

'I don't have one,' said Josie.

'Oh my goodness!' exclaimed Belinda. 'No script!'

'I suppose you "lost" it because you couldn't be bothered to learn your lines,' muttered Jim. 'Typical.'

'Fancy not knowing them on the first day of rehearsal,' declared Jim's mother.

'Fancy the post failing to deliver her script on time,' added Auntie Win, meaningfully.

As Belinda rushed off to fetch a copy, Josie spotted the balding actor raising an eyebrow.

'How can we work with a child who doesn't know her lines?' he muttered.

To Josie's dismay she overheard the director say, 'Let's see how these two sisters do in one of the scenes, Mrs Ellington.'

Mr Beauvoisin squeezed her hand. 'Your aunt told me all about it and I passed on the information to Mr Stanmore. Trust me, he knows what he's doing.'

'Susan, you will be Heidi, and you, Felicity,' said Mr Stanmore to her sister, 'will be Bridie. The chairs that Belinda is lining up for you at the other end of the hall represent the wall of a warehouse near the river. The fog is very thick. Heidi, this is the point in the story just after you and your brother have separated and you've seen what's happened to him. I want you to feel your way along the wall.'

'Which lines are these?' she asked.

The director smiled. 'This is a moment when you don't talk.'

The girl appeared lost for a moment and then nodded. She walked over to the end of the line of chairs, stretched her arms delicately in front of herself and moved slowly from one end of the chairs to the other.

'Thank you. Now, Bridie,' he said, looking at Felicity, 'if you would do the same from the other side.'

Felicity Bartholomew, her back as straight as a plank, walked slowly past the chairs to the other side.

'Thank you. I'd like you to do it again, only this time I want you to imagine that you are suddenly meeting a girl who looks exactly like you.'

'And I say the lines then?' asked Susan.

'No lines.'

Josie felt a massive wave of relief.

As the sisters pretended to meet their twin in the fog, they opened their mouths and threw the palms of their hands back in horror. Josie recognised the gesture as the one for surprise that Mrs Havilland had taught them.

'Well done!' she heard Mrs Ellington murmur to the girls. 'Your gestures were absolutely identical.'

And then it was Josie's turn.

'Good luck!' she heard her aunt whisper.

'Heidi first,' said the director.

Josie checked that her hat was on straight and moved towards what she was already beginning to believe was the river. *What I wish for is a telephone box.* She felt her way carefully along every brick, determined to find one.

'Now be Bridie,' said the director.

She pulled her hat to one side and marched over to the other end. *Where are you, Stan? You were supposed to wait for me outside the school!* Exasperated, she stopped every now and then to listen out for his footsteps. She was beginning to lose patience.

'Now you see Heidi's face coming out of the mist,' said the Director.

Josie gave a gasp. *Don't be so daft. It's just my reflection in a shop window.* She reached out to touch it. As her hand hit what she imagined was glass she touched Heidi's nose. She gave a loud yell, withdrew her hand and stared at the face in astonishment.

He then asked her to be Heidi coming from the opposite direction. She straightened her hat again and stood in a more upright manner. *Smells are important. In case I get lost. Speed is important. The man could be seriously injured.*

'Now you see Bridie,' said the director.

*Oh my goodness, there's someone else. Silly me! I thought she was me. Ow! She touched me. Oh my goodness! She does look like me. In fact, she is me! But she can't be me. I'm me!*

'Thank you, Josie,' said the director.

Not only were the cast laughing but the actor who had complained about her was actually smiling. As she re-joined her aunt, Miss Cogan leaned in her direction.

'If you don't have a script, how do you know Bridie touches Heidi in the fog?'

'I read Jim's script.'

'How did you manage to do that?' Jim burst out.

'I borrowed it from your desk and read it in the toilet. I mean, the *lavatory*.'

Terry laughed and Josie had a feeling they were going to get on very well.

Mr Stanmore thanked the two girls for coming, assuring them that they would probably be marvellous for other roles but that these ones were better suited to Josie.

Josie glanced down at the cast list.

### RIVER ADVENTURE

CHARLES.....................................JAMES ELIOT
HEIDI & BRIDIE................JOSEPHINE HOLLIS
STAN BIGGINS...................TERRY DAWSON
FRENCHIE................BERTRAM BEAUVOISIN
NOBBY..........................GERALD INCHPIN
GUS.............................ALISTAIR McBRIDE
SERGEANT PERKINS........GEORGE BROWNING
ROSALIND HAWKINS......HELENA PARTRIDGE

BERT HAWKINS . . . . . . . . . . . . . DEREK VALENTINE
MRS ADA BIGGINS . . . . . . . . . . ELVIRA HIGHGATE
INJURED CUSTOMS MAN . . . . . . . . SAM HUGHES
EXTRAS: POLICEWOMAN, POLICEMAN etc.

Seeing her name printed on the cast list, it suddenly dawned on Josie that she really was one of the company, and she felt so happy it was all she could do not to laugh.

'Right, everyone,' the director said, marching over to the end of the table and rubbing his hands together. 'Please accept my apologies for the arctic conditions. The oil heater is taking longer than anticipated to warm the place up. Belinda,' he said, turning to the young woman, 'would you like to introduce us to everyone before we begin?'

After the read-through, which Josie knew all about from Elsie, they spent the morning rehearsing the scenes in the police station before heading to a nearby café for lunch. Mr Beauvoisin pushed two tables together so that Josie, Terry and Jim, the three chaperones, Mr Beauvoisin and George Browning – the actor playing the police sergeant – could sit together. Within seconds, Jim's mother began regaling the entire table with tales about the wonderful parts and reviews Jim had been given when he was a little boy. She even had a dig at Josie for having been cast as Whitney when Jim was 'by far the most experienced pupil'.

'But Jim is fourteen,' Josie's aunt had pointed out gently. 'How could he play a nine-year-old boy?'

'Through the art of acting,' said his mother, in a manner

that conveyed she was speaking to a woman who was ignorant of such matters.

'With a broken voice?' asked Auntie Win.

Mr Beauvoisin bowed his head hastily, shaking with suppressed laughter.

In the afternoon, Mr Stanmore concentrated on the basement scenes in the bombed-out warehouse. To Josie's relief, aside from Mr Beauvoisin and her aunt, no one in the cast knew that Josie had experienced being kidnapped. It also helped that the two actors playing Nobby and Gus were more like a music hall comedy act than Scowler and Moustache.

NOBBY: That's the last bag of ivory. Take it while I take care of these little toe-rags.

GUS: What abaht cloth-ears 'ere?'

HE POINTS TO THE CUSTOMS OFFICER.

If someone finds him he'll squeal.

NOBBY: Don't worry. No one will find 'im till this smog 'as cleared. But to make sure 'e don't go off for a little stroll . . .

GUS: What you doin'?

NOBBY: A few minutes after we leave 'ere, those bricks by the door will come tumblin' dahn. We'll take the kids wiv us on the barge and dump 'em some place miles away from 'ere.

HE GRABS CHARLES AND BRIDIE BY THE SCRUFF OF THEIR NECKS.

CHARLES: You'll never get away with this!

'Don't forget to shake your finger at him,' said Mrs Eliot suddenly.

The actor playing Nobby swung round and glanced at the director.

'Thank you, Mrs Eliot,' said Mr Stanmore. 'I'll give your son notes later.'

'Oh, I'm sure you won't need to. Would you like me to prompt Josephine?' she added pointedly.

'No, thank you, Mrs Eliot. Now, Jim,' he said, turning, 'why are you smiling when you're telling the crooks they'll never get away with it?'

'I'm being brave,' he said.

'He's smiling through his fear, you see,' said his mother.

'Yes, thank you, Mrs Eliot. Jim, rather than think about how brave *you're* feeling, think about your ten-year-old sister, lost in the fog with no one to help her, and how angry that makes you.'

It was during a break that Mrs Eliot approached him.

'I wonder if James could have a few more lines, Mr

Stanmore,' she said. 'He's a child prodigy, you know. I've seen him give a magnificent speech warning members of the French Revolution that they will pay for their crimes. It was very moving. One line in this scene is so little, don't you think?'

'Films are more action than dialogue, Mrs Eliot,' he explained politely.

'Pity,' she said. 'But still worth thinking about, perhaps?'

Eavesdropping on this conversation, Josie was relieved that Auntie Win didn't interfere like Mrs Eliot did. It allowed her to concentrate on being both twins.

The following scene was where Heidi and Stan peer through the doorway into the rubble-strewn basement and discover the customs man tied up and gagged. As Jim wasn't needed, it was noticeable how his mother's absence made the atmosphere in the hall more relaxed. During a break, Auntie Win and Miss Cogan had a quiet word with Mr Stanmore.

'Would you like us to relieve you of young Jim's mother?' Auntie Win asked.

'Temporarily or permanently?' he said through gritted teeth.

'Well, neither of us is willing to pay with the hangman's noose,' Miss Cogan commented, 'but her constant interruptions and "directing" is spoiling it for the others.'

'What do you propose when legally she has to be here?'

'We'll think of something,' said Auntie Win.

The next morning Miss Cogan brought a skein of wool for

Mrs Eliot to hold apart with her outstretched wrists while she rolled it with painstaking slowness into balls. Forced to sit sideways, it prevented her from watching quite so avidly. Auntie Win sat happily beside them reading a brand new detective paperback, *Maigret Has Scruples*.

Unimpeded by interruptions from Mrs Eliot, the week's rehearsals whisked by, packed with scenes in the train carriage, on a bus, in a telephone box, inside the crew's quarters of an old sailing barge and in the bombed basement. When Josie wasn't happily absorbed in the rehearsals, she was having school lessons in any corner Mr Beauvoisin could find, or in Mrs Hale's kitchen. This left her no time to think about Scowler and Moustache. It was during one of their visits to Mrs Hale's flat that Mr Beavoisin made an extraordinary discovery. He had already met Mrs Hale, in 1929, when Mrs Hale had been staying in Paris for a week with her two sons.

Mr Beauvoisin's young American mother had gone into labour late at night while her husband had been playing the piano in a jazz club. Thousands of miles from her family, she had felt lonely and frightened. The landlady had asked Mrs Hale if she could sit with her while she went to fetch a midwife as she was the only woman who could speak English. Mrs Hale's older son, Oscar, had left his mother holding her hand while he went off to find Mr Beauvoisin senior. By the time he had returned with his father, Master Bertram Beauvoisin had been born.

'But my father told me that the English lady who had been so kind to my mother was called Mrs Beaumont,' he had said, over warm scones. 'I remember the name because it was similar to ours.'

'Beaumont was my first husband's surname,' she had explained. 'I was a widow then. Twenty years later I met Mr Hale.'

'And not a moment too soon,' he had said, beaming. 'I think this calls for a celebration, don't you, Josie?'

Josie who had been transfixed by this story had nodded in agreement.

'Any excuse for more cakes,' Mrs Hale added wryly.

'And why not?' he laughed.

On Saturday, at the end of her first week as a matron, Auntie Win met Ralph for tea between his matinee and evening performance at Wyndham's Theatre, eager to find out how he and Jessica were settling in at the Highgate flat and to reassure him that Josiè was safe and happy. They had just made their 'after tea' farewells at the stage door when she overheard two men having a heated discussion behind her. They were complaining about the closure notice of a play, *Look After Lulu*, at the theatre that backed onto Wyndham's Theatre, the New Theatre.

'It's insane,' one of them was protesting.

'But he wants to bring in another show,' said his younger friend. 'And there's no other theatre available for a transfer.'

'Noel is none too pleased.'

'I can imagine.'

She guessed they must have been speaking about Noel Coward and was about to head for the Tube station when she heard him add, 'Oh yes. It's one of Joan Littlewood's: *Make Me An Offer*.'

She froze and pretended to hunt inside her handbag for her purse.

'But it only opened at Stratford a couple of months ago,' exclaimed his friend.

'I know, but that's what he's decided. Opens here December sixteenth.'

'Good Lord! What with *A Taste Of Honey* and *The Hostage*, she'll have three of her productions in the West End at the same time.'

Auntie Win hovered until they had strolled out of sight before dashing down the alleyway alongside the theatre. She sprinted round the corner and there at the front of the building was the closure notice.

'Strike while the iron's hot,' she murmured. She pushed the heavy door open into the foyer and headed straight for the box office.

Climbing the stairs to her flat in high spirits, Auntie Win became aware of a hammering noise coming from the other side of her front door. Alarmed, she flung it open and moved briskly down the hall where she discovered that during her absence, Mr Beauvoisin had removed all the unmade furniture kits out of the spare bedroom and had spent all day busily assembling them. A waist-high cabinet stood along the back wall of the sitting room, and halfway across the room was a ceiling-high dividing wall of large box-size shelves.

'Now you can take your LPs and large books out of that spare bedroom and put them in here,' he declared.

A wooden step-ladder was propped by the window near the kitchen door on the other side of the shelves.

'The curtain rail is up!' she cried. 'And you've put the dining table together.'

'And brought out the superleggera chairs,' he said, indicating some tall, slim black chairs with cane seats. 'It's a crime to have those hidden away. And I thought your Mrs Jenkins might like to walk into more agreeable surroundings when she pops round here next Sunday.'

'But she's used to it looking unfinished.'

'Her friend won't be.'

Mr and Mrs Hale had invited Auntie Win and Mr Beauvoisin over to their flat the following Sunday evening and had suggested they stay the night as they lived so close to the Thames. It would mean they could have an extra hour's sleep before filming the following day,

The reason for the invitation was two fold. A ninety-minute play based on an Inspector Maigret novel was to be shown on the BBC. Mrs Hale's sons had already arranged to come round and watch it with their mother and stepfather and bring some early seventieth birthday presents for her. As well as watching the play, Mrs Hale thought it would be a wonderful opportunity for Mr Beauvoisin to meet the two men who, thirty years previously, had held him as a baby when they were young boys.

Knowing that Mrs Jenkins would be bitterly disappointed if she missed the programme, it being the first time a ninety-minute detective play had ever been shown on television, Win had invited her to watch it in the flat with a friend while they were away.

'It's very kind of you to go to all this trouble, Bertram,' she said.

'I am living here rent free,' he reminded her.

'As an unpaid bodyguard.'

'True, but my motives are a little more selfish. There's a bed in the room you've been using as a storeroom, and I'm tired of sleeping on the floor or on that settee.'

'Point taken.'

Win picked up one of the black and white curtains that for months had been draped over a box under the sill. She was halfway up the stepladder, attaching one of the hooks to the rail when the telephone rang. She jumped off the steps and headed for the hall.

'Another call from Detective Inspector Gallaway?' guessed Mr Beauvoisin, when she returned, smiling.

'Yes. The man Josie calls Scowler has recovered consciousness. After interviewing him, the police are convinced that whoever arranged the beating will have no idea it was Josie who disposed of the snow. And no, not because this Scowler chap cares a jot about *Larry*. DI Gallaway suspects it's because he doesn't want to be a laughing stock. All he's said to the police is, "*I told 'em the same as I'm tellin' you. I knows nuffin.*" It means Josie is safe. Put on the Perry Como LP again, will you?' and she climbed back up the steps to continue curtain hanging.

'*Catch a falling star and put it in your pocket,*' she sang. '*Never let it fade away.*'

# 6

# Interiors and Exteriors

JOSIE AND TERRY PEERED INTO A VAST STUDIO where small sets surrounded by high walls were set up in units ready for filming the interior scenes, and a few of the exterior ones. It was the first day of filming. Earlier Miss Cogan had pointed out the director of photography to them, the camera operator, the four men in the sound crew, the director, assistant director, the people in charge of props and many others. It would be pretty crowded, and all for a cast of nine and a few extras.

'That's for the camera operator to glide along,' Miss Cogan explained, as a man called the grip laid down what appeared to be a miniature railway track. 'He sits up high behind the camera which is mounted on a dolly. And it's not the kind of dolly girls play with. This dolly runs on the tracks so that the camera operator can be pushed smoothly towards an actor or actress for a close up.'

'And the reason the camera looks so enormous,' said Josie, 'is because of the huge case round it. Once the blimp is shut, it muffles the sound of the motor. My sister's fiancé told me that.'

'The blimp is like a wide door at the side of the case,' explained Miss Cogan to Terry. 'And do you see that young woman over there with the short black hair and glasses?' she added.

Josie turned to where Miss Cogan was pointing.

'The one carrying papers?' she asked

'Yes. That's Miss Tomkins, the continuity girl. Because the scenes won't be filmed in order, she has to make sure that when they're spliced together it looks right. For example, if a man in scene forty-two has his tie pulled to the right of his collar and they shoot scene forty-three two days after they've filmed scene forty-two, she has to study her notes to make sure that when they come to film it, his tie is in exactly the same place.'

Josie watched Miss Tomkins checking her lists, scribbling down new information and answering a stream of questions from people.

'When we've gone home to bed, she'll be typing it all up, ready to give to the editor who has to put the scenes in the correct order.'

'Look at those trolleys,' Terry gasped. 'The microphones on them look like they're hanging from giant fishing rods.'

It was all so noisy, thought Josie, what with the hammering, the technicians busily moving strange objects around, and the crews talking intently to one another. She gazed up at a narrow gangway where electricians were fixing lamps. A lighting gaffer below was giving them instructions through a series of hand signals. On the other side of the studio, in one of the units, stood a red double decker London bus. A man in overalls was puffing steam around it to make it look like fog.

They returned to their dressing room.

'Now remember, Terry,' said Miss Cogan. 'Don't scratch your chin, rub your eyes or wipe your nose. Your make-up has to last all day.'

Josie had two costumes. As Heidi she wore russet corduroy slacks, a bottle green jersey, a camel coat, brown lace-up shoes and a flat hat with a bobble called a tam o' shanter, knitted in a fair isle pattern with matching gloves. As Bridie she wore a dark blue woollen dress, a well-darned cardigan, long woollen socks, black plimsolls, a red jacket and a striped pom-pom hat.

An hour later, she and Jim were given their calls. Josie felt a rush of excitement as they entered the studio, followed by her aunt and Mrs Eliot, and headed towards the unit where their scene was to be filmed. The bus platform was being given some last minute touches by a man wielding a paintbrush.

She and Jim and the actor playing the bus conductor went over their moves while a chubby-faced man called Spud stretched a tape measure from the camera to where they were standing. The heat from the lights caused perspiration to trickle down Josie's face. A make-up lady stepped forward and pressed a small powder pad against her skin.

'Is this your first film?' she asked.

Josie nodded nervously.

'Thought so. You'll be fine. Just remember not to move from the area where Spud has measured or you'll be out of focus.'

'Has Josie's stand-in been told to keep her costume on?' she heard someone ask.

'What's a stand-in?' Josie asked.

'Someone who stands-in for a member of the cast while we sort out the lighting. It can take a long time so we use people who are the same height, wearing the same costumes to stand on the set while the cast waits in the dressing rooms. It's to make sure that the cast aren't too tired by the time we start filming. In your case, we'll sometimes be using your stand-in to play the back of one twin while you play the other twin talking to her.'

'What's her name?'

'Robin. She's very excited. Her mother works in the studio canteen. She heard we needed a girl of your height with short hair. She's thrilled to be chosen.'

'Josie, will you stop asking so many questions!' Jim muttered, once the woman was out of earshot. 'It's embarrassing. We don't need to know her name.'

'I do,' said Josie.

'Quiet, please, everyone,' said the assistant director.

There was silence but no one appeared to move. The film crew, Josie observed, seemed to be listening to the air. And then she became aware of a clickety-clicking sound. All heads swivelled towards the wall where Mrs Eliot was knitting rapidly on four needles.

'Quiet, please!' shouted the assistant director, staring in her direction.

Auntie Win gently covered Mrs Eliot's knitting with her hand.

'Oh,' said Mrs Eliot, looking up. 'Is the –?'

Hastily, Auntie Win placed a finger on her mouth indicating that there was to be silence. The clapper boy announced the scene number, called out, 'Take One!' and closed the clapperboard with a bang.

'Action,' said the director.

'You still need to be more angry,' said Mr Stanmore to Jim. 'And you're still wagging your finger. No one will see it. All we'll see is your face.'

They were rehearsing the bombed basement scene where Jim spoke his one line.

'What do you wish for?' Josie whispered to him as they walked back to a particular piece of tape on the floor.

'I wish I wasn't having to work with you,' he whispered back.

'As Charles.'

He sighed. 'I wish I could punch the crook on the nose.'

They rehearsed the scene again.

'Good,' said the director. 'Ready, everyone,' he warned. 'It's a take.'

'Cut!'

The crew moved to a unit where a brick wall had been built. A man carrying a high, swinging boom with a microphone dangling from it headed to where Auntie Win, Mrs Eliot and Miss Cogan were sitting, followed by an electrician with a large cumbersome light. The wires that were attached to the lamp began to slither towards their feet like speedily growing jungle creepers. The three women swiftly raised their legs, picked up their chairs and moved to another spot.

Within seconds, the camera operator asked them to move again. It was sometime later that Josie spotted them wedged into a corner by a blacked out window. Jim's mother was still knitting.

After the scene was in the can and they had eaten lunch, Mr Beauvoisin arrived in an exultant mood, having spent all morning chatting with African dockyard workers. Terry's tutor, a middle-aged man with a tattered briefcase in his hand made a little study in a corner of the dressing room. Jim had been given work to do on his own. Mr Beauvoisin asked if he would like to join Josie for French but his mother shook her head with a hurried, 'No, thank you!'

'Does Miss Dagleish know that Mr Beauvoisin is black?' Josie overheard Mrs Eliot ask Auntie Win.

'No,' answered her aunt, 'but she knows he has a law degree and is more highly qualified than the staff at her school.'

'Well, there's not much call for the law at such an establishment is there?' said Mrs Eliot. 'It's polish that is needed there.'

'Oh, Mr Beauvoisin has plenty of that, Mrs Eliot. Now, how's your knitting coming along?'

At which point Josie heard Miss Cogan smother her laughter in a handkerchief.

After countless takes of the train carriage scene, it was finally in the can, and Josie went off to change into her Bridie clothes ready for the moment when the twins first encountered each other in the smog. Because the phone call to her dad as Bridie was to be filmed with Josie's back to the camera, the first glimpse of her face emerging through the mist would be her shocked eyes above a smog mask smeared with soot from the polluted air. This was to be followed by her reaching out to touch Heidi and flinching when she realises that the face is not some strange reflection. Josie, as Bridie, then had to pull down the smog mask to reveal her identical face, followed by another shot of Heidi looking astounded. The director wanted the audience to be as surprised as the twins in the film.

It was quite complicated when they had to be filmed talking to one another. Heidi's side of the conversation had to be filmed first, and then Josie and Robin had to swap clothes to become the other twin for Bridie's responses, filmed with Robin's back to the camera. Remembering what she had learned with Joan Littlewood helped Josie concentrate on being two very different people.

At six o'clock everyone packed up and Josie was back in the dressing room talking to Robin and changing into her school uniform.

An outdoor night scene had been scheduled for filming late the following afternoon but owing to sleet the police station scenes were filmed instead. On Wednesday, the weather took another nosedive, bringing hail. This meant that the warehouse basement scenes where the wall above the door collapsed, trapping Stan and Heidi inside, were brought forward.

That evening Auntie Win received a phone call from Detective Inspector Gallaway. To her astonishment, he began to talk about the sudden dip in temperature.

'You didn't ring me to talk about the weather, Inspector Gallaway,' she said, detecting something more serious in the tone of his voice.

'Believe it or not, it is relevant. If the conditions had been more clement, the film company would have completed most of its outdoor filming by now. It's far easier to keep an eye on young Josie if she's spending most of her time in a studio surrounded by technicians.'

'There's bad news, isn't there?'

'I'm afraid so. The chap Josie calls Moustache was found unconscious this morning. Like Scowler, he's been badly beaten. We suspect that a message was passed on to one of the prison inmates to apply pressure on him for information about the missing snow.'

'Do you know if he talked?'

'No. And that's our main concern. We won't know if he's told anyone that Josie took it till he comes round. The snow, as you know, is worth a heck of a lot of money. If the owner thinks Josie has it on her person . . .'

'He'll come after her,' finished Winifred for him.

'And if he finds out she's thrown it away . . .'

'Let's just take one thing at a time, DI Gallaway,' said Winifred quietly.

'Which is what we're doing and why I haven't told Josie's

parents. There's no point worrying them unnecessarily. I'm only keeping you in the picture –'

'Because I'm Josie's chaperone.'

'Precisely.'

Early on Friday, on a bitterly cold dawn, Josie and a handful of the film crew departed from the Festival Pier on the South Bank in a launch – a motorised pleasure boat called *St Cecilia* – with Terry, Jim, their chaperones, the director, assistant director and camera operator. The heavy studio camera with its blimp had been left behind and in its place was a lighter portable camera mounted on a tripod. Within minutes, they were swiftly leaving the ferries behind and becoming part of the river traffic.

As they huddled together on the deck, the launch swept under Waterloo Bridge and headed for the three Blackfriars Bridges. The massive carved buttresses supporting them reminded Josie of pictures she had seen of Greek temples. One bridge had traffic flooding across it, the latter two bridges, trains. It was exciting to be moving underneath them and watching the hundreds of boats clustering round one another and moving up and down the Thames. Beside her, Miss Cogan was yelling above the din, attempting to teach Terry about the other bridges and pointing out old buildings on the shore.

'And remember,' Josie heard her shout, 'when you write about what happened today for your homework and you're talking about the Thames, you must always remember to call it "the River", with a capital R, because it's a very special river.'

Above Josie's head hungry gulls hovered and dived, their squawks drowned out by the boats' engines.

'London Bridge!' she heard Terry yell.

'Are we near the Pool now?' Josie shouted to Mr Stanmore.

He nodded. 'Almost there!'

It was all so confusing, she thought. The River was divided into areas. Within each area were sections alongside it like little roads, with different sized watery parking squares for vessels alongside the wharf called docks. There was an Upper Pool and a Lower Pool, an east dock and a west dock, and they were joined to the River through massive locks that were like gates under the surface, which kept the water levels high when the River was at low tide.

'How will we know when we're there?' Josie yelled.

'Because you'll see large ships that have travelled across the ocean to reach here,' Mr Stanmore yelled back. 'And cargo boats and barges and liners.'

Her aunt put her arm round Josie's shoulders.

'Isn't this wonderful?' Josie shouted.

They passed a team of men scooping up water near a salvage vessel.

'They're taking samples to examine in a laboratory,' explained the director. 'This river is filthy. Not the sort of water anybody should swallow. You can get blood poisoning if you do. That's why we're making sure you don't fall in.'

Josie screwed up her nose. 'What's that rotten egg smell?'

'Pollution. People think it comes from the thousands of worms in the river but they're only here because they love what's in the water. You should see it when it rains. The worms lying in the mud make the banks look red.'

'Tower Bridge!' Terry interrupted excitedly.

He was pointing to a long bridge with steel spires. The tall, narrow towers at each end resembled two miniature castles. What appeared to be two drawbridges rose and separated, allowing a massive liner pulled by three tugs to glide through. The tugs seemed like tiny toys in comparison. The drawbridges came down like a trap behind them and it was a bridge again, with red double decker buses, pedestrians in bowler hats, and cyclists streaming across it. Josie stared up at the bridge's massive chains, their boat rocking from the wash caused by another launch sweeping past them.

'It's so busy,' yelled Josie.

'Yes. Sea-going ships mingling with the little ships of the river. And we need to keep out of their way. The tide only gives two hours of high water to dock the very large ships.'

'How on earth are you going to film the children here?' Auntie Win asked.

'With great difficulty,' replied Mr Stanmore. 'It's the busiest port in the world. This area is what they call the *turn around*. It's where they dock and undock. It would be far easier for us to film on a Saturday or a Sunday when it's not so busy but we've been told it would cost twice as much, so we have to make the best of it. Being a children's film we have less money to play around with. We have a lighterman with us today, showing us the safest places to film. We don't want to be in people's way, though I doubt they'll notice us. That's why we've chosen St Katharine

Dock. So many of its warehouses were destroyed by bombs we're hoping there won't be so many boats there. You'll see it on your left as soon as we've passed under Tower Bridge.'

'Are we going to Wapping police station to be filmed?' asked Josie.

'No. Their work is far too important to have their pontoon flooded with a film crew. But we've taken shots of it from a distance so that when Terry points during the scene on the Thames barge, it will be in the next shot.'

'So it'll look as though that's what I can see,' Terry said.

'Exactly. And we'll also be filming the scenes where Nobby and Gus are taken off the barge in a part of the River where it's less crowded.'

Josie spotted a landing stage near St Katharine Docks, its massive chains at the edges attached to heavy, cylindrical bars. She gazed across at the dozens of long, flat boats surrounding the towering hulls of ships. Cargo from the ships was being lowered mechanically down to them.

'Those flat boats are called lighters,' Mr Stanmore explained. 'They carry the cargoes to and from the docks and wharves.'

They were everywhere, Josie observed.

The reason they were filming so early was because the camera operator wanted to catch the early morning mist to create the appearance of the children being in a fog. Equipment had already been tied down and set up on one of the lighters, although most of the small scenes were to be filmed in long shot from the launch.

'The lightermen can cross the river by jumping from one lighter to another.'

'But isn't that dangerous?' interrupted Mrs Eliot.

'It is if you don't know what you're doing but we have some of them helping us, ready to keep a grip on Jim and Josie. The lighters can be quite slippery but we're filming at low water. They'll be steadier then.'

Mrs Eliot looked aghast.

'As long as they follow instructions they'll be safe enough,' he added.

'It's so noisy,' she heard her aunt yell to Mr Stanmore. 'How will you be able to hear the children speak?'

'There's no dialogue in this section. We'll have music over it.'

Josie glanced across at Jim, who was clutching the side of the boat. He looked terrified. As though reading each other's minds, she and her aunt turned to look at his mother who was trembling so violently that the strange whimpering noises she was making appeared to be emanating from the open fangs of the juddering fox's head around her neck. 'The BBC would never c-countenance these sorts of c-conditions,' the fox seemed to stammer. 'They would use doubles.'

*This isn't the BBC*, thought Auntie Win, feeling exasperated. *It's a film! And the director must have his reasons for wanting Josie and Jim to do it themselves.*

'Cup of hot sweet tea for everyone,' she said briskly, ushering Mrs Eliot firmly towards the hatch.

'But I have to stay . . .' she protested.

'Wonderful idea,' exclaimed Miss Cogan, joining her. 'Come on, Terry!'

Josie noticed the camera operator give a relieved smile and she gazed back at the river. It had changed from green to a murky chocolate brown, only it didn't smell like chocolate. As the camera crew began talking about the changing tides, she found herself mesmerised by the living theatre on the next bridge – the army of lorries and motorbikes weaving their way past carts and horses, and the hundreds of men walking to work.

*This is the life*, she thought.

Handbarrows were being wheeled through the crowds along the dockside and gangs of men were loading or removing cargoes to and from the large ships. On both shores, swivelling from side to side, lines of towering cranes were raising and lowering wooden crates in large nets. A man was climbing up one of them towards a cab that was perched about a hundred feet from the ground.

'Up he goes to his seat in the sky,' muttered Mr Stanmore.

*St Cecilia* had been booked in advance to enter a lock. They queued in orderly fashion with other river craft. As the giant lock gates drew apart for them to enter, Josie noticed that the second pair of gates to the dock was still closed.

'We all have to be locked in and wait till the water inside the lock has reached a certain height before it's safe for us to go into the dock,' the captain explained.

Small tugs were now towing more boats behind and alongside them.

'How long will we have to wait?'

'Long enough for you to get your schoolwork done,' said Mr Stanmore.

There hadn't been enough room on the launch for the tutors to travel with them so they had been given work to do under the supervision of the chaperones. Josie moved down the steps to the cabin with Jim and Terry just as the lock gates shut behind them.

Auntie Win was supposed to remain with them and help supervise but every now and then she found an excuse to *reconnoitre* up on deck. Surrounded by so many different sized vessels it all seemed chaotic but it didn't take her long to realise it was highly organised. In addition to PLA harbour master's staff, she spotted policemen both on land and in police boats all keeping an eye on the proceedings. She prayed that the man referred to as Moustache hadn't spilled the beans about Josie throwing the snow away, but if he had, and Josie's whereabouts came to light, it lifted her spirits to know that surrounded by so many uniforms, she would be well protected.

Once filming had begun in the dock, Auntie Win and Miss Cogan kept Mrs Eliot below deck since they sensed there would be more risk of Jim and Josie falling into the water if she was up on deck having screaming hysterics. Whenever it appeared as though she was about to ascend the steps, they would rapidly ask her about Jim's past successes in the theatre world. Once she was in full throttle, Auntie Win would sneak up on deck again. It was during one of these sorties that she watched one of the lightermen stepping deftly from one lighter to another, carrying Josie while she hung cheerfully onto him, her arms around his neck.

*She's loving it*, Win observed.

A massive, burly man had draped Jim over his shoulder like a sack of potatoes. There had obviously been a change of plan once they were on the lighters. She suspected that Jim had been too paralysed with fright to move.

*Thank goodness his mother can't see him looking so undignified*, she thought.

And then Win heard the director say the scene was in the can. More tiny scenes needed to be filmed from different angles but Auntie Win could see that the children were in safe hands. She relaxed, drew up the collar of her coat and listened contentedly to the creaking of the barges, the water slapping against the hull of the boat and the rhythmic *dugger dugger dugger* of a boat engine passing.

By the time Auntie Win dropped Josie off at Mr and Mrs Hale's flat at the end of the day's filming, Josie was ready to drop. Aware that Josie's family always had fish and chips on a Friday night, Mr and Mrs Hale had it waiting for her in their warm kitchen but Josie found it so difficult to keep her eyes open that she asked if she could have it cold for breakfast.

As she fell into bed, her head hitting the gloriously soft pillow, she was conscious of a warm sensation on her face from being out on the River all day. Outside, the rain was falling heavily, rattling the window. That was lucky, she thought sleepily. If it had rained earlier they wouldn't have been able to film her and Jim crossing the lighters. She rested the soles of her feet on her hot water bottle and pulled the chunky feather eiderdown up to her nose. In two days' time she would be outside again being rescued from the bombed basement.

'Smashin',' she murmured and closed her eyes.

The following afternoon Mr Beauvoisin nipped out of Auntie Win's flat by the fire escape and slipped round to the street opposite the entrance, where a plain-clothes detective constable was sheltering under an umbrella.

'May I have a word?' he said quietly, avoiding eye contact.

The man hid his mouth in a handkerchief and pretended to blow his nose.

'I'm listening, Mr Beauvoisin.'

'The major and I have had an invitation to stay at Mr and Mrs Hale's flat tomorrow night which means we won't be here.'

The man nodded and Mr Beauvoisin walked on.

When he returned to the flat, he found Auntie Win gazing out of the window in the dining room area.

'All in order?' she asked him.

'Message received and understood,' he said, smiling.

She ran her fingers up and down the curtains with satisfaction.

'It feels like a proper home now that these are hanging up.'

Just then the phone started ringing.

'I'll get on with the omelettes,' said Mr Beauvoisin.

* * *

'And when the men on the lighters say, "The tide is away",' Josie told Hilda on the phone in Mr and Mrs Hale's hallway, 'it means the tide is ebbing, which means going down. And when the tide is beginning to rise and flow again they say, "The tide's making" or "It's flooding".'

'It sounds like a foreign language,' said Hilda.

'How's Esmeralda?'

'Worse than ever. She's been telling everyone about the protests over a man called Lionel Bart and that woman called Joan Littlewood. And she keeps glaring at me as though it's all my fault because I'm your friend. I didn't understand it at first but I suppose it's because your brother is in *The Hostage*.'

Josie felt awkward. Hilda still didn't know she had been working with Joan Littlewood. She began to jig up and down in Mr and Mrs Hale's hall in an attempt to keep warm. In spite of wearing her duffle coat, she was freezing.

'What did she say exactly?' Josie asked, her teeth chattering.

'Oh, something about them casting people for a musical called *Fings Ain't Wot They Used T' Be* and that they don't want anyone from a drama school or a stage school to play the East End kids. Instead, they've chosen some teenagers they found in a coffee bar in a place called Soho who've never done any acting and haven't had any training.'

'I wonder why Esmeralda is so cross about it? I can't imagine her wanting to play a cockney, can you?'

At which point they collapsed into giggles.

'Wot's up, Guv?' said Josie in her most upper class voice.

'Blimey and love a duck, me old china! Someone 'as poured me a cuppa cha wiv the tea leaves floatin' and they're stuck to me nashers.'

By now they were both helpless with laughter.

'Thank you for letting me know, Inspector' said Auntie Win quietly.

She replaced the receiver and walked slowly back to the kitchen.

'Has he died?' Mr Beauvoisin asked, taking in the expression on her face.

'It might have been better if he had. No, I'm sorry. That's a dreadful thing to say.'

'He's recovered consciousness, I take it?'

She nodded.

'He's told the police that whoever arranged for him to be beaten up will know by now that it was *Larry* who ran off with the snow and that he's thrown it away. If it was Mr Lovatt-Pendlebury . . .'

'He knows that the *Larry* who was kidnapped . . .'

'Is Josie.'

They fell silent. They both knew what each other was thinking. Josie was in terrible danger.

# 7

# Maigret's Television Debut

MRS JENKINS LET HERSELF AND HER ELDERLY friend Ida Jones into Auntie Win's flat.

'Oh, it's so modern!' Miss Jones sang out as they entered the sitting room. 'And so colourful!' She took in the radiogram and the slim, red, curved settee with its matching armchair and footstool.

'Those legs,' she said, gazing down at the settee, 'they're a bit on the thin side. Do you think they'll take our weight?'

'Oh, yes. No need to worry about that,' said Mrs Jenkins.

'Everything's so neat. And the wood, it's so light.'

'Teak,' said Mrs Jenkins. 'Scandinavian style. Winifred told me she wanted to escape from dark, heavy Victorian furniture.'

'I feel as though I've walked into a film! And I've never seen a lamp like that before,' she said, pointing to a squat bottle with a lampshade above it.

'She made that herself. She covered a wire frame with raffia and stuck that electric socket thing for the light bulb in the neck of the bottle.'

'How clever!'

'Wait till you see her kitchen,' Mrs Jenkins said and waved Ida through the dining room area. 'She's got a refrigerator and cabinets.' She stepped into the kitchen and gave a cry. On the Formica-topped table was a tray with two sherry glasses and plates piled high with square sandwiches and strange-looking pastries.

'There's a note,' said Ida, handing it to her.

Mrs Jenkins glanced at it and laughed.

'It's from Winifred, telling us not to be afraid of the pastries as she didn't make them. Monsieur Beauvoisin did. He thought we should have something French to eat while we watch *Maigret*. He once worked in a kitchen in Paris and the chef taught him how to make brioche and chocolate éclairs. He calls them *patisserie*, she says.'

'Oh!' said Ida. 'This is lovely, isn't it?'

'Come on, let's lay everything out on her coffee table.'

Josie sat curled up in the armchair by the fire, her hair still damp from her bath. Mr Hale had given her one of his cardigans to wear over her pyjamas and a pair of his woollen socks.

Seated on the enormous settee, Mr Beauvoisin and Auntie Win were talking enthusiastically to two middle-aged men. They were Mrs Hale's sons. One of them, Max, had sandy hair and a laughing sort of face and turned out to be a camera operator. He was bombarding Auntie Win with questions about the filming on the Thames. Oscar, his brother, a dark-haired plump man with a quiet smile, was telling Mr Beauvoisin how inspiring it had been to hear his father play the piano in a Parisian jazz club when he was a boy and that it had been his introduction to the world of jazz. Josie eavesdropped, relieved to be tucked away in the armchair, because for some reason she felt shy.

The telephone in the hall began ringing, and within minutes Mr Hale poked his head round the door.

'It's your parents, Josie,' he said.

'Hello, love,' said her mum. 'Who are all those people I can hear? It sounds as though you're having a party there.'

'They're Mrs Hale's sons, and Mr Beauvoisin and Auntie Win. Guess what! Mrs Hale helped Mr Beauvoisin be born.'

'What's that?' she heard her father say. 'Mr Beauvoisin's had a baby?'

Josie began to giggle.

'Take no notice of him,' said her mum. 'We wanted to ring you before the Hendersons arrive here.'

'Are they coming round to see *Maigret*?'

'That's right.'

'I hope Mrs H brings those nice ginger biscuits,' Josie heard her father call out.

'I'm providing the food this time,' her mother called back.

Josie smiled. Elsie said that sometimes her parents were like a music hall act. It was difficult to believe that things had been bad when her dad had come home after the war, and that he and Auntie Win were always having arguments, although Auntie Win seemed to have arguments with quite a few people.

'So tell us about the filmin',' said her mother excitedly.

'Yeah, don't keep us in suspenders,' she heard her Dad butt in.

'John, behave yourself! He means in *suspense*, Josie.'

But Josie had a vision of her dad wearing a woman's corset with stockings attached to suspenders and she couldn't stop laughing.

'Now look what you've started, John.'

'Is everything laid out, Ida?' asked Mrs Jenkins.

Ida began to giggle. 'Oh dear,' she said waving a hand across her flushed face. 'I'm not used to drinking.'

'Which is why I've made us a nice pot of tea. We don't want you falling asleep do we? This should keep us going,' and she placed a mat on the coffee table and thrust a teapot swathed in a tea cosy onto it.

'How many minutes to go now?'

'Two minutes after the last time you asked me,' she said, kneeling in front of the fireplace and switching on the electric log fire. 'Nine.'

'Oh my goodness! We'd better start warming the TV up and getting the aerial sorted out.' She looked around. 'Brenda, where's the television?'

Mrs Jenkins waltzed over to the rosewood cabinet. With a flourish she opened the two doors at the top revealing a small screen.

'Oh my!' cried Miss Jones, sinking onto the sofa which earlier she had convinced herself was unsafe to sit on.

Josie gazed out from her bedroom window at the lights on the Thames, listening to the tugs hooting in the distance. Music was seeping through the wall from the sitting room. Jazz. It seemed to belong to the city she was observing. It was people drifting on the streets at night, cars moving past them in a stream, their dazzling headlamps like giant eyes moving swiftly past shadowy alleys. It wasn't a twirling on your feet kind of jazz. It was a pounding, thinking to yourself sort of jazz.

Everything was perfect, she reflected. Her mum and dad had made her laugh. Auntie Win was about to watch one of her favourite detectives solve a mystery and tomorrow, if it didn't rain, they would be filming on an old sailing barge.

'That's odd,' said Mrs Jenkins, hearing the doorbell. 'I wonder who that is.'

'P'raps someone's set has broken down and they want to join us,' murmured Ida, her eyes fixed to the screen.

Mrs Jenkins rose to her feet.

'I'll see who it is. You keep watching, Ida, so you can tell me if I miss anything important.'

Mrs Jenkins flung back the hall door to be greeted by two tall, burly men with thick black hair. They were identical except that one looked as though his nose had been broken. *Rough types*, she thought. Not the kind of person who resided in the flats. Before she could ask them what they wanted, she felt a hand grip her mouth with such ferocity that she was unable to speak and she was lifted off her feet. The other man flew past her, opening the bedroom doors.

'She ain't there,' he barked to his brother.

'She's in there watching telly. Quick!'

Mrs Jenkins tried to cry out a warning to Ida but she could hardly breathe.

'Who are you?' she heard Ida ask. 'What are you doing in here? Mrs Jenkins!'

'Where's the red-headed kid?' the man yelled.

*These monsters were after Josie!* Mrs Jenkins realised. *A small girl a third of their size! How dare they!*

'And what business is that of yours?' she heard Ida demand.

'Cos we want her, that's why. Now where is she?'

*Please don't tell him*, Mrs Jenkins prayed, remembering she had mentioned that Winifred was watching *Maigret* in a flat south of the Thames where Josie was staying to be near the film locations.

'In Timbuktu, you cowardly brute!'

*Good for you, Ida!*

To Mrs Jenkins' horror, she heard a sudden shriek followed by a thump. This was followed by heavy footsteps thundering back towards the hall.

Mrs Jenkins was flung back against the wall and her glasses fell to the floor.

*Don't let him break my back*, she prayed.

'So, tell us where your niece is!'

*They think I'm Josie's aunt.*

The man took his hand briefly away from her jaw and she gasped for breath. And then she had a brainwave. Winifred was always joking about her and her darning needles but they did come in jolly handy.

'The address,' she mumbled.

'Hear that,' the man said to his brother. 'That's the way to do it.'

'But I'll need my spectacles,' she added. 'Perhaps you could find them for me?'

'Get them yourself, but no funny business.'

'I'd need to put them on to find them,' she explained.

She was suddenly lifted off her feet again.

'Are you trying to take the mick, lady?' the man threatened.

'I can't see them,' she said politely.

The man dropped her, marched down the hall and picked them up from the floor. He thrust them in her direction. Mrs Jenkins was careful not to touch the lenses when she put them on. She moved deliberately slowly to make herself appear feeble but also to give herself time to think more clearly. When she reached the sitting room, it was all she could do not to cry out. Lying on the floor with a red mark across her face was Ida, her eyes closed. Mrs Jenkins had no idea if she were dead or alive. But she was angry, very angry. She picked up her handbag and opened it.

'It's in my address book,' she explained. Inside her head she said a small prayer. *Dear Lord, please forgive me for what I am about to do, but for Josie's sake, needs must.*

She found the packet where she kept her darning needles, carefully slipped out what she hoped was the sharpest one and gathered it into her fist. All she had to do was to find a way of reaching him.

'Come on! Come on! We ain't got all night!'

'My handwriting is somewhat small,' Mrs Jenkins began in her shakiest 'old lady' voice. 'If you could come a little closer?'

The man who had grabbed her mouth gave an impatient sigh and bent down.

*Please, Lord, direct my hand so that it gives him a minor and not a fatal injury.*

And she swung her tiny fist, thrusting the darning needle into the side of his throat.

The man gave a loud yell. Mrs Jenkins felt a heavy weight, like an iron bar, careering into her forehead, and her spectacles flew off her face. As she fell to the floor she found herself thinking about her friendship with Winifred. They both had a love of detective fiction and were always swapping books. Determined not to miss a moment of *Maigret*, Mrs Jenkins had rinsed her spectacles and dried them with a clean tea towel before coming to the flat to make sure that she would be able to see the screen clearly, which was why she had been keen for the man to pick them up from the floor because she knew that his fingerprints would be the only ones on the lenses. Then it went dark.

'Was it good?' murmured Josie when she heard her aunt climb into the other bed.

'Good? It was absolutely marvellous! If they have any sense they'll make a series.'

'P'raps you could write the BBC a letter,' yawned Josie.

'That's not a bad idea,' she commented. 'I wonder if

Inspector Gallaway watched it.'

Josie was curious as to why her aunt should be interested in knowing that.

'What was that jazz-sounding music?' she asked sleepily.

'A new LP Oscar brought round for his brother and the Hales to hear. Apparently, everyone's talking about it. *Kind of Blue*. Josie?'

But Josie was asleep.

Within the walls of a London telephone box, Mr Lovatt-Pendlebury slowly replaced the receiver. So the kid wasn't at her aunt's flat. It meant he would be forced to use his trump card – a little trip to a place he knew young Josephine would be attending the following morning. And this time he would deal with the matter himself.

Mrs Jenkins heaved herself forward on her stomach through the doorway of the sitting room. Her journey to the door had already taken an inordinately long time. Thankfully the lights in the flat were still ablaze. She realised she must have been kicked while she had lain unconscious, for whatever they had done had made it impossible for her to walk. The pain in her leg was so acute that it sent her head spinning. She smiled wryly. Why was it that some men thought it tough to attack a person half their size? As far as Mrs Jenkins was concerned, a man was someone who used his superior physical strength to protect those weaker than himself. The two intruders were not men in her eyes. They were mice. On second thoughts, indeed they were not! That was an insult to mice.

It was this inner fury that gave her the determination to try to reach the telephone. She had to warn the police that those two devils were after Josie.

She forced her chin upwards, and through blurred eyes struggled to focus on the hall table.

'Come on, Brenda,' she told herself firmly. 'Not far now. You can do it.'

From outside she could hear the dawn chorus and the distant hum of a milk van from down in the street. She must have fainted again because she was woken by the sound of the doorbell ringing. She attempted to call out but could only manage a whisper. It rang again. She almost wept when she heard footsteps fading away. Minutes later, it occurred to her that it was rather odd for someone to be calling so early. Whoever it was must have expected Winifred to be home.

'The milkman,' she whispered. 'With his bill.'

But it was Monday and it was on Fridays that he came to be paid.

The pain in her leg was unbearable. By now she was pulling herself along the carpet using her elbows. And then, at last, she had arrived at her destination and was touching the table. All she had to do now was to manoeuvre herself into a sitting position, pick up the receiver and dial 999. So simple, and yet in her condition, so seemingly mammoth a task. She rolled onto her back and pushed herself up. And then she felt giddy. She stretched up one arm and placed her other hand on the floor to support herself. She was about to lift the receiver when the phone rang. She gripped it and dragged it to her ear.

'Is that Major Lindsay?' said a man's voice. 'I rang your doorbell but you didn't answer.'

'Help!' whispered Mrs Jenkins.

'I'm a driver from the film company. Hello? Major?'

*He can't hear me,* she thought. *I must use every bit of strength I have left.*

'Ambulance!' Mrs Jenkins gasped and promptly collapsed.

Inspector Gallaway was leaning wearily over his desk gazing out at the Embankment, the city lights skimming the surface of the Thames as the first signs of dawn began to throw its colours across the sky. Due to a complicated criminal investigation and an accumulation of paperwork, he had been up all night. One of his three phones rang. He picked up the receiver.

'Detective Inspector Gallaway speaking.'

'There have been further developments on the drug case, sir,' said DS Mason at the other end of the line. 'I've just received information regarding Major Lindsay and a female friend. They've been taken to hospital.'

DI Gallaway sat up sharply. 'What!' he yelled. 'When did this happen?'

'Last night. A driver hired by the film company called round at her flat this morning to pick up her and Mr Beauvoisin but when he rang the doorbell there was no answer. When he looked up at the window above the door he noticed the lights were on and phoned her from a local telephone box. The major picked up the phone and asked for an ambulance. She's badly beaten up, sir.'

Much to DI Gallaway's surprise he felt as though someone had punched him in the stomach. *Pull yourself together, man,* he told himself.

'Forensics are on their way to her flat,' added DS Mason.

'How did the intruder get in?'

'There was no sign of a break in. The door to the kitchen was still locked. The major must have answered the door.'

'And how about our man on duty? Did he spot anything?'

There was an awkward pause.

'Hello? Mason?'

'He wasn't there.'

'Wasn't there!' Gallaway roared. 'Well, where the dickens was he then? Sunning himself in the Bahamas?'

'Mr Beauvoisin had told him that he and the major were staying at the Hales' last night. The other person found unconscious in the flat was a female neighbour,'

'That'll be Mrs Jenkins,' murmured DI Gallaway. 'He lied so that the major would be unprotected. The little –'

'The detective constable did report that he was no longer watching the building,' DS Mason interrupted, 'but the man at the station who took the message failed to pass it on, which is why we have only just found out.'

'He failed to . . .' DI Gallaway spluttered.

'He was suffering from food poisoning from a ropey piece of haddock.'

'I am not in the least bit interested what kind of fish –'

'And to be fair, sir, he spent most of the night running into the ablutions,' added the detective sergeant hurriedly.

DI Gallaway took a deep breath and counted to ten.

'The major . . .' he began. To his annoyance he found his voice shaking. 'How bad are her injuries?'

'One leg broken, sir, but no internal injuries.'

'And she's said nothing yet about her attacker?'

'No, sir. She's still unconscious, as is her female friend.'

When the phone conversation was over, DI Gallaway cursed his stupidity. It was obvious that Mr Beauvoisin had been up to his neck in it all along and was probably halfway across the country by now.

'He lied to us all,' he muttered angrily. 'But I'll catch him, and when I do . . .' He clasped his hands tightly in an attempt to control his rage.


'Detective Inspector Gallaway!' whispered Mrs Hale in her dressing gown. 'And DS Mason. What brings you here so early?'

'May we go somewhere more private?' asked Gallaway.

'Yes, of course. Come into the kitchen. It's warmer there.'

'Is Josie asleep?' he asked as she closed the door behind them.

'Yes. But she'll need to be woken in half an hour. Oh dear, it's bad, isn't it? I can see by your face. You're as white as a sheet.'

'I can assure you, Mrs Hale, it's nothing that a good night's sleep won't cure.'

'Sit down both of you,' she insisted, and she hurriedly placed a large black kettle on the range and joined them at the table.

It was at this moment that the door opened and Mr Beauvoisin walked in. DI Gallaway's jaw dropped. Within seconds he had sprung to his feet, grabbed Mr Beauvoisn's collar and flung him against the dresser with such ferocity that the china rattled on the shelves.

'You!' he roared.

'Guv!' cried DS Mason in alarm.

The detective inspector hastily released him, glaring at him with venom.

'Well, your little plan worked. But to have the gall to hide here beggars belief!'

'Hide?' But I told the plain-clothes man where we would be staying,' said Mr Beauvoisin angrily. 'Didn't he pass on the message?'

'You told him that *both* of you would be staying here. Because of your lies, the major is now lying injured and unconscious in hospital.'

'What's going on here?' said a voice at the door.

The DI swung round and his face went ashen.

'Major!'

Auntie Win hastily shut the door.

'You'll wake up Josie with all this noise and she has a long day ahead of her.'

The DI continued to stare at her, astounded.

'But who is the woman in hospital?' he demanded.

'Can I suggest that for Josie's sake we all sit quietly round the table over some hot sweet tea?' suggested Mrs Hale gently. 'She needs to see that the grown ups in her life are calm.' She gave a quick glance at the detective inspector.

'Although *you* look like you could do with a brandy.'

'So it appears that while your man was watching the flats, someone else was watching him, spotted he was off duty and took their chance,' said Auntie Win.

'I still can't understand why you didn't inform me personally,' said DI Gallaway.

'You're far too busy for me to tell you that I'm off to watch a television play at Mr and Mrs Hale's.'

'A television play! Are you telling me that the only reason you came here was to watch a play?'

'*Maigret.*'

'I don't care what it was called.'

'It was very good. Pity you missed it.'

'I thought . . .' he snapped. He stopped to compose himself. 'I thought you had been attacked.'

'Yes, I understand that,' said Auntie Win quietly. 'But we didn't want your officer wasting his time watching the flat when we weren't there. We assumed the message would be passed on.'

'Which it would have been if it hadn't been for some off-colour haddock,' said DS Mason.

The detective inspector gave him a withering look.

'So do you think this suspect of yours attacked Mrs Jenkins and Miss Jones, Inspector?' asked Mrs Hale.

'No. His sort always hire other people to do their dirty work.'

After Mrs Hale had seen the detectives to the door, Auntie

Win crept into the spare bedroom and gazed down at Josie, who was fast asleep totally unaware of how much danger she was in.

*And that's the way it will stay*, she thought.

'Wakey, wakey,' she murmured, giving her niece a gentle shake.

Josie opened her eyes sleepily.

'There's porridge and warm clothes waiting for you in the kitchen. Hurry up!'

# 8

# The Return of
# Mr Lovatt-Pendlebury

MR LOVATT-PENDLEBURY NIPPED ACROSS THE road to Miss Dagleish's stage school. Hardly had he reached the steps when he spotted a young girl, head held high, walking in his direction. Instinct told him she was the perfect source of information.

'Good morning,' he said, giving a small bow. 'You must be one of the talented pupils at Miss Dagleish's stage school.'

Esmeralda beamed.

'Well, yes. I am actually.'

'Allow me to introduce myself. I am Miss Merryweather's fiancé. You may know her.'

'Oh, yes. She's one of our matrons.'

He raised his hat. 'Mr Lovatt-Pendlebury,'

'Pleased to meet you. I am Miss Esmeralda Havilland,' she said politely, and she gave a small curtsy.

'I was hoping to catch her before she arrived but I think we must have missed one another.'

'I believe she's looking after one of the juniors. She's probably taken him off to a rehearsal somewhere.'

'Ah, yes, of course!' He gave a little laugh. 'I remember

her telling me now. How foolish of me. Having an artistic disposition I am apt to forget practicalities such as timetables. As a writer I don't ascribe to one. I write when I can.'

'A writer!' exclaimed Esmeralda, awestruck.

'Yes. But aside from that, I'm delighted that Miss Merryweather has recovered enough from her ordeal that she is able to return to her duties.'

'Her ordeal?' said Esmeralda, puzzled.

'That dreadful kidnapping business. Oh. Unless . . . Of course, you don't know. Please accept my apologies. How very remiss of me.'

'That's quite all right. My mother is the acting mistress. She told me all about it. But I'm not supposed to mention it.'

The man gave a slow smile.

'I can see just by looking into your eyes that you are a remarkably intelligent girl.'

'It has been said,' said Esmeralda with false modesty.

'I must say, the pupil involved had none of your charm. Looked like a boy.'

Esmeralda scowled and then forced herself to smile, remembering that anger made a girl look ugly.

'Not quite top drawer enough for this establishment, perhaps?' he murmured in a conspiratorial manner.

Esmeralda glanced around hastily.

'I quite agree with you, Mr Lovatt-Pendlebury.' She drew closer to him. 'No poise at all. And so conceited! She only gets parts because her brother and sister are in the theatre.'

'Oh yes, I remember now. Her sister was in *Life With*

*Father*, wasn't she? But surely that type of girl is hardly likely to be in work again.'

'Oh, yes she is!' Esmeralda burst out.

'No!' he said, shocked. 'You astonish me. Theatre job, is it?' he added vaguely.

'A *film* part. Two parts, actually. She's playing twins! Makes me sick.'

'I can see it does.' He paused. 'So she's off to Hollywood and warmer climes . . .'

'Hollywood!' she interrupted. 'No. Nothing like that. It's a cheap little film for the Saturday morning pictures. That's what my mother told me. What they call a Quickie.'

'A Quickie?'

'Oh, yes. Decent films take ages to film. A Quickie only takes one or two weeks.'

*Which means I'll need to move quickly*, thought Mr Lovatt-Pendlebury.

'And it's being made here in London. On the Thames.'

'So close? Still, I suppose that must be more convenient for her, living in London. But I'm surprised Miss Merryweather isn't chaperoning her.'

'Her aunt is.'

*Not any more*, thought Mr Lovatt-Pendlebury, if the account of the two brothers' visit to her flat was correct. She must be in hospital by now. He wished their temper hadn't erupted before they had acquired some useful information, but then it was because of their streak of nastiness that he occasionally employed them, so he couldn't complain.

'Ah. That's a shame. Miss Merryweather would have

enjoyed chaperoning her on the Thames. She is very interested in old architecture – Big Ben, the Houses of Parliament . . .'

'Oh, they're not anywhere near all that. They're filming in some slummy area where there are lots of bombed warehouses. The Puddle, I think my mother called it.'

'The Pool?' he suggested.

'Yes, that's it! Not a very nice area at all. Serves her right.'

'Upper Pool or Lower Pool?'

'Goodness! Are there two kinds?'

'There are indeed.'

'I had no idea. All I know is that it sounds like a church, Saint something or other.'

'Saint Katharine?'

'Why, yes!' said Esmerelda astounded.

'It's the name of one of the docks.'

'Oh, I see.'

'So I've helped you solve the mystery of her whereabouts then?'

'You have indeed, Mr Lovatt-Pendlebury.'

'Delighted to be of service.'

'Yes,' she said thoughtfully, 'the docks would be just up her street. So lower class.'

'I can see she's been the cause of much distress to you.'

'Mr Lovatt-Pendlebury, can I tell you something in the strictest confidence?'

'You most certainly can.'

'I had to go to the *police* station with my mother and answer all sorts of questions because of her, as though I were a common criminal!'

'No!'

'Yes!'

'But one glance at you and it's clear you don't have an ounce of criminality in you. No wonder you feel aggrieved.'

'One day, she'll get her comeuppance, Mr Lovatt-Pendlebury.'

'Oh, I'm sure she will.' He gave Esmeralda an agreeable smile. 'And now I won't disturb you a moment longer. Thank you so much for giving up your valuable time to speak to me.'

He raised his hat, bowed and crossed the road. Esmeralda watched him walk away feeling a great deal happier than she had felt all week. *What a gentleman*, she thought. It was only when she turned to walk up the steps that she felt puzzled. Why on earth was he so interested in knowing where Josie Hollis was working?

'Oh, who cares!' she muttered to herself and carried on up the steps.

That afternoon, the skies opened, tarpaulins were thrown over the film equipment and dozens of large umbrellas appeared as if from nowhere. The crew and cast, together with the wardrobe mistress who was holding a suitcase packed with sets of twins' clothes for Josie and Robin, huddled beneath them in little groups on a jetty near the warehouse. There was nothing they could do but be patient and wait for the sky to clear.

In a classier part of London, in a small tea house in Kensington,

Miss Merryweather gazed out at the gloomy, late afternoon sky as the rain streamed in rivulets down the window. That would put paid to any outdoor filming, she thought.

'I hear our young Josephine is working again,' said Mr Lovatt-Pendlebury.

Alarmed, Miss Merryweather nearly dropped her teacup. Could he read her mind?

'Oh, is she?' she remarked casually.

'I wonder why they didn't ask you to be her chaperone.'

She glanced quickly out of the window again. 'Oh dear, I hope this wind isn't going to turn my new umbrella inside out. My last umbrella was ruined that way.' And then she turned back to him. 'Perhaps the jobs clashed. I'm chaperoning one of the juniors at the moment.'

'Ah yes, so one of your pupils said.'

'One of my pupils?'

'At the stage school. Yes. No love lost between them, is there?'

Miss Merryweather did her best to look blank.

'I'm so sorry, Cedric, what do you mean?'

'She seemed to hate her.'

'Really? I can't think why.'

'She told me she had to go to a police station and answer questions because of her. Did you have you go to a police station too?'

'No,' she said carefully. 'A detective inspector and his sergeant came to the school.'

'Did they ask you questions?'

'Oh, yes, but I don't think I helped them much.'

'Did they ask about me?'

Miss Merryweather was taken aback by this direct questioning.

'Why would they want to know about you, Cedric?'

'Oh, I just wondered, seeing as I was someone she had met recently. A stranger really. They sometimes ask about that sort of thing.'

'Do they?' Miss Merryweather said, feigning innocence. 'Oh, Cedric, let's not talk about my young charges. It's so lovely to have you back here in England again. Can you imagine my surprise when I returned to the school with young Jimmy after his rehearsals to find you waiting for me on the steps and then being whisked off in a taxi to this lovely tea house. I don't want to waste any of this precious time thinking about work, my dear. I want to hear all about your trip to Italy.'

Miss Merryweather knew it was imperative she should telephone the police and leave a message for Inspector Gallaway, letting him know that Mr Lovatt-Pendlebury had returned from Europe, but it would be too risky to use the telephone in the hall because the other lodgers might hear her. And she didn't want to risk using a public telephone box in case Mr Lovatt-Pendlebury was lurking outside her lodgings or she was followed.

She remembered his parting words to her that evening.

'I've missed you so much, my dear,' he had said. 'Now that I'm back, I'm not going to let you out of my sight for a moment.' He would be calling for her early the next morning to accompany her to the stage school where she would be collecting the little boy she was chaperoning. 'After all, with this dreadful kidnapping business, I don't like to think of you walking the streets unprotected.'

*Or be able to talk to the police*, she added internally.

Miss Merryweather suspected he would continue to keep an eye on her. Once she was back in her room, she wrote a letter to the inspector to let him know that if the police wanted to find Mr Lovatt-Pendlebury, they would only need to look for her and he would be close by. She gave details of where she would be and when. The next problem that faced her was how to get the letter to him. If Mr Lovatt-Pendlebury intercepted her on the way to a postbox, he might spot the name and address on the envelope.

She felt frightened. The letter and its contents resembled a time bomb. It was visible evidence that she was deceiving him and she had no doubt that there would be a terrible price to pay if he ever found out. But Josephine's safety had to come first.

She thought long and hard. And then she had an idea. To test the waters, she would write another letter to a friend and fill it with chaperoning news about the play young Jimmy was appearing in, and hide the envelope addressed to DI Gallaway before posting it. After all, she might be worrying unnecessarily. But where could she hide it? Her handbag? No. That would be too risky. It might be taken away from her.

'My brassiere!' she thought.

* * *

She hardly slept a wink that night. Once up, she washed and dressed. She felt too nervous to eat any breakfast. All she could think of was the envelope with the letter to DI Gallaway in it.

'One step at a time,' she murmured.

She had hardly opened the front door of the lodging house when Mr Lovatt-Pendlebury stepped into view, a warm smile on his face.

'I told you I'd be here,' he said gallantly.

'Oh, Cedric! You're being too kind,' she sang out with all the gaiety she could muster.

'I'll post that for you,' he said, spotting the letter in her hand. 'I insist.'

She handed it over to him and observed him staring intently at the address.

'Anymore letters to post?' he asked politely, indicating her handbag.

'No. It was just that one, thank you.'

With relief she knew she had made the right decision.

As they travelled on the bus, now filling rapidly with people on their way to work, she was acutely aware of him glancing at her bag. Struggling to keep her feelings to herself, she asked him to talk about his travels, although by now she suspected they were all gleaned from travel guides.

'I'll say goodbye to you from here, my dear,' he said on the pavement opposite the stage school, 'and meet you after your young pupil's rehearsals.'

'I look forward to it, Cedric,' she lied.

She stepped across the road, unaware of the sharp nod

her fiancé was giving to someone in the distance and of the sudden acceleration of an approaching car. Within seconds the car had knocked her to one side. Lying sprawled and unconscious across the road, the seemingly distraught Mr Lovatt-Pendlebury ran to her aid.

'I'll phone for an ambulance,' he cried to a nearby pedestrian, but only after he had slipped Miss Merryweather's handbag under his raincoat. With any luck he would find some useful information inside it.

That afternoon, shivering by the dockside warehouses in the bitter cold, Auntie Win held Josie's script in her gloved hands. It had taken all morning to film one tiny scene by a narrow path near the remains of a bombed basement. Luckily Josie was only playing Heidi that day so wouldn't need to change into her Bridie clothes.

Win glanced at the small group of onlookers where a large well-built man with black hair was listening to Mrs Eliot.

'Miss Cogan, that person with Mrs Eliot, do you know him?'

Miss Cogan shook her head.

'I thought he was one of the production team. He could be a driver. The film company have so many vans and cars taking people and equipment to this location. Whoever he is I could hug him. I overheard him asking her questions about the star of stage and screen.'

'Her son?'

Miss Cogan nodded.

Still, Mrs Eliot had a big mouth, thought Auntie Win,

and there was something about the man's manner that made her feel uneasy.

Jim was only needed for one more scene that day. From then on, it would just be Josie, Terry and Mr Beauvoisin. By now, more people who had heard about the film company had come along to watch. One of them, she noticed, was a policeman. He left the group and walked up to Spud.

'I'd like to speak to whoever is in charge,' she heard him say.

She watched the assistant director heading his way and continued to eavesdrop.

'We're making an adventure film for children,' he explained. He then proceeded to show the policeman various documents and to inform him where and when they would be filming. The policeman asked if he needed any help with preventing members of the public from getting in the film company's way. After a brief conversation and much nodding he shut his notebook, beamed across at Josie, and gave her and Jim a wave. They waved back. And then he was off, walking past the half a dozen spectators.

The black-haired man, Auntie Win noted, had disappeared.

Terry was taken out of the car where he had been sitting with a rug over his knees with his tutor. He was joining Josie for the scene where Heidi would be taking Stan to the remains of the bombed basement to show him where she and her brother Charles had discovered the bound and gagged customs man and the bags of ivory.

The scene where the bricks had fallen and blocked the opening had already been filmed in the safety of the studio. Mr Stanmore now needed to film the scene where the African dockyard worker, Frenchie, hearing their shouts for help, pulls the bricks away and hauls the two of them out of a hole.

Josie glanced at the crowd of onlookers and Auntie Win whipped her head round to see what had caught her attention. Standing in the front were four young African men all wearing woollen caps and old jackets buttoned tightly over their collarless shirts to keep out the cold. One of them had a pipe in his mouth. They were smiling. They were dressed similarly to the way Mr Beauvoisin was dressed as Frenchie.

'They're seamen,' she heard Mr Beauvoisin explain to Mr Stanmore. 'I told them we would be filming here today. They're the men who allowed me to observe them working.'

'Do they have any friends?' asked the director.

The camera operator was now by his side. 'Why? What are you thinking?'

'How about if Frenchie blows a whistle for some help when he discovers the opening to the basement has been filled with bricks and . . .'

'*Hue and Cry?*' finished the camera operator for him.

Josie and Terry looked puzzled.

'Don't ask me,' Auntie Win overheard Josie say. 'I don't know what they're talking about either.'

'You know the film, Bertram?' Mr Stanmore asked.

'Where hordes of boys run amok over the bombsites after a gang of crooks?'

'Yes.'

The three men went into a huddle and there was a lot of technical discussion about cameras.

'Bertram, do you think you can find . . . ?' began Mr Stanmore.

'*Bien sûr*. Leave it to me.' He walked over to the seamen. They all began to talk rapidly to one another, translating and exchanging different forms of French amongst themselves. Within minutes they were nodding and laughing.

Mr Stanmore waved the children towards him.

'I'm going to film the basement rescue scene tomorrow instead of today.'

'Is it because it's too dangerous?' asked Terry nervously.

'No, I want to film the scene with some extra people in it who aren't here today.' But the director could see that Terry was worried. 'Do you want me to explain it to you again?' he asked.

Terry nodded.

'First we'll film you and Josie walking into it. Then we'll stop filming to pile the bricks up to make it look like the doorway's fallen in. I'll give you and Josie a signal to call for help, which will be Bertram's cue. We'll be filming Frenchie in long shot as he runs over to the bricks to rescue you. We'll stop filming to make a hole, and then we'll film Bertram hauling you both out of the basement. There's no danger whatsoever. You'll be quite safe, I promise you. You won't really be trapped.'

'Wanna bet?' muttered a voice from one of the glassless windows on the floor of a nearby warehouse. 'You will be after a good mate of mine has fixed up a loverly little booby trap for you.'

The owner of the voice was a big man with thick black hair, his brain still fresh with useful information from Mrs Eliot.

'Hello,' said Auntie Win, picking up the receiver late that night.

It was Inspector Gallaway and he came straight to the point.

'It's about Miss Merryweather. She's been involved in a hit and run accident, though we believe it to be no accident.'

'Oh, my goodness,' interrupted Auntie Win. 'Please don't tell me she's been killed.'

'Luckily, no. A fraction of an inch more in one direction and she would have been. But she's very badly bruised and her arm is broken. At first it looked like some kind of robbery. Her handbag was missing. But one of the nurses at the hospital came across a letter addressed to me hidden in her bra. Her matron had the foresight to telephone us to collect it rather than put it in the post.'

'Are you allowed to tell me what was in it?'

'That's why I'm calling. Miss Merryweather wanted me to know that her fiancé had spoken to one of the girls at the stage school. It was clear that Josie had been the topic of conversation because he let it slip that this girl hated her. Apparently she blamed her for being made to answer questions about her at the police station. Miss Merryweather knew immediately that the girl in question must have been –'

'Esmeralda Havilland,' finished Auntie Win for him. 'Who also happens to know where Josie is working,'

'Exactly. Our forensics man has also traced the identity of the fingerprints on Mrs Jenkins's spectacles. They belong to a very nasty piece of humanity who usually works hand in glove with his twin brother. So I'm suggesting we have a plain-clothes detective to be her chaperone instead of you. This is no place for a woman.'

'Oh, so I'm weak and feeble, am I?'

'May I remind you that three other women have been attacked already.'

'Not only women, Inspector,' said Win. 'Moustache and Scowler too. Besides, all the chaperones are female. If you put a man in my place, I guarantee Mr Lovatt-Pendlebury will smell a rat. And so will Josie, and that will alarm her.'

'But he must believe that you've been attacked in your flat, so it would natural for someone else to take your place.'

'Nonsense. He'll just think I have a very thick head and have recovered, although I'm a little concerned to hear you plan to use Josie as bait.'

'Sadly, this man is like a dog with a bone. He will never give up. This is the best chance we have of catching him. There's usually a group of people watching film crews when they're filming outside. We'll put one of our plain-clothes men among them.'

'But Josie's safety isn't the only reason you want to catch him, is it? You've been keeping another piece of information rather close to your chest.'

'Nonsense.'

'His identity, for instance,' pressed Win. 'I'm guessing Scotland Yard have a pretty shrewd idea of his real name, that he's not the kind of man who sells drugs to addicts in Stepney; that he's more of a West End dealer than an East End dealer; that he probably sells to the upper classes where he's picked up all the right kind of etiquette and social manners that help him infiltrate the higher echelons of society and some extremely wealthy clientele. Am I right?'

Inspector Gallaway made no reply.

'I'll take that crashing silence as an affirmative.'

'You can take it anyway you like,' he told her.

'So,' Auntie Win carried on, 'do we warn the film company?'

'We?' said Inspector Gallaway. 'I am in charge of this investigation. Not you.'

Auntie Win smiled. She enjoyed making the inspector hot under the collar.

'But to answer your question, no. If we do that, Josie will be taken off the film. By keeping quiet about it, it'll be easier for us to keep an eye on her. Thames Division Headquarters in Wapping is close by. As soon as I received Miss Merryweather's letter, I informed them and they've alerted all the boats on patrol in the area. She's in expert hands. The River Police keep an eye on the river twenty-four hours a day. Most of the men are ex-navy and what they don't know about the tides, currents and conditions on the river . . .'

'You could squeeze through the eye of a needle?'

'Indeed. And they have children of their own so they're

very keen to catch this man and protect Josie. The police boats have radio telephones and can contact the Yard immediately should they need to do so and vice versa. They'll be keeping an eye on the film-makers under the guise of making sure there are no accidents. Meanwhile, *we'll* keep an eye on land matters. It's the school that's the problem. They'll have to be kept in the dark, I'm afraid. If Miss Dagleish gets wind of anything, it will inevitably be passed down to the staff and that means . . .'

'Esmeralda Havilland will know everything.'

'In a nutshell. Yes.'

'If only we could keep her occupied and out of the way,' said Auntie Win. 'A nice little film part in the Outer Hebrides would come in handy.'

This was followed by another silence.

'Yes, Inspector? Is there anything else you wanted to say?' she added innocently.

He gave an exasperated sigh.

'You're a fool.'

'Oh, I've been called far worse,' she retorted.

# 9

# In the Pool

'BEAUTIFUL,' JOSIE MURMURED.

Sitting in mud at the end of the jetty was *Vanessa*, a spritsail Thames sailing barge with her long, narrow, flat deck and two masts. The smaller mizzen mast aft, at the back of the boat, had a rectangular red-tan sail that sloped upwards at a diagonal. The main mast had what appeared to be another mast attached halfway up, a bowsprit, with four red-tan sails – some triangular, some like the slanting rectangle. As Josie gazed upwards, it was as though the sails were part of the sky. The main mast was so high that she was surprised it didn't pull the barge over onto its side. Crowded round the vessel, the film crew were almost laughing with exhilaration.

'I agree,' said Mr Beauvoisin beside Josie, an overcoat covering his dockyard worker clothes. 'She is a beauty.'

Two men accompanied by a small, scruffy, square-faced dog stood at the end of the wharf, grinning. The skipper was in his fifties, his mate a nineteen-year-old youth. Under woollen hats, both had faces the colour of brick, their eyebrows bleached by the sun. It was obvious they were enjoying all the attention *Vanessa* was receiving.

'And the smugglers are taking the ivory away in this?' Josie asked.

'Yes,' said Mr Stanmore. 'Most of these barges aren't used for carrying cargo any more so the police assume that this one is manned by sailing enthusiasts. They have no idea it's being used to smuggle stolen goods.'

'And it's a wonderful excuse to film her,' added the camera operator.

Mr Stanmore gave a broad smile.

'That too. And I thought children in the cinema might enjoy seeing her as well.'

'Everyone on set, please!' cried the assistant director.

Josie walked dreamlike to the end of the jetty and stepped onto the sailing barge.

Hearing a cry, Auntie Win glanced up from her book, startled. But there was no need to worry. They were filming the scene when the twins and Charles discover they are related and Josie had flung her arms around Robin, who had her back to the camera, dressed as Heidi.

'Cut!' said Mr Stanmore. 'That cry is not in the script, Josie, but I like it.' He turned to the assistant director. 'Can we pencil that in? Robin, you'll need to hug her back. Let's rehearse that.' He turned to the wardrobe mistress. 'Annie.'

'More costume changes?' she finished for him.

He nodded and then he noticed that Robin seemed upset.

'Robin?' he said gently. 'What's the matter?'

'It's so lovely,' she blurted out, tears streaming down her face. 'Them suddenly finding one another after seven years.'

He smiled.

'Good job she doesn't have to wear powder,' laughed the make-up lady.

It had been a productive morning. Determined to make the best of the good weather, Mr Stanmore had not only managed to film the scene where Stan and Heidi clamber on board *Vanessa* to find Charles and Bridie tied up and gagged in the hold but also the scene where Stan and Charles push the crooks into it with the stolen ivory and seal the hatch over them.

It was Robin's last day playing the back of the twins, and she and her mum, who had been allowed time off from the canteen to chaperone her, joined Josie and Auntie Win in a working man's café nearby for a farewell lunch.

While Auntie Win chatted to Robin's mother, the two girls swapped information about each other's schools. Josie was hunting for a scrap of paper to write down Robin's address when she became aware of a big, burly man with black hair standing outside the window, staring at her. She was about to tell her aunt when plates of steak and kidney pie, mash, cabbage and rich dark gravy appeared on the table and from that moment nothing else mattered except eating. Working outside in the freezing cold made you ravenous.

After lunch, Josie and Terry returned to the remains of the bombed basement. There was talk about the extra people he had mentioned arriving later but Josie didn't take much notice.

She and Terry entered the basement as directed. Within seconds, bricks and large stones tumbled from above the opening behind them, blocking it completely and plunging them into darkness. It was so unexpected that Josie gave a yell. It had been very clever the way it had been filmed inside the studio but they had been told it was already in the can. Perhaps Mr Stanmore had changed his mind about wanting to build the bricks in the entrance by hand and wanted to film them falling here too. She waited for it to be cleared.

'It's collapsed!' they heard Mr Beauvoisin say on the other side.

'It's supposed to,' called Josie through the wall.

'No. It's really collapsed!'

Josie could hear him scrabbling.

'There's been a bit of an accident,' he shouted. 'I'm going to ask Mr Stanmore to phone the fire brigade to help pull these bricks away.'

And that's when Josie became aware of the water rushing round her ankles.


'Any minute now,' said a pair of watchful eyes from a window high up in a nearby warehouse.

'You sure this is gonna work?' said his black-haired brother.

'Course I am. The man I got to fix it is a genius. He ain't never failed yet. As soon as them bricks collapse, a wire gets pulled. Out comes a stopper like a giant cork from a pipe through a hole in the brick wall and *whoosh*! In pours the water from the river. Soon she'll be swimmin' abaht like a goldfish in a bowl.'

'There's water comin' in!' yelled Josie.

'Water?' Mr Beauvoisin called back.

'Yeah and it's coming in fast,' shouted Terry. 'It's just gone inside me wellies.'

'And up to me knees,' said Josie. 'It's risin' really quickly.'

'No time,' she heard Mr Beauvoisin mutter and there was the sound of a whistle being blown.

'Did you hear a whistle?' said one of the black-haired twins from their hideout.

'Well, if it's a copper there ain't nuffin much he can do on his own.'

'Wot the . . . !' exclaimed his brother. 'I don't believe this!'

In the distance, from behind every broken wall and jagged door of the bombed warehouses, there appeared dozens of African men, and they were all running towards the collapsed building.

'There must be a hundred of 'em!' groaned his brother.

Within seconds, the African seamen and dockers were hauling the bricks off while the others lined up and formed a human chain, passing one brick speedily to the other.

'They ain't never . . . ?' the man squealed incredulously.

The two men watched stupefied as a girl in a soaked camel coat, slacks and tam o' shanter was pulled out through a gap, followed quickly by a small boy. The children were now being hugged by the crowd of men.

'That's twice we ain't got her,' said the one with the broken nose.

'He don't like failure,' said his brother. 'Watcha gonna tell him?'

'Third time lucky, that's what.'

'It better be or . . .' He paused and they threw each other a look.

'He'll hire someone else to do the job,' finished his broken-nosed brother.

'And he'll take care of us, an all.'

'What do you mean I forgot to say "Cut"?' said Mr Stanmore. 'Oh. I see what you mean. Cut!' He whirled round to the camera operator. 'Are you telling me it's all in the can?'

But the broad smile on the camera operator's face had already answered his question.

And now every member of the film crew was cheering.

*So, it was deliberate*, thought Inspector Gallaway, replacing the receiver. The call from the forensics department confirmed it. The inspector knew that someone had been extremely anxious to get hold of Josie, but had put aside the possibility that the raid on the major's flat might have been attempted murder until he had more evidence. Now he had the evidence. The ingenious little flooding device in the warehouse that forensics had discovered within minutes of their arrival was intended to drown her and it mattered little that young Terry was to have been taken with her. If

Mr Beauvoisin hadn't spoken to the seamen earlier and if he hadn't been able to tell them rapidly in French that the children were in real danger, Josie and Terry's family would have been making funeral arrangements.

It beggared belief that a grown man would want to murder a child to ensure that all who did business with him had to toe the line or pay the ultimate price. Loss of face, that's what it was all about. If it ever got out that a twelve-year-old girl had thrown his drugs away he would be a laughing stock and his wealthy, drug-addicted clients might go elsewhere.

But should he tell the major? She might insist on withdrawing her niece from the film, as would his superiors, and he couldn't let that happen. He was absolutely convinced this was the best chance the police had of catching this man. He knew he was risking his job by putting the children in so much danger, not to mention losing his pension, he thought wryly, but it was as clear as crystal to him that Josie would be more at risk if they didn't catch this man – and soon.

'Where on earth is he?' Auntie Win repeated.

It was after the lunchbreak, the following day. The crew had left in advance to set up the camera again on *Vanessa*. The three children had followed them with Mr Beauvoisin and one of the regular drivers. The driver was supposed to have returned to collect her, Mrs Eliot, Miss Cogan, Miss Tomkins and Annie. Over an hour had passed and there was still no sign of him. It didn't make sense. Mr Stanmore would be unable to start filming without them present, so why hadn't the driver returned to pick them up?

'Angela,' she said to Miss Cogan. 'I'll go and see what's going on by the jetty.'

'How are you going to do that?'

'I'll make my way through one of the bombed warehouses and take a look on the other side.'

'Isn't that a bit dangerous?'

Win smiled. 'If I'm not back in three days, call mountain rescue.'

She chose one of the warehouses where the sheets of lead had been stripped from the roof. It let in more light to see by. Using a ladder, she cautiously manoeuvred her way, section by section up through holes in the floor. After climbing and descending repeatedly, she finally managed to haul herself up several floors. She hung on firmly to anything that was solid, grabbing stone pillars, protruding brickwork and iron rings. Half sliding, half padding along the slippery floor, she made her way through a thick and slimy carpet of pigeon droppings until she was standing gingerly on the loading bay, scanning the busy skyline of funnels and cranes to the jetty half a mile away.

'Ah,' she exclaimed, having at last spotted *Vanessa's* two masts. Aside from a tiny sail showing on the mizzen mast, all the other sails were lashed down. This struck her as odd. They were usually untied for the filming so that they could be seen billowing about. She was beginning to wonder if the Thames sailing barge she could see wasn't *Vanessa* when she spotted a man standing next to three children on a small jetty. She could just make out the splash of red and green on the tam o' shanter Josie was wearing.

But there was no sign of the crew or any plain-clothes detectives or river police.

Suddenly her scalp began to tingle and she knew instinctively she had to get out of the building as quickly as possible. Acutely aware that one slip could result in her skidding backwards, hitting her head and knocking herself out, she patiently and methodically began to make her descent.

Once she had reached ground level, she sprinted over loose bricks and headed towards a small, pitted road towards the building where the others were waiting. She was about to dash round the corner when she heard men's voices. At first she was relieved, assuming they were the drivers returning to pick them up, but their aggressive tone made her retreat rapidly.

'Do as I say and no one will get hurt!' one of them yelled.

Immediately, she pressed herself against the wall.

'Where are you taking us?' she heard Mrs Eliot cry out. 'Oh! But you're the nice man I spoke to about Jim.'

Auntie Win groaned inwardly.

'That's right, lady.'

'But I don't understand . . .'

She was interrupted by the sound of a dog barking. She recognised it immediately, having heard it many times during the film breaks. It belonged to the skipper of *Vanessa*, and if the dog was there, so also must be its owner.

'Keep 'im quiet or I'll put this knife in his throat!' the man ordered.

'What about Win?' Mrs Eliot began.

'Yes indeed, what about *win*ning?' interrupted Miss Cogan

swiftly. 'Well spoken, Mrs Eliot. Are we going to allow these bullies to defeat us?'

This was followed by a slap, a cry from Mrs Eliot and the loud slam of a van door being shut. Auntie Win didn't move a muscle. Within minutes she heard the engine starting. She peered round the corner in time to spot an ambulance driving away.

*Good old Angela Cogan*, she thought, as it disappeared out of sight. If she hadn't interrupted Mrs Eliot and prevented her from spilling the beans, the two men would have come looking for her and taken her along with them. She now had to make a quick decision: either find a telephone box and call the police, or make her way to the jetty so that she could warn Bertram.

'The River,' she muttered, remembering its icy, polluted waters. 'I have to get the children away from the River.'

'It doesn't make sense,' said the camera operator. 'I can understand someone wanting to steal our equipment but why shove *us* with it inside an ambulance?'

'It's no good,' said Spud, turning to the other technicians. 'I can't unlock the door and even if I could it's too dangerous while we're still moving.'

'Shush! What's that?' said the camera operator.

'Birds,' said Spud. 'We must be in the middle of the country.'

'That explains the bumping up and down. I bet your bottom dollar we're in a field.'

The ambulance came to a sudden halt, followed by silence

as the engine was turned off. A door was being opened. They stared at the back doors, expecting them to be flung open by the driver, but all they could hear was the faint sound of a motorbike speeding away.

'He must have had a motorbike waiting for him 'ere,' said Spud. 'Hello! What's that?'

'Another vehicle!' said the camera operator.

They began hammering on the walls of the ambulance.

'It's slowing down,' yelled one of the location drivers. 'The driver must have heard us! Keep hammering.'

'Listen!' said Spud.

In the distance they could hear the familiar sound of another motorbike revving and fading away.

'Are you thinking what I'm thinking?' asked Spud.

'Another stolen vehicle,' said the camera operator, 'with another convenient motorbike for the driver to get the 'ell out of 'ere?'

They all gazed at one another.

'No,' they chorused. 'Don't be daft.'

This was followed by a pause.

'Well, there's only one way to find out,' said the camera operator. 'Who's got the loudest voice?'

The chosen big mouth yelled out. Within seconds they could hear a voice in the distance answering. It was Mr Stanmore.

After much shouting between the two vehicles, they discovered that Mr Stanmore and the others had been bundled into another ambulance, having been told that their vehicle had broken down but had been temporarily replaced by an ambulance from their film company store of vehicles. They also found out that the chaperones, children, make-up and continuity ladies, and Mr Beauvoisin were absent.

'Maybe they'll be arriving soon in another "ambulance",' said Spud.

'But why on earth would anyone drive a film company here?' said the camera operator. 'And why lock us up?'

'P'raps someone wants to remove us from the docks because they think we're in the way,' said Spud.

'In the way of what?'

'I dunno.'

'What do we do?' asked the clapper boy.

'Let's have another go at that door,' said Spud.

Auntie Win attempted to make her way to where *Vanessa* was moored, but she realised pretty quickly – after wasting valuable time running across vast bombsites, only to be met by impenetrable walls and locked gates – that she had to find someone who knew their way around. She moved swiftly away from the River. As soon as she hit the nearest road, she stood on the pavement, glancing round urgently at the cars and bicycles streaming past. She spotted four youths with shiny red and white Lambretta scooters surrounding a young lad who was hanging grimly to a battered bike.

'Workin' dahn the docks is a mug's game,' one of the youths jeered at him, swaggering in front of him in his smart Italian suit and tie. 'I can earn more in a week that you can in a month. That heap of rust on wheels should be on a scrapyard.'

'Don't know why you bovver tryin',' added another member of the gang, 'they ain't ever gonna give you a job. You ain't exactly Charles Atlas, are you?'

'Yeah,' added a third member. 'With muscles like yours, you couldn't lift a doughnut.'

And they laughed at him and started up their engines. One of them pushed the boy over as they roared off, sending him sprawling across the pavement. The bike went spinning into the road. Auntie Win leaped forward and grabbed it, whisking it away from an approaching car. She could see from the look of horror on the boy's face how valuable the bike was to him. It was clearly his ticket to work. He scowled up at her, humiliated.

'Do you know the docks well?' she asked sharply.

'Like the back of me 'and,' he said, pulling himself to his feet and taking the bike roughly from her. 'What's it to you?'

'I need to get to Harrison's Wharf on that bicycle.'

He stared at her as though she were demented. And that's when she decided to bend the truth a little.

'My name is Major Lindsay.' *Well, at least that part is true.* 'I'm on a secret government mission. I need to get to that wharf pretty damned quickly. And . . .' She paused for dramatic effect. 'I could make it worth your while.' She produced a large silver coin.

'I ain't sellin' this bike for 'alf a crown!'

'I don't want you to sell it to me, I want you to take me there side-saddle on the cross bar, or me on the saddle and you cycling standing up. I guarantee you've more strength in those legs than those four youths put together. That's why they have to ride with a motor.' The boy fought down a smile. 'Of course if you're too scared, I quite understand. I admit it could get dangerous.' And she looked him straight in the eye. 'But if you decide to help me, it's top secret. Do you understand?'

'If you're a major,' said the boy suspiciously, 'prove it.'

Whereupon Aunt Win stood to attention and gave him a smart salute.

'Blimey!' he whispered.

'Yes, you've guessed. I'm ex-army but I'm in civvies now, working undercover. And there's no time to waste.'

*You can say that again*, she thought.

'Yer on!' said the boy, brightening.

After what seemed like a lifetime of juddering along on the bike and leaping off at intervals to carry it at breakneck speed over obstacles, Auntie Win finally reached the entrance to the wharf. She handed over the half crown and shook the boy's hand.

He gave her a rough salute back and grinned. He had hardly turned to wheel his bike away when there was a loud 'Oi!' and a man with skin the texture and colour of leather grabbed him by the ear with the intention, it appeared, of lifting him off his feet.

*Perfect*, thought Auntie Win, a diversion handed to her on a plate, and she hastily manoeuvred herself past groups of men in overalls who were now busily watching this young intruder being given a ticking off. Once out of their sight, she broke into a sprint, determined to reach the wharf before anyone could grab one of her ears.

* * *

'If it gets any darker,' commented Mr Beauvoisin, 'they'll have to film this scene tomorrow.'

'Where is everybody?' asked Terry yet again.

'You don't think the driver has got lost, do you?' said Josie.

The driver who had brought them to the jetty had also been puzzled by the absence of the film crew, so had decided to go in search of them, but had never returned. The empty *Vanessa*, now rocking gently from side to side at the lower end of the jetty, resembled a ghost vessel.

Auntie Win was only yards away from them, having run without stopping along the wharf. Panting breathlessly she waved her arms frantically in an effort to attract their attention but because they had their backs to her, they couldn't see her.

'Bertram!' she gasped, stumbling along the creaking timbers 'Get off!'

Mr Beauvoisin and the children turned.

'What a very good suggestion,' said a rough voice.

Win whirled round. Standing behind her were two large men with thick black hair. Legs astride, they filled the entire width of the jetty. *How the hell had they managed to get there without her seeing them?* she asked herself. They couldn't have followed her. She and the boy would have noticed them. She recognised the man she had seen talking to Mrs Eliot during the filming down by the bombed warehouse, the man she suspected was also the one who had forced Miss Cogan, Mrs Eliot, Annie and Miss Tomkins into the ambulance.

'Winifred, you take care of the children,' said Mr Beauvoisin quietly. 'I'll look after these two.'

'Funny that,' said the twin with the broken nose, cos we planned to look after you.'

'Yeah,' said his brother, and he gave a malicious smile.

By now Auntie Win had slipped behind Mr Beauvoisin.

'And we want you off the jetty too,' he added.

'We're even gonna give you an 'elpin' hand, and chuck you off it ourselves.'

'See that mooring buoy,' whispered Auntie Win to Josie.

She was pointing to a massive object some distance away, bobbing in the water. As tall as Josie, it had a large mooring ring on top and was tipping over on its side like a giant can. Surrounding it were wooden slats with chains looped between each one. *Vanessa*'s stern appeared to be resting on it.

'Get into the dinghy with Terry and Jim, and row as close to it as you can. Lucky for us *Vanessa*'s leaning on it, but I doubt she'll be there long. Once the tide begins to rise, she'll probably be lifted off it, so we need to move quickly to get you away from the jetty and over to it in time. I'll jump onto *Vanessa*, toss the lifebelt down to you on a rope and haul you onboard.' She turned to Terry. 'You go first. I'll help you.'

'I'm scared . . .' he began tentatively.

From behind came the roar of the two men as they threw themselves at Mr Beauvoisin. Terry gave a startled jump and allowed Auntie Win to take his hand and lower him into the boat.

'Sit down at the end. Whatever you do, don't stand. Josie, you next.'

Josie stepped into the dinghy and hurriedly sat in the middle.

'I'm not getting into that,' protested Jim.

'You're not tall enough to reach *Vanessa* by foot so it's that or swimming in the River. Take your pick.'

But before anyone could move, one of the men shoved his way past Mr Beauvoisin and grabbed the dinghy's mooring rope.

Further down the Thames by Irongate wharf, swinging on bosun's chairs around one of the soaring funnels of a general steam navigation ship, and working higher than a trapeze artist but minus a safety net, three painters in their overalls were dipping their brushes into the small buckets attached to the chairs. Luckily, with there being no frost, they had been able to repaint the funnel all day, but it was now beginning to grow too dark to see what they were doing.

Ted Parks rested his brush against the inside of the bucket.

'Time to pack up,' he said to his companions, and he revelled in the thought of the mug of hot sweet tea and the baked potato waiting for him on the dockside.

He was feeling pleased with the day's work. They'd got a lot done. He took a last glimpse at the old Thames sailing barge moored down the River. He had been admiring her on and off all day. *Must be thirty years old*, he thought. *Lovely vessel.* And then he caught sight of something that nearly rocked him off his perch. Two burly thugs were fighting an

African dockyard worker who seemed to be protecting a woman and three children. To his alarm, he saw one of the men throw himself at the nippers!

Hurriedly he began to lower himself down the funnel.

'Steady on, Ted!' yelled one of his workmates. 'You'll kill yerself going down at that speed.'

'What's yer rush?' yelled the other.

'Got to find a copper,' Ted yelled back. 'No time to explain!'

But his fingers were shaking. He had seven kids of his own and the thought of some thug going for one of them, and right by the River, enraged him.

'Nearly there,' he told himself, as the perch swung precariously.

Mr Beauvoisin dragged the man off and threw him screaming into the Thames. As the brother in the water struggled to reach the jetty, his twin hurled himself with fury onto Mr Beauvoisin's back. But Mr Beauvoisin was ready for him and sent him backwards with a sharp elbow thrust in the stomach.

'Move!' commanded Auntie Win.

Jim gingerly lowered himself into the dinghy. Auntie Win took a few steps back, ran to the end of the jetty and hurled herself onto *Vanessa*. Nervously, Josie looked up, expecting to see her slip off the hull and into the River, but she had somehow managed to haul herself onto the deck and had disappeared.

\* \* \*

Angry with frustration, Ted Parks forced his way through the crowd of dockyard workers.

''ere, whatcher think yer doin'?' shouted a docker.

'Kids attacked,' he yelled breathlessly, 'on the River. I need to get to the copper on the dock gate!'

'Let him through!' yelled the man to the other dockers. 'Kids in trouble on the River! Let him through!'

From the dinghy, Josie could hear the thwack of fists, splashing and yells from the jetty. The dinghy jerked away and rocked from side to side. Jim must have undone the mooring rope. She grabbed the oars.

'Keep still,' said Josie, realising that it was Jim who was causing the violent motion. 'You'll have us over.'

She glanced over her shoulder at Terry. He stared silently back at her, his face white.

Back on the jetty, she saw that Mr Beauvoisin was still fighting one of the men but there was no sign of the one who had fallen in the water and she was terrified he would suddenly shoot upwards like a rocket beside the dinghy and tip it over. And then she spotted the rope from the dinghy in the water. Jim hadn't undone it. It had been cut, and by someone who must be carrying a very sharp knife. She shivered. Ahead of them towered the mooring buoy. She pulled on the oars.

'Terry,' said Josie, 'when we reach the buoy I want you to grab one of the chains.'

'What are we going to do then, O mighty one?' Jim asked sarcastically.

*Shut up for a moment*, she wanted to yell. *I can't think straight*. But she could see that Terry was petrified. The last thing he needed was to see them arguing with one another. They drew nearer to the buoy and Terry grabbed a chain.

'That's good, Terry,' she said. 'Hang on to it.'

It was at that moment that a rope with a lifebelt attached to it slid down *Vanessa's* hull and hit the water. Josie looked up to see her aunt leaning over the side.

'I've fixed up a pulley device,' she shouted.

Jim pulled it out of the water and hauled it into the boat. To Josie's astonishment, he hurriedly untied the knot around it.

'What are you doing?' she cried in disbelief.

'I'm putting the lifebelt on, of course,' he snapped.

'No!' Auntie Win shouted. 'Tie it back on again! The rope is there so that I can haul you up!'

Suddenly, shots rang out. Jim gave a cry and in his panic dropped the ring overboard. Helplessly, Josie watched it slip away on the ebb tide. More shots rang out. One hit the dinghy. Within seconds, water was trickling around her feet. She looked around to find out where the leak was coming from only to discover that a bullet had dislodged one of the planks.

A police constable sprinted along the dockside with Ted Parks running alongside him. Up ahead by an arch was a police box. He unlocked it, flung open a small door and grabbed the receiver from inside. Ted stood impatiently beside him, his shoulders heaving.

A banging in the distance caused them to swing round sharply.

'Someone's letting off fireworks,' said Ted.

'Those aren't fireworks,' said the policeman, alarmed. 'That's gunfire.' And he swung back towards the box. 'I can hear gunshots,' he yelled into the receiver.

'Tell the River Police to come quick!' Ted pleaded.

'He's hit the boat!' yelled Jim.

'But not us,' said Josie firmly. She racked her brains trying to think of something they could do which might save them. In desperation she asked herself what Nancy would have done in *Swallows and Amazons*. Bail out! That's what Nancy and her sister did in rough weather, when water slapped over the sides of *Amazon*. After scrabbling around, she found a small bucket and rapidly began hurling the water out. The boat started rocking again.

'I can't swim!' screamed Jim. 'I'm going to drown! I'm going to die! I don't want to die!'

*Die?* thought Josie. *No! Never say die!* And she was flung back into a school gymnasium on a Friday night when her patrol leader was teaching her how to tie a . . .

'Bowline!' she yelled.

The rope was now dangling by the boat in the water.

'Shut up, can't you?' Jim screamed out.

'I can tie a bowline knot.'

'So what?'

Immediately, Josie knew that Jim had to go first. The way he was rocking the boat and panicking, he would soon have all three of them in the water and they'd all drown. She thrust the bucket at him.

'Keep bailing while I make the knot. She fished the rope from the water. *Main part in left hand. Make the loop.* She paused. *Make the loop a bit higher up. Thread tail through and round and through and pull.* She checked that it wouldn't slide shut under pressure and it didn't!

'Put your head and arms through this,' she ordered Jim, snatching the bucket from him and bailing in a frenzy. 'Hurry! We're sinking!'

It was that which moved him into action. Auntie Win was peering down at them through the dusk and Josie placed her arms into two semaphore positions.

'Why are you waving, you stupid girl?' Jim cried. And then Auntie Win disappeared. 'Where's she gone?'

'I've just given her the semaphore message for *Up.*' Josie explained.

The rope gave a sudden jerk and he began flailing his arms.

'Stay still!' Josie cried.

It was growing darker. On the jetty, Mr Beauvoisin was still fighting one brother and then Josie noticed another man standing nearby, coolly observing them. It was Mr Lovatt-Pendlebury and he was holding a gun! So that's where the shots had come from. But what on earth was he doing there? And which man was he trying to help? Mr Beauvoisin? Or the horrible man with the black hair?

As Auntie Win was about to haul Jim up onto *Vanessa*, a

Thames firearms team was moving swiftly towards one of the police boats moored at Wapping police station, and in a street outside Scotland Yard, DI Gallaway and DS Mason were climbing into a radio car.

'There's a second witness, Inspector,' said the voice on the car radio. 'A workmate of the first witness. He watched what happened after his mate went off to find a policeman. Three youngsters forced off the jetty into the River. Some kind of fight going on. Four men involved. We could be looking for three kiddies heads in the water.'

'Any more shots reported?'

'No, sir.'

'Nothing more about the woman?'

'No, sir.'

DI Gallaway turned the radio telephone down and slammed his hand against the receiver. One of his men was supposed to be keeping an eye on the film company, disguised as one of the drivers. How on earth had he lost sight of them?

He stared out the window at the darkening winter sky. *What had he been thinking of?* If they were in the water they had little chance of surviving. If the pollution didn't kill them, hypothermia would. He would never forgive himself if lives were lost because of a reckless gamble that hadn't paid off. And why, oh why, had he allowed the major to remain a chaperone?

'Idiot,' he snapped. 'Just because she's been in the WRAC she thinks she's the same as a man!'

Meanwhile, on a police boat, a sergeant at the wheel was

on the look out, his eyes peeled as the narrow beam of his searchlight swung across the River amongst a crowd of vessels. It was going to be tricky to spot any heads above the surface. With *Vanessa* having left her moorings and with a strong tide running, it was vital that he find these children quickly but he knew he had to be cautious to avoid mowing them down or cutting them to pieces with the boat's propeller.

The rope jerked Jim upwards so that he was standing with his knees bent. Clinging tightly to it, he gave an agonising shriek as he began to rise from the boat. Josie turned away swiftly because she didn't want him to know that she had seen him beginning to cry.

Terry was still hanging on to the buoy's chains.

'Well done, Terry!' she shouted.

Jim was now suspended above them. He swung across towards *Vanessa*, his feet skimming the water. There was another jerk and he bumped into the hull.

'The water's still coming in,' said Terry fearfully.

'But it'll be much better now that Jim isn't in her, isn't it?

'He's goin' to be all right, ain't he, Josie?'

'Course he is,' she said, bailing even harder.

'You won't leave me on me own, will you?'

It was as though she was back with Larry again.

'No, course not,' she said.

In the distance there was the faint sound of a boat approaching. As it grew louder, she was blinded by a searchlight sweeping across the water. Then a bullet whistled by her head.

'We're going to be killed, Josie!' cried Terry.

'But we're still alive now. And I think he's used up all his bullets,' she added hopefully. Whoever Mr Lovatt-Pendlebury was trying to help, firing bullets all over the place was really stupid and very dangerous.

The boat with its searchlight passed them by, but its sudden absence made the sky seem even blacker and the stench of the River even more revolting. She glanced up. Jim had almost reached the deck and was stretching out a leg to touch it. The rope gave another jerk and then shuddered to a halt. Auntie Win reappeared, hauled him over, and within seconds, she was lowering the rope again. As soon as it touched the water by the dinghy, Josie pulled it in.

'Your turn, Terry,' she said cheerily, her voice shaking like a baby's rattle. In spite of the bailing, she was acutely aware that the water had crept up to their waists. 'But don't let go of the chain yet,' she added quickly. 'Wait until I tell you.'

Terry nodded, his teeth chattering with the cold. It was a good job he was wearing a coat, Josie thought, otherwise, being smaller than Jim, he might have slipped through the loop.

Gingerly, she passed it in his direction.

'Take one hand off and put your arm through the loop, but keep hangin' on to the chain. Now slowly pull it over your head.'

The dinghy juddered as he manoeuvred his head through the loop, struggling to keep hold of the rocking buoy.

'That's good! You're almost there. Now swap arms and

hold the chain with the other hand.'

She didn't need to say any more. He understood. As he slid his free arm through the loop, Josie almost wept with relief. She peered up at *Vanessa*, gave her aunt a thumbs-up sign and bailed with even more ferocity. But the water continued to creep upward and she could feel the boat sinking.

'Hang on to the rope,' she told Terry.

'But the chain!' he began. 'The boat will drift away if no one is hangin' onto it.'

'As soon as you're out of the way, I'll grab it.'

'I want me mum,' he whimpered.

'You'll see her soon,' Josie said.

His knees rose above the surface of the water. In the distance she could hear the sound of another boat engine. The rope gave a jerk, and Josie dreaded the next moment.

'Terry, let go of the chain.'

As his hands loosened their grip, he swung towards the hull of the boat. Suddenly, the searchlight appeared again, and at that moment another shot rang out. Terry who was now dangling alongside the sailing barge, let out a howl. The searchlight swung away from him to the jetty and Josie saw Mr Beauvoisin give one almighty punch to the burly man's jaw. The man staggered backwards against Mr Lovatt-Pendlebury. They careered towards the edge of the jetty but not before the black-haired man had grabbed the lapel of Mr Beauvoisin's coat, causing all of them to fall into the water. The jetty was now empty. All Josie could hear were shrieks and violent splashing.

IMPOSSIBLE!

It was when the dinghy collided into a hard object that she remembered she should have been hanging onto the buoy. But it was too late. The boat sank beneath her. Flinging her arms out she grabbed one of the chains. To her shock she discovered it was as cold as a block of ice. How Terry had managed to hold on to one for so long astonished her. She glanced over her shoulder to see if her aunt had flung the rope back over the hull, only to see *Vanessa* drifting away from her, its aft sail flapping. The tide had turned and lifted the sailing barge clear of the buoy.

She struggled to look at the jetty again. Even if she had had the strength to cry out for help there was now no one to hear her. And then she spotted the outline of *Vanessa*'s rope drifting in the water. It too must have been cut from its moorings.

In desperation she made cycling movements to keep herself afloat, but it caused the massive buoy to tip in her direction, dragging the chain under the icy surface of the water so that it was almost impossible for her to hang on to it. By now, the strain of gripping it while the river sucked her away from the buoy caused her arms to ache with a pain so intense it was unbearable. She struggled to keep her chin above the water to prevent it from slopping into her mouth. But her fingers had other ideas. Helplessly, she felt them slip away from the chain, all power and strength frozen and numbed out of them. Cold and exhausted, she had an overwhelming desire to close her eyes and go to sleep. She could feel the dark, greasy river sliding inside her nose and over her forehead. *Oh*, she thought wearily, *I'm drowning*.

She was drifting into unconsciousness when a jolt beneath her thrust her violently upwards. Some force gripped the back of her coat and hauled her to the surface. In seconds she was twisted onto her back, spluttering and blinking the slime out of her mouth and eyes. A human mattress seemed to be swimming powerfully underneath her, pulling her backwards, cupping her chin in a strong hand. She began coughing and retching so hard she thought she would be sick. Above her head, the stars were obliterated by a dazzling searchlight. A boat was approaching. *We are going to be smashed to pieces*, she thought, *and there's nothing I can do to stop it.*

But its engine was soft and slow like a purr, and there were men's voices and they sounded kind. Within seconds, hands were gripping her from above and pulling her upwards out of the water.

With two wet and frozen boys cowering in the crews' quarters, *Vanessa* leaned and tossed while Auntie Win fought to control her with the wheel, praying that she wouldn't crash into another vessel. The fact that most of *Vanessa*'s sails were tied down was in her favour. If they had been flapping all over the place, what little control she had would have been lost, and at least she could see Jim and Terry from where she was standing. It was then that she had the most glorious piece of luck.

'Wapping police station!' she breathed.. Ahead of her, coming into view, were police boats moored on a pontoon, the steps running up from the foreshore to an alleyway alongside it.

As she drew nearer, she spotted a man sitting at his desk up on the first floor. He was peering out of a large open window. She waved frantically at him. The man smiled and waved back.

'Silly man,' she muttered. 'Can't he see we need help?'

But all the chief superintendent could see was a magnificent spritsail Thames sailing barge with its soaring masts, one small tan red sail fluttering like a flag on the mizzen mast and a friendly woman waving to him on a late December afternoon. *Unusual to see a woman at the wheel*, he thought. *Lucky girl. But she should really have her navigation lights on.*

'Hang on a minute!' he exclaimed and he leaned forward. 'Are you *Vanessa*?' he yelled down at her.

'Yes. There's a child in the River,' she shouted, pointing urgently behind her. 'I've two more onboard in the cuddy.' But already she could see the he was barking orders into a telephone. He looked up and gestured to her that help was on its way.

*By George, the woman has guts*, he thought, but she would never have the strength to moor *Vanessa* single-handed.

Terry and Jim were peering out of the crew's quarters. Terry was whimpering with the cold.

'Don't you worry,' Win said firmly, 'we'll find somewhere to moor soon.'

Jim crawled out on his hands and knees, too terrified to stand. He manoeuvred himself towards her, clinging on to anything that appeared to be fixed to the deck.

'Why are those men after us?' he shouted.

'They're not after you. They were trying to steal this barge and we were in their way,' she lied, struggling to hang on to the wheel.

'So they could still be after us . . .'

'What's that?' she interrupted, pointing over his shoulder.

It was a broken-down landing stage, sadly just out of reach. *If only*, she thought. But even if she had managed to steer the boat in its direction and jump onto the jetty she would have needed Jim to help her. The rope on the forrard deck was as thick as her wrists and so heavy that it would have been a struggle for him even to lift it, let alone throw it at her.

'Look out!' yelled Terry. He was pointing at a police boat drawing alongside them. 'It's going to hit us!' he screamed.

'No, she's not,' Auntie Win said excitedly. 'We're being nudged towards the jetty!'

Within seconds, a river policeman had climbed up on deck.

'Throw the forrard rope to me!' Auntie Win yelled, running.

'Come on, lads,' he ordered.

They followed her to where the heavy rope was coiled, and scooped it up in their arms.

'When I give the word,' she called out, 'throw it to me as hard as you can.' And she ran for the bow. 'Here goes, girl!' she muttered to herself and leaped off *Vanessa* onto the landing stage, rolling over commando style onto the broken wood in an effort to break her fall. Clambering to her feet, she shouted, 'Now!'

The policeman and the boys threw the rope at her with all their strength. Auntie Win dived at the tail end, which was now rapidly slithering along the wooden boards and back into the Thames.

'Got you!' she snapped, grabbing it. Using her hand and elbow as a cleat, she wound it speedily into a loop and passed it over a weather-beaten bollard where she made fast. Relief swept over her as the sailing barge swung round into the tide and faced the river. *Vanessa* was attached to terra firma again.

'Have you done it?' cried a small voice.

It was Terry, shivering on the deck.

'I certainly have.'

The river policeman was now standing with a hand on each of the boys' shoulders. He was grinning.

'You'll be getting the George Medal for bravery for this,' he joked.

She couldn't see the funny side of this remark but she forced herself to look happy for the boys' sakes. Hastily she turned away and pretended to check the knot round the bollard so that they wouldn't be able to see her mouth trembling. How was she going to explain to her sister that she had managed to save these boys but had failed to save her lovely Josie?

Inside the cabin of the police boat, wrapped in a heavy blanket and drenched in filthy, foul-smelling water, Josie sat juddering with the cold. There were three peak-capped river policeman onboard. One of them was holding an oxygen mask over her nose and mouth, another was at the wheel, while a third was speaking into a radio telephone. She stared at the man holding the mask. On both sides of the collar of his dark navy uniform, was the word *THAMES* in white block capitals. It struck her as strange. She pushed the mask gently away so that she could take a closer look.

He smiled.

'She's fine, guv,' he said, over his shoulder to the sergeant.

Unable to stop her teeth from chattering, she was convinced her insides must resemble frozen peas. A large blanketed figure sat opposite her, the man who had saved her from drowning. Mr Beauvoisin. He winked at her.

There was a murmuring in the background on the radio telephone about some other people who hadn't been found yet. More river police were out looking for them with dragging apparatus. Josie guessed they must have been talking about the men who had attacked Mr Beauvoisin. And then she gave up trying to make sense of it all. She was too numb and too tired to care.

She was about to drift off to sleep but was jolted into wakefulness when the boat gave a slight bump. Before she could ask where they were, she was scooped up like a baby and carried with speed from the boat. By the thumping of feet on creaking wood she guessed that they were on some kind of pontoon. Her face must have been very cold because as the river policeman carried her up some steps, she could feel the warmth of his breath on her face. There were more voices now and a sense of urgency, as if there were some kind of race. She was taken at breakneck speed into Wapping police station, up several flights of stairs, and into a room. Out of the corner of her eye she could see two steaming baths. Her sodden blanket was removed and she was lowered into gloriously warm water, coat, shoes and all.

She heard one of the policeman say, 'French gent, guv. Looks African but talks English like royalty. Army background. Good fighter.'

'Army,' murmured Josie, and she had an image of her aunt's green uniform hanging in the wardrobe.

Mr Beauvoisin was now sliding into the second bath, also fully clothed.

'Auntie Win?' Josie managed to get out.

A flicker of sadness crossed Mr Beauvoisin's eyes.

'They're still looking for her and the boys in the River,' he said gently.

'*Vanessa*,' she grunted.

Mr Beauvoisin looked at her, puzzled.

'*Vanessa*,' she repeated, struggling to get the word out. 'When you were . . .' But it was too much effort to speak. She clenched her fists and made boxing movements.

'While I was fighting?' And then he sat bolt upright. 'Wait a minute! Are you saying she managed to get onto the sailing barge?'

Josie nodded wearily and let the warmth eke into her bones. It was only when she found herself taking a breath that she realised that, being so cold, she must have been holding it in.

She closed her eyes. Mr Beauvoisin was calling out for a

policeman and there was talk about Mr and Mrs Hale, and a fire, hot water bottles, woolly socks and hot chocolate with a visit from a doctor, rather than a trip to a hospital.

'You're a lucky boy,' said a voice.

Josie opened her eyes. A ruddy-faced river policeman was beaming down at her.

'Lucky *girl*,' she croaked.

'Yes, that is good news,' said Inspector Gallaway and he replaced the radio telephone.

'Sir?' queried DS Mason from the behind the wheel of the car.

'The dredging apparatus will be looking for three people, not six. A Thames Four has picked up *Vanessa* with the major and the two boys onboard. The major moored her onto a bombed landing stage only a few hundred yards from Wapping police station. Middleton's Wharf.'

'How on earth did she manage that?' asked Mason.

'I don't know, but I expect she'll give me all the details.' He gave a wry smile. 'Army style.'

'This film, it's not about smugglers, is it?' asked the River CID inspector, sipping tea on the settee in Mr and Mrs Hale's sitting room.

'How on earth did you know that?' asked Auntie Win. She was leaning back in an armchair by a roaring fire with Josie wrapped in a blanket on her lap.

He raised an eyebrow.

'Because nearly everybody who writes about crime on

the River, invents endless tales about smugglers, despite there being very little smuggling.'

'So what does go on then?'

'Boat thefts, recovery of timber, petty pilfering, people jumping in, thefts from nippers who've been sent out by their parents to steal food from barges. And we often have to chase off youngsters larking around the foreshore. It's particularly dangerous if there's a rising tide. And then of course there's members of the public having trouble with their boats that we then have to rescue.'

'Like me,' said Josie.

'That's right.'

'And you reached her just in time,' said Auntie Win, giving her a squeeze. 'By the way, Inspector, about *Vanessa*?'

'Don't worry. We'll explain to the skipper that you didn't steal her.'

'Still no sign of *Vanessa*'s crew?'

He shook his head. 'Nor the film crew.'


Early the following morning, a party of workmen with a group of tourists approached a brick building with a central archway. Painted in white, below a large clock in the wall, were the words *Crescent Wine Vaults*. A man in a suit and tie wearing an official-looking peaked cap was waiting for them there. One of the tourists had a camera.

'I'll need you to come in pretty sharpish when we enter the vaults,' said the guide. 'So's I can close the door quickly to avoid draughts blowin' in from outside. The vaults have to be kept at a constant temperature cos of all the wine.'

'A friend of mine was told by some coopers and vault keepers that there's a ghost in there,' said the amateur photographer.

'Oh, stop it!' protested a smartly dressed young woman beside him. 'You're making me nervous.'

'Is that true?' asked her plump friend, a pale-faced woman who wore vivid red lipstick.

'Ah,' said the guide, 'you mean the ghost of the Grey Lady.'

'Have you actually seen her?' she squeaked.

'Not recently. Have we, Fred?' he called out to a workman who had joined them.

Fred grinned.

The visitors stared at the oil lamp mounted at the end of the long, flat, wooden handle he was carrying.

'Safest kind of lighting is oil,' he explained. 'It's so's you can light your feet,' he added casually in the manner of one who had rehearsed and given this explanation many times. 'Its difficult to see the rails sometimes cos of all the barrels.'

Once inside the underground vault, the visitors gazed at the arches and tunnels with their rows of gigantic wooden barrels lined up on the rails.

'Twenty-eight miles of gangways,' the guide began.

'But no ghosts,' interrupted the amateur photographer. 'Yet,' he added, teasing his well-dressed companion. 'But what a wonderful smell! And it's all wine down here, you say?'

'And port and sherry,' said Fred. 'We had one poor lad who were workin' dahn 'ere and he got drunk from just smellin' it. He had an awful lot of explainin' to do when he got home!'

'Someone's dog is barking rather a lot outside,' said the plump lady.

'That's not outside,' said Fred, alarmed. 'That's inside.'

'Don't tell me it's a ghost dog!' she squealed.

But the guide looked serious.

'Move that lamp around, Fred.'

Suddenly, the smartly dressed lady screamed.

'What the . . . ?' Fred began. 'Ben,' he yelled over his shoulder to one of the other workmen. 'You'd best call down the PLA inspector.'

'PLA?' whimpered the plump woman. 'Is that who deals with the ghosts?'

'No, madam. Port of London Authority. And I think it's best if you all leave.'

But the amateur photographer was already lining up a shot of the other group of people huddled together there, the collars of their overcoats turned up to their ears.

A man from the PLA in a peaked cap and naval uniform appeared. He looked taken aback. 'How the blazes did you manage to get locked in here?'

'I thought you said these vaults were safer than the Bank of England, sir,' piped up Fred.

At that moment, a police constable ran in.

'You're not the other members of the missing film crew are you?' he asked eagerly.

'The crew is missing?' cried Mrs Eliot.

'I'm the wardrobe mistress,' said Annie swiftly, 'and this

is the continuity girl, Miss Tomkins,' she added, waving to her friend.

'And we're chaperones,' said Miss Cogan, introducing herself and the traumatised Mrs Eliot, her chin sunk deep beneath her fox fur. 'And we're very concerned about the children in our care.'

'One of them is my son,' Mrs Eliot whimpered.

'Don't worry, madam,' said the policeman. 'They've been rescued.'

'Rescued!' she shrieked.

'And I'm one of the hired drivers from the film company,' butted in a middle-aged man with a moustache. 'I took the kiddies with a chap called Bertram to the location. I thought it were odd when there was no crew waiting there for 'em so I turned back to look for 'em, but were kidnapped and bundled into an ambulance.'

'One of two ambulances that were reported missing yesterday,' added the PLA Inspector.

'Where he found me and my son,' continued a voice from the darkness, 'and we were all driven here. I'm the skipper of a Thames sailing barge called *Vanessa*.'

Just then the dog leaped through the arch and stood barking at them.

'And this is her burglar alarm.'

'But what did you mean when you said, "the missing film crew"?' asked Miss Cogan.

'Oh, they're found now. The Essex police received a phone call early this morning from a farmer who found them in one of his fields locked in the two stolen ambulances along with the kidnapped ambulance and film crew drivers and a PLA inspector in his underwear. One of the thieves had stolen the inspector's uniform.'

'Ah,' said the PLA man. 'That's how they managed to smuggle you in here.'

'But what were they doing in a field?' asked the continuity girl. 'What's this all about?'

'Seems someone was out to get one of the kiddies on your film. A little girl called Josie.'

At which point Mrs Eliot gave a loud harrumphing sound.

'I knew she would be at the bottom of all this!'

The rescued driver, Miss Tomkins, Annie, the skipper, his son, Miss Cogan, Terry and the dog thawed out in the warmth of the Hales' kitchen. They each took turns to lean against the large range, their frozen hands cupped around cups of hot tea laced with something a little stronger than sugar, while Mr and Mrs Hale cooked scrambled eggs, bacon and tomatoes. Josie and Mr Beauvoisin were put in charge of buttering piles of toast while Auntie Win kept an eye on the fire in the sitting room. Mrs Eliot and Jim had been taken home in a taxi, his mother protesting loudly that she never wanted to set eyes on 'that girl' ever again.

Josie was in her element. Wrapped in Mr Hale's dressing gown, which trailed along the floor behind her like Dopey in *Snow White and the Seven Dwarfs*, she carried chairs into the kitchen to put around the table.

'But how did you keep warm?' she heard Mrs Hale ask.

'They cuddled up to me,' said the skipper, beaming.

'And me,' said his nineteen-year-old son, holding the well-fed dog in his arms.

'And me,' added the driver happily.

'We all cuddled up to one another,' said Miss Cogan. 'Even Mrs Eliot.'

'Telephone call for you, Winifred,' said Mr Hale, poking his head round the doorway, 'from Inspector Gallaway.'

Auntie Win was careful to close all the doors behind her so that no one could eavesdrop. She quickly picked up the receiver.

'You've had some news, haven't you?' she asked.

'Yes. Mr Lovatt-Pendlebury's body was found ebbed dry at low tide early this morning'

'Ebbed dry?'

'Washed up on the mud. We don't have much hope for his accomplices. It's unlikely the river police will find their bodies for at least a fortnight.'

'Which means the children won't have to appear in court and testify against them?'

'That's right. And I'll make sure that young Josie will never know that those men were out to kill her.'

'Oh, thank you! I told her after breakfast about Scowler and Moustache being arrested, as you suggested. Let's hope they won't want to carry out their revenge again when they come out of prison.'

'I doubt it. They've become so superstitious they think that anyone connected to Henry Carpenter will bring them bad luck.'

*  *  *

By the time Mr Stanmore had arrived at the Hales' flat, the
fire in the sitting room was well banked up and throwing
out a good heat. Those who couldn't fit into the settee and
armchairs sat on the carpet, clasping more hot drinks and
yawning.

'Josie, do you think you'll be fit enough for filming on
*Vanessa* again tomorrow? We still need to finish the sailing
barge scene.'

'On a Saturday?' asked Auntie Win. 'I thought it was too
expensive to film at the weekends.'

'It is but *needs must* and our producer thinks that the
publicity will more than cover the extra costs.'

'What publicity?'

'Oh, didn't I tell you? There are a couple of journalists
downstairs who'd like to have a chat with our young heroine.
So how about it, Josie? Think you could put in a morning's
work tomorrow?'

And Josie could hear her father's voice inside her head
saying, "You get back on that horse," and her mother adding,
"Oh, John! You and your horses."

She beamed.

'Rather!' she said in her best *Heidi* voice.

# 10

# One Door Closes

MISS DAGLEISH SLID THE NEWSPAPER ACROSS her resk in Josie's direction.

*NEVER SAY DIE!* the headlines announced in capital letters. *Girl Guide Saves Lives Of Two Boys.*

Josie reddened.

Miss Dagleish picked it up and began reading it aloud.

'"*I learned how to tie a life-saving bowline knot in the Bullfinch patrol*," *young Josie explained. When asked if she had any immediate ambitions she replied*, "*Yes, I'd like to learn how to swim.*"'

She flung the paper back onto the desk.

'Would you care to explain that last comment, Josephine?'

Mrs Havilland stood regally by her side, her nose held so high that Josie could see the hairs inside her nostrils.

'What Miss Dagleish is pointing out,' said Mrs Havilland, 'is that when the director recently had a conversation with Miss Dagleish, it transpired that after you were asked if you could swim at the audition, you answered in the affirmative.'

'Which is a very serious matter, Josephine,' added Miss Dagleish. 'At first I thought that a firm reprimand was all that was needed but the more I've discussed it with Mrs Havilland, the more I've come to realise that the only recourse is expulsion.'

Josie stared blankly at her.

'You are to be expelled,' said Mrs Havilland, struggling to control a self- satisfied smirk.

'Expelled?' repeated Josie dully. 'But I've been workin'. That's good, isn't it?'

'We have our reputation to consider, Josephine,' said Miss Dagleish. 'We cannot have future employers thinking that pupils from this establishment are liars. I have written a letter to your parents informing them of our decision. As soon as the bell has been rung, you will remove your belongings from your desk and the cloakroom, and leave post haste.'

'But couldn't I stay till the end of the week when everyone else breaks up?'

'Certainly not. You must be made an example of,' said Mrs Havilland. 'The other pupils need to be made aware of your misdemeanour.'

'But if I don't go to a stage school, how am I goin' to get actin' work?'

Mrs Havilland gave a short laugh.

'Oh, you can rest assured that no one will *ever* want to employ you again. I suggest you cast aside all thoughts of entering the acting profession, learn how to cook and sew, and get married.'

'But I'm only twelve,' Josie protested.

'Don't be ridiculous, girl! I am talking about when

you're an adult. As I was saying before I was so insolently interrupted, if you are fortunate, you might find a husband who can take you in hand.'

'You may go now,' said Miss Dagleish, giving Josie one of her dismissive flicks.

Josie curtsied, suddenly realising it would probably be the last time she would curtsy for anyone ever again. She was about to leave when Miss Dagleish held up her hand.

'There is one other matter I would like you to clarify. Why was James lifted first?'

Josie instantly realised Miss Dagleish was trying to find out if he had lied about being able to swim too. It would be an excuse to get rid of him as well, as there was less work for him now that he had grown taller. She knew he had had been in loads of work when he was little and had done the school proud, and it didn't seem fair to chuck him out just because there were less parts for him. Well, if she were a liar, she'd leave them with a whopper.

'Because he was the heaviest and the boat was sinkin'.'

'I see.'

'And he wanted to show us it was safe.'

'So why didn't you go next?'

' I couldn't leave Terry on his own, madam.'

'No, of course you couldn't. Well, I suppose that's something in your favour.'

'But not enough to excuse telling lies,' butted in Mrs Havilland hurriedly.

Josie hovered outside the classroom, stepping back quickly

to avoid two girls colliding into her as they rushed out of the door. She slipped inside and walked over to the Form III row, her head bowed, and sat next to Hilda. They remained silent until the rest of the pupils had left the room.

'I've been expelled,' she whispered. 'I have to leave straight away.'

Hilda gasped. 'The beasts!'

Josie gave a tight smile. Hilda was beginning to sound more like the girls she read about in the Lorna Hill ballet books every day.

'They just want you to look bad in front of everyone.'

Josie nodded. 'It's to warn everyone not to do what I did.'

'What, save the lives of two people?'

'No. Tell lies.'

Hilda's mouth fell open.

'But Esmeralda is the queen of the liars! I don't see them expelling her.'

'Anyway,' said Josie despondently, 'I've got to pack all my stuff up.'

'I'll help you. If we do it really quickly, you'll be gone before they return from break.'

Josie smiled. 'Would you?'

'Come along, let's *beat the clock*!'

They flung back her desk lid, grabbed her exercise books and shoved them in her attaché case.

'What if I can't get everything in here?'

'Put it into my cubby hole and I'll bring them round to your aunt's place later. Run!'

They raced down to the basement, her case full of books,

flung her dance tights, leotard and ballet shoes into her shoe bag, shoved her tap shoes in with Hilda's tap shoes, bolted up the stairs and headed for the hall. As soon as they were through the front door they hugged one another.

'We did it!' laughed Hilda. 'I'd better get back to the yard before Esmeralda and her gang smell a rat and come out here to jeer you off.'

Josie watched her friend dash back into the school, slamming the door behind her. She was halfway down the steps when she heard someone call out her name. She swung round, dreading who it might be. It was Jim Eliot.

'I heard,' he said.

'From Esmeralda?'

He nodded. 'It's all over the school.'

'Miss Dagleish asked me why you were hauled up first,' said Josie, and she quickly repeated what she had told the headmistress so that he was forewarned. 'I didn't tell her you couldn't swim.'

He shoved his hands deep into his trouser pockets. 'Thanks.'

She turned away and carried on down the steps.

'Jo!'

She looked over her shoulder.

He grinned sheepishly.

'Good luck.'

By the time the bus drew up, she felt too drained to climb upstairs. She sat slumped in the nearest seat to the entrance, her head resting against the window. She had been in such a hurry to avoid being seen by the other pupils that the full impact of being expelled was only just beginning to hit her.

'Fares, please!' said a bright voice.

A young conductor was beaming down at her. Josie scrabbled around in her pocket for money, swallowing down the ache in her throat.

'Cheer up, my darlin'!' he said. 'It might never happen.'

She forced herself to smile.

When it was time to get off at her stop she stood motionless on the pavement, staring across at the road where her aunt lived, the London traffic roaring past her. It felt strange to be standing there in the middle of the day. It was as though she had been sent home early because she had the flu.

'Are you lost, dear?' said a voice. It was an elderly woman. 'Broken up from school, have you?' she said, indicating her bags.

'I was just daydreamin',' she explained.

'Ah. About the holidays, eh?'

Josie nodded, and crossed the road.

She hauled herself up the stairs to her aunt's flat but when she attempted to open the door, she discovered it was locked. She rang the bell. There were footsteps and voices.

'Oh no!' she murmured. 'Not visitors.'

She would hide in the bedroom until they had left.

'Josie!' cried her aunt, flinging back the door. 'You're early! Now stay in the hall and don't move. I've a lovely surprise for you.'

Josie dropped her case and shoe bag onto the floor. She

didn't even have the energy to remove her duffle coat. There were now muffled noises coming from the sitting room. *Mrs Jenkins*, she thought. After much whispering, her aunt peered round the door.

'You can come in now,' she said.

Josie walked in but the room was empty.

'Sit down there,' her aunt commanded, pointing to the settee.

Reluctantly, Josie did so.

'Auntie Win . . .' she began.

'We weren't expecting you to be back so early but now you're here you can come with us and we can have a special lunch together.'

'We?' said Josie puzzled. 'Auntie Win, I don't feel like –'

'You can come in now!' her aunt sang out.

The door to the kitchen was thrown open and in strode Josie's mum and dad.

'Surprise! Surprise!' said her mother, beaming.

''ave we got a lot of news to tell you,' said her dad.

'But I need to explain why I'm early,' Josie interrupted.

'You'll have your turn in a minute,' he laughed. 'You go first,' he said to Josie's mother.

'We've missed you so much this term,' she said. 'And as you know it's been difficult for us to come up and see you.'

'Especially as we've been very busy,' added her father, looking mysterious.

'Get on with it,' said her aunt.

'We've left Sternsea and moved to London!' announced Josie's mum. 'We've got a flat near the Thames.'

'And this mornin' I been given a job in Fleet Street,' said her dad. 'I've even been able to get an allotment.'

'We thought there'd be a queue a mile long for them,' said her mother.

'But it seems no one wants to grow their own veggies any more,' he added.

'So you'll be able to live with us,' said her mum.

'Of course you'll stay with me sometimes,' said Auntie Win. 'And at Molly's on Fridays for Guides.'

'Isn't that wonderful?' said her mother.

At which point Josie burst into tears.


At midday, Hilda ambled across to the tea house and sat on her own in a corner. Esmeralda was in her element, telling everyone about the latest goings on in the theatre world.

'Your friend nipped off pretty sharpish,' she announced suddenly.

Hilda swung round and looked her full in the eye.

'She couldn't wait to leave.'

Her friends sniggered.

'She wasn't given much choice, was she?' said Esmeralda.

'No. But at least she won't have to listen to you pretending to know all those people in the showbiz world when you don't really know any of them.'

There was a communal gasp. Esmeralda went scarlet.

'How dare you?' she spluttered angrily. 'Do you know who I am?'

'Yes. A great big liar! You get all your information from *The Stage* newspaper and pretend you've been told it all by mixing with the stars. Shall I bring in some old copies for people to read? I'm sure Josie's sister will have some.'

'I could have you thrown out. Do you realise that?' hissed Esmeralda.

'I'm leaving, anyway.'

'Can't cope with the competition then?'

'No. I've been offered a place at another stage school,' said Hilda.

'I don't believe you. Why would anyone offer you a place?'

'Because, thanks to Josie, I auditioned for it.'

'And did they offer her a place?'

'Yes. But her dad couldn't afford the fees.'

'And your dad can?' Esmeralda smirked.

'He doesn't have to,' said Hilda quietly. 'I've been offered a scholarship.'

Esmeralda and her friends stared at her in silence.

'At Aida Foster's,' she added.

'You're making this up,' Esmeralda said haughtily.

Hilda shook her head and stood up to leave. She didn't feel like eating.

'My father wasn't going to tell Miss Dagleish till the end of term but now that Josie isn't here, I don't want to stay any longer.'

As she stood up to leave it suddenly occurred to her that this was probably the first time Esmeralda had ever been struck dumb. She slung her coat over her shoulder, threw open the tea-house door and stepped out into the street unable to stop herself from smiling.

* * *

Josie sat on the settee between her parents, twisting her dad's handkerchief in her hands.

'I'm so sorry,' she sniffed.

'Why didn't you tell us you were unhappy at the school, love?' her mother asked.

'Because you were so proud of me getting in there. And I liked the bits when I wasn't there.'

'When you were workin' with the actors an' that?' asked her dad.

Josie nodded. 'I loved those times,' she said sadly. 'I wanted to stay with them for ever.'

'You were too good for that school,' he said.

'They didn't think so, Dad.'

'Then how come you got that job at Winford rep?'

Josie had never thought of that.

She shrugged.

'But they seemed so cross when I got work.' She looked at her mother. 'And you're sure you're not ashamed of me for getting expelled? You still want me to be a bridesmaid at Elsie's wedding?'

'Course I do. I've brought the kilt with me for you to try on. It's blue and dark green and I've got a lovely dark green velvet jacket for you to wear with it.'

'But aren't you angry with me for making you leave all your friends behind in Sternsea? You won't be able to catch a bus to the sea now.'

'No. But we'll be able to walk to the Thames. And the flat is big enough for your gran to stay with us sometimes.'

'If she condescends to come south of the river,' added her dad.

'She will,' said Josie's Mum. 'She's so lonely in that new town place.'

'But what about your job?' Josie asked her dad. 'And all your friends there?'

'Thanks to you, I'll be making new friends pretty quick.'

Josie was puzzled.

'Tell her,' urged Auntie Win.

'When I had me interview this morning, the boss says, "Hollis? No relation, I s'pose, to that little nipper who saved those two in the Thames?" And I says, "Yes. I'm her dad." And a couple of blokes passing by overhears and comes over for a chat and asks me questions, and I told 'em all about you and the stage school.'

'And now you'll have to tell them I've been chucked out.'

'You know what, love?' said her dad. 'They'll think any school that threw out someone like you don't deserve to have you in the first place. You're well shot of 'em.'

'Here, here,' said Auntie Win. 'Now, Josie, are you sure you can cope with coming to the Lyons Tea House with us? I could always cook us something here instead.'

Josie hurriedly blew her nose.

'No!' she said quickly. 'I can manage.'

'There's no need to look quite so alarmed,' her aunt protested. 'My cooking isn't that bad!'

'Oh, yes it is, Win,' said Josie's mum, and she and Josie's dad caught each other's eye.

Josie smiled. She was beginning to feel better already.

*  *  *

Jim Eliot didn't know what made him hover outside Miss Dagleish's study to eavesdrop on her and Mrs Havilland, but once he heard Josie's name being mentioned, he decided to stay put. They had been furious when she had managed to leave the school unseen by the rest of the pupils. Now, hearing the subject of their conversation, he knew he had to tell someone about it and soon. Unfortunately, Hilda had already gone home, having decided to pack her belongings and go after lunch, and he couldn't ring Josie's aunt as he didn't know her telephone number. He wracked his brains desperately trying to think of who he could phone, and then he had a brainwave.

He nipped down the street during the afternoon break, headed for the nearest telephone box and dialled 999.

'Scotland Yard,' he blurted out as soon as it was answered. 'It's urgent.'

'And Miss Dagleish was going to keep quiet about it?' said Auntie Win on the phone.

'It appears so,' said the inspector.

'But how do I get in touch with these people?'

'Done and dusted. I asked Wapping police headquarters to give me the details of the film company, then I called the director and gave him Mr Hale's number. I explained that Mr Hale has kindly offered to let Josie's parents use his phone for emergencies. The director will be arranging a time to speak to Josie's father on his telephone.'

'I'm staggered that she was going to keep it a secret,'

said Win. 'That's pure malice.'

'I agree. Luckily the pupil who overheard her talking to the acting mistress was determined not to let her get away with it.'

'That'll be Josie's friend, Hilda.'

'Oh no,' said the inspector. 'It was that boy, Jim Eliot. He said he owed her.'

# II

# And Another Door Opens

AUNTIE WIN STRODE BRISKLY PAST PICCADILLY
Circus in a green tweed suit with matching velvet-
brimmed hat and crossed over to Great Windmill Street. A
tall woman and a short, stocky man wearing a monocle were
approaching her. It was only when they drew nearer that
she realised that the woman was a man dressed in women's
clothes and 'her' companion with the severely short haircut
and dark three piece suit was a woman. The 'woman' gave
her a wink as they passed and Auntie Win laughed. Already
she could hear people around her speaking in different
languages. As she breathed in the aroma of Italian coffee
and Turkish cigarettes, a man in evening dress dashed out in
front of her and dived into a nearby restaurant.

The smell of Cypriot food wafted out of the door and
she smiled, absorbing the glorious mix of tailors' shops and
jewellers, boot repair shops and coppersmiths, laundries and
jazz clubs. With its French shops and bars, its scents from
the East mingling with the smoke billowing out of blackened
chimneys, walking into Soho was like stepping into another
country. She passed the stage door of the Lyric Theatre and

made for the corner of Archer Street, where the Windmill Theatre stood.

Archer Street was a tiny road tucked behind Shaftesbury Avenue. Nipping past the Apollo's stage door and a swirling striped barber's pole, she crossed over to the other side, heading towards a small row of tall buildings from where a cacophony of music was erupting from one of the first-floor windows at Number Fourteen. Written on the wall underneath were the words *Orchestral Association*. A handful of musicians were standing on the street outside having an animated conversation.

'All the jobs went yesterday, mate,' one of the men was declaiming to a haggard-looking man. 'Today's Tuesdee. Where you bin? You know all the jobs get picked up on a Mondee.'

'I thought today was Mondee.' He gave a groan. 'I must have slept for twenty-four hours!'

'Well, you look like you could do with another twenty-four hours.'

'I didn't have much sleep last week. You know what it's like. Nothing for months, then a whole load of offers come at the same time. I bin going from a studio to all-night gigs and back to the studio. I mean, you can't turn jobs down, can you?'

Auntie Win hurried towards the building before it, Number Twelve. Glancing at the windows, she calculated that above ground level there were four more floors. She stared at the school in astonishment. Because of its reputation she had assumed that Italia Conti would be in far grander premises in a quiet, more refined area. During her telephone conversation with Miss Conti earlier that morning, she had been instructed to make her way upstairs where she would find a little waiting room outside an office. She checked her watch. She was ten minutes early.

She pulled back her shoulders, opened the door and stepped into a narrow corridor. Countless assorted coats were hanging from hooks on the walls. No spacious hall like Miss Dagleish's establishment, she noted. The floor was littered with dozens of attaché cases where she guessed the pupils kept all their school possessions. The walls were in need of a good lick of paint. In fact, the school was rather shabby in appearance. It was mystifying. Why were the fees higher?

She hovered at the foot of a narrow flight of stairs. Piano music was coming from the next floor. It was then that it suddenly occurred to her that she hadn't seen a piano in Miss Dagleish's school. The dance display she had witnessed on their open day had been accompanied by a gramophone record, as had the singing. The music stopped abruptly. She crept up the stairs to where a door had been left ajar and peered in.

There was a long room with dance barres fixed to a wall of mirrors above a scuffed wooden floor that had seen better days. About forty boys and girls of all ages were shrieking and larking around. It was pandemonium. *No discipline at all*, she thought disapprovingly. She was about to turn away when a young woman in a jersey and slacks gave two sharp claps. Immediately there was silence, followed by a few introductory chords from a piano. Seated behind it, wearing a generous application of face powder and bright red lipstick, was a heavily bejewelled elderly woman. Her hands glided with rapidity along the yellowing keys, the ash from the cigarette in her mouth falling onto the jangling rings on her fingers, and the children, in their assortment of leotards and tunics, danced.

It didn't take Auntie Win long to realise that it wasn't a class. It was a rehearsal. Mesmerised, she found it impossible to take her eyes off the children's faces. The pupils at Miss Dagleish's school were poised and elegant, whereas these pupils appeared to be electrically charged with an exuberance that made her smile. At Miss Dagleish's school, the children were like little adults. The Italia Conti children had the curious combination of being childlike yet having the professionalism of adults, and it was obvious at a glance that their standard of dancing was far superior. And then the penny dropped. Perhaps the reason why their fees were more expensive was because they employed more experienced teachers.

'Major Lindsay,' said a voice. Standing on the landing above her was a small, slim, dark-haired woman about the same age as Win, with vivid blue eyes and a high forehead. 'I'm Miss Ruth Conti.'

Auntie Win followed her up more stairs into a tiny, badly lit, book-lined office on the third floor.

'Thank you for agreeing to see me,' said Auntie Win.

A woman was sitting squashed in a corner, darning a pair of dark green tights. Stacked high on the small table next to her were more tights and a cluster of wings.

Miss Conti sat behind an enormous wooden desk and indicated that Auntie Win should sit in a chair opposite. Auntie Win lowered herself onto it, unable to take her eyes off the costumes by the needlewoman's feet.

'They're for our annual Christmas production, *Where The Rainbow Ends*,' Miss Conti explained. She removed a cigarette from a small lizard-skin-covered box and held it out to her. Auntie Win shook her head. 'Bar the five years during the war, it's been a tradition at Italia Conti every year since 1911. The school has provided fairies, elves, dragons, toads, mice . . .'

'Frogs,' said the needlewoman absently. 'Spiders, caterpillars, hyenas . . .'

'Rainbow children, mortals, immortals. It's a huge cast', said Miss Conti. 'And they perform twice daily. Anton Dolin is in it this year. He's playing Saint George. And there's a wonderful Swedish ballerina called Gerd Andersson who will be the Spirit of the Lake. Professional actors play the other roles. Even the pupils who are working all over the country take part in it, if it's possible. For some of our youngest pupils, it's their first professional production.'

'So instead of having an old school song to remember when they leave, they have their production of *Where the Rainbow Ends*?' murmured Win.

'I'd never thought of it quite like that,' Miss Conti said, tapping the lizard-skin box with her cigarette. 'Your niece might like to see it. We open next week, December twenty-second at Sutton Granada.'

Auntie Win fell silent. She didn't think *Where The Rainbow Ends* would be Josie's cup of tea.

'I'm guessing from the expression on your face that fairies and elves don't feature much in your niece's life,' said Miss Conti. 'But it's as much fun as *Peter Pan*. Lots of comedy and boisterous goings on as well as lovely things to watch, and I doubt we'll be putting on so many performances of it from now on. You see, your niece is not alone, and themes like patriotism and Saint George are beginning to sound a mite old fashioned. But in case you think we live in the dark ages, Major, we have had a teacher from America giving modern American ballet classes to our pupils in our basement studio for five years.'

'That isn't the kind of dance they perform in *West Side Story*, is it?'

Miss Conti nodded.

'Oh, Josie would love to learn that.'

'Major Lindsay, during our telephone conversation you mentioned that your niece was expelled from a stage school yesterday. Why did you need to see me today? Why the urgency? Do her parents wish her to audition for this school?'

Win shook her head. 'Waste of time. Her father couldn't afford the fees, even with my help. But I heard that you were an agency as well as a school.'

'Only for our pupils.'

'So how does a child get an agent when he or she is not at a stage school? Or not in a school at all?'

'Her parents will need to find one or pay for her to go in

*Spotlight.* That's a casting directory.'

'But her parents don't know how to tell a good agent from a bad agent. That's why I've come to you for advice.'

'Major Lindsay, a good agent prefers to take on a child who has had some experience, otherwise they would be inundated with demands from every doting and pushy parent –'

'But she has had some experience,' Auntie Win interrupted. 'She was in a play called *Life With Father* in Winford rep. Then she did a fortnight's work at the Theatre Royal with Miss Joan Littlewood.'

'Miss Littlewood!' she exclaimed.

One look at Miss Conti's face and Auntie Win remembered that Miss Littlewood didn't approve of stage schools.

'On second thoughts, perhaps she's not the best person to ask for a letter of recommendation.'

There was an awkward silence.

'My niece learned a lot with Miss Littlewood,' added Auntie Win firmly.

After all, she thought, since Josie wouldn't be attending Italia Conti, she had nothing to lose by telling her so.

'Major Lindsay,' said Miss Conti, frowning, 'I happen to have seen a performance of *Life With Father* at Winford rep because an ex-pupil played one of the four red-headed brothers, and there is no role in the play for a girl of your niece's age.'

'She wasn't playing a girl,' said Auntie Win. 'She was the nine-year-old brother. Her name is Josephine although she prefers to be called Josie. In the programme she was down as

Joe Hollis. She played a boy called Whitney.'

The woman looked startled. 'The boy who loves baseball?'

'That's right. So you've seen her perform?'

'I don't know. It might not have been the night it was her turn to play the role.'

'She has masses of freckles, if that helps.'

'Ah yes,' Miss Conti said, 'I have seen her then.'

'Then there's the film she's been in. And now this offer of a part in another film, which is why her parents need advice.'

'She's been offered more work, you say?'

'Yes.'

'Major Lindsay, can you please explain why her parents aren't here? I take it they know that you're asking questions on their daughter's behalf.'

'Oh yes. It's because they've only just moved to London and Mrs Hollis is busy trying to find out about other schools in the area for next term.'

'And the real reason?'

Auntie Win stared at her awkwardly.

'They thought there would be a better chance of you meeting me if you heard my voice on the telephone. They're working class.'

'We make no class distinctions at this school. Our pupils come from all grades of society. It often happens that the humbler the upbringing, the better the raw material.'

'Really?' said Auntie Win.

'Oh, yes. Children from what used to be called the upper-middle classes, for example, would appear to have all the advantages. However, we frequently find that the very care of their education goes against them. They lack the easy self-expression and the general naturalness of movement so essential to an actor. In fact, many here are what you might call bilingual.'

'They speak two languages?'

'Two accents. Their local one and –'

'Received pronunciation,' finished Auntie Win for her.

'And they learn to speak other dialects too. Now, tell me about this film.'

'An organisation called the Children's Film Foundation have asked a film company to make it. It's all double Dutch to me, which is why we need advice from someone who knows about contracts.'

'The Children's Film Foundation?' said Miss Conti, looking interested.

'Yes. Have you heard of them?'

'Oh yes indeed. A very reputable organisation, and they're rather fussy about which film companies they give contracts to. How did she get this job? Did she audition for it?'

'No, it's the same film company she worked with before. She played two very different girls. Twins. I suppose they were pleased with her work.'

'Ah,' said Miss Conti sagely. 'And it all went to her head. She thinks she has aspirations of being a film star and started to misbehave. Is that why she was expelled?'

'She would hate to be a film star!'

Miss Conti looked surprised. 'And why is that?'

'Because she would have to wear frocks and smile all the time. She's a tomboy, happiest in trousers. She just wants to act. She would hate to be set apart in that way. She likes being part of a team. Being famous would make her feel very lonely.'

'Then why was she expelled?'

'It was the newspaper business.'

'She was in the newspaper!' said Miss Conti. 'Has she been in trouble?'

'No. She helped rescue two boys in the Thames.'

Miss Conti looked startled. 'You don't mean the Bullfinch patrol girl?'

'Yes. She's my niece.'

'She saved young Terry's life!' Miss Conti exclaimed. 'But I don't understand. Why was she expelled?'

'She lied about being able to swim. To get the job.'

'Ah.' Miss Conti looked thoughtfully at Win. 'Tell me more about her. It might help if I know what kind of girl she is.'

So Auntie Win told her how Josie loved dancing, how she was desperate to go camping and sailing, and how she liked reading and scribbling down the odd story.

'Major Lindsay, I need to make a few phone calls,' she said after Auntie Win had finished, 'and then I will be in touch with her father.'

'Her parents don't have a telephone. Could you ring a Mr Hale?' she asked, handing her a slip of paper with his number on it. 'He and his wife live ten minutes' walk away from them and they're both happy to be a go-between.'

Miss Conti accompanied her down the stairs to the front door where they shook hands.

'Your niece has a natural comedic talent,' said Miss Conti. 'Probably because she lives the part and doesn't think she's funny. I'll do my best to solve the agent problem.'

Auntie Win thanked her and watched her disappear down the dark corridor. She was about to step out into Archer Street when it suddenly occurred to her that it wasn't only piano music she hadn't heard at Miss Dagleish's establishment.

'So that's what was missing,' she murmured.

It was the sound of children laughing.

Early the following evening, Auntie Win and Josie stepped out of Leicester Square Tube station into the chilly air, crossed the road and headed towards the alley at the side of Wyndham's Theatre. A long queue of people were waiting on the pavement to find out if there were any returned tickets for *The Hostage*.

'That's what I call optimism,' Auntie Win commented, indicating a noticeboard with the words *SOLD OUT* written in large black capitals.

'It'll be strange me sitting in the New Theatre watching *Make Me An Offer* while Ralph's performing in *The Hostage* in the theatre behind me,' said Josie.

On the last day of filming *River Adventure*, Auntie Win had asked the wardrobe mistress if she could buy the russet corduroy trousers and tam o' shanter that Josie had worn as Heidi. To her surprise, the wardrobe mistress had given them to Josie free with the film company's compliments. This meant that Josie could attend the West End opening looking smart without having to wear a dress.

They were about to walk past the stage door of the New Theatre when they spotted Joan standing outside it. Still wearing her woolly hat, and waving a cigarette, she appeared to be giving a pep talk to an actor. Their conversation over, she whirled round and gave them a broad smile.

'Jo! My little chick.' She strode towards them. 'We're having another opening night!'

'We have tickets for it,' said Auntie Win.

'Marvellous!' She looked at Josie with a twinkle in her eye. 'You wouldn't like to join the cast in the market scenes, would you?'

Josie laughed. 'No, thank you. I want to watch it with my auntie.'

'So, how are you getting on in that institute for stuffed shirts?' Joan asked.

Josie felt a lump in her throat. 'I've been expelled.'

To Josie's surprise Joan threw back her head and roared with laughter.

'Wonderful! That's the best news I've heard all day. Well done! You've had a lucky escape.'

'But what am I going to do now?'

'I told you before, go to an ordinary school and make up your own plays with a group of friends.' She turned and dived through the stage door.

'I wonder if she'll be taking notes from the gallery,' said Josie.

They were halfway down the alleyway alongside the New Theatre when they heard voices coming from St Martin's Lane. Turning the corner, they stopped in stunned amazement, for what they were witnessing was a million miles away from the opening of *Make Me An Offer* at the Theatre Royal.

Lines of shiny black Rolls Royces were rolling up at the front of the theatre, depositing men in evening dress and women in long gowns and furs. It was strange to see so much glamour so close to the bombsite down the road. As if reading Josie's mind, a well-spoken woman in front of them complained to her fur-coated companion, 'I see they still haven't done anything about that site. It attracts every grubby little urchin and guttersnipe in the area. They treat it as a cross between a playground and an assault course. After all these years I can't understand why nothing is done about it. It really does lower the tone.'

'I doubt they have many other places to play,' whispered Auntie Win to Josie. 'If Joan lived round here I suspect she would use it as an open air theatre with the so-called ragamuffins as her cast, don't you?'

Josie nodded, smiling, transfixed by all the glittering necklaces, brooches and earrings adorning the ladies.

'Aren't you glad now that I persuaded you to wear the tam o' shanter rather than your old pom-pom hat?' said Auntie Win.

They made their way under the chandelier, through the throng of first-nighters in the packed foyer.

'I think I'm the only girl here,' said Josie, scanning the

theatre-goers. 'Everyone else is old.'

'Including me?' asked her aunt sardonically. 'On second thoughts, don't answer that.' She squeezed Josie's hand. 'Let's move over there.'

They manoeuvred their way through the crowd with lots of 'excuse me's and 'thank you's towards a staircase blocked by three men deep in conversation. Two of them were giving advice to an earnest young man in a shiny old evening suit.

'The best place to find out about acting jobs,' said the taller of the two, 'is Joe Lyons in Piccadilly.'

*Interesting,* thought Auntie Win. *I wonder if that includes acting jobs for children.*

The crowd began to nudge the men and they carried on up the stairs talking excitedly as people from every side jostled against Josie. Auntie Win grabbed her hand.

'Ah!' she cried. 'That's what I'm looking for. Quick!' She pulled Josie towards a young woman dressed in black carrying a tray of programmes.

'And my parlour maid is so rude,' Josie heard a woman behind her in the programme queue complain.

'You're lucky to have one, my dear,' said her female companion. 'You just can't get 'em nowadays.'

Stepping into the vast, ornate, cream and gold auditorium, the New Theatre made the Theatre Royal seem tiny in comparison. And 'New Theatre' was a funny name for it, thought Josie. It wasn't new at all. It was old.

'Such a pretty theatre,' she overheard one of the theatre-goers remark, 'and so French. The interior is Louis Seize, I believe.'

Josie had a strong desire to giggle. Auntie Win caught her eye.

'You're wondering what they're going to make of Portobello Road, aren't you?' she whispered.

Josie nodded.

As soon as they were seated in the upper circle, Auntie Win handed her a glossy pale pink and cream programme. Josie gasped.

'It cost a shilling!'

'I don't care. It's so that you can remember this evening.' She flicked over the pages. 'Look here.'

There in small print were the words, *First Produced by Theatre Workshop at the Theatre Royal, Stratford, E15 on October nineteenth, 1959.*

'And me and Mr Beauvoisin were there,' she murmured.

'A lot has happened since then, hasn't it?'

It was a completely different programme to the one at the Theatre Royal. There was no mention of the box office staff or cleaning ladies.

Josie glanced round the theatre. People were talking about Joan, peppering their conversation with the names of the writers and composer. She knew that amongst the ordinary theatre-goers, there were famous actors, actresses and directors and newspaper men who would be writing reviews, but she wasn't interested in them. The only people she wanted to see were the familiar faces of the cast on stage. She spotted the pianist sliding in behind the piano, accompanied by the accordionist and the trombone player. Two more musicians followed.

'The EP of that new film *Expresso Bongo* with Cliff Richard is being advertised in the programme,' said the excited voice of a young woman in front of her. 'Oh, Mummy, please can I have that for Christmas?'

'Perhaps,' she answered. 'I'll have to ask your father first. He might not approve.'

Auntie Win gave Josie a nudge.

'Only five more minutes to wait,' she said, surprised to feel nervous.

Most musicals began with a big song and dance number, which heralded a romantic story about a couple falling in love, marrying and living happily ever after. *Make Me An Offer* opened in the early hours of the morning in a tiny flat where a young married couple lived in cramped conditions with their baby. Josie wondered how a West End audience would take it.

The lights dimmed and a pool of light hit a small kitchen table with a large pram alongside it. The silence was shattered by an alarm clock ringing loudly and the appearance of a sleepy young couple struggling to wake up in order to give their baby a feed. A bleary-eyed young man in pyjamas stumbled towards the kitchen area, manoeuvring his way round the table searching for the milk.

*This is real life*, thought Auntie Win. It was as though she was peering into someone's private world.

'Ow!' yelled Charlie as his leg hit the pram.

There was a wave of laughter, and he and his wife Sally began to argue about the size of the pram and how it kept getting in the way.

'*Before the pram,*' sang Sally.

'*We never rowed at all.*

'*And your voice was never loud at all.*'

'*Till one day you brought it home,*' Charlie sung back.

'*That coach built*

'*Silken fringed*

'*Suspension sprung*

'*Two position*

'*Safety-braked*

'*Anti-social monster*

'*In chrome.*'

'Beautiful!' Josie heard a man murmur behind her.

Hardly had *The Pram Song* ended when the lights dimmed and moved to another part of the stage where stallholders were making their way with their loaded barrows.

The cast were utterly convincing, thought Auntie Win. And that Dan Massey chap playing Charlie was even better now.

Josie spotted Marjie Lawrence in her green top, flared red, black and white skirt and small brimmed hat. She was standing with her hands on her hips in front of Harry Green in his loud black and white checked jacket, his tweed cap pulled over his black hair. Soon she would see Sheila and Roy dancing together. And then she forgot who they were. They were other people now.

'Mrs Hale!' said Josie's mother, welcoming her into their new flat. 'What a lovely surprise!' And then her face fell. 'Oh my goodness! What's happened to Josie now?'

'Nothing. A Miss Conti has rung me and wants to speak to your husband. I said I would pop round and ask if –'

'We'll come over straight away. John!'

Josie's dad poked his head out of one of the doors, his dirty overalls covered in white paint, a paint roller in his hands.

'I've started decoratin' Josie's bedroom,' he said, beaming at Mrs Hale. 'She won't want brown walls.'

'Put that roller down, love,' said Josie's mum. 'There's been a phone call for you. Quick!'

'Encore!' the audience roared yet again. 'Encore!'

And the actress who had stopped the show yet again with her rendition of *It's Sort of Romantic* yelled back at the audience in exasperation as she had done at the Theatre Royal opening.

'I think we'll see a lot more of that young woman,' Josie overheard the man behind her say as the audience fell apart laughing. 'Someone's bound to give her a leading role once this is over. What did you say her name was? Sheila what?'

Josie couldn't resist turning round in her seat.

'Hancock,' she said airily to the surprised man. 'Sheila Hancock.'

But it was all moving too fast, thought Josie. Before she knew it, the population of Portobello Road were half yelling, half singing the last number out to the audience.

'Well, gel,' they sang,
*'We've about shot our load
'Flogging in the Portobello*

'Schlapping in the Portobello
'Punting in the Portobello Road.'

The roar from the audience said it all.

'Best musical I've seen all year,' the man behind her
shouted above the deafening applause. 'If this doesn't win
the Evening Standard Award, I'll eat my hat!'

It was while Josie and her aunt were laughing and clapping
that she suddenly remembered Miss Dagleish telling her
that Joan's productions were only for a *certain class of adult*.
Well, she was wrong. They were for everyone.

Josie's Dad could hardly contain himself. Clutching the
telephone in the Hales' hall, he beamed at his wife who,
along with Mrs Hale, was peering out of the sitting room
door, attempting to eavesdrop.

'Ta very much, Miss Conti!' he said. 'No, she ain't.
She's with her aunt at the theatre. I'll tell 'er soon as she
gits back . . . Yeah. Goodbye.'

He replaced the receiver and gazed glassy-eyed into the
distance as though paralysed with shock.

'John?' said Josie mother. 'What is it?

'You look like you've been hit on the head with a
sledgehammer,' exclaimed Mrs Hale.

He shook his head from side to side, his eyes glazed.

'It's like a blimmin' dream.'

'What is?' chorused Josie's Mum and Mrs Hale.

But he was miles away.

'My little Josie,' he murmured.

* * *

'Look who's here!' shouted Auntie Win, struggling to make herself heard over the excited din of first-nighters streaming out of the theatre into St Martin's Lane.

'Ralph!' Josie yelled.

She could see his wiry brown hair sticking up and his big friendly grin. He must have raced round to meet her after *The Hostage* had finished. He pushed his way through the crowd, scooped her up in his arms and planted a big kiss on her cheek.

'Hello, trouble,' he said.

'Oh, Ralph,' said his aunt as the theatre-goers jostled around her. 'It was absolutely wonderful!'

'I gathered that from listening to what people are saying. Another hit, I think.' Because her brother continued to hug her Josie was able to have a good bird's eye view of the audience coming out of the theatre.

'Brilliant!' she heard them saying.

'That *Lock Up* song was my favourite.'

'Wonderful characters!'

'Captivating!'

And Josie agreed with them all.

Mrs Hale flung the door open before Josie and Auntie Win had time to ring the bell.

'Hurry into the warm, Josie. Your parents are waiting for you in the sitting room.' She turned to her husband. 'Take their coats and I'll make more hot chocolate.'

Josie found them sitting by the fire. They were smiling.

'Good news?' guessed Auntie Win.

Josie's mum nodded. 'Go on, John.'

He rose and stood in front of the fireplace, his face flushed. It was obvious he was enjoying being the centre of attention.

'You've got that Jim Eliot to thank for it really,' he said.

'Jim?' Josie exclaimed, puzzled.

'Yeah. 'E phoned Detective Inspector Gallaway at Scotland Yard, who phoned the Wapping lot. The Wapping lot give 'im the number of this bloke who'd phoned Miss Dagleish. Then the DI phones this bloke and, tells 'im to call Mr 'ale – which 'e does on on Mondee night.– and tells 'im all abaht it. Mr 'ale tells me. I tells yer aunt. Then, you'll never guess, Mrs 'ale pops round to our flat tonight to tell me and yer mum.' He broke off beaming. 'They were all cockahoop when I spilled the beans at work yesterday mornin'.'

'Yesterday?' asked Josie. 'What beans?'

'John, if you don't tell her soon,' threatened Josie's mum, 'I will!'

'You've been offered a part in another film. In May,' he said, his voice rising to a squeak. 'You'll have to play a girl who's a bit like Nancy in *Swallows and Amazons*, they said. Does that mean anything to you?'

Josie was speechless for a moment.

'Er, y-yes,' she stammered. 'But how can I have a part if I haven't auditioned for it?'

'You have in a way, love,' said her mum. 'It's got the same director as *River Adventure* and he was very impressed with how you coped. There is one snag, though. He wants you to learn how to swim by then because it'll be in boats again. This time, small sailing boats. All the children will have a week of sailing lessons before they begin filming.'

Josie gasped. 'You mean I'll be *sailing?*'

'So that'll be swimming lessons as your Christmas present from me, I think,' said Auntie Win.

'And that's not all,' said her dad. 'Tell her, Ellen.'

'The thing is, love,' said Josie's mum, 'we don't know anything about the business side of all this so when yer dad told Auntie Win about this film offer she remembered that school Terry goes to with the Italian name, so she went there yesterday and had a chat with a Miss Conti to ask for advice.'

'I didn't say anything to you, Josie, in case she couldn't help us,' said Auntie Win. 'I didn't want to raise your hopes and then have them dashed.'

Her dad looked at Josie intently.

'Josie, that Miss Littlewood hates stage schools, don't she?'

'Yes.'

'And I know you think a lot about her, love, but the thing is, there ain't a lot of choice.'

'You see, yesterday I also tried to find out about other schools for you,' interrupted her mother.

'We might be able to get you into a grammar school,' said her dad. 'You got the brain. But me and yer mum think you'd go mad with all that sittin' behind a desk for 'ours and we think you'd go even madder if you 'ad to do a lot of sewin' and cookin' in a secondary modern school. We did 'ear about a big new school in 'olland Park called a comprehensive . . .'

'Lovely, it is,' her mother said.

'But it's got two thousand pupils in it and we think you'd be miserable in a school that big so . . .'

'Dad?' said Josie, exasperated.

'Well, as I said, Auntie Win visited this Miss Conti . . .'

'And she's offered you a place,' her mother burst out.

'At *Italia Conti*?' cried Josie in disbelief.

'That's right. She saw you in *Life With Father* with one of the teachers at the school and they not only remembered you but they'd talked about you too.'

'But, Dad, I can't go there. It costs too much!'

'Reduced fees. And yer first job will cover most of your first term, although the pupils 'ave to put a third away in a post office account and they're not allowed to touch it till they're fifteen, which is what that Miss Dagleish should 'ave been doin'.'

'John,' warned Josie's mother.

'Anyway, I've told Miss Conti yes. It'll be up to you to make the best of it, although this Miss Conti seems to know her onions. And you're doin' a pretty good job of educatin' yourself, what with yer readin' and pickin' things up as you go along, and then there's all this tutoring when you're workin', so if the book lessons aren't up to much . . .'

'And it's so near,' said her mother excitedly. 'It's only about a thirty-minute walk from our flat! We've really landed on our feet, love!'

'So now you can get back on the 'orse,' finished her dad for her.

'I'm going to Italia Conti?' asked Josie, still unable to take it in.

'That's right,' he said, getting out his handkerchief and handing it to her.

'What's that for?' she asked huskily.

'You look as though you're about to start cryin' again.'

'Italia Conti,' she whispered. Who would have thought that being expelled would have been the very best thing to have happened to her? But instead of bursting into tears she started laughing. She had no idea why, but the image of Mrs Havilland's furious face once she heard the news might have had something to do with it.

When Josie entered the gymnasium early Friday evening in her Girl Guide uniform, nothing had changed. The same ladders were fixed to the wall, there was the same smell of floor polish and the same girls chatting and laughing in their blue and navy uniforms with badges sewn down their sleeves. She and Molly separated as they had done every Friday at the beginning of the term and Josie walked over to the Bullfinch patrol corner. Two girls were pouring over a map, and Penelope, who was sitting next to Carol, was showing her how to cast wool onto her knitting needles. The wool was pink mohair. Josie smiled. Typical Carol. There was one difference, though. Now Carol was in uniform.

'You passed the tenderfoot tests then?' Josie asked.

Carol looked up. 'Josie!' she cried. 'We've all been reading about you in the newspapers.'

Sheila immediately came over to her.

'I think I can do the bowline test tonight,' Josie said, and she beamed.

By the time the patrols had lined up to be inspected it was as though she had never been away. The Bullfinch patrol was the last to be given the 'once over'. Captain remained her dignified upright self but Lefty stood behind her with a smile the length of a cucumber. She caught Josie's eye and winked at her. Josie gave her a quick glance and then looked straight ahead as Captain came closer.

'Very smart, Carol,' she was saying.

And then she was standing in front of Josie.

'I see you've given that badge a good polish,' she began. Suddenly she thrust out her left hand and Josie realised that she wanted to give her the Guide handshake. 'Nice work,' she added gruffly as they shook hands. 'We're very proud of you. Well done.'

But Josie noticed a hint of moisture in her eye.

'I now pronounce you man and wife,' announced the Reverend Mr Hailsham.

Josie spotted her mum scrabbling in her handbag and her dad handing her his handkerchief. Molly gave Josie's kilt a tug.

'I have two sisters now,' Molly whispered, beaming.

There was a tap on Josie's shoulder.

'You look more like 'er bruvver,' muttered a voice.

Josie turned to look at a round-faced woman in her sixties who was giving a disapproving shake of her head before breaking into a broad smile.

'Only jokin',' she mouthed. 'You done well, gel.'

'Thanks, Gran,' Josie mouthed back.

The church organist played the opening bars of the next hymn and the congregation rose to their feet. Josie couldn't take her eyes off her sister, now standing at the altar in her lacy, billowing white dress, gazing happily up at Henry in his tails. Earlier, when they had been walking in a procession up the aisle, she had overheard one of her aunties saying that Elsie looked like the film star Grace Kelly, only a smaller version. And then she suddenly remembered what Molly had said to her.

*And I have two more brothers*, she thought.

'I'll never remember who everyone is,' said Molly.

She was squashed in the back of the car between Josie and Mrs Carpenter, who was holding Larry on her lap. Her white flouncy dress with the pink rose buds was so rucked up that it began to sail up towards her face. She attempted to pull it down to cover her ballet shoes, causing the crown of pink petals on her curly blond hair to become lopsided.

'Don't worry. Even I find it difficult,' said Josie reassuringly. 'Mum was so old when she had me that all my cousins are grown up, and their children who are about my age are my second cousins. There's only one person you need to remember and that won't be difficult. She's the boss.'

'Your grandmother,' Molly guessed.

At that moment a car overtook them and through the window they could see Gran having an animated conversation with Mr Beauvoisin and the Hales. She had insisted that they sit with the family at the church and be

573

included in the wedding photographs. She and the other members of the Hollis family referred to Mr Beauvoisin as Bertie.

As soon as the relatives and friends arrived at the house where the Carpenters' lived, they piled into the large double room on the ground floor and sat at rows of trestle tables. They laughed at the silly speech from Josie's dad and listened to him reading the telegrams from the people who hadn't been able to make it, like Josie's other brother, Harry and his wife, after which the trestle tables were cleared and folded away and the Philip Hart Jazz Quartet appeared, accompanied by Grace Hart, a young singer with long, black, wavy hair. Within minutes they had begun to play and sing their way through old favourite song and dance numbers, the wedding guests jigging around on the floor, their faces growing ever pinker while small children ran underneath their waving arms.

'That's Uncle Ted, Aunt Lilly and Aunt Dolly,' said Josie to Molly, pointing into the crowd. 'They're my dad's brothers and sisters. Uncle Ted doesn't have any children but my aunts have got eight of them. And that's my brother Ralph and his wife Jessica. And that's cousin Kitty,' she added, pointing to a dark-haired woman. 'She's married to Frank and they have two children, Alan and Deirdre. Alan's my age. And over there,' she said, pointing to a woman near the piano, 'is Joan. She married a German POW after the war. She's got four children, Birgitta, Erica . . .'

But Molly had already given up trying to remember and glanced across at Larry, who had found another sputnik fan amongst Josie's second cousins. The wedding day had been like a grand reunion with relatives hailing one another and smiling at the children, and saying, 'My haven't you grown?'

Josie listened transfixed to all the East End accents mixed in with the ones from Kent, the Hertfordshire ones mixing with the BBC vowels of the actors and actresses, and all the myriad accents among the film crews who had turned up. On the other side of the room were her two great aunts. In their eighties, they sat bolt upright in their Sunday best, insisting that they keep on their hats, each holding a tiny glass of port.

Because Christmas was only six days away, the room had been decorated with holly, and red and green ribbons. A wave of laughter caused her to swing round. Henry was carrying a camera and was being chased by his best man, Roger Jeffries.

'No, you don't,' said Mr Jeffries, snatching it from Henry. '*I'm* taking the snaps today. Not you!'

By now, Molly was surrounded by girl cousins who were admiring her frock. Josie decided to search for Gran. She spotted her by the door chatting to Elsie and Mr Beauvoisin.

'So once a month we gits a lift dahn the docks,' she heard her say, 'and we 'ide in one of them empty 'ouses with our candles, thermoses and pies, and has a good old natter.'

'But you're in a lovely new town in a house with an indoor bathroom,' said Elsie. 'I thought you'd be pleased.'

'I am, but you can't 'ave a chinwag with fancy plumbin' can you? There's no corner shop, no chippie. I don't know me neighbours no more so's there's no one I can pop round

and 'ave a chat wiv or have a gossip wiv on the doorstep.
And I miss the sounds of the docks. The quiet eats you up
inside.'

'Well, now you have us, Mrs Hollis,' said Mr Beauvoisin,
and he held out his arm for her to take. 'May I have the
pleasure of this dance, madam? Or should I say, "'ow's abaht
a bit of a knees up, ma?"'

She looked at him, impressed. 'That's very good!'

They walked regally into the centre of the room where
Mr Beauvoisin began to guide her round the room, waltz
style.

Elsie laughed. Josie glanced aside at her sister.

'You still haven't said anything about me going to Italia
Conti,' she said, awkwardly. 'Do you still think I shouldn't
go to a stage school?'

'Not any more,' Elsie said, and put her arm round her.
'I can't see you spending the next few years day in day out
with children who are all the same age as you. Being at stage
school means you can work with those who are both younger
and older, and I think you're happy being with adults too,
aren't you?'

That thought had never occurred to Josie but Elsie was
right.

'Yes!' she said, surprised. 'I am.'

'And later, you can join my acting classes for young
people.' She smiled. 'I plan to start giving them next year.
After some training from Joan, I hope. I'm going to follow
her example and call them *workshops*.'

Auntie Win tapped Josie on the shoulder.

'Time for us to leave. Best just to say goodbye to Molly and Gran. It'll take all day if you say it to everyone.'

They collected their coats from the study across the hall. Mr and Mrs Carpenter accompanied them to the front door and quietly observed them as they walked down the steps to the pavement.

'I suppose we ought to tell Molly the truth about Josie *not* being with her sick mother and the non-existent mumps epidemic at her school,' murmured Mr Carpenter.

'I'm not looking forward to telling her we deceived her.'

'Let's wait until next weekend,' said Mrs Carpenter. 'Just in case she's upset.'

'Next weekend is Christmas,' he reminded her.

'Let's leave it till 1960 then.'

To their surprise, Henry suddenly appeared and raced down the steps. 'Hey!' he called out. 'Josie!'

Josie whirled round. Before she could answer him he threw his arms around her.

'Thanks for hidin' Larry in the theatre skip. I couldn't risk sayin' anything earlier in case he overheard. If those men had kidnapped him instead of you, he would never have been able to escape. You saved his life, Josie, and I'll never forget it.'

# 12

# Curtain Calls

JOSIE HAD TO ADMIT IT WAS A RELIEF TO BE back in her comfy trousers and jersey again, padding around Auntie Win's kitchen in her socks. They had laid food out on the hostess trolley but after having prepared it all the room looked wrecked, as though a gang of juvenile delinquents had broken in and had attacked every square inch of it with sledgehammers.

'Once they begin arriving,' said Auntie Win, 'we'll keep this door shut.'

Josie scooped up a dollop of Shippam's fish paste with a knife and spread it onto a slice of buttered bread.

'Auntie Win, can you explain something to me?'

'I'll try. Fire away.'

'In the newspaper it said how I'd rescued Jim and Terry but it didn't say anything about Mr Beauvoisin rescuing *me*. He told me that at his school there were people who didn't like him doing better than them because he was black. Do you think newspaper men are like that too?'

'I don't know. Perhaps he just preferred to stay out of the limelight.'

Auntie Win couldn't help noticing that Josie hadn't mentioned that the newspapers had also failed to report that Win had helped rescue the boys as well, and was relieved, otherwise she might have had to suggest that their omission could have been due to the fact that she was a *mere* woman.

They were interrupted by the doorbell.

'That'll be the first of our visitors,' she said, wheeling the trolley into the sitting room. 'Would you like to welcome them in?'

Josie ran past the coffee table now filled with apple-green plates piled high with fish paste, ham and mustard, and egg and cress sandwiches, shop cakes and glasses of sherry. Auntie Win had explained that Mrs Jenkins and her friend Miss Jones had been involved in some kind of accident and that this was a little treat to help them recover from their injuries. It was also a little surprise thank-you party, but she kept that to herself.

Josie had been prepared for a sprained ankle and perhaps an Elastoplast on a finger, so was somewhat taken aback on opening the door to find Mrs Jenkins wearing new bright blue winged spectacles, with one of her legs in plaster. Gripping a crutch under one armpit, she was resting her free hand on the arm of a young woman in nurse's uniform. Her face lit up when she saw Josie.

'Safe and sound,' she trilled.

Beside her stood Miss Jones, her arm in a sling. Both of them had bruises around their eyes and cheeks.

The nurse helped Mrs Jenkins hobble towards the settee

and Auntie Win placed a chair beside it for the nurse.

'This is Nurse Thomas,' said Mrs Jenkins.

'I've poured a glass of sherry for you too,' said Auntie Win, smiling at the young woman.

'I shouldn't really,' she said. 'I'm on duty.'

But Josie noted that she was eyeing the cakes with longing.

'But if you filled up first on food . . .' suggested Auntie Win.

'Well, if you're sure,' said the young woman, eagerly reaching for a plate.

Josie helped herself to sandwiches and fig rolls. The television had been switched on and the aerial placed perfectly on two books on the radiogram in preparation for an episode of *The Invisible Man*. Auntie Win drew the striped curtains across the windows, put on the log-effect electric fire and settled in the armchair while Josie joined Miss Jones and Mrs Jenkins on the settee.

Within seconds, Josie's eyes were hooked to the screen where glass bowls and tubes were bubbling with chemicals. Accompanied by eerie, pulsating music, the bandaged face of Peter Brady – the Invisible Man – appeared, his dark shadow thrown up against the back wall with hollows where there should have been eyes.

Auntie Win's doorbell rang.

To Josie's astonishment, Mrs Jenkins and Miss Jones jumped and clutched one another.

'Can you answer that?' Auntie Win asked Josie cheerily.

Josie ran down the hall, puzzled by their behaviour.

Perhaps *The Invisible Man* was too scary for them. She flung open the door.

'Miss Merryweather!' she exclaimed, glancing at her right arm, which was encased in plaster and resting in a sling. A bandage covered half her forehead and she was leaning on a stick. 'What's happened to you?' asked Josie.

'Bit of an accident,' she answered lightly. And to Josie's surprise she smiled. 'Oh Josephine! I mean, *Josie*. I'm delighted to see you safe and sound.'

'That's what Mrs Jenkins said. I'm sorry about your fiancé,' she added politely. 'Auntie Win told me about the quarrel between him and the two men on the wharf.'

'Did she now?'

'And how they wanted to steal *Vanessa*. Only just when they'd got the owner and the film company out of the way, Mr Lovatt-Pendlebury goes and turns up and he's after it too. A falling out of thieves, she said.'

'And you happened to be at the wrong place at the wrong time?'

'Yes. I'm sorry he was a bad 'un, Miss Merryweather.'

'Well, yes. Indeed.' She cleared her throat. 'But better to find out early than later. We've both had a lucky escape in different ways, haven't we? And seeing you here has cheered me up no end. Your aunt obviously wanted it to be a lovely surprise for us both.' She looked serious for a moment. 'I was very sad to hear about your expulsion.'

Josie beamed up at her.

'I've been offered a place at Italia Conti.'

'Oh!' Miss Merryweather cried, and she threw her

unfettered arm around Josie and gave her a hug. 'That's splendid!'

'Come in quick and take a seat,' Josie urged.

'A seat? Am I interrupting something?'

'No. You're just in time.'

Auntie Win welcomed her into the sitting room and indicated that she should sit next to Miss Jones.

'Josie can sit on the floor.'

The three women waved their slings and walking sticks at one another in greeting, and Mrs Jenkins and Miss Jones moved aside to let Miss Merryweather squeeze in next to them.

'The police have discovered a case containing dangerous chemicals in the wreckage of a plane,' explained Mrs Jenkins, nodding at the television.

'Half as much as you'd need to make an atomic bomb,' added Miss Jones.

'And they think that whoever is responsible for trying to smuggle it into the country will use an innocent person to smuggle in more,' said Auntie Win, rising from her armchair. 'Sherry, I take it?' she added, deftly removing a small glass from her sleek drinks cabinet.

'Oh, thank you,' said Miss Merryweather.

'See that slim, very beautiful woman?' said Mrs Jenkins, pointing at the screen. 'That's Lady Peversham. That's who they're using.'

'But she doesn't know it,' added the nurse.

Auntie Win handed Miss Merryweather her sherry as the elegantly dressed Lady Peversham slid her luggage along the custom officer's table. It was as the machine beneath it crackled into activity, detecting something sinister in her golf clubs, that the doorbell rang again. This time all three women jumped and Miss Merryweather spilled some sherry on her skirt. Josie headed for the hall again.

This time it was Detective Inspector Gallaway in his trenchcoat and trilby hat. He was holding a bunch of flowers.

'Major,' he began. 'Oh,' he said, looking down at Josie, 'I thought you were staying with your parents.'

'No, because Elsie and Henry got married today. They're having a late party so that the friends who are performing in shows can come after work. Mum and Dad will be there too so I'm staying the night with Auntie Win. Come on in,' she said hurriedly. 'It's already started.'

'What's started?' he said.

Auntie Win's face peered round the doorway into the hall.

'Richard. At last. Oh, how lovely!' she said, noticing the flowers. 'Josie, put them in the kitchen, will you?' She turned hastily towards him. 'Hang your raincoat on a hook. Can I talk to you afterwards?'

'After what?' he began, but she had already disappeared into the sitting room.

Josie ran to the kitchen and dumped the flowers in the washing up bowl with the dirty dishes. As she rushed out of the kitchen into the sitting room, she caught sight of the detective inspector's startled expression on finding three injured women on the settee but they didn't even acknowledge his presence, so riveted were they by the drama on the screen.

'She's carrying uranium 235 in her golf caddy,' said Miss Merryweather when Josie re-joined them on the floor.

'And the Invisible Man has removed his bandages and spotted those men putting tools in the boot of Lord Peversham's car,' added Miss Jones.

'I think they're double-crossing him,' murmured Mrs Jenkins.

'You don't look like a sherry man, Richard,' Josie heard her aunt whisper. 'Whisky and soda?'

He nodded.

'Sit!' she said bossily, indicating the armchair. 'I'll go on the foot stool.'

'And Lady Peversham suspects something untoward is going on in the basement,' said Mrs Jenkins ominously, as Auntie Win sat down.

Josie looked over her shoulder. What with the nurse sitting there as well, she could have been in the middle of a scene from *Emergency – Ward 10*. She glanced across at Inspector Gallaway, leaning comfortably back in the armchair, the whisky and soda in his hand and Auntie Win sitting like a young girl by his feet. Josie's mother always used to say that there was a Jack for every Jill, and her dad used to add, 'But there are some exceptions,' meaning her aunt. But to Josie's surprise, Auntie Win and DI Gallaway seemed to slot together like two pieces of a jigsaw. *I hope he likes burned toast*, she thought.

At that moment, the image of a telephone receiver

hovering in the air caught her attention and the disembodied voice of the Invisible Man was heard to say, 'Hello, Sir Charles. Brady, here.'

Drawn back into watching the police fighting to prevent a gang of ruthless men from putting a bomb under the city of London, Josie sat totally absorbed, completely unaware that the trio on the settee behind her had each done something equally as courageous to protect her from harm.

'Nice work, Brady!' said Sir Charles once the criminals had been rounded up.

And as the credits began to roll, Auntie Win swivelled round and said, 'Anyone for ice cream?'

## CURTAIN

# Acknowledgements

Special thanks to:

Murray Melvin (actor, writer, director, lecturer and theatre archivist).

Doctor/ Dame Sheila Hancock (actor, writer, director and cast member of *Make Me An Offer*).

Harry Greene and Marjie Lawrence (fellow cast members).

Dudley Rogers (actor, director, writer).

John 'Joz' Joslin, (curator of the Thames Police Museum, Wapping, Wapping High Street, Wapping, London E1W 2NE) who helped me understand the Pool and River Police procedure.

Patrick Connolly, Metropolitan Police Service, Marine Policing Unit. (Liason officer at Wapping police station for matters concerning the Thames Police Association and Wapping Museum.)

Terry Broomfield for sharing his experiences working for the London Port Authority and Betty Wiles, John Wiles and John McCallum for script layout and film procedures.

Brian Glanvill and Bev Thomas (Student welfare at Italia Conti Academy of Theatre Arts Ltd) for introducing me to Sue Gallagher and Derek Brampton who shared their memories of school days at Italia Conti in the fifties.

*The Stage* newspaper, Nadia Stephens, Matilda Ferry-Swainson and Talia Pick.

Inspiration from Wole Soyinka's *Telephone Conversation*.

The author has been unable to trace writers of the following:

*Voyage to Vulcana* and *End of the Line* from *Film Fun Annual*, 1958.

*Be Prepared: The Official Handbook for Girl Guides* by AM Maynard OBE.

*Stars of Tomorrow* by Cecil Wilson (an interview with Miss Conti) from *The Daily Mail Annual for Boys and Girls*, edited by Susan French.

'The Big Plot' from *The Invisible Man* by Ian Stuart Black, from an original story by Tony O'Grady (pen name for Brian Clemens) and Robert Smart.

*Advice to a Player* by Denys Blakelock, published by Heineman (1959).

# About the Author

Michelle Magorian is the much-loved and highly acclaimed author of *Goodnight Mister Tom*. She has also written *Back Home*, *A Little Love Song*, *Cuckoo in the Nest*, *A Spoonful of Jam* and *Just Henry*. She has won many awards, including the Guardian Children's Fiction Award for *Goodnight Mister Tom* and the Costa Prize for *Just Henry*.

*Goodnight Mister Tom* has recently been re-issued as A Puffin Book, Stories to Last a Lifetime. It has been translated into thirteen languages and has been televised and made into a play as well as a musical.

Her writing has been described as 'masterly' (Philip Pullman), 'exhilarating' (*Sunday Times*) and 'gratifyingly emotional' (*Independent*).

Michelle is an actress as well as an author and trained at the Rose Bruford College of Speech and Drama and Marcel Marceau's L'École Internationale de Mime in Paris. She lives in Petersfield, Hampshire with her two sons.

www.michellemagorian.com

# Also available by
# Michelle Magorian